UNDER THE CLOUD

A Thriller

B.R. Erlank

D1738831

Under the Cloud

Copyright © 2022 by B.R. Erlank

ISBN9798838292773

Edited by Mary Hargreaves, through Jericho Writers

Cover Design by Reese Dante

This is a work of fiction. Any resemblance to persons living or dead is entirely coincidental. The events are purely fictional, so is the Church of Holy Redemption, the Renaissance Institute and many of the other entities referred to in the book.

Visit www.brerlank.wordpress.com to learn more about the author and his work. Sign up on his email list to receive information about upcoming books.

Dedication

For my family: Philippa, Lara and Richard. They are a
constant source of inspiration and support.

About Under the Cloud

They call themselves *The Settlement Bureau.* A faceless, soulless organization coercing individuals with threats to expose their improprieties and vulnerabilities. Inhumanely persistent, they've secretly driven hundreds of victims into bankruptcy, despair – and several even to suicide.

But when this organization tries to blackmail IT expert Terry Reynolds, they make a serious mistake. Terry is down on his luck. He is penniless, divorced and in a dead-end job. Yet, the abuse of his personal information stirs Terry out of his lethargy and he fights back. He embarks on a digital game of cat-and-mouse with the cold, calculating minds behind *The Settlement Bureau* – and in doing so, uncovers a sprawling criminal conspiracy.

***Under The Cloud* is a chillingly plausible new thriller by B.R. Erlank. With a plot ripped straight from the headlines, readers warn, "this book delivers a roller coaster ride right up to the final pages."**

Table of Contents

Prologue
San Francisco, California

LILY

Lily parked the red Jeep Wrangler and patted the steering wheel. The vehicle still had that new-car smell. It had been her mother's final act of defiance. *I'll beat this cancer thing. You'll see. You and I will cruise up to the Sierras and go camping.* The only place they'd ever driven to was the hospital.

A foghorn wailed. Lily clutched the decoupage box that held her mother's ashes and joined a trickle of tourists as they braved the Golden Gate Bridge on a gloomy January afternoon. Despite her jacket, her slim frame shivered. Cars whizzed by with their headlights on. The thick woven cables between her and the sea, made Lily think of boa constrictors wrapped around a tree trunk – or a person. The foghorn sounded again.

At the first pillar, Lily let her hand glide over the smooth rivet heads, each as big as a quarter. Such a simple yet effective way to hold this monumental structure together. Their squared pattern reminded her of the spare tacks on the notice board in the classroom where she used to teach. That was before. She shut out thoughts of the adoring second graders. That was life before Lily had taken on the full-time care of her cancer-stricken mother two years ago.

A woman in a long coat and sensible shoes stopped and spoke with an accent that Lily recognized as Swedish, "Can I trouble you to take my photo?"

Lily nodded, and the woman handed her an iPhone, then posed against the pillar. She said with an apologetic smile, "It is not a good day for a photo, but I have to show my children I was here."

The tourist moved on, and Lily propped her elbows on the railing, looking out into the nothingness – so many shades of white and gray. A gust of wind shredded the fog, and she glimpsed the sky. The light turned the clouds below into an gigantic duvet, beckoning her. She was so tired.

Lily opened the box. She was at a loss. Should she pray? Hum a hymn? She'd given up on the whole incense and confession thing a long time ago, and her mother had refused, right up until the end, to discuss "the end".

I'm sorry, Mom. Sorry for all the times my patience failed me. Sorry for those dark moments when I wished it were over. You always said I was a wonderful caregiver but not much of a fighter. I gave up on you long before you did.

She had expected to feel relief when her mother finally passed, but there had only been an overwhelming void for the last two weeks. Lily had sat alone in the apartment, waiting for the calls from the sickbed. They had gone forever.

She wiped tears from her eyes and slowly let the contents trickle down towards the clouds. The wind picked up the ashes and played with them, and with Lily's hair. It made Lily think of days on the beach with her mother.

When the container was empty, she sighed, reached into an inner pocket of her jacket, and took out a bundle of official-looking envelopes. "Personal and Confidential" was printed in bold above her name. Lily knew the contents of the letters by heart and the hateful logo of *The Settlement*

Bureau was burned into her retinas. Thank God her mother never saw these letters. Never saw the cold demands for the "ill-gotten gains" her father had "sealed away in a trust fund" in Lily's name. She had tried to reason with the faceless organization; tried to explain that they were welcome to the money, but it was untouchable till she turned thirty-five. It was no use. Their threats had become unbearable.

Lily grimaced as she tore the letters in half, then watched the pieces disappear into the clouds below. Then she firmed her grip on the railing and pushed herself up. Out of the corner of her eye, she glimpsed the Swedish woman, waving and shouting, *"Vänta! Gör det inte!"* She remembered enough of the language to understand that the woman was trying to stop her. She cast an eye to the heavens, begging for understanding. *I'm coming, Mom.*

The last thing Lily registered was the irony of leaving this world with the language of her father in her ears. The language of the father who had not spoken to her in years.

Chapter 1, San Francisco
Thursday Afternoon, 2nd Week of June

TERRY

Terry rubbed his eyes and rotated his aching shoulders. He sat up to look across the gray cubicle farm to the windows at the far end. With luck, he would get out in time for a bicycle ride, or at least a run.

An instant message pinged on his computer.

Alison: *The User Acceptance Test results are in. All-hands meeting – now!*

Terry sighed and picked up his shaker bottle. A dozen team members had already assembled in the large conference room. Alison sat at the head of the table, working on her iPad. The bun in her hair was threatening to unravel, and the rings under her eyes were more pronounced than usual. She took off her reading glasses and started without preamble, "Go-live is next week. The tests show that we have work to do – lots of work."

A collective groan sounded around the table as Alison flicked on the large, wall-mounted monitor. Terry soon realized that the NorCal bank's new customer portal had failed response time tests. He groaned inwardly. This was notoriously hard to fix; like shoring up the foundations of a house after it had been built. All eyes turned to the IT architect, who appeared fascinated by his fingernails.

The team went through the test results in detail for the next half hour. Terry was relieved to see that the work he was responsible for had passed with flying colors. But, when they got to the results from the user interface tests, there were pages and pages of change requests. Randy, who had been working on the user interface, complained, "This is ridiculous! These aren't bugs – these are new requirements! How can the users come up with new requirements a week before go-live? We can't work like this."

Alison ignored him and looked at her watch, "We'll have to get cracking tonight; I've ordered pizza." She turned to Terry, "Can you stay and help Randy?"

"Sure," Terry said, "no one but the dog waiting for me at home anyway."

Tricia, next to him, brushed her hand over his arm and shot him a sympathetic smile.

The pizza arrived and filled the room with the smell of garlic, pepperoni, and cheese. Terry fought a gag reflex. He hated garlic. His father had insisted that "the stinking rose" was the cure-all for everything and had always reeked of garlic. Terry's therapist had once tried to help Terry figure out whether he had transferred his irrational dislike of garlic to his father or whether it was the other way round.

Terry couldn't give a shit. He was just grateful for the supply of protein shakes on his desk.

Once Alison had left, Randy launched into a tirade. He had a pasty complexion and the fuzzy beginnings of a beard. Between mouthfuls of pizza, he complained about the imbecile users who changed their minds more often than their underwear. Terry sipped from his shaker bottle and wished Randy would hurry up eating so that they could get started. But it was evident that the whole team needed a little time to regroup and pick themselves up for the long night ahead.

"What kind of dog do you have?" Tricia asked.

"A black lab," Terry said.

"I love dogs," she said and smiled. "But with the crazy hours we work here…"

"It's not easy," Terry agreed. "And thanks, you've just reminded me that I'd better get hold of the dog walker to take Charlie out again."

He took out his phone to message the dog walker and felt the familiar pain when he saw the screen saver – him and Chloe. Since the divorce, he had got rid of everything that reminded him of her, except this screen saver. The photo had been taken three years earlier at Yosemite. For their seventh anniversary, Terry and Chloe had spent the night at the Ahwahnee Lodge and had set off on an early hike to Glacier point. There they had encountered a Yosemite ranger who happened to be a professional photographer.

The couple in the photo, each carrying their daypack, exuded vitality and good looks against the backdrop of Yosemite Valley. They complemented each other perfectly. Chloe was only a few inches shorter than Terry's 6' 1". She had a broad, open smile, perfect teeth, and an upturned nose. Her blonde hair was tied into a ponytail while the wind tucked at the waves of Terry's dark hair. His features were more Heathcliff – an aquiline nose, a strong jaw, and only a slight smile curling at the edges of his mouth. The real magic of the photo lay in the way the photographer had captured the morning light in their eyes. Chloe's eyes seemed to reflect the green of the forest, while Terry's had the earthy brown of fertile soil.

The ranger had asked permission to use the photo for marketing purposes. When it appeared on the Yosemite website with the heading, "Honeymooners on top of the world," they had been amused and thrilled. He remembered

Chloe saying, "Seven years later, and we still look like honeymooners – that calls for some kind of reward." That evening they had cracked a bottle of champagne and ordered Uber Eats from their favorite Nob Hill restaurant. Afterward…

He felt a light touch on his arm, and Tricia said, "She's beautiful. Your ex?"

Two hours later, Tricia stopped by his cubicle and handed him a Poke bowl. He looked at her in surprise. She smiled and pointed at his shaker bottle, "Man cannot live on green juice alone."

She brushed off his thanks and handed him an official-looking envelope, "This came for you; I know you never check your pigeonhole."

As Tricia left, he contemplated whether it was time to break out of his celibacy, but decided it was unfair on Tricia. What he needed was sex – only sex. Any involvement with someone from the office would complicate things.

He opened the envelope.

Dear Mr. Reynolds

At the behest of various women's rights groups, our department recently conducted a study to assess the fairness of financial settlements in divorce cases. Publicly-available divorce details were cross-checked against IRS information. In your case we have found that the settlement received by Ms. Chloe Reynolds is considerably less than half of your declared assets for the financial year….

Terry stared at the letter; what the hell was this? Was this her latest little trick to demean him? She knew very well why there was less money in the settlement. She had cleared out their joint accounts before filing for divorce. His unwillingness to fight had cost him his home, his car, and most of his savings. Now this!

Our researchers are under no obligation to make this information available to the IRS or the courts. However, as concerned citizens, we find ourselves in the moral dilemma of wanting to see justice prevail. Therefore, we would greatly appreciate it if you would make a voluntary contribution of $8,000 to the organizations that initiated the study. The funds can be remitted via our website www.settlementbureau.org.

We look forward to…

Terry closed his eyes. His breathing became shallow and perspiration formed on his forehead. A claw growing inside his chest, clutching his heart. The grip tightened, and as the pain spread, he tried to steady his breathing. He eyed the phone. At what point should he call for help?

Deep breaths, Terry, deep breaths. Think of the ocean, the rolling waves.

If he hadn't experienced this before, he'd be convinced that he was suffering a heart attack. He reached into his backpack for a pill container that, lately, never left his side. It took a while to steady his hands enough to extract a Xanax and gulp it down. For several minutes he sat hunched and trembling over the keyboard, blood pounding in his temples. Then the magic of the anti-anxiety tablet prized the claw from his heart, and he could take a few breaths.

He had no idea how long he had sat staring at his monitor before he got up so abruptly that his chair shot back against the cubicle wall. A bespectacled head, crowned by a mop of brown hair, appeared to ask, "Hey, are you okay?"

Terry ignored his colleague and strode to the common area, which was crammed with a watercooler, refrigerator, microwave, coffee paraphernalia, and the most temperamental printer/scanner he'd ever used. Mercifully, there was no one around. He scanned the letter.

Back at his desk, he attached the electronic copy to an email addressed to his ex and wrote in 44-point font, "WHAT THE F%#K?" Then he angled his monitor to shield it from passing co-workers and started to Google *The Settlement Bureau.*

Chapter 2, Tracy, California
Friday Afternoon, 2nd Week of June

JEREMIAH

The catering committee at the Church of Holy Redemption had their hands full. Despite meticulous preparations, they struggled to keep up with the demand for coffee, tea, juice, and snacks. At 3:30 p.m., an usher informed them that the overflow parking lots had been opened and that six golf carts were in service to ferry parishioners from those far-flung lots. Sarah Bates had made an emergency dash to Safeway to buy three more gallons of half-and-half, juice, paper cups, and the store's entire stock of brownie bites. Now, Sarah gritted her teeth against the pain in her feet caused by her decision to wear new shoes for this special occasion.

The tables in the gathering hall looked like a biblical locust swarm had hit them, and Sarah was relieved when the tolling bells summoned the crowd into the church. She wished she could just get off her feet, but instead, she helped clear away the debris.

Sarah hated to disappoint Pastor Jeremiah and told herself that the insufficient catering was not her fault. These were exceptional circumstances; the timing of the service – 5:00 p.m. on a Friday – was unusual and, of course, there was the presence of TV cameras. She suspected that many of the non-familiar faces were there purely in the hope of seeing themselves on TV. Immediately she chided herself for this uncharitable thought. Just last Sunday, Pastor Jeremiah had warned them to beware of hasty judgment. Why, hadn't she herself gone to have her hair colored and set?

She was about to admonish two boys for licking crumbs off the platters when she felt a hand come to rest on her shoulders, and a deep voice said, "Let the children be, sister."

She turned, flustered, "Oh, Pastor Jeremiah, I didn't see you." After all these years, she still felt elated and intimidated whenever he addressed her directly, especially when he was clad in full splendor. Today he wore an ivory-colored robe and a green stole. The latter was intricately embroidered with silver hand-stitching that complemented the streaks in his hair, which was swept back and reached down to his shoulders.

Sarah took a deep breath and said, "I'm sorry we let you down – especially on this special day. We ran out of food, and…"

"Let me down?" His chuckle boomed and filled the space. "I couldn't be happier; the sanctuary is packed. Imagine if we had sat here with a fully-laden table and no one had come to share it. No, no, you have nothing to apologize for."

"Well," she said, "it would have been a good day for a miracle of fish and bread to feed the thousands." She gave a nervous laugh and felt goosebumps on her arms when his gray eyes looked directly into hers. It felt as though he could see right into her soul.

He said, with a hint of a smile, "Miracles come in many shapes, sister. Please convey my thanks to the catering committee."

A tall young man rushed towards them. It was Isaac O'Neill, the church's Operations Manager. His cheeks were flushed as he said, "Pastor Jeremiah, the TV crews are ready, and the procession is waiting for you."

"Thank you, Isaac. I assume you have double-checked everything?"

"Yes, sir," Isaac replied.

"Well then," Pastor Jeremiah squared his shoulders and smiled, "let's go, then."

***

An acolyte handed Jeremiah his earpiece and pinned on a microphone. Another assistant reverently placed a white miter on the pastor's head and gave him his silver shepherd's staff. Pastor Jeremiah stood 6' 3" in his socks; with these adornments, he towered above everyone else in the processional train.

The organ started low and softly but quickly built up to a full-throttle crescendo. Jeremiah savored the sensation of its sound as the Bach Fugue in G minor (578) thundered up to the rafters. At $4,000,000, it was the most expensive organ west of the Mississippi. It employed state-of-the-art virtual pipe organ technology, capable of simulating any major organ from Milan Cathedral to St. Paul's in London and St. John's in New York. Top organists from around the world clamored for an opportunity to play on the fabled instrument. *Worth every penny*, Jeremiah thought. He felt the vibrations travel through the floor, up his legs, and into his chest – *God's voice.*

The ushers opened the double doors, and the procession moved towards the altar, which was precisely one-hundred-and-eighty feet from the door – just like King Solomon's temple. Jeremiah knew every dimension, every corner, door, and beam of this church as though he had built it with his own hands. The procession was led by eight altar youths carrying baskets of bread and stone jars filled with wine. Behind them came the incense bearer, the flame carrier, and the four assistants who would conduct readings and help distribute holy communion. They all wore narrow trousers and dark blue jackets that bore little resemblance to the flowing tunics seen in churches for millennia. Instead, these jackets, with their stand-up collars, looked more like the uniforms of some futuristic movie. Epaulets in various colors denoted everyone's rank.

Jeremiah watched the backs of his blue-clad army of God's soldiers, as he liked to refer to them. He saw with satisfaction that everyone's hair was neatly trimmed and combed; the silver torch, which would not have been out of place at an Olympic ceremony, was polished to perfection. However, the pastor noticed that an epaulet of one of the altar boys appeared to be missing. Jeremiah suppressed a sigh; *I'll have to speak to Isaac about it. When you represent God, it must be done right – no room for sloppiness.*

Behind the assistants walked the cross-bearer. Congregants took it in turn to volunteer for the honor of bearing the six-foot cross in procession. Today, the cross was carried by a stout man in his forties, a local farmer. He was barefoot and dressed in a plain-brown monk's cassock.

Jeremiah walked, as though insulated by an invisible bubble, ten paces behind the cross-bearer. The church elders kept a respectful distance behind him. He heard

Isaac's steady voice in his earpiece. "Slow the pace a little, sir, to reach the altar with the end of the prelude."

Jeremiah nodded left and right to the congregation and smiled; he slowed the pace. Again, he heard the voice, "The opening hymn is *A Mighty Fortress is our God.*"

He had personally devised the scheme of prompts from the operations manager. It allowed him to conduct the service without the encumbrance of any paper or notes. The primary rule was no interruptions during prayer or his sermon. Those he spoke freely from the heart. For everything else, he relied on Isaac's prompting.

As they progressed down the aisle, Jeremiah felt seven thousand pairs of eyes on him – every seat was taken. He shook his head imperceptibly; on days like today, it was hard to imagine that he had come this far. He, Jeremiah Blanchard, a carpenter's son from Biloxi, Mississippi, who had not even owned a pair of shoes until the day he was confirmed.

Chapter 3, WNET Studio, New York
Friday Evening, 2ⁿᵈ Week of June

KATIE

Katie Blanchard stood backstage, waiting for her cue. On a bank of monitors, she could see various angles of the studio audience and the show's host seated on one of two comfortable chairs. Meredith de Frey, the host of *A Better Tomorrow,* exuded calm and confidence.

On a large screen behind Meredith was an aerial view of the Church of Holy Redemption and its associated buildings. Katie's heart swelled with pride, especially when she looked at the recently-completed women's shelter. The photograph captured both the tranquility of the courtyard garden and the security of the ten-foot military-strength wall surrounding the compound.

Katie saw herself on one of the backstage monitors and wondered whether the producers had put a camera in the green room to keep an eye on show guests that might get cold feet and bolt. It was an out-of-body experience to perceive herself the way thousands of viewers across the country would see her. How would they judge her? She had opted for a knee-length, navy dress with a pale jacket. Discerning viewers would realize that this outfit, molded to her body, had not come off a rack. The studio's team had persuaded her to wear her long, dark hair in loose curls, and they had applied more make-up than she would have.

Her mind wandered to an incident, ten years earlier, after graduating from East Bay University in Oakland. Grandmama Montgomery had summoned her to the mansion in Pacific Heights, where she held court. Katie had hated being "Exhibit A" to be paraded in front of Grandmama's friends. But the matriarch had needed to make a performance out of handing over an admittedly generous check as a graduation present to her only surviving blood relative.

Katie had dutifully poured tea, served cake, and made small talk till her cheeks hurt from smiling. Then, when she had gone to find the sherry, her grandmother's friends had discussed her in the insolent manner of the old.

"She's got good posture; I'll give her that."

"Quite patrician looks, though not exactly pretty."

"Can she sing or play an instrument?"

Her grandmother's voice, "I've had poodles who were more musical." Laughter. "It is so sad that my Amelia did not pass a scrap of her musical gift on to Katherine."

"Very brainy; not exactly marrying material, is she?"

Not exactly marrying material. Would that be her epitaph? Katie's mouth twitched in a smile. At least it would be more honest than the "Beloved wife and mother" on Grandmama's tombstone in the Montgomery crypt, where she lay next to her husband, as icy in death as she'd been in life.

The makeup team had softened Katie's features. They had accentuated her heart-shaped face and highlighted her healthy skin as a backdrop for three intense points of green – her eyes and the delicate golden cross, set with tourmalines that she had inherited from her mother. She wore it night and day on a thin gold chain around her neck. Katie's heels brought her up to six feet and as she surveyed herself, she confronted the inner voice that chided her vanity. This had nothing to do with her. This was all about the church and the good they could do if they expanded their reach and increased their income.

Her phone beeped. *Not now!* She thought, and could have kicked herself for not turning it off. She stole a quick look at the text from the IT Manager at the Church of Holy Redemption.

Kim: *I have double and triple-checked. Pastor Jeremiah has personally authorized $30 million for the new technologies. Orders have already been placed.*

Katie gasped. What was Pastor Jeremiah thinking? The church's reserves were utterly depleted after the construction of the women's shelter. How could he?

She heard Meredith de Frey say, "Our special guest tonight has come all the way from California. Please welcome Ms. Katie Blanchard, Public Relations Officer of the Church of Holy Redemption."

Katie crossed herself and set her face in a smile before stepping out in front of the cameras. The living, breathing audience was more intimidating than it had appeared on the monitors, and the intensity of the lights hit her. She remembered not to squint, crossed the stage, and took the seat opposite Meredith.

The host welcomed her before addressing the cameras, "It's no secret that the United States is a deeply divided country; the rift cuts through every conceivable social, economic, and political issue. We are divided on immigration, health care, police reform, abortion, LGBTQ rights – you name it. And the tone of discourse is getting ever more strident.

"It is vital to seek out and listen to the organizations and voices that work to span the chasm in this divided nation. One such organization is the Church of Holy Redemption, based in the Republican heartland of the Democratic state of California."

She turned to Katie, "Tell me, Ms. Blanchard, isn't it rather unusual for a church to have a Public Relations Officer, a Chief Operating Officer, and I don't know what all else? It makes the church sound...what's the right word...mercantile?"

Katie was relieved to start off with a question she'd had to field numerous times before. She said, "The intent of most Christian churches has always been to provide a refuge and spiritual guidance, but also to be an active part of the world and the community. Even the medieval monasteries sold honey, mead, and vegetables, and," she smiled, "one of the nuns would have been responsible for the selling. They just didn't call her a Public Relations or Marketing Officer."

Meredith said, "There have been various rumors about the scale of the Church of Redemption, that the budget runs over a hundred million dollars a year. Give us a sense of the size of the operation – how big is your budget?"

Katie leaned forward in her chair. "Now, this is where we differ from a traditional business. Of course, money is important, but we don't measure our success in terms of dollars. We measure it in terms of what those dollars achieve. We regularly have more than five thousand people attend our Sunday services; the Pastor Jeremiah has a following of more than a million on social media and his radio talk show. At any time, we have seven hundred people in our various residential programs."

Meredith said, "But you are vying against hundreds, if not thousands, of other organizations for donations. People want to know that their charitable giving is spent wisely. There have been accusations of first-class travel by church leaders and excesses such as the millions spent on an organ."

Katie felt a trickle of sweat forming between her shoulder blades. She maintained a smile and said, "I was very blessed to inherit money from my grandmother. Therefore, let me state for the record that I do not draw a salary, and I traveled here in coach." Before Meredith could follow up, Katie continued, "What does it say about us as a society that it is perfectly acceptable for any wet-behind-the-ears financial analyst or business consultant to travel in first class? While at the same time, we expect teachers, nurses, firemen, and other service personnel to work for such a pittance that they can barely afford their daily commute, let alone fly anywhere."

Katie saw people in the audience nod their heads. She continued with one of her favorite topics, "Imagine a society with a different value set. A society where we say Kindergarten teachers and hospice workers *always* travel first class." She paused. "You might ask, why? I'll tell you. They are the most important people in the world. They shape our children into responsible human beings, and they give us comfort when we depart this world. Isn't it about time we aligned recognition with true value provided to society?"

The audience applauded, which allowed Katie to relax a little. She continued, "As for the organ – what are the hallmarks of a civilized society? Firstly, it is compassionate and takes care of the most vulnerable. Secondly, it invests in music and other arts. What sort of human beings would we be if we did not make music to praise God and the creation?"

Again, the audience applauded.

Meredith said, "You just spoke about taking care of the most vulnerable. Let's get back to the residential programs and why they're so important."

"They are the manifestation of our deep-seated belief that Christians have to *act* to alleviate the suffering in the world – Jesus role-modeled action. Hence, we have a home for orphaned and abandoned children and a shelter for abused women.

"Not many people are aware, but we have also built the Renaissance Institute to educate and rehabilitate troubled young men. The institute is located on forested land in the Sierra mountains, a hundred miles away from our main campus. Many of the three hundred residents have had brushes with the law. We are proud to have saved them from a prison system that focuses on punishment rather than rehabilitation."

Meredith nodded, "We are now going to give our viewers a live look right inside the workings of the church, where a service is underway."

Katie looked over her shoulder at the large screen, where the scene changed to the Church of Holy Redemption. The camera panned across the congregation, who were on their feet and singing *A Mighty Fortress Is Our God*. The sheer power and force of the music filled the church and the television studio. Pastor Jeremiah stood with outstretched hands behind the altar. Katie felt a lump in her throat. Thousands called him "Father", but she was the only one who could call him "Dad".

Pastor Jeremiah's voice filled the studio. "Brothers and sisters – we all have many, many blessings for which we must thank the Lord. And we all have our share of burdens to carry and challenges to overcome. I want to invite some of you to join me here at the altar so that we might pray for you. I call on brother Fred de Vos, on Isabella Fernandez, Davy Washington, and Clara McGill."

The camera moved from one chosen congregant to the next. The expressions alternated from ecstatic I've-won-the-lottery enthusiasm to shock and reluctance.

"Come, brother Davy," the pastor urged a young African-American man who sat unmoving with his hands over his face. "God knows what is in your heart and promises you redemption if you pray and unburden yourself."

The young man was cheered as he sauntered down the aisle to join the others. Pastor Jeremiah and his four assistants surrounded the group and laid hands on their shoulders. Then, the camera zoomed out, and the pastor's praying voice faded away.

"There are seven thousand people at the service today," Meredith said. "Is it true that the church has sophisticated data gathering and analytics capabilities to decide whom to call forward? That is, who might need special prayers?"

Katie let her fingers glide over the tourmalines on her cross. How did Meredith know this? It was one of the church's best-kept secrets that Isaac would prompt Pastor Jeremiah with detailed and pertinent facts that tended to cause awe, wonder, and shock among the congregants called to the altar.

On cue, young Davy Washington broke down in sobs and clutched the pastor's hands like a drowning man. The camera tactfully panned away to focus on a stained glass window.

Katie looked directly at the audience and said, "We believe the church must move with the times. So yes, we do make use of data analytics and social media to enhance the effectiveness of our programs and interventions."

"That sounds terribly theoretical. Can you give us some examples?"

Katie tugged at her earlobe and thought for a moment, "A week ago, I left my office at the church rather late. On the steps, I encountered a frightened six-year-old girl. All she would say was, "My mommy is hurt." She led me to a car in the deserted parking lot, where I found a woman whose face was so badly beaten that both her eyes were swollen shut. She had bruise marks around her neck and was barely conscious. In the backseat sat a bewildered four-year-old clutching a huge Panda bear. That woman had gotten herself and her daughters to us through sheer willpower."

The audience was so quiet, one could hear the hum of the air conditioning. Katie continued, "We had that woman and her children in our shelter within minutes. In the past, it would have taken us forever to figure out what was going on in her life. But now, we have an information network that instantly lets us access police reports, social services, employment, medical, and banking information to assess the situation. Are there guns in the home? Does the partner have a record of violence or alcohol abuse? Has the woman suffered injuries that required medical attention in the past? How many days of school have the children missed? Putting all this information together – obviously with the victim's consent – we employ an Artificial Intelligence agent to come up with a risk score."

Katie had to stop to take a breath. The audience was like a single living entity – waiting. It was difficult to gauge whether they approved or not. She pushed on, "Within fifteen minutes of Mrs. L. entering our shelter, we had a fact-based assessment of the situation and an action plan. Such a plan can include counseling, foster care, or housing the victims in a secure facility – particularly when firearms are involved."

Katie pointed at the aerial picture of the church and shelter behind her. "Let me just say that we were grateful to have those sturdy walls when the husband appeared alternately begging his wife to come home and threatening to kill the whole family." She took a breath, "Our predictive ability continues to grow, and this is what helps us to be Christians who can *act* effectively and decisively to improve the lives of the people we serve."

"What a novel concept," Meredith said with a wry smile, "allowing facts and data to influence the decisions and actions of people in power." She consulted her notes. "Let me switch gears and go straight to one of the most divisive issues in our nation. Ms. Blanchard, can you tell us where the church stands on the issue of abortion?"

Katie poured herself a glass of water, took a sip, and paused before she said, "Before I answer your question, I want to go back to one of your original comments – how is it that we manage to bridge the divide in our country? We do it by valuing action above words. The deeds of our church and our ministries inspire people from all walks of life to trust us. When it comes to abortion, nothing goads me more than to see a group of politicians or evangelists – usually men in suits – wring their hands and pontificate about the sanctity of life."

The studio audience had gone completely quiet, and the cameras zoomed in close on Katie. On a monitor near her feet, she caught a glimpse of her blazing eyes and the pink glow rising from her chest to her neck. She did not try to conceal the contempt in her voice.

"My question to them is, how many unwanted babies have you adopted? How many drug-addicted youths have you picked up off the streets and rehabilitated? Unlike most politicians, we earn our stripes by climbing in and *doing*. Mother-Child is our most extensive ministry. We do everything possible to help and encourage women to go through with the pregnancy and assist them afterward. Everything from daycare, career counseling, skills training, and shelter for women in abusive relationships."

She took a deep breath, "We can offer all these things, but we ultimately respect a woman's right to choose. And if her choice is to terminate her pregnancy, we will support her with the care and compassion that Jesus would want us to bestow on everyone in their hour of need."

She looked out at the audience. It was hard to read their expressions. Then the applause started. It quickly grew to a crescendo, and Katie allowed herself a slight smile of relief.

Meredith said, "Thank you for that eloquent explanation. You have shown us how, with action and compassion, we can all…"

A shout came from the audience, "Murderers!" Then again, two or three voices, "Murderers, murderers!" A banner was held aloft by two women. It read, *SAY NO TO BABY KILLERS.* The words were painted in red ink on a bedsheet. Then a volley of tomatoes was hurled at the stage and splatted on the ground in front of the host. One came flying and landed on the coffee table.

Security guards swarmed toward the protesters. Meredith De Frey took it in her stride and announced, "Well, that certainly confirms the need to continue the dialogue across the great cultural divide in this country. We'll take a break."

She took off her microphone and turned to Katie, "Are you okay?"

Katie hadn't moved a muscle since the protest had started. She nodded, then looked at the tomato splatters on her cream jacket and said, "Such a waste of good food."

Chapter 4, San Francisco

Saturday Morning, 2nd Week of June

TERRY

Charlie sat near the front door and thumped his tail. He kept his eyes fixed on Terry's every move and gave an occasional bark.

"Good boy," Terry said, "don't wake the neighbors; we'll go in a minute." He sipped his coffee, tied the laces of his running shoes, and strapped on a belt with a water bottle. The dog vibrated with anticipation when Terry led him down the stairs and out of the apartment building.

Baker Street was quiet and shrouded in fog. They walked one block and crossed Fell to reach the panhandle of Golden Gate Park, where Terry let the Labrador off-leash and proceeded to do his stretches. Charlie sniffed among the Eucalyptus trees. When he got too close to the homeless – cocooned in plastic, cardboard, and sleeping bags – Terry's whistle brought him back to his master.

Terry's friend, Jake, approached from Haight Ashbury. They greeted each other with a fist bump and set off jogging towards the ocean. After a while, Jake commented, "Charlie's picked up weight."

"Yeah," Terry said, "you're welcome to take him for a run anytime you like. Chloe and I used to take it in turns, so I guess he's now only getting half as much exercise."

"Just feed him less. You're at the opposite extreme – wasting away. How much weight have you lost?"

"Don't start on me at this time of the morning. I haven't even had a full cup of coffee yet."

"Just saying. You two bachelors are going to seed. Speaking of which, Britney wants you to come round for dinner tonight. She's got a friend…"

"No, no, no!" Terry said. He scowled and picked up his pace. Jake was half a head shorter than Terry but carried twenty pounds more. After a few minutes, Terry slowed for Jake to catch up. "Look, I know you guys mean well, but I really, really do not need to be fixed up with any dates."

"Don't you miss it?" Jake asked, panting.

"Miss what?"

"Sex, of course. Jeez, the only reason I go out running with you at this godforsaken hour in the cold and mist is to improve my sex life."

Terry rolled his eyes, "What makes you think I'm not getting any? But right now, I can't handle any of the baggage that comes with a relationship."

"Care to share what you're getting?" Jake asked, his voice tinged with envy.

"No," Terry said as they passed a homeless man scratching his backside while relieving himself against a tree. Charlie joined the man and peed against the opposite side of the tree.

They ran along JFK drive, past the conservatory and the De Young Museum, till they reached a bench at Spreckels Lake that marked their turning point. The fog had assumed a shredded quality with shafts of sunlight playing hide and seek across the lake's mirror surface. Charlie plopped down at their feet, panting.

Terry said, "How're things going at Facebook? I see Congress has got your fearless leader up for yet another hearing. What nefarious scheme have you guys dreamed up this time?"

Jake chuckled, "You're just jealous because I'm having fun while you're still on the NorCal job. How can you stand the boredom of working on a bank's IT system? Its so… yesterday." He continued, "We've only just begun to scratch the surface of what can be done with the new metaverse data lake. The latest analytics tools are mind-blowing, and it's incredible to find the weirdest correlations. Often, they make no bloody sense at all, but then you sit back and think, wait a minute. And even if a correlation doesn't make sense, you can still use it."

"Like what?"

"Like, people who drive Teslas have a disproportionate liking for ice cream – it makes no sense, but it's a statistically valid correlation." He looked out over the lake and continued, "Or people who bank with NorCal are more likely to be gun owners than the rest of the population. Or, here's a good one: what do you think, who is more likely to take statin drugs for high cholesterol – people who eat at hamburger joints or those who shop at Whole Foods? Go on, take a guess."

Terry shrugged, "Um…people who eat at hamburger joints?"

"Wrong!" Jake laughed. "It's the people who shop at Whole Foods – by a huge margin. The Wholefoodies are concerned about their health and more likely to get annual checkups. Those who eat in hamburger joints don't give a shit till they fall off the perch or end up in the ER."

He bent forwards to hold his toes and stretch, then continued, "It's phenomenal. Instead of bombarding people with all manner of advertising crap, we give them only what they want – razor-sharp precision."

Terry snorted, "So, you guys are utter saints, on a mission to rid the world of unwanted advertising. How very noble." He shook his head. "Anyway, something completely different, have you heard of an organization called *The Settlement Bureau*?"

Jake asked, "Why, are you in trouble? Have you fallen for some scam?"

"No, no, it's nothing like that," Terry reassured. "It's… it's one of the guys at the office. I think there was some attempt at blackmailing him or something. Don't worry; I just thought you might have heard about them – you guys are normally so on top of this sort of thing."

"If you like," Jake said, "I could ask our boys in cybersecurity."

"Would you? That would be awesome, man."

Jake asked, "How much longer is your stint with NorCal?"

Terry grunted, "The contract is coming to an end next week."

"Seriously? Have you got something else lined up?"

Terry shook his head, "Nope. I'm going to be divorced and unemployed. That's why Charlie and I are always nice to the homeless." He attempted a laugh that came out hollow. "Hoping for some good karma when we join their ranks."

Jake said, "Something will turn up."

"Yeah, yeah. That's what the agency keeps saying."

Jake looked at his watch, "Shit! Look at the time. Britney will have my balls for breakfast. I'm supposed to go to the garden center with her."

The fog had yielded, and they kept Charlie on the leash as they threaded their way among joggers, bicyclists, dog walkers, and people with baby strollers. Terry was amazed at the number of babies. How did young people with babies afford to live in the city?

They passed a group of men playing basketball. Terry slowed to watch, and one of the players spotted him. The youngster shouted, "Hey, Irish, come join us. We need you!"

Terry shouted back, "Another time. Have fun!"

He turned to Jake, "You'd think six-foot-one would be a good height. Another inch or two, and I might have made the UCLA first team. Might have made it to the major league."

Jake snorted, "An inch or two more in another department, and Chloe might not have left you."

Terry spun around, enraged, but when he saw the smirk on Jake's face, he just shook his head, "I don't know why Britney puts up with you."

Jake shot back, "Maybe it's those extra inches."

Terry rolled his eyes, "Where do you keep your brain? In a jar somewhere – pickled in sewage? Or have you joined Facebook's censorship group to watch porn all day?"

Jake panted, "Nothing wrong with a bit of porn now and then."

"Jake Fullerton, you're going to rot in hell."

Jake tried to laugh but instead had a coughing fit. He wheezed, "You'll…always be…a good Catholic choirboy. That's why I hang out with you."

Terry gave him a quizzical look, and Jake grinned, "I'm hedging my bets. If it turns out there really is a big daddy up in the sky, then you're going to intercede for me."

They parted ways at Fell Street, and Terry stopped at a Starbucks to pick up a coffee and bagel.

As he neared his apartment, he saw an older man busy packing his blankets into a supermarket cart. The man was a head shorter than Terry and wrapped in an oversized coat. He had a weather-beaten face, sharp gray eyes, and strands of equally gray hair protruding from under a woolen cap. Charlie barked, wagged his tail, and strained on the leash towards the man.

"How's it going, Joe?" Terry asked and handed the man a paper bag containing the coffee and bagel.

Joe's face creased into a smile as he bent down to stroke the dog's velvety black coat. He peered into the bag and said, "Better now, Sonny – a cuppa Joe for Joe Doe." He grinned at his joke, then clamped the paper bag shut and asked in a whisper, "You didn't give them my name, did you?"

Terry shook his head and let the familiar charade play out.

Joe looked over his shoulder and said, "Never give them your real name, Sonny, never tell them *anything*. They're everywhere."

"Who's everywhere?" Terry asked.

Joe brought his finger to his lips, "I'm not saying another word." His hands trembled, and he shook his head vigorously. Then he started to push his cart towards the panhandle.

"See you, Joe," Terry called.

Chapter 5, Renaissance Institute, Sierra Foothills California

Saturday Morning, 2nd Week of June

DANNY

Danny Gunderson woke to the muffled sound of gunfire and helicopters. He squinted at his watch and saw that it was only 6 a.m. Then he remembered that it was Saturday, rolled over, and tried to go back to sleep. Finally, after ten minutes of tossing and turning, Danny got up and went to the bathroom. Afterward, he leaned against the doorpost to look at his roommate, Timothy, who sat at a small desk playing *Rainbow Six Siege* on his laptop. The sound of violence continued to seep out from the roommate's headphones.

Timothy was the same age as Danny – seventeen – and the same height at 5' 8". But that was where all similarities between the two ended. Danny had the physique and looks of a stereotypical California surfer – blonde hair down to his shoulders, blue eyes, a smile to melt a glacier, and an aquiline nose in a perfectly symmetrical face.

31

Timothy was hunched over in his striped pajamas, and with his glasses and unruly black hair, he looked like an awkward teen version of Harry Potter. Danny moved toward the desk and slowly leaned his head into Timothy's field of vision. He gave a small wave and smiled.

Timothy removed the headphones and glanced at Danny, then fixed his gaze onto the computer screen.

Danny said, "Morning, Tim. Since what time have you been up?"

"I got up at four to help my friend Mykyta."

"Mykyta – the Russian hacker?"

"He is not Russian," Timothy said in a monotone, "he's Romanian. And he is not a hacker anymore. He now works for a cybersecurity company."

"Ah-ha, a hacker turned cybersecurity specialist in Romania. That sounds fishy."

"No, it doesn't. Mykyta told me he doesn't work on phishing attacks anymore."

"How did you get out of the controlled network and onto the internet this time? You know you're not supposed…"

"It was easy," Timothy interrupted. "I used coach Jamey's account. He's very predictable. I cracked his password in eight minutes and twenty seconds."

Danny became stern, "Timothy, I worry. If you get caught hacking again, the judge won't send you to a nice facility like this. He's going to send you to a proper prison. Don't you understand? It would be a horrible, horrible place for someone…someone like you. And it was a specific condition of your being here that you stay away from those Eastern European hackers like Mykyta."

Timothy raised his voice and stamped his foot, "He is not a hacker." He reached for his headphones and fixed his gaze on the screen.

"Okay, look, I'm sorry," Danny said. "Just tell me what you were doing with him."

Timothy avoided looking at his roommate's face and said, "He and his friends needed help debugging some code." Then, with a furtive glance towards Danny, he added, "For his cybersecurity job. And I was able to debug it for them in twenty-nine minutes."

There was a hint of self-satisfied triumph in Timothy's smile.

"That's…that's awesome," Danny said with fake enthusiasm. "But let's just keep it between us, okay? You know how thick all the meatheads are around here. If you talk to them about it, they wouldn't understand."

"You're right; they don't even understand Kerckhoffs's principle of cryptography. When I tried to explain to…"

"Hey, do you want to come for a run?" Danny interrupted, knowing full well what the answer would be. Timothy declined all physical exercise except his forty-four-minute walk around the athletics track *every* afternoon at four. Danny asked because it was part of their routine; it was his role to ask, and Timothy's to shake his head and say, "No."

Timothy waited for the next question, and Danny obliged, "Do you want me to see if I can rustle up a bagel and a banana from the kitchen on my way back?"

Timothy nodded. Danny knew that if Timothy could, he would avoid all meals in the dining hall. He cherished weekend mornings when he could stay in their room and eat the cream cheese bagel and banana Danny always brought for him.

At the door, Danny turned and said, "While you're on the internet, can you see if you can spot any signs of life from my father?"

Timothy answered, "You don't need to ask; you know I always do."

Danny did a few stretches on the lawn in the courtyard, then jogged out through the carriage gate. The gate reminded him of a trip to France during which he and his mother had visited various castles and walled cities. He had marveled at the ingenuity of the thousand-year-old designs to keep out enemies.

He set off along a paved road heading north. The sun had just peaked across the Sierras on his right, and the air was cool and fresh. He inhaled deeply, grateful for the cool air because he knew that the temperature would be in the nineties by noon. Half a mile from the campus, he reached the boundary fence, which looked like the border fences he had seen on a visit to Israel. It was made of twelve-foot-high metal palisades with barbed wire and security cameras along the top. After nine months at the "Institute," Danny did not even think of the fence as something extraordinary anymore.

He approached the main gates, where two Rottweilers were tethered to a post under a sheltering roof. The dogs leaped up, barking and straining at their chains, but when they heard Danny's voice, they calmed down and wagged their tails.

A guard, with a semi-automatic slung across his shoulder, emerged from the gatehouse and said, "Hey, Danny, how's it going?"

Danny replied, "Hola Carlos. Que va muy bien."

They fist-bumped.

The guard grunted, "Your pronunciation is terrible, but it's good to see you."

Danny produced a handful of cookie pieces, and the dogs sat up and watched his every move with rapt attention. He made them sit, lie, stay until the treats were depleted.

"You're turning them into pussycats," Carlos said, but he didn't seem concerned.

"What's up around here? Anything interesting happening?"

"Nothing interesting ever happens. It's boring as shit, but I'm not complaining. It's a job."

"And the other side?" Danny gestured towards a road that led to the neighboring property. The guardhouse had been placed in such a way that it could serve the gates of two adjacent properties, with the guard able to direct traffic from the main road into either. The one that adjoined had a similar fence with cameras.

"Why you so interested?" Carlos asked, "You always want to know about this other place."

Danny produced his most innocent smile and said, "No reason; I'm just a naturally curious guy and as bored as you are. It's a puzzle to me."

"Agh, go play Tetris."

"Carlos," Danny said, "no one plays Tetris anymore. And besides, you know very well that we're not allowed cellphones." He added, "You wouldn't happen to have a cellphone for sale, would you?"

Carlos chuckled and pointed at the camera in the corner of the guardhouse, "Nice try, amigo. You carry on like this – trying to corrupt an officer – and you'll spend the rest of your days locked up."

Danny laughed, "God, does no one have a sense of humor anymore? Nice talking to you."

He patted the dogs and started jogging up the dirt path that hugged the northern fence. The terrain got steeper, and after twenty minutes, Danny veered right onto a dirt road that wound its way up the mountain in long, lazy serpentines. He maintained the steady pace of a cross-country runner, overtook a group of three younger joggers puffing up the path, and nodded acknowledgment to two young men on their way down.

After forty minutes, he reached a level shelf carved by nature into the side of the mountain. Sweat ran down his back, and his lungs burned as he pushed himself to sprint the last quarter mile towards a clump of trees. He scrambled up a pile of boulders wedged between two ancient pines. The top boulder had a natural hollow that reminded Danny of a chair, shaped like a hand, that he had seen in the New York Museum of Modern Art. The hollow held a cushion of pine needles and dried leaves. He sank into this hideaway and inhaled the scent of pine. When his panting subsided, he could hear the gurgling of a creek. It seeped through beneath the boulders and then disappeared underground.

Before him lay the Renaissance Institute, bathed in the golden light of morning. It faced west over California's central valley and was completely isolated from civilization, hours away even from "The Mothership", that is the Church of Holy Redemption. The institute looked like any small liberal arts college with three red-brick quadrangles, three stories high, and several smaller buildings overlooking sports fields. The quad on his left was the dormitory where three hundred boys lived. Danny observed a team of gardeners starting up their lawnmowers and thought of Tim, who would now be turning up the volume of his computer to drown out the intrusion.

The central block had classrooms and a plethora of workshops for vocational training as well as administrative offices. The third block housed the dining hall, kitchen, clinic, and staff accommodations. The quarters with the best views on the top floor facing west were reserved for the principal, the vice-principal, and the two resident psychiatrists. Danny could see several guys jogging around the track that encircled a football field on a terrace below the central building. To the left was a gym, and to the right, a swimming pool and two basketball courts where he could make out one lonely figure shooting hoops. One noticeable difference from other schools was that there were no stands or seating at the sports facilities – it was not the sort of place that parents would visit for sports days.

The peaceful tableau was completed by a white building with a squat, square steeple – the chapel of Holy Redemption. It was situated on the road leading from the school to the main gate. Danny was convinced that the location of this structure was no accident. It was a not-so-subtle hint that the road to freedom could be found through the church.

Once Danny had caught his breath, he clambered down and, with a quick look behind him, pushed through a thicket next to the left-hand tree. Behind the boulders lay a ravine – his hidden valley. The boulders had rolled down to block the valley's mouth and form a natural dam in ages gone by. Light bounced off the water and a family of ducks swam by. The valley was only fifty yards across, and the craggy granite sides showed the cracks and fissures brought about by eons of earthquakes and erosion. A creek cascaded down several waterfalls and ended in the dam. Ferns and wildflowers flourished along the stream, and silence enveloped Danny like a comforter. It was a place that could make one believe in fairies.

Danny was not thinking of fairies – he walked up to a level area where he had found an abandoned patch of cannabis. He had re-cultivated the field, the size of a classroom, and the plants stood in neat rows on the southern side of the stream. On the northern side were the drying racks for the leaves. He spent half an hour checking his rudimentary irrigation system, pulling out weeds, and repositioning drying racks. Finally, he filled two small zip lock bags with dried leaves, tucked them in his pants, and made his way back to the secret exit.

He emerged back onto the main track and nearly collided with another boy running, head down, along the path. The runner was even more startled than Danny. He removed his headphones and asked, "Where...where on earth did you just come from...? What's back there?"

Danny recovered his composure and said, "I was just taking a leak."

The boy peered past Danny, "Funny; I didn't see you running on the path ahead of me."

Danny quickly extended his hand and introduced himself, "I'm Danny Gunderson. I haven't seen you before. Are you new here?"

"Gerald Myers. Yes, I've only been here a week."

"Join you for the run back?" Danny asked. Anything to divert Gerald's attention from his secret valley.

"Sure."

Danny set the pace and found that Gerald, who was taller than him, kept up easily while maintaining a steady flow of conversation. He established that Gerald was eighteen years old and from Sugar Land in Texas. He was close to his three older sisters, and his father was a logistics manager. The family had a cabin by a lake north of Houston and, other than cross-country running, Gerald was into swimming. He'd spent the last few summers working as a lifeguard.

Gerald said, "The other thing I really like doing is spelunking."

"What's that?"

"Spelunking. You know, exploring caves."

"Oh. Where in Texas do you go spe…lunking? I thought Texas was all flat and full of cattle."

Gerald laughed, "We have some of the world's biggest cavern systems north of San Antonio. There are still tracts that haven't been fully explored."

After ten minutes, Danny had secretly dubbed his running mate "Captain America" and had to resist the urge to ask why such a clean-cut, all-around wholesome Texan boy had been sent to the institute.

"And you?" Gerald asked, "Where're you from?"

Danny had to think for a moment. He had started to think of the institute as home. He said, "My folks are divorced. My father travels a lot, though I guess his base is in the Middle East. My mother is remarried; she and her new husband live in DC."

Gerald said, "That sounds pretty…modern America. And do you have brothers or sisters?"

"Not really."

"Not really?" Gerald appeared amused. "I thought the answer to that question was a simple 'yes' or 'no.' I've never heard anybody say, 'not really.'"

Danny felt defensive. He didn't usually talk about his family but, since Gerald had freely volunteered information about his own, he said, "My father had a son and a daughter with his first wife. They were already out of the house at university and boarding school, respectively, when I was born. They spent most of their vacations with their mother, so I pretty much grew up like an only child."

Gerald nodded, "Well, I've learned something new."

"What's that?"

Gerald smiled, "There is such a thing as not really having siblings."

"What are you doing for passion time this afternoon?"

Gerald looked at him, "Passion time?"

Danny had to laugh at the bewildered expression of Captain America. He said, "I'd love to play poker against you. I bet you suck at it." He paused, "You must've had a lousy induction. Saturday afternoon is deemed *passion time* around here – a time to develop new interests. They open the workshops, the art studio, the recital rooms, and we're encouraged to do woodwork, paint, play sport; anything except sit and watch TV."

Gerald shrugged, "I might swim."

With an affected voice, mimicking his therapist, Danny said, "The idea, my boy, is to try something new. You're here to learn new behaviors, new methods of coping. So, it is rather counterproductive if you just keep doing what you've done before."

Gerald laughed, "Looks like I have a lot to learn. But I'm not really here to change…" Then, he caught himself, and said, "What are you doing for passion time?"

"Today, I'm going to bake cookies." On an impulse, he added, "Want to come? I usually have the whole place to myself."

Gerald shrugged, "Why not? I've never baked anything in my life, but my sisters have certainly subjected me to enough baking shows."

They jogged on in silence and, as they neared the campus, they both picked up their pace. They tore down the asphalt at a full sprint for the last quarter mile, reaching the dormitory block neck and neck. They both bent over, panting for breath before shaking hands and parting ways.

Then Danny doubled back to the kitchen to pick up the bagel and banana for Timothy.

Chapter 6, Tracy, California

Saturday Afternoon, 2nd Week of June

KATIE

Katie opened her laptop and started a Zoom session with her father. Pastor Jeremiah was finishing up some paperwork, and Katie could observe him in his domain. Even as a small child, she had been content to simply be in his presence. Pastor Jeremiah, dressed in sandals, jeans, and a white buccaneer shirt, sat at a large birchwood desk. His office was a mix of the traditional and the innovative. Behind the pastor was a floor-to-ceiling stained-glass window reminiscent of a Picasso design – a joyous explosion of cubist flower petals. On a table to the pastor's left was a collection of "singing bowls" he had brought back from Nepal. Smoke from an incense burner wafted lazily up into the light. To his right was a yellowed globe of the world. The ten-foot-high double door to the study bore replica panels of Giotto's famous portal to St. Peter's. The doors were flanked by a replica of Michelangelo's *Pieta* and a copy of *The Crucifixion* by Salvador Dali.

The serenity of the scene struck Katie. The light caught the pastor's head from behind and illuminated him. She wished she could paint to capture the timeless quality of a scholar at his desk – a man toiling for wisdom and enlightenment.

On one side of the room was a sleek conference table with a state-of-the-art audiovisual system, including a 72" TV screen. She was observing the room through a fish-eye camera mounted above the TV.

Eventually, Pastor Jeremiah looked up to the TV screen and smiled. "Where are you calling from?"

"I'm in a taxi on my way to the airport," she said.

"You're going to be arriving late at SFO," her father said. "Shall I send someone to pick you up?"

"Oh, not to worry, Dad. I'll go to my place in the city. I'll be fine with an Uber."

"As you wish."

They both expressed their satisfaction with the televised service and the previous evening's TV interview. It had generated a great response on the church's social media platforms.

After a few minutes, Katie said, "Did you look at the spreadsheet I sent this morning? We must talk about these numbers. We can't sustain this kind of expenditure…"

"Hush," he said. "It's all under control."

"You keep saying that," she answered, and tried to keep the petulance out of her voice. "But we are as accountable as anyone. I'm concerned about the *God's Eye* project. It's hemorrhaging money. I spoke to the IT team, and they told me you'd given them a blank check; they're acting like the church's money is Monopoly money." She held up a hand to stop her father from interrupting. "You heard some of the questions Meredith asked last night. We have to be mindful of public perceptions if we want to retain the trust of our donors."

"You look just like your mother when you get stern," he said with an affectionate smile.

She sighed, "And you are once again trying to change the topic."

"I told you, have faith. I am meeting with our potential technology investors next week; when they see our progress, they *will* want a stake and will provide the necessary funds."

That certainty! Katie wondered about it for the thousandth time in her life. How did he do it? How could he be so confident that he and he alone was right? She knew that this was the essence of his charisma. It was what people craved in an uncertain world; it was why they flocked from near and far to hear him preach. It was a quality that she used to admire, but she had come to worry about it in recent months. She feared that this certainty was a delusion that fed on itself and became ever stronger – blurring the line between fantasy and reality.

"Thirty million dollars?" she asked, her voice rising.

"Why don't you come with me? Then you can assure yourself."

"What, all the way to Africa? I still don't understand why you must meet them in – what's that country again – Namibia? It's ridiculous."

"Isn't it rather obvious? Namibia is famous for hunting. CAFCA – Civil Action for Carrying Arms – is all about weapons. The board members are into hunting. I would hazard a guess that this is a hunting trip in the guise of a tax-deductible business trip."

"And that doesn't bother you at all? The fact that they're a gun advocacy group?"

Pastor Jeremiah became stern. "We are not having the discussion about the second amendment again. I've told you, CAFCA are blown away by our work and want to invest in our *defensive* capabilities. I have no problem

43

sharing our insights, learnings, and experience with them. It's all for the betterment of humankind." He paused, then added rather petulantly, "It is a great honor and opportunity for us to be invited to present in person. Most other projects just submit written proposals."

"I don't know," Katie said. "I've a bad feeling about CAFCA and I have so much going on..."

There was a knock at the door, and Isaac entered. He looked at the screen, "Oh, hi Kate." He smiled broadly and gave a thumbs-up. "Well done on that interview yesterday. It's caused an enormous buzz on Facebook and Twitter."

Katie liked Isaac; he was two years younger than her, and she viewed him as the little brother she never had. Her father always called her Katie, but Isaac wouldn't presume to call her that. To him, she was Kate, or even her full name, Katherine. She smiled at the thought of characterizing him as 'little.' He was a lanky six foot two and had the demeanor of an oversized puppy. With his sandy-colored hair and endless enthusiasm, he made Katie think of a Golden Retriever – always eager and ready to 'go fetch'. It was obvious that he idolized her father; he'd even started to grow his hair longer to emulate the pastor. The flowing locks and short beard gave him the look of a modern disciple.

She smiled and asked, "Is 'buzz' good or bad?"

"No such thing as bad publicity," he quoted. "There are the usual cranks who are upset at any pro-choice view, but most people commended you for the balanced perspective. We're jumping in and riding the wave with extra fundraising."

Pastor Jeremiah said, "I was just trying to persuade Katie to join us on the trip to Namibia."

"That would be so amazing." He placed his palms together in front of him, tilted his head, and begged, "*Please* come."

Katie found it hard to resist those soulful brown eyes. She said, "I'll think about it and will let you know tomorrow. Got to run now; I'm at the airport."

***

Jeremiah listened as Isaac went over the schedule with him. Then, he walked over to the globe and spun it around. "Wow, Namibia is literally on the opposite side of the Earth. Which way are we flying?"

Isaac replied, "We're going via Frankfurt, where we have an eight-hour layover – I've booked us a hotel – from there, it's an overnight flight to Windhoek, the capital city."

Jeremiah traced the route and said, "Lots of time for reading and meditation." It was going to be torture to have his tall frame squashed into a coach seat for that length of time. But, especially after the interview last night, he knew that business-class travel would detract from their fundraising efforts. He sighed. Maybe someone at the airline counter would recognize and upgrade him. That's what usually happened.

Isaac said, "We had numerous requests for you to stop over in Lagos and in Johannesburg, but we just don't have the time. When we reach Windhoek, we freshen up at a local hotel and then have a three-hour journey by SUV into the wilds of Africa, to the Oshinawa Game Lodge. That's where CAFCA are holding their retreat."

Jeremiah had his finger on the globe, "I wish they'd picked somewhere a little closer." He sighed, "I'm trying to placate Katie; tell her as little as possible."

Pastor Jeremiah had little interest in operational detail and readily accepted Isaac's offer to prepare presentation material and to compile bullet points for the negotiations. He patted the younger man on his shoulder and said, "Very well then, good work. This should be quite an adventure."

Isaac headed to his office in the basement, and Jeremiah crossed the church foyer toward the sanctuary. The twelve-foot tall oak doors, with their sleek pewter handles, were locked. He pressed his finger against a reader next to the wall, and the doors swung open. Inside, the church's facilities manager met him. The man immediately pressed a remote control to shut the heavy doors before greeting the pastor.

"And how's it going here, Larry?" Jeremiah asked as he surveyed the activity around him. "I trust you'll have everything back in order for tomorrow's morning service."

"We're on schedule," Larry said.

Jeremiah liked this man; he exuded trustworthiness. His close-cropped hair, faded jeans, and tight-fitting brown T-shirt screamed "army vet", and a weather-beaten complexion made him appear older than his thirty-seven years. Larry had served with the bomb squad in Iraq. He'd been discharged with a string of commendations, shrapnel in his left thigh, and PTSD. Jeremiah viewed Larry as one of his personal success stories. He had lifted the man out of the depths of despair and brought him back into the light.

Larry gestured to a group of technicians working near the back of the church, "We're reaching the end now. Only about five hundred seats to go."

"Where are the cameras?" Jeremiah asked.

Larry gestured up to the hundreds of spotlights and said, "Among the lights up on the catwalks. It's easy to get to them for angle adjustments – and they're impossible to spot from down here."

Jeremiah shielded his eyes and looked up. He counted seven more technicians busy stringing cables along the catwalks. He nodded his approval.

Larry introduced the pastor to two young men bent over a disassembled chair. The red carpet had been peeled back, laying bare conduits and cable trenches. Similar pairs of technicians were working on other chairs, and Jeremiah had the fleeting image of a field hospital in a war zone with multiple operations being performed.

Larry and Jeremiah exited through a panel door behind the altar, through the sacristy, where vestments, candles, hymnals, and other support materials were arranged in designated spaces. At the far end of the room, a door gave them access to a stairwell leading down into the basement. They descended to where a wide corridor, with walls ten feet high, stretched ahead of them. The passage ran directly under the altar and the center aisle of the church. At the third door on the left, Larry pressed his finger on the reader. They entered a room that could have been a NASA mission control center or a military operations command post. One wall was covered in monitors, and there were rows of desks with computer stations.

Larry veered towards a group of people huddled in front of their computers. A young Asian man got up to greet the visitors. Pastor Jeremiah shook his hand and said, "Great job last Friday, Kim."

"Thank you, sir," Kim said. "Were you comfortable with the subjects that we picked out for the special prayers and blessings?"

"Oh, yes. Definitely. I could clearly hear Isaac relaying the key points of personal history to me. They all seemed thoroughly surprised. How did you decide on those individuals?"

"The facial recognition in the sanctuary is operating at ninety-eight percent accuracy and, with the power of the God's Eye database, we can pull pertinent information in real-time. Of course, we also collect all the sensory data from the chairs – heart rate, body temperature, blood pressure. The algorithm does the rest in terms of identifying who is in a state of stress." His lips stretched into a smile. "The software zips through the sensor data and narrows down the search to people displaying stress symptoms. They are either guilt-ridden sinners or in despair – our target groups."

Jeremiah nodded, "Yes, it was quite something when I told that young man – what was his name, Davy? – that God had seen him break into a car in Stockton last week. And of course, Clara McGill was totally overcome that we singled her out for special healing prayer when it was only two days ago that she found out about her cancer."

Jeremiah pointed at a bank of computers with blinking lights behind a glass wall and asked, "Are those the new computers?"

"No," Kim answered. "This is a backup that only holds a fraction of our data for rapid access. You should come and see the new offsite installation." His eyes shone, "It's truly magnificent."

The pastor nodded, "Well, then, I won't keep you. Let's all get on with God's work."

Chapter 7, San Francisco

Saturday Afternoon, 2nd Week of June

TERRY

Terry looked up from his laptop and noticed the gloom in his north-facing apartment. He felt clammy and sensed the familiar twitching in the region of his heart that could evolve into a full-blown anxiety attack if he let the darkness overcome him. However, he didn't want to take more medication, so he turned on lights, searched for Beyoncé on Spotify, and furiously finished his ironing. Then he rinsed out his tea mug, wiped the spotless kitchen counter and, much to Charlie's annoyance, ran the vacuum cleaner through the apartment.

Tobacco smoke wafted up from the apartment below. Terry rammed the windows shut, picked up his laptop, and took himself to the coffee shop on Fell, where he continued to research *The Settlement Bureau*. He learned that it was a collection agency providing outsourced services to various companies, including major retailers and banks. The company was headquartered in San Francisco but had its call center in Tulsa, Oklahoma, where it was lauded as a major employer. It appeared to be a division of a privately-owned company; hence there was scant information. He came across one interesting piece from the Washington Post.

Have the Regulators learned nothing from the 2008 Financial Crisis?

Our regulators seem doomed to be at least one step behind Wall Street and other greedy entrepreneurs. While they have attempted to curb specific practices that led to the financial crisis, they sorely lack the imagination to identify shenanigans that will precipitate the next debacle.

There are, for example, companies like the San Francisco-based Settlement Bureau. The company buys questionable debt from reputable retailers at a deep discount and then aggressively pursues the debtors. They employ online bullying tactics reminiscent of the mafia. We spoke to several major corporations who declined to confirm or deny any association with the bureau.

The journalist noted that The Settlement Bureau had declined an invitation too. In another article, a whistleblower alleged that Facebook sold consumers' personal information to collection agencies such as *The Settlement Bureau*.

Terry made a note to quiz Jake about these allegations.

On his way home, he picked up a lean cuisine microwave dish. In typical San Francisco fashion, the weather had changed since he'd left home. Fog was rolling in from the Pacific, and he shivered in his T-shirt. He was ten paces from his front door when a dark figure peeled away from a midnight blue Volvo and blocked his path.

"Hello, Terry."

Terry nearly dropped his shopping. He had not seen or spoken to his ex in the three months since their divorce.

"Chloe?" Was all he managed, his mind reeling and his innards coiling up, ready for a fight. The first thing he noticed was the coat. They'd had an argument about it when she bought it at Niemann Marcus for a ludicrous amount of money. But she'd loved the fabric and the high collar that gave it the feel of a highwayman's cape. In her leather boots, she was nearly as tall as him, and he had to concede that the coat, with its broad belt, did justice to her figure. The fading light reflected her blonde hair, and she looked like a superhero, ready to kick the hell out of someone – him?

As he drew a step closer, he caught a whiff of her perfume, and it gave him a kick to his gut. God, she was beautiful.

"Are you going to invite me in?"

He was too dumb-struck to answer, and Chloe started to pick imaginary fluff off her coat. For a moment, he saw her self-assurance slip before she said, "Sorry, this was a dumb idea." She spun around.

"No, wait," Terry reached for her elbow. The familiar touch sent a jolt through him. She jerked her arm away.

"I was just…surprised."

She hesitated, and he realized that he wanted to – needed to – talk to her. Up until this moment, he hadn't realized how much time he spent talking to her in his head. It was driving him crazy.

Terry said, "Charlie will never forgive me if I let you walk away."

They looked at each other. Then she nodded, and he led the way up to his apartment. Halfway up the stairs, he could hear the dog whimper. As the door opened, Charlie launched himself at Chloe, his tail wagging like the wing of a hummingbird.

She knelt to hug the dog. "I missed you, too, Charlie boy."

Terry unpacked the shopping and asked, "What can I get you? Tea, coffee, sparkling water?"

Chloe peeled off her coat to reveal tight-fitting black jeans and a cream, silk blouse. She took a seat at the table that served as desk, dining and kitchen table.

"Do you have any wine open?"

Terry crouched down and found a lone bottle at the back of his pantry cabinet. He held it up for her inspection, "This okay?"

"Oh," she beamed, "My favorite, Chateauneuf Du Pape."

He coughed, "Last one from the case we ordered before..."

He poured the wine. Chloe took a big swig while he hardly touched his, watching her.

"Go on, then," Terry said, "I'm sure you're dying to comment on my new abode."

Her eyes widened, "What do you mean...?"

"Oh, come on, Chloe, I can practically see the wheels turning as you look around, thinking that your mother would faint if she saw you in a hovel like this."

"Two minutes," she snapped. "It took you less than two minutes to bring my mother into the conversation."

"That's because she's lived between us, either physically or in spirit, from the day I met you."

"Oh, yeah, you want to talk about ghosts that live between us."

It hit him like a whiplash. Cold sweat sprung up between his shoulder blades, and he put the wine glass down with a clank. He rubbed his temples.

"I'm sorry," Chloe said, "that was uncalled for." She reached across the table and touched his wrist. He put his hand in hers, which felt cool and soothing. He missed her touch, missed it so much. When he looked up, her eyes were filled with concern. "Are you still seeing the psychiatrist?"

He nodded, "But I don't want to talk about it."

He withdrew his hand, picked up a sheet of paper from the table and smoothed it out in front of her. "You want to tell me about this letter I got? This letter that alleges I ripped you off in the divorce settlement?" He tried to keep his voice neutral, businesslike. But the bitterness could not be contained when he said, "Look around; does this look like the apartment of someone who scored big in a divorce?"

She stabbed a finger onto the paper, "This is why I came. You must believe me – this has absolutely nothing to do with me. I immediately forwarded it to my lawyer." She looked at him, and he detected the faintest smile when she continued, "Without your color commentary, of course. My lawyer was as surprised as you or me."

He tried to read her expression.

"Don't do that," she snapped.

"What? What am I doing? I'm not doing anything." Even as he said it, he sounded to himself like the kid who'd tugged a girl's ponytail and then pretended he'd done nothing.

"Yes, you are! You're doubting my word – and that's not fair!"

Instinctively he put up his hands, but her temper – always on a hair-trigger – had been activated.

"I've never ever lied to you. Tell me one time that I lied to you?" Color rose up her neck and into her cheeks. "I didn't need to come here at all. I could have just let you stew with this; I know as little about it as you do, and frankly, it's not my problem. It's got nothing, zilch, nada to do with me." She paused for breath and looked at him with a frown, "Terry, are you listening to me?"

He blurted, "You're so hot when you're angry."

She leaned back in her chair and gave a dry laugh, "And you are so *exasperating*. How is a girl supposed to have an argument with a guy who goes all gooey at the first sign of conflict?"

"Not gooey," he smirked, "hard and horny."

He saw her blush before she pulled herself together and said in a calm tone, "Seriously, what do you think this is? How do we get to the bottom of it?"

Terry pulled up some of his research on the laptop and told her what he'd found out about *The Settlement Bureau*. Together they spent an hour digging deeper, and the more they looked, the more puzzled and intrigued they both became.

"This looks like a serious scam," Chloe finally said. "Shall I run it by some of the experts in our firm, see what they know?"

He nodded, overcome by strong emotions: gratitude, and the relief of having an ally, of not carrying this burden alone.

Chloe emptied the wine bottle into her glass and asked, "Why didn't you fight?"

"What?" Terry was dumbfounded and confused. "What do you mean?"

"Why didn't you fight during our divorce? It was a no-fault divorce. You could have had half of everything, but you didn't fight. Why?"

"Why?" He noticed an embarrassingly squeaky pitch in his voice. He got up, rammed his chair under the table, and walked to the sink.

"You have one of San Francisco's largest law firms behind you, not to mention your parents and the whole damn political establishment. What's the point of fighting when you had clearly made up your mind to flay and fillet me and then grind what was left into the dust?"

"Is that what you thought?" she asked, her voice low and calm, "that I was out to vindictively destroy you?"

"What do I know what your intentions were?" He waved his arm and looked about the apartment in a dramatic gesture. "But I do know what you did, and I'm living with the consequences."

"After ten years, you should have known me better." Ice had crept into her tone. He hated her lawyer's voice. "You never seemed to find the time or inclination to get to know me, really get to know me. I felt like a stranger in my own marriage; you shut me out." She took a gulp of wine. "You know what I wanted? I wanted you to fight. I wanted you to notice me and to fight for our marriage. I couldn't believe it when I asked for the house, the car, the money; your answer was always, 'whatever.'" She spat out the word and splayed open palms out in front of her.

"The only thing," she continued, "the only thing that got any sort of reaction out of you was when I demanded custody of Charlie."

The dog, who had taken refuge next to the couch, looked up. Chloe slammed an open hand on the table and got up. "You care more about the dog than about me."

Her voice had risen to a level where Terry was sure the neighbors could hear every word. He didn't care.

"Bullshit!" he spat back. "I was in it for the long haul; you were the one who hit me with divorce papers out of the blue. Who put you up to it? Your mother never liked me."

"Give me some credit!" With two steps, she crossed the room and grabbed the front of his T-shirt. "I am perfectly capable of figuring out for myself when my marriage is untenable."

She shook her fists, and he thought the T-shirt might rip as she continued, "Do you have any idea what it's been like for me, sharing you with the ghost of your sister? I'm very sorry about Lily's suicide; you know I am. But you couldn't let it go, and I couldn't deal with it anymore."

Her face was inches away from his, and it was so familiar that he felt like he was looking at a part of himself. He saw tears in her eyes, but he could not tell whether they were tears of anger, frustration, or hurt.

"I love you," he said and brought up a hand to massage her scalp the way she liked it. He heard her catch her breath. "I love you so much," he repeated and embraced her.

His lips sought hers, and he kissed her lightly. She tasted of red wine and tears and...Chloe. He nipped at her lower lip, hesitated, and continued to stroke her hair. And then, with her hands still wrapped in the front of his T-shirt, she parted her lips and allowed him in. Terry was overwhelmed by how familiar it felt and yet how exhilaratingly new. The last year, since he'd moved out of their joint home, he had harbored so much anger and resentment that he hadn't realized how much he'd missed her. It seemed she felt the same way. How could he have been so stupid as to let her go? Why hadn't he fought harder?

A cellphone rang. She pulled away, and they looked at each other.

"Yours or mine?" Chloe asked. For years they had discussed that one of them ought to change their ringtone, so they wouldn't always both leap up when a phone rang. It had become a power struggle to see who would succumb and change theirs in deference to the other. As with so many things in their relationship, neither had budged.

Terry pulled her back toward him and said, "We'll just ignore it." He sought out her mouth, but she was distracted. The ringing stopped. Desperately he tried to regain the mood. The phone rang again. Chloe pushed him away and walked across to the kitchen table.

"Yours," she said and handed him his ringing phone.

It was Jake. Terry sighed and pressed the green button.

"Hey, Terry, what's up? D'you want to come over for dinner? Britney and I hate to think of you moping by yourself on a Saturday night."

"Thanks, Jake. Appreciate the thought, but I'm fine – really." He mouthed "two minutes" to Chloe before walking into his bedroom, phone pressed to his ear.

"Suit yourself. Listen, there's something I want to run by you. How quickly can you get out of your current contract? I have a potentially brilliant opportunity for you. Have you heard of BDA – Big Data Analytica?" Without taking a breath, he rushed on, "They've ramped up hiring like crazy – they're always hiring; the demand is just ridiculous – but these last two weeks, it's like they've gone nuts. I mean, normally, we have a gentlemen's agreement among the tech companies not to poach from one another, but..."

More like honor among crooks, Terry thought.

"...over the last two weeks, they've hired five of our top data analytics people. This has gone all the way to the top at Facebook. Zuck has steam coming out of his ears. There's something big going on at BDA. So, here's the deal. I can get you in there through a recruiter friend, but they need you to start like, yesterday..."

"I haven't done much big data," Terry interjected, impatient to finish the conversation.

"Even an old mule like you can learn new tricks. We've pulled all your info, and the recruiter will work up your resume. She feels you know enough to get in the door, and then you'll just have to learn fast."

"What? I know enough to get 'in the door?' Jake, what do you take me for? I do have *some* professional integrity, you know."

"Yeah, yeah. And look where it's gotten you. In a week, you'll be the only unemployed IT professional in a

57

red-hot market in San Francisco. You're lucky to have a friend like me. You'll be thanking me."

Terry was about to protest when Jake cut in, "Did I mention that you'll be making twice as much as you're making now?"

Terry ran his hand through his hair. Twice as much! He looked around the bare, uninviting bedroom and sighed, "What's the catch? Why me?"

"Jeez, you're one ungrateful and untrusting son-of-a-bitch. I told you, I'm worried about you, and I'm your friend. I'm looking out for you."

"Jake – what's the catch?"

Jake sighed, "Okay, it's not really a catch, but we do have a small favor to ask."

"Who's we?"

"Me and a few of the leaders here at Facebook. We want to know what's going on there at BDA – and we can't exactly ask the traitors who jumped ship. So, all I need is for you and me to continue to go for our weekly jog and to chat a bit about work. No one expects you to share any trade secrets or compromise your precious professional integrity; just give us some sense of what's happening. What d'you say?"

Terry closed his eyes and thought hard. The money would certainly be welcome, but why did it feel so wrong?

Then Jake said, "Did I mention that *The Settlement Bureau* is closely aligned with BDA? We think all this activity might have something to do with them. They're ramping up for something big."

Without hesitation, Terry said, "I'm in. I can wrap things up and start by the end of the week."

They agreed to finalize the details on Monday.

Terry hung up and returned to the living room. He found Chloe with her coat on, giving Charlie a goodbye cuddle. She crossed the room and silenced his protestations by placing a finger on his mouth.

"We should thank Jake for the interruption," she said. "Kissing, at this stage of the game, is not a good idea." She turned at the door and added, "I'll let you know what I find out about *The Settlement Bureau*." Then she was gone.

Terry flopped onto the couch, trying to figure out what had just happened. "Fuck, fuck, fuck!" What did she want? Was this another test to see if he would run after her, fight for her? He punched the cushions and muttered his annoyance at the door, the empty wine bottle, the crappy apartment, and the whole world beyond.

Charlie slunk onto the couch and put his head on Terry's lap.

Chapter 8, Renaissance Institute, Sierra Foothills California

Saturday Afternoon, 2nd Week of June

HOLLY

Holly Banks was a stout woman in her fifties. Her mop of reddish hair, with an inch of gray showing at the roots, defied being corseted into a bun; half of it curled about her face. The sign on her office door off the kitchen read, "Chief Matron." After six years at the institute, it still gave her a kick to see that sign. Holly was an only child and had spent her entire life caring for her parents. Her mother had suffered from MS for as long as Holly could remember, and it had never occurred to her that anyone but she should nurse her mother. By the time Holly's mother had died, her father had been diagnosed with Alzheimer's. He was a physically fit man and took nearly a decade to succumb. By then, she had reverse mortgaged the family home and had spent every penny her parents had ever possessed on medical care.

At age forty-eight, Holly had found herself thrown into the job market without any qualifications. In her view, it had been God's will that, through the church and Pastor Jeremiah, she had found a job at the institute. She'd started as an assistant cook, worked her way up to housekeeping supervisor, and was now the Chief Matron. The Renaissance Institute was her salvation, her home, and her family.

Laughter came from the kitchen, and she smiled. Danny had won a special place in her heart, and it was nice to see him with a friend; hear them laughing. There was a loud clatter, and Holly yelled, "Don't make me come out there! If you make a mess, you'd better clean it up."

"Roger that, Chief," Danny shouted back and laughed. "The new boy is a clumsy klutz."

"Am not," came the indignant reply.

Minutes later, she was distracted by more noise from the kitchen and got up to investigate. Danny and Gerald were chasing around the workstations, trying to whack each other with wet kitchen towels.

Her heart lurched when she observed Gerald. He was beautiful and stirred her most cherished memories. There'd been a boy once, many, many years ago, when she was in her senior year at Fresno High. They'd laughed and played much like these two – spent hours together reading, talking, doing homework together. He'd taught her how to cook. She remembered how happy she'd been, bathing in the glow of his attention and waiting with mounting anticipation for the day when they would be more than friends. One moonlit evening, when her young, loving body could wait no more, she'd taken the initiative and kissed him passionately. It was then that he had confessed that he was gay, confused, and scared.

She raised her voice, "Enough, let me see what you've done before I sign off on your attendance sheet."

Danny presented two glassware containers with brownies.

"Hmph," the matron grunted, "they're not very even in size, and the texture looks kind of strange. What flour did you use?"

"The normal flour – baking flour," Danny said. "Do you want to taste?"

"No, thanks. What's the obsession with brownies? You've done them two weeks in a row. Next week I want to see you do something a little more challenging – I know you can."

Gerald said, "I was hoping you might have a good recipe for a baguette. I've seen them do it on TV, but I've never baked any."

Holly beamed, "Good idea. I'll show the two of you how to work with yeast. And Danny, I've told you before, I don't want you taking my glass containers. Please make sure you bring them back."

***

They finished cleaning and said their goodbyes before Danny headed to the center's administration area, where there was a room set up for the boys to conduct fortnightly calls with their families. He took his place in one of the twenty cubicles and braced himself. All calls were recorded, and some were monitored live by counselors.

"Pombo residence," the housekeeper said when she picked up on the third ring.

"Hi, Florence," Danny said, "Can I please speak to my mother?"

"I'll see if she is in."

As he waited, Danny tried to calm his breathing. The time for these calls was set – 5 p.m. every second Saturday – yet he always had to go through the same farce with Florence.

The phone clicked, and his mother came on the line, "Danny, darling, how are you? Are they feeding you properly? How's the weather in California? It's beastly hot in DC already, and we've had the air conditioning people in twice, but they can't seem to get it right. The weather is killing me. That reminds me, how are your allergies?"

"Fine, Mom."

She launched into another monologue that covered her bridge group, the garden, and a redecoration project that was giving her gray hairs. Then she moved on to various social engagements.

When she took a breath, Danny asked, "How's Laurence?"

"Oh, he's right here; we're about to go out for dinner."

Her voice was muffled then; Danny presumed she had her hand over the phone.

"Laurence," he heard her say, "You cannot possibly wear that tie – too garish. No, no, not that one either…yes, that one, the gray and blue."

Her voice was back to normal, "Honey, I so enjoyed chatting with you. Got to run now. We've been invited to dinner with a Japanese trade delegation. It's going to be boring as all hell, but at least we get to eat at Barmini's – there are usually interesting people to watch. Now, I hope you're going to be good; I'm so glad you're happy in this school. Bye, darling. Love you."

There was the *smack, smack* sound of fake kisses.

"Bye, Mom," Danny said.

He looked at his watch – 5:08 p.m. Everyone around him was engrossed in their allotted half-hour phone conversation. Quietly, he got up and made his way back to the dormitories.

***

On Sunday morning, Danny woke at six and got into his running gear. He left Timothy fast asleep, curled up like a hedgehog, with his face buried in the crook of his arm.

Danny followed the usual path to the main gate, spent some time making the dogs perform tricks for treats, and exchanged a few words with Carlos.

"Here," Danny said as he retrieved a glass container from his backpack, "I baked some brownies. Thought you might like some."

"You baked?" Carlos seemed to waver between incredulity and disdain. "Where did you learn to bake?"

Danny shrugged and grinned, "These are an experiment. Let me know what you think." He waved goodbye and started along the track. Then he stopped and turned, "Oh, I nearly forgot. Matron wants that container back; I'll pick it up later. No need to wash it. I'll pop it in the kitchen's dishwasher." He pushed his pace up the mountain and was pleased with his time when he crashed through the foliage into the secret valley and flopped on the mossy bank of "his" pond. The sounds of nature enveloped him – water gurgling, rustling leaves, and a series of splashes as the ducks launched themselves. From far away came the sound of a woodpecker and something that sounded like a coyote. As he lay on his back, he kept his eyes on a pair of hawks circling above. What was it that they could see so far below them – a mouse, a squirrel, a rabbit?

After a while, he rummaged for a water bottle and the second cookie container in his backpack. He munched a brownie and then another before tending to his plants. The soil had the right moisture level, but there seemed to be a never-ending need to pull out weeds. Danny hummed to himself as he crouched along the rows of marijuana plants and worked the soil.

The sun hadn't even reached the valley floor, but Danny felt flushed and hot within twenty minutes. He ripped off his clothes, left them where they fell and strode into the pond. It was too shallow for a swim, but the water was wonderful. He saw rainbows when he splashed about before lying down to float on his back in the warm shallows. It was the strangest sensation, lying there with submerged grasses stroking his back. His senses were in overdrive, and he focused on six falcons above, going around in lazy circles. Suddenly it was as though he was among them, looking far into the distance, all the way to the ocean, and then down to where his naked body lay splayed like a sacrificial offering on a circle of velvety green.

He smiled. Man, the marijuana brownies had turned out good.

Danny closed his eyes and lost all sense of time as he lay suspended between the warmth of the sun and the coolness of the water. His mind soared above the daily rut of anger, concern for Timothy, anxiety, and scheming. Instead, he felt nothing, and yet he felt everything; it was as though he could sense every nerve ending of his body – and they all coalesced into a song his mother used to belt out: *Let the world turn without me tonight.*

Through a fog came a voice, "Danny…Danny, are you okay?"

He opened his eyes, and Gerald's concerned face was looking down at him.

Danny nodded and managed to swallow a mouth full of pond water. As he spluttered and struggled to sit up, a pair of strong arms gripped him under the shoulders, hoisted him up, and lay him down on the mossy bank. He coughed a few more times.

"Are you sure you're okay? I thought…"

Danny noticed how pale Gerald was. "You thought I was dead?" He gave a little laugh, "I'm sorry, man. I wasn't expecting anyone. Guess I just had one brownie too many." He gave another laugh and pointed at the container, "D'you want one?"

Gerald shook his head and turned away, staring up the side of the ravine.

"Oh, shit," Danny said and pointed at Gerald's shoes. "Your shoes are all wet."

"Doesn't matter."

Then Danny noticed the small backpack that Gerald had dropped on the ground. He stretched and reached past Gerald to pull the bag towards him. But, as he brushed against the older boy, Gerald stiffened. His gaze fixed somewhere in the distance.

"What's in the bag?" Danny asked, rummaging through the backpack. "I'm starving."

"You'll be disappointed; it's just basic spelunking gear I scavenged. I want to see if there are any caves up here."

"Cool," Danny said and struggled into a seated position. "Can I come?"

"No," came the immediate answer.

Danny reached out and touched Gerald's back, "I'm sorry I gave you a fright, but why are you so mad at me?"

Gerald looked over his shoulder and said, "I'm not mad. It's just…can you please put on some clothes. Seeing you… like this. It makes me uncomfortable."

Danny retrieved his clothes from where he had dropped them. He pulled them on, sat next to Gerald, and followed his gaze to where the falcons were still circling. He said, "Would I be right in guessing that you're here for the pray-the-gay-away program?"

Gerald seemed to ignore the question. Instead, he sat and stared ahead of him, then said, "It's called the sexual re-assertion program."

They sat in silence. Eventually, Danny said, very slowly and deliberately, "They sent you on this program because you are a committed Christian and you believe in God. Is that right?"

Gerald turned towards him and nodded.

There was so much anguish in his eyes that it threatened to make Danny choke up. His belief in God had evaporated about the same time as his belief in Father Christmas. Neither had listened to his fervent, desperate prayers.

He looked at Gerald and was thankful for the pot-induced hyper-clarity in his mind, which guided him to be very calm. He sensed that he was dealing with a wounded individual.

Danny said, "God made you the way you are. Never forget that God loves you and, in his eyes, you're perfect."

He touched Gerald's cheek and repeated, "You're God's beloved. You have to believe that."

Then he turned and held Gerald's face between his hands. When the older boy did not resist, he leaned in and kissed him on the mouth. At first, it was a gentle brushing of the lips, but soon he felt the stirrings of response. Gerald's mouth opened, and they were entwined in a deep kiss, unleashing the full force of Gerald's longing. His breath came in gasps, and he moaned, digging his fingers into Danny's back.

Danny was the one to break away. He smiled, put a finger on the tip of Gerald's nose, and breathed, "You're perfect. And we're not going to let them fuck with your brain. D'you hear me?"

67

Gerald's expression was a mixture of confusion and gratitude. He was still breathing hard, but he mustered a smile and nodded.

"Good," Danny said and winked. "I have to get back – Timothy will go nuts if he doesn't get his bagel and banana soon. You enjoy your spelunking."

He punched Gerald on the shoulder, turned, and set off down the mountain.

When Danny peered into the guardhouse, Carlos was sprawled in a chair, his feet on the desk right next to the control panel, and his head lolling back as he snored. There were only two of the original six brownies left in the container. Danny smiled when he saw several unmistakable fingerprints on the glass. He slipped on a surgical glove – courtesy of his last visit to the clinic – and took a zip-lock bag from his backpack. He was about to take the container when he heard loud honking. One of the monitors above the control panel showed a large truck waiting at the main gate. Carlos snorted and opened his eyes, "What...what are you doing here?"

Crap! Danny tucked his gloved hand and zip lock bag into his pocket. He said, "Just came by to pick up the container for matron." Pointing at the screen, he continued, "You'd better deal with that truck."

Carlos rubbed his eyes and peered through the window. He tapped on a keyboard to pull up what looked like a visitors' schedule. After a minute of scrolling and clicking, Carlos placed his index finger on a reader. It took a few seconds for the system to authenticate him. Then he pressed a button to open the gate. The truck rumbled into the triangular no-man's land between the "outside world," the institute, and the neighboring property. Carlos grabbed a clipboard and went out to meet the driver. The dogs stirred from their weed-induced slumber and gave a few half-hearted barks.

As soon as Carlos was outside, Danny placed the glass container into the zip-lock and stowed it in his backpack as carefully as if he were putting a premature baby into an incubator. Next week's passion time would have to be spent in the science laboratory.

He looked up to where the driver and Carlos were talking to each other. There was something strange about the truck. Then it struck him – there were no markings. Every other truck he had ever seen was a rolling billboard for something or other, but not this one. On the computer screen he read, 11:00 a.m. Cisco Delivery for La Cave – 240 Servers.

Two hundred and forty servers!? *Holy Shit!*

Carlos ambled back to the guardhouse, and Danny dashed outside and gave the dogs a pat.

He waved, "I'll be on my way then, adiós."

Ten minutes later, bagel and banana in hand, Danny raced up the stairs of the dormitory block where he was greeted by raised voices and shouting. Near his and Timothy's room was a small common area with a TV, a couch, and a coffee table. TV at the institute was restricted to a few sports channels and a meager offering of "wholesome" entertainment. Most inmates watched sports on the big screen in the recreation center, where there was a pool table, fuzzball, table tennis, and other amenities. Danny and Timothy were the only ones who ever used the small common area when Danny dragged his roommate away from his computer to watch the History channel. Danny was therefore surprised to hear the TV blaring at full volume.

He took in the scene and cursed himself for being late. Juanito Gonzalez and his cadre of sycophants had made themselves at home in the common area. Juanito, one of the oldest "boys" at the institute, reminded Danny of Jabba the Hut in Star Wars. He fancied himself a self-styled mafia boss and would tell anyone who cared to listen that he had "connections" and that he could "get stuff". Juanito was instantly recognizable by his bald head and fat neck rolls. He was sprawled on the couch with three younger boys draped around him – on the floor, the coffee table, and the couch's armrest. Though alcohol was strictly forbidden, they all held beer bottles – a testament to Juanito's "connections".

Their attention was not directed at the TV but at Timothy, in his pajamas, standing against the wall. He rocked back and forth on his feet, his face red and his arms clutched around his laptop.

"Stop making a noise," Timothy pleaded, his voice desperate. "Please stop. You are giving me a headache."

"Fuck off, freak!" One of the boys said.

"Your mother dresses you funny," the next mocked. "Funny, funny, funny," he intoned. "You don't fucking belong here; you belong in a funny farm." They all cackled with laughter.

"Please," Timothy implored, "go somewhere else."

The youngest guy of the group, who sat perched on the armrest, piped up, "You go somewhere else, arsehole. We have every right to be here."

Danny crossed the room and switched off the TV. He conjured up a smile, turned to the four, and said, "Show's over. Give the guy a break. He asked you nicely."

One of them pointed at Timothy, "Why does the freak get to have a laptop, and we don't? We're not even allowed a fucking cellphone."

Danny maintained the mock demeanor of an elementary school teacher, "It's part of Timothy's therapy. His psychiatrist has authorized it."

"Why don't I get therapy like that?"

"Oh, you've had your therapy," Danny said and smiled. "You just don't remember. It's called a frontal lobotomy."

The three youngsters turned to Juanito. The older boy glared at Danny through thin slits. He snorted, took a long swig from his beer bottle, and said, "You're fucking with the wrong guys." He pointed his beer bottle at the TV and said, "Turn it on." His voice was high and reedy.

The dark-haired youngster sitting on the coffee table also took a swig from his bottle, burped, and said, "Yeah, turn it on."

Danny displayed his teeth in a toothpaste-ad smile, "I hear an echo. The TV noise is obviously not good for one's health." He looked at them one by one, then said, "Why don't you guys just fuck off to the rec. center and watch TV there? Oh, I forgot, the mother's milk you're sucking from your bottles might attract attention."

The youngest of the boys lurched up from the armrest and aimed a fisted blow at Danny's head. Danny wasn't sure whether the guy was drunk or just a hopeless fighter, but he blocked the punch and brought his knee up into the youngster's groin.

"That's for calling my friend an arsehole," Danny said as the boy howled and collapsed in agony.

"Get him!" Juanito hissed without moving his bulk. The boy who'd sat on the coffee table reached Danny before his friend managed to get up from the floor. Danny knew that he only had seconds to deal with the first aggressor if he didn't want to deal with two of them simultaneously. Every muscle in his body was tensed, and he was transported back to New York – running. Running had always served him well. He remembered running down a narrow street, pursued by three older jocks from his school. He could hear their taunts, "Your father belongs in prison; you bastard son of a cock-sucking whore; spawn of scum." He could still feel the breath of a wolf pack closing in on its prey. Wolves hunt to survive; these boys, however, had been fueled by nothing but naked hatred. Years later, he'd developed some understanding of it. But, as a twelve-year-old, he'd been utterly bewildered, especially since he'd done nothing wrong.

On that muggy day in New York, he'd led the wolf pack straight into a police station. They were so blinded that they crowded around him, shouting obscenities, pummeling him from all sides. To his immense relief, the plan had worked; two officers stepped in and shoved the perpetrators away.

One police officer asked, "What's the meaning of this? Shame on you ganging up on a kid." She'd kept her hand on her baton. "Explain yourselves." Danny had been gratified by the sympathetic look she'd shot him as he stood bent over, panting.

"He's Carl Gunderson's son," one of the boys had shouted.

Danny would never forget how the police officer's face had transformed from sympathy to something that was a mixture of awe and disgust. "*The* Carl Gunderson?" she had intoned, and her knuckles had gone white on the grip of the baton. She'd looked at her colleague and said, "The police pension fund lost millions in the Gunderson scandal."

The colleague had eyed Danny like he'd just spotted a chopped-off finger in his chili and said, "The sins of the fathers…"

Danny hadn't waited to hear anymore – he'd dodged out of the police station and disappeared into the maze of alleys that would become his refuge for the ensuing months.

Now he looked up and saw that same look of hatred and disdain in the eyes of the brown-skinned youngster. Danny dashed to the open door of his room. The predator gave chase. They shot past Timothy, who was crouching motionless against the wall. Danny ran into the room, spun around, and crashed against the door with his shoulder. This was another escape maneuver he had perfected over the years. A door smashing shut was bound to do some damage, and this time was no exception. The door hit the pursuer's head – hard – and his arm got trapped between the door and the frame. He cried out a string of expletives in Spanish. Danny opened the door, grabbed his assailant's neck in a tight arm lock, and kicked his legs out from under him. The boy lay still where he had fallen.

When Danny looked up, the third sycophant, with a maniacal grin on his face, had grabbed Timothy around the neck with one arm. In his other hand, he held the jagged remains of a smashed beer bottle. There were glass shards on the coffee table, and the rancid smell of beer filled the room. Danny had to suppress his gag reflex and fight off a whole other set of memories.

Danny breathed hard and fought to keep his voice level. "Leave him," he said.

The boy merely grinned.

Danny crouched and took a step forward. He held out his hands and beckoned in a *come, come* motion. "Yellow," he taunted. "Juanito's little lapdog is scared."

Juanito intervened, his voice wheezy, "Don't let him goad you into…"

But it was too late. The enraged boy flung Timothy aside and lunged across the room. Danny squatted low, went into a one-legged spin, and ducked. The cut-off beer bottle ripped into his backpack, where it connected with matron's glass containers. In a fluid motion, Danny continued spinning as though he were performing a Cossack dance. His outstretched right leg connected with the boy's knee, and they went down together. Danny's muscle memory took over. He was on top, and before the other boy knew what hit him, Danny's fist smashed into his face. Blood gushed from the older boy's nose. Danny was about to plant his fist again when a searing pain shot through his shoulder and filled his vision with a blinding

73

light. He gasped, screamed, and rolled over to get out of the way. He was convinced his arm had been ripped off by a grenade. Danny gasped, ground his teeth, and writhed until finally, the source of the pain seemed to be withdrawn.

He had no idea how long he lay there in a convulsed heap before he could make out the figure of a gray-clad security guard towering above him. "Get up," the guard said and nudged Danny's leg with his boot. He yanked Danny to his feet and held up the taser as a warning. His colleague had meted out similar means to subdue Danny's adversary, who looked even worse than Danny felt, with blood splattered all over his shirt.

Danny managed a wan smile in the direction of Timothy before the two boys were marched off to the security center, with Juanito's curses and weaselly protestations of innocence ringing down the corridor.

Chapter 9, Berkeley

Sunday Afternoon, 2nd Week of June

KATIE

Katie handed the keys of her Audi convertible to the valet, perched her sunglasses on her head, and strode into the Claremont Hotel in Berkeley. The lobby exuded old-world charm and quiet efficiency. Entering the private lounge with its parquet floors was a step back into a genteel era. Fresh flowers were on each table, and well-heeled clients sat in velvet-covered chairs, sipping their afternoon teas. Katie was pleased that she'd decided to wear a skirt and heels rather than her usual weekend gear of jeans and trainers.

A waiter led her to a table near the windows, where a middle-aged woman with meticulously-coiffed hair gave a tiny wave.

"Katie, darling," the woman said. "So good of you to come all the way from the city to see me."

"Eleanor, you look wonderful," Katie bent down for an air kiss. "No bother at all. I quite enjoyed the drive across. I could drive with the top down – such glorious weather."

"Ah," Eleanor said, "that would explain your radiant complexion. And here I was thinking that maybe you'd finally found a suitable beau."

That didn't take long, Katie thought. Eleanor McGrath was her godmother and since Katie's own mother had died when she was fourteen, Eleanor had seen it as her duty to instruct her goddaughter on the finer points of womanhood – all with the goal of finding a suitable husband.

Katie settled into her chair and studied the woman across the table. Eleanor wore a two-piece cream suit, a pale green silk blouse, and a long pearl-and-gold necklace. A layer of expertly applied make-up and – Katie suspected – regular doses of Botox gave her a smooth complexion, except for the crow's feet around her dark eyes. Eleanor had once sued a tabloid for printing her age, even though they had understated it by three years. Katie, however, knew that Eleanor's sixtieth birthday had passed with no fanfare five months earlier.

"That's a beautiful necklace," Katie commented. "I don't think I've seen it before."

"I'm glad you like it. I've found this marvelous young jeweler who does the most original things." She fingered the necklace. "I inherited the pearls from my grandmother and collaborated with the jeweler on the design."

"You still keep surprising me with new talents," Katie said and smiled.

They ordered tea, admired the sweeping views of the Bay and the Golden Gate Bridge, and discussed the décor of the refurbished hotel. All the while, Katie wondered why Eleanor had invited her to this "cozy little chat".

"How's Mitch?" Katie inquired. She thought back to sleepovers and weekends spent at the McGrath home in the

Berkeley hills when she and her best friend, Chloe McGrath, were in elementary school. Eleanor had taken them on outings to the MoMa, the Legion of Honor, and other art galleries. She had taught them how to set a formal dining table and had encouraged them to read. Katie could not remember ever watching TV at the McGrath home. But when Mitch McGrath, Chloe's father, was home, the pall of seriousness lifted. He taught them to play baseball and shoot hoops. He took them to the merry-go-round or on hikes in Tilden Park, where they pretended to be explorers. When Mitch was around, there was laughter and light.

When Katie was in middle school, and Mitch was campaigning for state senator, he would sometimes take the girls with him when he met with constituents in coffee shops, restaurants, and shopping malls. Katie had always admired the easy way he connected with strangers, listened attentively, and found the right things to say. He was a pillar of stability and empathy, and the people of California kept re-electing him.

Despite his numerous obligations, Mitch had always been there for her – a rock. Katie's thoughts drifted to that summer's day, the most horrible day of her life when Mitch had been the one to deliver the worst news possible. After sixteen years, the emotions were still so raw that they could be triggered by a word, a phrase, a memory. It had been a day like any other. She'd been late for school and had raced out the door, blowing a kiss at her mother. After school, she'd gone to Chloe's because her parents had to meet with some legislators in Sacramento.

Katie and Chloe were busy with homework when Mitch had arrived. Chloe had jumped up to greet her father, but his eyes had been on Katie even as he'd hugged his daughter. There had been such tenderness and pain in his expression that she knew, just knew, something terrible had happened.

77

Mitch had taken her hands and said, "Katie, I'm so sorry. There is no easy way around this. There's been a terrible car accident. Your father's walked away without a scratch, it's like a miracle, but your mother...she died at the scene."

She remembered distinctly, saw it like a movie reel, the way he had shaken his head, looked down at his lap. She remembered feeling grateful that he'd used the term "died" and not the euphemistic "passed away." He'd squeezed her hands and said, "The EMTs said she died instantaneously and would have felt no pain."

And no time to think, let alone say a word of goodbye, Katie had thought. And then her mind had raged. *God in Heaven, Dad loves you so much; why didn't you call him to you and leave Mommy for me.* And instantly, she'd regretted this thought, had never uttered it to anyone, but had tried to atone for it by honoring and respecting her father.

Eleanor interrupted Katie's thoughts, "Mitch is fine. Though it did shake him that the last election was such a close race." She sighed, "There's such an obsession with youth and change that, no matter how good you are, people want something new and fresh."

"Give him my regards," Katie said.

Eleanor looked at her watch, "You might see him later. He'll be picking me up; then we head out to Sacramento for the week."

She took a nibble of a tiny cookie, dabbed her mouth with a corner of the cloth napkin, and said, "I do miss your mother, you know."

Katie's back stiffened, but she kept her face neutral.

Eleanor continued, "I could so use her advice on dealing with Chloe."

"Divorce is never easy," Katie said. "I'm sorry things didn't work out between her and Terry."

Eleanor's jaw tightened. She made a dismissive gesture, "Oh, I think she's over him. Good riddance, I say."

Katie was not surprised. Eleanor had never made a secret of the fact that she had deemed Terry Reynolds an unsuitable match for Chloe who, from a young age, had been groomed "for greater things". Chloe had been a good student in high school but not outstanding. Katie suspected the McGraths had made a substantial donation to Harvard to secure Chloe's place at the law school. It occurred to her that she could easily ask one of the data analysts at the church to find out. Immediately, Katie reprimanded herself. That was over; she had sworn to herself that she would never again abuse access to sensitive personal data. The data analytics capabilities of the church were to be used strictly to further the church's mission. That had been her bargain with God.

"I tried to warn Chloe," Eleanor said with a shrug, "but of course, she never listens to me."

Katie suppressed a smile. "Tried to warn" was the understatement of the decade. She had witnessed some of the exchanges between mother and daughter. It had been like two ice queens dueling with daggers of pinpointed, hurtful jibes.

Eleanor had said, "You're throwing your life away. He's pleasant enough but not suitable."

"You sound like a Medici queen – making *suitable* political matches. I'm not throwing *my* life away; I'm throwing away the fantasy life you've dreamt up for me."

"At least get your facts straight. The Medicis weren't monarchs."

Chloe had spat, "Does every conversation with you have to be an educational intervention?"

"You were born into privilege; with that comes duty."

"For God's sake, spare me the sanctimonious drivel. Has it occurred to you that I might actually love Terry, or is marriage for love a totally alien concept to you?"

Katie shook her head to dispel the memories and said, "Aren't you being a bit harsh on Terry? He's had an awfully rough time."

Eleanor gave a dainty snort, "He's got more baggage than a porter on the Orient Express – that whole scandal with his father, then his mother dying of cancer, and of course his sister dying by suicide." She made a gesture in the direction of the Golden Gate. "It's all so…so unsavory."

The words hit Katie like a whip. She clenched her hands into fists and thought they might start bleeding where her nails dug into her palms. Inside, she was wailing with despair, and yet she maintained a neutral expression. She was good at this game; she'd learned from a young age that showing fear or sorrow made things worse, and hence she had learned to cry on the inside while maintaining her composure. She was going to need a long run this evening to flush out the shame and self-loathing.

Eleanor was oblivious. She continued, "It's just no good. We all have our crosses to bear, but the way Terry then went and had a nervous breakdown…" She trailed off. "That would always be dragged up when Chloe runs for office." She declared, "A politician's spouse can never show weakness."

Showing a little human compassion would be nice, Katie thought. She coughed to see if she could trust her voice and said, "It might backfire. Voters might think that Chloe abandoned her husband in his hour of need?"

"*Hour* of need?" Eleanor's voice rose, "More like a *life* of need. No, we must just message this correctly. Chloe has the strength of character to make tough decisions when necessary."

So much for the idea of in sickness and in health, Katie thought as Eleanor continued, "The more distance she can put between herself and that yours-mine-and-ours clan, the better."

"Do you really think it matters that much? There are so many non-traditional families in California – single, blended, re-married. I don't think people care."

Eleanor looked around, leaned forward, and dropped her voice, "I am not talking about California. That is just step one. I am talking about the long game. She has to appeal across the country."

Katie raised an eyebrow and waited. Eleanor said, "Think about it; one term as state senator, then a term or two in Congress. At forty-five, Chloe will be ready to run for president. She brings the perfect blend of tradition and freshness. Her grandfather was a congressman, her father a state senator. That is an impeccable pedigree. And Chloe will add the vigor and youth that this country craves. We just have to map out the right set of perspectives and policies. I see her as a socially progressive and fiscally responsible democrat – someone who can hold the middle ground."

Katie leaned back in her chair and studied the woman in front of her. She glimpsed something behind the mask of genteel sophistication, something raw and hungry. Katie knew that Eleanor had always been ambitious for Chloe, but this was new. The goal – the presidency – had never been mentioned before. And now there was a timeline. Could Eleanor's sixtieth have caused her to reflect on her own mortality? If she was going to see her daughter in the oval office, she had to get moving.

Katie sipped the tea, which had grown cold, and asked, "What about Chloe? Is she now all ready and raring to throw herself into politics?"

"Well, that's where you come in. You know Chloe has always idolized you, like an older sister. If you, and the church, could publicly endorse her, that would give her a great start." The words came tumbling out, "You see, the Church of Holy Redemption is exactly the kind of bipartisan, middle-of-the-road organization that would align with the political position that Chloe needs. By the way," she leaned across and patted Katie's hand, "you did a great job the other evening with that TV interview. Very poised; you would make such a great coach and ally for Chloe." For a second, there was something almost akin to pleading in her eyes.

Then Eleanor withdrew her hand and said, "And of course, Jeremiah wields great influence – way beyond California. Plus, there's…"

Katie interrupted, "But Eleanor, we've been very deliberate in keeping the church out of politics, in not endorsing any political candidates. That's part of why we can function across the entire spectrum. I don't need to lecture you on the importance of the separation of state and church – it works both ways."

Eleanor snorted, "Katie, I don't mean to be crass, but we all know how the game is played. How do you think your father got all that industrial land in Tracy rezoned for a church? And how did it happen that state-owned land in the Sierra foothills was suddenly available for establishing a privately-run juvenile detention center?"

"Institute for troubled youth," Katie corrected automatically, but her mind was in a whirl. She had been a high schooler when the church had acquired the land and, if she'd thought about it all, she would have assumed that wealthy donors had made these acquisitions possible.

Eleanor continued, "Mitch worked tirelessly to support your father in his dreams. You know how it was after your mother died. He was consumed with guilt about the accident and obsessed with the idea that his God had spared him to take his little congregation and turn it into something meaningful – something to honor the memory of your mother. I don't mind telling you that Mitch…we – we were concerned. If the church had failed, I don't know what your father might have done. And where would that have left you?"

She paused while a waiter cleared away the tea things. Katie was trying to process all she had heard. Her nerve endings were on fire. She registered every clink of cutlery, music drifting in from the lobby. The streaming sunlight felt hot and oppressive, and she had to control her breathing.

"It's a long game," Eleanor said. "And sometimes one is forced to call in old debts."

"What exactly is it that you want from me?"

Eleanor's response was immediate, "Two things. Spend some time with Chloe and help her recognize that she has so much to offer; that she should seriously consider a run for office."

"And the second thing?"

Eleanor placed her elbows on the table and pressed her steepled fingers together. She appeared to be studying the tablecloth pattern. Then she looked Katie straight in the eye and said, "I do not profess to know everything about social media and data analytics, but I do know that they are crucial weapons in any election. Obama and Hillary started it, Bernie took it to the next level and," she shuddered, "Trump, clearly, was a master at it."

She paused, apparently thinking carefully about her next words. Katie felt nausea rising from the pit of her stomach. The biggest mistake of her life was about to come back and haunt her. No, not the biggest mistake, the second-biggest – the fact that she had confided in this woman what she had done. Years ago, as a student, Katie had been in terrible trouble. She wanted to unburden herself, confess, and atone for her shameful action. And of all the people in the world, she had chosen to talk to the woman in front of her. Eleanor's shocking response had been, "As long as no one knows, it didn't happen."

In a trance, she heard Eleanor say, "I remember a conversation you and I had some years ago. That leads me to believe that the church, particularly you, have exceptional capabilities in data analytics and social media." Her face was a question mark, and Katie could do nothing but nod.

"So why don't we start there? You bring that power to bear on shaping Chloe's platform. How do people feel about divorcees? What is the right age to be youthful and fresh, yet old enough to be trusted? What do the voters feel about the death penalty, global warming, traffic congestion, housing? What are the issues worth taking on? You can provide the answers, and for the time being, you don't even need the church to be publicly associated with Chloe's campaign."

She paused, inclined her head, and said, "As long as no one knows, it didn't happen."

Katie felt perspiration collect near her neck and trickle down her spine. What could she do? Eleanor was a master strategist. A flash of anger in a remote corner of her mind triggered a thought – there had to be something out there in the data lake that she could use for leverage over Eleanor; fight fire with fire. But for now, she needed to buy time.

Slowly she nodded and said, "I'll talk to Chloe. As to the rest, I'll think about it."

"Don't think too long; time is press–"

A voice boomed across the quiet restaurant, "There you are!"

Mitch McGrath strode across the room, and Katie rose from her chair to meet his outstretched arms. He kissed her on both cheeks and said, "You look marvelous. Congratulations on that interview; you were great! Have you considered going into politics?"

She laughed, "The field might be getting a little crowded. I don't fancy taking on some of the competition."

"Ah, you've been talking about Chloe," he said.

Eleanor touched his forearm, "Keep your voice down, Mitch."

Indeed, heads were turning throughout the restaurant as people recognized the popular politician. Mitch, in his early sixties, was a man in his prime. He was six-foot-two, dressed in designer jeans and a golf shirt that showed off the toned body of a life-long athlete. He had a strong jaw, and his short, gray hair, streaked with the original black, made him look distinguished. It was his eyes, however, that made him approachable. The gray-green eyes always reminded Katie of the ocean. They were bright and alert, and he had a way of looking at people that made them feel like they were the only thing in the world that mattered to him. When he smiled, as he did now, laughter lines appeared.

A waiter raced across the room and pulled up a chair for Mitch. He thanked the man as he folded his frame into the tub chair.

Mitch looked at Katie and asked, "Do you have time for a drink?"

Eleanor cut in, "Mitch, you're driving."

Katie said, "Thanks, but I really need to get going. Got a busy few days ahead. I've decided to join my father on his trip to Africa, so now there's a hundred-and-one things to sort out."

"Don't forget your vaccinations," Mitch cautioned, and Katie added that item to her mental to-do list.

"She's only going to Namibia," Eleanor said. "It's a desert country – very few bugs. So Katie doesn't need any special vaccinations."

Katie reflected that Eleanor was probably the most enigmatic person she knew – a maelstrom of contradictions.

Her knowledge was encyclopedic and, to further Mitch's career, she had practised advanced data analytics in her head years before the term had even been invented. She could be very empathetic when engaged in a cause but ruthless in the face of any opposition.

They said their goodbyes, and Katie headed back over the Bay Bridge. The traffic was light, and the wind was in her face. The city skyline was etched in black against the sunset. Stray clouds showed their orange-golden underbellies.

For the thousandth time, she recalled Eleanor's words from long ago, "Sometimes the end *does* justify the means. As long as no one knows, it didn't happen." But the words meant nothing; she knew the truth. She, Katie Blanchard, was responsible for the death of three people. Of course, it had not been intentional, but still... three young lives cut short because of her youthful arrogance and ignorance. Despite the glow of the sun, a familiar darkness enveloped her. It was going to take more than a jog to dispel the demons.

She veered off onto Howard street and made her way into the South of Market area to a building that had once been a warehouse. As she passed, music reverberated down the street. Katie pulled into a side street and parked. Then she slung her jacket into the car's trunk and retrieved a reddish-brown wig, which she pulled over her hair before applying a matching lipstick that gave her pale face a vampire-like quality. Finally, she opened the top three buttons of her blouse and pulled it sideways to leave one shoulder bare. She pressed a button to shut the trunk and strode into the nightclub.

Most of the bar stools were empty this early on a Sunday night. Katie picked a seat in the middle of the bar and ordered a double vodka on the rocks. The conversation with Eleanor played itself over and over in her mind. It was just the sort of complication she didn't need right now – not with all the effort going into system upgrades, her father's outrageous spending, the trip to Africa…

"Hey, pretty woman. Can I buy you a drink?"

She eyed the smiling stranger. *What a pathetic pick-up line*, she thought. The guy was probably in his mid-forties, good-looking, with a dimpled chin. She sensed his mixture of bravado and insecurity. Her eyes flitted to his hand, and sure enough, a pale marking indicated that the wedding ring was stashed somewhere out of sight for the night.

She smiled, "Sure, mine's a vodka."

He settled in next to her and asked, "You come here often?"

She could hear his New York accent and shrugged, "What about you?"

"Visiting; I'm here for a convention." He eyed her over his scotch.

Perfect, Katie thought. Twenty minutes later, she and the stranger were on their way to her apartment.

***

The town of Livermore was exactly halfway between San Francisco and the Church of Holy Redemption. The town was home to the famous Lawrence Livermore atomic research labs. Lately, it had also strived to build a reputation as a wine-growing region. Critics argued that it was all rather wannabee compared to the famous Napa and Sonoma valleys further north. One of the wine estates, Ruby Hills, boasted a gated community with oversized houses set in manicured gardens.

Isaac O'Neil lived in one of these houses. Four of the five bedrooms were never used. The kitchen counters were uncluttered, and the great room ultra-tidy. An eclectic mix of magazines lay neatly arranged on the coffee table: GQ, Conde Nast, People, National Geographic, and Wine Spectator. The walls were a pale beige and the furnishings unremarkable – except for a single large painting. It was a portrait of a woman in Andy Warhol style. The artwork bore an uncanny resemblance to Katie Blanchard.

Isaac had settled down in front of the TV with a pizza and his second glass of eight-year-old Syrah. He was flipping through the channels when his laptop pinged. It only took a few keystrokes, and the screen filled with a live feed from a CCTV camera that had been triggered by the geolocation transmitter he had planted on Katie's car. Time for the evening ritual of making sure that she got home safely.

He watched her Audi roll into the parking garage of her apartment block. He hit a few buttons and got a feed through the camera in the lobby. Katie was not alone. "Damn!"

She was wearing the wig – God, how he hated that wig. He beat his fist on the table and swore.

When Katie and her companion got into the elevator the feed automatically switched to the camera inside. The man with Katie was clean-shaven, with brilliant white teeth and a hint of gray in his short hair. His biceps strained at the sleeves of a designer golf shirt. When the elevator doors closed, the man put an arm around Katie's waist and bent down to kiss her. She did not resist.

The elevator door opened, the two pulled apart, and Isaac captured a screenshot. Methodically, he cropped the image and fed the stranger's portrait into a database. Isaac had to steady his hands and will himself not to think about the scene unfolding in Katie's apartment. Were they going to settle down for a drink and a chat? He doubted it, and unbidden pictures crept into his mind – the stranger unbuttoning Katie's blouse, kissing her...

Stop it! He wanted to roar as much to himself as to Katie. His computer pinged – it had found a match. The man was a stranger no more. His name was Brian Stewart from upstate New York, an account executive with an advertising firm. He appeared to be happily married and the father of two teenage girls, with whom he went cross-country running. The family had a Labrador and two Lexuses. His bank balance drew a whistle from Isaac, who topped up his wine and settled down in front of the computer to do more research.

Forty minutes later, he watched the lover boy descend in the elevator and wished he could put his fist into the man's dimpled, smiling face. Isaac drafted a quick note to his team leader at the Settlement Bureau. He muttered to the screen, "Brian, my friend, you might think you got lucky tonight, but you've just fucked with Karma. And Karma is a bitch." Brian Stewart was going to make some hefty payments to atone for his sins.

Chapter 10, Renaissance Institute
Sunday Afternoon, 2nd Week of June

DANNY

The door of "The Cooler" slammed shut behind Danny. The windowless cell had a high ceiling with a single fluorescent light, a bunk with a thin mattress, and a stainless-steel toilet and washbasin. It also had a table and a chair. Danny massaged his arm where the guard had gripped him so hard that the blood had stopped flowing. Fucking arseholes. He slumped into the chair and slammed his fist on the table. "Fuck it!"

His main concern was for Timothy. There was no telling how Tim would react. Danny hoped that his roommate would take himself to the clinic. Nurse Kelby was among the few people Danny respected at the institute. He tried to think whether any of the other boys on the floor might help Tim but didn't hold out much hope. At best, they ignored him; often, they mocked him.

He hated feeling so helpless and yelled at the door, "Wankers! Imbeciles! Arseholes! Go fuck yourselves."

On the desk were a pad, pen and envelope. From previous "visits", Danny already knew the contents of the single sheet of paper that was taped to the desk.

> *Take this opportunity of quiet time to reflect on your behavior, its impact on others, and what you might want to do differently. You are encouraged to write down your thoughts and share them with your counselor.*
>
> *Anything you write will be held in the strictest confidence by your counselor.*
>
> *Duncan Hughes, Principal*

Principal wanker, Danny thought.

He stared at the green wall for a few minutes and thought, *okay, you want to know what I'm thinking? I'll give you what I'm thinking.* He started writing in a frantic scrawl.

> *Dear Dr. Roberts*
>
> *I trust you will forgive me if I do not start with <u>my</u> behavior but rather the behavior of the people who have influenced and shaped me. This is pertinent since my actions are a reaction to their actions – that's a basic universal law.*
>
> *My "Dear Papa" is a notorious crook who swindled thousands of people out of their pensions and savings in an elaborate Ponzi scheme. You may recall the scandal when Carl Gunderson was a household name, bandied about on CNN and every other cable station in the country. Who can forget the baying crowds in front of the New York courthouse, chanting "lock him up; hang him; lock him up; hang him"?*
>
> *Our house was put up as collateral for bail. So, when Carl Gunderson skipped the country, we lost our home.*

I know you consider yourself to be ever-so empathetic, but I'm not sure you can appreciate what it meant to bear my father's name and to find one day that my mother and I had been abandoned, penniless, reviled, and ostracized by everyone we knew.

Except, did I mention that my oh-so-clever father had locked up money in trust funds for me and my half-sister? The ultimate fucking joke! He made those trusts as tight as Alcatraz so no one could get at them till they turned thirty-five. But, of course, he never intended for us to have any of the money; it was just his piggy bank of last resort.

"Dearest Mama" did the only thing she's ever learned to do – played the victim and prostituted herself to a series of very unsuitable men till she hit rock bottom with the slime ball that is now my "stepdaddy". Said lowlife is a third-rate loser of a lobbyist and spends his time figuring out how to get his hands on the millions in the trust fund. He actually found a loophole – direct expenditure for education can be taken from the fund. And, since the venerable Renaissance Institute provides a generous "referral fee" kickback on the cost of "education" (I use the term loosely, given the Gestapo methods employed here), Mama and the uber arsehole can now keep body and soul together. The trustees even allow them to take the occasional vacation on the West Coast to visit me – except they always seem to get stuck at some Napa Valley spa and never quite make it here.

As for my brother, Terry...

Danny put down the pen and pressed the palms of his hands against his eyes. He was used to raging against his parents. It had become a conditioned response, and it brought him neither satisfaction nor relief. They had long since lost any ability to hurt him. He didn't forgive them – he never would – but he couldn't give a shit.

But Terry – what would he say to his big brother if ever he met him again? What do you say to someone who is probably unaware that they've hurt you deeply, someone you want to simultaneously kick in the balls and embrace so hard that they can never ever leave you again?

He scowled at the page, ripped it into confetti, and flushed it down the toilet. Then he lay on the bunk for a while. His stomach grumbled, reminding him that he'd missed lunch. Finally, Danny concluded that there was no point in self-pity and decided it was time to have some fun with the dickheads in charge of the institute. He got up and started writing again.

Dear Dr. Roberts

You have been urging me to let go of my anger against my parents. I have decided to follow your advice and do my dear Mama, who wants nothing more than money, a favor. During passion time, I assembled a bomb that will go off this evening in the science lab. Dearest Mama will get the usual percentage kickback when my trust fund pays for the damages.

Please do not be alarmed. I have taken care to choose a time and place when damage to property will be maximized and the risk to human life not too great.

Since all communications are confidential, this note will only reach you on Monday – long after the explosion. I look forward to discussing my progress with you at our next session.

With kind regards,

He signed the page with a flourish and sealed it into the envelope. Then Danny lay on the bunk and grinned. This cooler thing really worked; he felt much better.

He must have fallen asleep because he woke with a start when the guard came to release him with gruff comments about staying out of trouble. It was dark and past dinner time when he got back to his room, where he was startled to find Gerald sitting, reading a book.

"Where's Timothy? What are you doing here?"

Gerald closed the book and said, "I took Timothy to the clinic; they're going to keep him overnight. He was pretty upset, but I got the gist of what happened."

"Thanks, man," Danny said and flopped down on his bed. "That's a relief. I was worried about him."

"The nurse says he'll be fine. They called his counselor and gave him something to sleep." He shifted in his chair and looked at Danny, "But what about you? I gather it was quite a fight. Shouldn't they have taken *you* to the clinic?

"Nah," Danny said. "A few scrapes and bruises. I'm used to it."

Gerald's eyes searched out the bruises and crusted blood on Danny's forearm, but the older boy did not pursue it any further. Instead, he said, "I snagged you some food from the dining hall."

Danny was instantly up, "Oh, man, you're a saint. I'm starving." He reached for the plastic container that Gerald produced and stuffed a boiled egg into his mouth while picking lettuce and tomato off the ham sandwich.

Gerald watched with a bemused smile, then asked, "What's it like?"

"Wha' wha' like?" Danny asked through a full mouth.

"You eat like a pig," Gerald observed.

Danny grinned, "I use my time efficiently. Besides, my eating habits drive my stepfather crazy. I found it an effective way to be excused from the dinner table so I could eat in front of the TV."

Gerald rolled his eyes, "What's 'The Cooler' like?"

"Oh, that," Danny made a dismissive gesture. "Like being sent to time out in kindergarten. They even want you to sit and reflect on your sins, write them down and share them with your counselor. It's like writing punishment lines. I just wish they'd paint the walls a different color. They're a *soothing* green. Makes me want to vomit."

Suddenly, a piercing alarm went off, warbling like an ambulance. It was followed by the sound of clanking metal. Gerald leaped up and rushed to the door.

"What the blazes…" Gerald looked utterly bewildered.

Danny hadn't moved from his seat. Instead, he chuckled and mimicked Gerald, "What the blazes? You must be the only person on the planet who still says that."

"What's going on?"

"Relax. It's just the lockdown alarm. See those iron grates coming down? That's to lock everyone into their sectors. Standard crowd control procedure in prisons."

"But what… why…?"

"It's a bomb scare. They're looking for a bomb that is set to go off…in the science block."

Gerald gaped, wide-eyed. "What… how? We're trapped." He stared at Danny in disbelief, "How do you know this?"

"Because I," he paused, feeling pride and a pang of guilt, since Gerald looked seriously freaked out, "because I *allegedly* planted the bomb."

Gerald backed into a corner of the room, shaking his head.

Danny walked over, took hold of Gerald's shoulders and squeezed them. "Hey," he said, "get a grip. Don't worry – nothing's going to happen. It's just a hoax."

Gerald eyed him with suspicion, and Danny led him to sit on the edge of the bed. Then he scooted behind Gerald and started massaging his shoulders.

"But why?" Gerald asked.

"Because the principal, the staff, the counselors, my parents...the whole fucking world is pissing me off." Danny was surprised to hear the venom in his own voice. He'd meant to keep it light. "So, I decided to have some fun and yank their chains."

Gerald groaned as Danny's thumbs dug in beneath his shoulder blades.

Danny continued, "Everything you write down in the cooler is supposedly confidential – only to be shared with your counselor. Well, I've just proven that it isn't. The counselor isn't here tonight; it's not like *he's* alerted security. This place is a goddamn gulag, and I'm going to get out of here and expose these bible-punching hypocrites for the money-grabbing Pharisees they are."

Gerald peered over his shoulder, "Do you think that's wise? I mean, the Renaissance Institute is part of the Church of Holy Redemption – a very respected and powerful organization."

"Yes, and the Catholic church is also a powerful organization and condoned priests fucking altar boys for centuries. It's precisely because they are powerful and arrogant that someone has to stand up against them."

Gerald winced as Danny pressed down hard.

"Sorry," Danny said and leaned down to kiss the spot he had bruised.

"You must really hate God," Gerald said.

Danny paused in his massaging and let an arm rest on Gerald's shoulder. He leaned in closer and was aware of the smell of Gerald's hair – something fresh and lemony. He stroked his hair, which felt as smooth and velvety as it looked.

"No, I don't hate God, because I don't believe he exists. But, if he did exist, I wish he'd pay a little more attention to what's going on down here. It would be nice if he could occasionally fire off a few lightning bolts to incinerate the arseholes who give him a bad name." He sighed, "But I guess he's busy with more important stuff."

Gerald said, "He works in his own way – I know you're rolling your eyes – and I still don't think it's wise for you to play such a dangerous hoax."

"Wisdom is greatly overrated," Danny said, "and truth be told – it gives me a thrill; it gives me pleasure to yank their chains." He leaned in closer and whispered in Gerald's ear, "Now pleasure, that's a noble goal. Don't you agree?" He stroked Gerald's chest while letting his lips and tongue ghost along his neck.

Danny whispered, "Has anyone ever told you that you're hot?" His lips touched Gerald's, whose eyes were shut. The older boy's cheeks flushed, and his breath came in shallow, ragged gasps. His indecision was palpable, but slowly, tentatively, his lips parted.

Then they both heard boots clanking along the corridor and pulled apart. Danny crossed the room and peered down the hall. Two security guards were stopping at every door to take a roll call. Over his shoulder, he said, "It'll be cool. Just let me do the talking."

In response to the guards' questions, Danny explained that Timothy was in the clinic and that the nurse had sent Gerald to get a few of Timothy's things. Just as he was about to leave, the alarm had sounded. One of the guards made a notation on his iPad and muttered, "We're watching you," before they moved on. Danny made a rude, fisted gesture to their retreating backs.

When the guards had gone, the boys looked at each other, and both began to speak.

"I just…"

"That was…"

"Look. What happened…"

Danny gestured for Gerald to start. The older boy sat on the bed and spoke in a calm tone, "Danny, I really like you, and I want to be your friend, but not like that. It can't happen again."

Danny looked at the unwavering blue eyes and bit his lower lip, "But… it's nothing, just a bit of fun. If I like someone, I want to give them pleasure."

"That's exactly the point. I don't believe that…intimate contact…" He swallowed and blushed before forcing out the words, "that kissing or sex should be *nothing, just a bit of fun.* I think it's something reserved for people in a committed relationship."

Danny had heard of people who held this kind of worldview, but he'd never actually met one. It was like seeing a strange new species. Gerald was so pure, innocent, and vulnerable – especially in this place – that it caused Danny an almost physical pain. But he didn't say any of this, he just shrugged.

"Friends?" Gerald asked with an outstretched hand, and they shook. Then, Gerald said, "Turn off the light and come sit here." He propped up the pillow against the headboard, stretched out his legs on the bed, and patted the mattress next to him.

"What? I thought you just said…"

Gerald cut him off, "I know. But you see, when *you* like someone, you want to give them pleasure. When I care for someone, I want them to talk to me to understand them better. And it's much easier for people to talk in the dark. Trust me – turn off the light."

They lay side by side in the darkness. Danny could hear Gerald's steady breathing, and slowly his eyes adjusted to the moonlight. He waited, unsure, until he couldn't stand the silence anymore. Finally, Danny asked, "What do you want me to talk about?"

"Anything. Why don't you start by telling me why you're so angry?"

It was weird sitting in the dark, unable to read Gerald's expression yet feeling the warmth of his body. So very different from his encounters with a succession of school counselors and psychologists. He'd always viewed them as adversaries, had watched every twitch of their faces, looking for expressions of judgment or shock. He'd told them all lots of things – half-truths, outright lies, preposterous dreams. It was a game. This, however, was new for Danny, and he had to think hard to find the right words because it mattered what Gerald thought of him. He didn't want to sound whiny or pathetic, and he didn't want to lie.

He cleared his throat and started, "Have you ever heard of Carl Gunderson, the guy who swindled thousands of people out of their pensions and savings?" He told the whole story, dispassionately, and Gerald did not interrupt him.

It hadn't been all bad. In the summer, when his mother was at her wit's end with constant hounding by the media, they'd packed a suitcase and gone on a road trip from New York to L.A. Danny was thirteen. He smiled when he thought back to that trip, "We had the top down on my mom's convertible and we were singing along to her favorite Spotify playlist. She has a good voice, my mother. I got to learn all those songs from the nineties." He paused and picked at the scabs on his arm. "But she had absolutely no plan. We ended up in some cheap motel in Santa Monica. She got a job as a cocktail waitress. The next thing I knew, the first of many boyfriends moved in."

Even with Gerald, he couldn't bring himself to say out loud how ashamed, angry, frustrated, and helpless he'd felt, pretending to be asleep on the couch while his mother fucked yet another stranger.

"One of the things I remember is the smell of booze. It just seemed impossible to get away from it. I don't think I'll ever drink alcohol – just a whiff of Juanito's beer this morning made me feel ill."

Gerald put an arm around Danny's shoulder and squeezed him. Danny felt a lump in his throat and did not dare to continue for fear that his voice would betray his emotions.

"What about your brother and sister?" Gerald asked. "You explained this morning that you didn't see much of them, but you had some relationship with them?"

"They lived with their mother – my father's first wife. But they did spend some of the holidays with us. Like I said, Lily was already in high school when I was born; I suspect she thought of me like a puppy or a doll, but to me, she was like a fairy princess. She had a beautiful, soft voice and would crawl under the covers with me and read me goodnight stories." He paused, then plowed on with a little laugh, "She even taught me a good night prayer: 'Father, we thank thee for the night, and for the pleasant morning light...' I forget how it carries on."

Gerald picked up the prayer, "For rest and food and loving care, and all that makes the day so fair."

Danny nodded in the dark, "When Lily was around, there was a smell of Thanksgiving, a Christmas glow, and happiness around the house. Even my father would come home early from the office and look less stressed."

He sighed, "Lily and my mother didn't get along. I think my mother was jealous. And Lily was too gentle to deal with confrontation. So she just stopped coming."

Danny's mind held a gallery of Lily pictures – smiling in the snow; helping him paint a card for his father; making him hot chocolate; humming to herself; lifting him up so he could put an ornament on the Christmas tree. All these mental pictures had the softness of fading sepia prints. He knew that the mist of time had embellished the truth –

made everything seem more wonderful than it probably had been. But he cherished the memories of his sister and would never let anything tarnish them.

As he lay with his head in the crook of Gerald's shoulder, he was suddenly aware that this was what it had felt like to lie next to Lily – safe, cherished. His eyes stung, and he was glad that Gerald could not see his tears.

"And your brother?" Gerald asked.

"Terry was already at UCLA studying computer science when I was still in elementary school. Then he got his first job. His visits were brief – a few days for Thanksgiving or Christmas. He was like a distant God to me, mostly holed up in his room with his computer. But occasionally, he would take me into the yard to kick a soccer ball. He also spent patient hours in the driveway teaching me how to shoot hoops. He was great at basketball – I think he was on the UCLA team. I, of course, sucked at it."

"What was he like?" Gerald asked.

Danny bit his lip and searched his memory. "With Lily, everything came from the heart. Terry was more methodical, purpose-driven. If I'm honest, I wonder if he ever saw me as a person. It was more that I was a project – see if he could teach this kid ball skills. He never called me by name. I was always 'Kiddo' or 'Runt.' Terry and my father used to fight. I have no idea what it was about. While Lily was there, they kept it civil, but the fights got bad once she stopped coming. I remember lying in bed, with the blanket pulled over my head, listening to them shout downstairs. Then he stopped coming for the holidays, too."

There was a long silence before Danny continued in a low voice, "When my mother and I were in LA, I hoped and prayed that Terry would come and find me and take me away. I prayed so hard! Every night I would get on my knees and say the prayer Lily had taught me over and over.

101

And then I bargained with God. I told him that the only Christmas present I ever wanted ever again was to go live with my brother so that I would not be such a burden to my mother."

He felt Gerald's arm tighten around his shoulder in encouragement and continued, "Well, Christmas came and went – no sign of Terry. That's when I decided there was no point in relying on God or anyone but myself. So I packed a muffin and an apple from the motel breakfast buffet and ran away to look for him." He paused and chuckled, "I might even have succeeded. A very nice Sikh man at a service station got on the internet for me and tried to help. One snag, though – I didn't know that Terry and Lily had taken their mother's name after the divorce. So, I was looking for Terry Gunderson when I should have been looking for Terry Reynolds.

"The police picked me up three days later. My mother was more embarrassed than anything else; she packed up the car and drove us back to the East Coast."

They sat in silence before Danny asked, "You're close to your sisters, aren't you?"

He could feel Gerald nodding before he said, "Yes, very."

Danny cleared his throat and said, "Can you imagine one of your sisters dying and nobody in the family deeming it necessary to tell you?"

For the first time, Gerald lost his calm demeanor. He turned, and in the ghostly light, Danny could see the intensity of his emotions when he said, "You're not serious? Surely…are you telling me…is Lily…?"

Danny nodded, "She died by suicide – jumped off the Golden Gate bridge." He paused, then continued in a strangled whisper, "And I happened to read about it online – some article about the high suicide rate in the US – two weeks later. Long after the funeral."

"That's unbelievable! Your father, your mother? Why didn't they…?"

"My father was hiding from the authorities somewhere in Asia and apparently didn't dare contact me for fear of exposing his whereabouts. My mother literally said, 'It slipped my mind. I didn't think you'd care after all these years.'"

They sat in silence before Gerald asked, "And Terry?"

"I traced him via LinkedIn and got through to his wife – I didn't even know he was married. It took a lot to persuade her to let me speak to Terry. He'd only vaguely mentioned a half-brother to her."

The memory of that realization still seared his insides. He had just lost his sister, and his one and only brother had barely thought to acknowledge his existence. Who or what was he in the eyes of the world, of his family? That night, he had helped himself to a bottle of Vodka from his stepfather's cabinet and, a few hours later, lost consciousness on a park bench where the police had found him.

"When I finally spoke to Terry, he was heavily medicated in hospital. He'd had a breakdown and kept saying, 'I'm so sorry, Kiddo, it's all my fault.' I did eventually gather that Lily had been blackmailed because of my father's scandal. Of course, she and Terry weren't immediately associated with it because they'd taken their mother's name. But someone had figured out who her father was and had threatened to tell the school where she taught second-graders. You know what people are like – the parents would have hounded her out of the school with pitchforks and burning torches, convinced that these terrible moral faults in the family would taint their precious darlings."

They sat in silence for a long time. Then Danny turned to Gerald, "I could have helped her, you know. It's not Terry's fault; it's mine. I lived through that whole scandal, and I survived. I could have been there for her and shared my experience – told her it would be okay. But I was sulking, waiting for her to come find me when I should have reached out to her."

"That's preposterous. Circumstances drove you apart; you can't put this on yourself," Gerald said.

Danny thought of Lily – beautiful, gentle, smiling Lily – and suddenly, he felt something welling up inside him. It was as though a coil, too tightly compressed for too long, had snapped. Sobs escaped his lips, and a shudder went through his chest. He hadn't cried for her, not once – had buried his grief under a thick layer of anger. Gerald wrapped his arms around Danny and held him tight. Danny's whole body convulsed, and he started to cry like a puppy in the midnight hours of the first night away from its mother.

Chapter 11, San Francisco

Wednesday Morning, 3rd Week of June

TERRY

Terry arrived at One Embarcadero Center too early for his interview with BDA – Big Data Analytica. He decided to get a cappuccino at a Starbucks brimming with the stylish dress and self-importance of the financial district. He was pleased to be wearing his suit and tie. Hissing coffee machines competed with the music, shouting baristas, and people talking into their phones.

Terry escaped the din and found a table outside from where he could witness the city's awakening. In various doorways, homeless people lay asleep, unperturbed. BART exits disgorged commuters who rolled like a river to be swallowed by towering buildings. A delivery van double-parked, and a cyclist had to swerve into the traffic when the driver opened his door. The cyclist swore and gave the driver the finger.

San Francisco in the morning exuded the putrid ambiance of a hangover. Terry tried to ignore the smell of garbage wafting up from the gutters and inhaled the aroma of his coffee. He picked up snippets of conversation from the table next to him, where two men were pouring over an iPad. He pricked his ears when he heard them mention BDA.

One of them was tall, with thick brown hair. His brown eyes radiated with intensity as he leaned across the table and said, "Rajiv, you know I've always been one hundred percent behind you. But the rate at which you're expanding...I don't know..."

Rajiv was of Indian descent and looked like he might have stepped out of a GQ magazine. He wore designer jeans and a European-style cotton jacket over a white shirt. He exuded self-confidence from his expertly-styled hair and the Patek Philippe on his wrist to the black loafers –no socks – on his feet. His voice was calm and melodious when he said, "Isaac, we've done this before. I have a great team, and the business model is sound."

Isaac tapped his finger on the iPad, "Why did you have to go and take out a lease on *seven* floors? You only need three right now. And why here in downtown? You could have rented space at half the price in the East Bay."

"We've ramped up our hiring, and it's a competitive market. The top talent wants to work in the city."

Isaac shook his head, "I don't know. It's diverting attention from the main goal. The cash flow is going to kill us."

Rajiv's voice was smooth, "We have no choice; we have to get to critical mass and corner the market." He gave his opposite a smile, "I have full faith in Pastor Jeremiah getting us that investment. If you need me to speak to the investor angels – just call."

Rajiv looked at his watch, and Terry realized he'd better get moving.

As he ditched his cup, he heard Rajiv say, "Give Katie my love..."

Terry crossed the street and rode the elevator to the 30th floor. It opened onto an expansive lobby that was so out of keeping with the bland, forty-year-old exterior of the building that Terry did a double-take. For a moment, he thought he'd stepped onto a Star Trek set. Two receptionists with headsets sat behind an oblong glass counter with metal accents. They appeared robotic with their synchronous, "BDA, please hold; BDA, please hold; to whom may I connect you?" Behind them was a frosted glass wall sporting the company's logo – B.D.A. surrounded by blinking LED orbs, spinning like planets around a sun. The effect was both futuristic and retro.

Terry was asked to wait and settled on an orange-and-turquoise couch that had been purchased for aesthetics rather than comfort. He watched as the elevators delivered batch after batch of workers, who entered through security turnstiles and disappeared behind the glass wall. In contrast to the financial district crowd at Starbucks, the dress code was mixed – predominantly jeans, sneakers, and T-shirts. There was an abundance of hair streaked in bright colors, ear and nose piercings, tattoos, Doc Martens and backpacks. And there were also tailored suits, pencil skirts, and high heels – the full diversity of San Francisco's trendiest and brightest on display. Terry was struck by how young everyone looked and the one unifying feature – earbuds. They appeared to be a standard accessory for everyone.

Terry's phone buzzed with a message from Tricia back at the office. *Hi, sleeping off a hangover?*

He texted back. *Toothache, waiting at dentist, should be in the office by lunchtime.* She answered with a sad emoji.

He felt a little guilty about the white lie, but he couldn't stand the idea of his teammates crowding around, wanting to know how the interview went. Especially if he didn't get the job or didn't even make it to the next round of interviews.

He had just opened his laptop to take another look at his resume when a clanging noise made him look up. A man with a bicycle emerged from one of the elevators. A mop of red hair protruded from under his cycling helmet, and he wore a yellow shirt, a green tie, and impossibly-tight black jeans.

One of the receptionists looked up and intercepted him, "Simon, your nine o'clock." She nodded in Terry's direction.

The man looked at his watch and cursed. Then, he extended his hand to Terry, "Simon Osborne." They shook, and the man continued, "Sorry to keep you. Traffic was abysmal. I don't know what's going on with people – it's like the zombie apocalypse down there."

"Tell me about it," Terry said, "I live up near the panhandle where you have to dodge commuters *and* tourists all the time."

"You cycle?"

Terry nodded, and Simon said to the receptionists, "Hear that? Another cyclist. When are we getting the cycle racks installed in the basement?" He looked at his watch again and said to Terry, "We've got our daily standup meeting in a few minutes – bring your stuff."

The space behind the screen was a hive of desks on wheels arranged in clusters with at least a hundred people bent over their computers. One third of the floor was cordoned off with yellow tape, and workmen were busy assembling furniture. On one wall, a bank of silent TV screens provided non-stop news coverage from every major channel. A giant screen at the far end showed two digital clocks counting down. The screen proclaimed,

Sprint Ends - 04 days: 23 hours

75% Complete vs. Target of 79%

Next Standup - 00 hours: 01 minutes

As Terry watched, the clock reached 00:00 and started flashing. Everyone on the floor got up and, as though performing a ritualistic dance, rearranged themselves into groups of six to ten people near various whiteboards. Simon led the way to a corner where six co-workers joined them.

"Morning all," Simon said. "This here is Terry; he's joining as of today." No one but Terry looked surprised. Simon continued, "And Indira – he nodded to a young woman – started yesterday. For you newbies, there are two rules to remember. Firstly, if you don't know, try and figure it out on the internet, and if you still don't know, ask! For God's sake, don't make assumptions and fuck up – we don't have time for that. Secondly, if you have any spare capacity, put up your hand and take on more work. That's what this meeting is for – we pay for output and, as you can see from the board, we're behind target."

He looked to a young man to Terry's right and said, "Okay. Clock starts now. Go!" The stand-up clock reset to twenty minutes and started to count down as the team, one by one, gave status updates. Terry was surprised by how concise they were.

The fourth person to report out was a woman in a short skirt and Doc Martens. She wore her purple, green, and pink hair in a thick, psychedelic braid. Terry was reminded of when Chloe had dragged him to the opera to see Wagner's "Ride of the Valkyries." A tattoo winked from beneath her shoulder strap. *Concentrate,* Terry told himself.

The woman gave Terry a broad smile. She exuded something very wholesome, despite the garish hair – like someone out of a chocolate commercial. She said, "We've started work on the API to extract data from the new master feeds, and we should be ready to start testing…"

109

Simon interrupted, "Sandy, I don't want to hear about activities. Finished work and obstacles only."

Sandy seemed unperturbed, "We're shorthanded. I need at least one more resource."

Simon replied, "Terry here has done loads of ETL and some API. He can join your scrum. We'll give it till Friday and make a final decision." He turned to Terry, "That okay with you?"

Terry nodded, dumbfounded. He wished he'd told Tricia he was in hospital with appendicitis.

They moved from status reporting to reviewing a list of "backlog stories" on an iPad. One by one, a young man pulled up the description of discrete work packets, and team members volunteered to take on the respective tasks. When the count-down clock reached 00:00 again, the entire room dissolved and rearranged itself till everyone was seated back at their desks, headphones on and eyes glued to the screen. The only sound came from a white noise generator.

Sandy proved to be an excellent teacher. Throughout the day, she made Terry review completed work items, research techniques on the internet and perform various programming tasks. She checked his work without judgment and adjusted his learning program. At four o'clock, she went into the backlog on her computer and assigned the first real task to Terry. He read the description.

> **Client:** *Big West Insurance Company*
>
> **Requirement:** *Client wants to correlate data from Alcoholics Anonymous membership with motor vehicle accident history.*
>
> **Hypothesis:** *Number of years as an AA member is a predictor of increased motor vehicle accident risk.*

By now, Terry knew enough to extract the required data from various portions of the data lake. He was astounded how easy it was – a simple point, select, click in one database, and another point-and-click in a few more, and he had the report. He was grateful for the courses in applied statistics he'd taken at UCLA. They now allowed him to appreciate the elegance of the graph, complete with a correlation coefficient of 0.4, that appeared on his screen.

Sandy leaned over his shoulder to study his screen. Terry caught his breath when her breast brushed his shoulder, and her perfume enveloped him. He resisted wrinkling his nose when he also detected the smell of cigarettes.

"I guess that's what they wanted to prove," she said. "The longer people stay with AA, the more likely they are to have accidents."

"That's kind of sad," Terry said. "I was expecting the opposite. I thought that people who stuck with AA would stay sober and would be less likely to have accidents."

She touched his shoulder, "Beware of confusing correlation with causality – it's the most tempting mistake in this line of work. We can only speculate but if you think about it – people who are long-time AA members are likely to be the ones that fall off the wagon repeatedly. So it might stand to reason that they're more prone to having DUI accidents."

She mused, "Poor suckers, now anyone who's faithfully going to AA will find their insurance premium going up."

Terry was outraged, "Seriously? But how? Surely the insurance companies aren't allowed to do that? That's private information. They're not allowed to discriminate."

She straightened up and gave him a pensive stare, then said, "But *we* are. Welcome to our world." Then she stretched and smiled, "You've done great. Time for a break – follow me."

Minutes later, Terry found himself on the rooftop of the building. Sandy led him through the utility jumble of satellite dishes, aircon fans, water tanks, and elevator gear to a corner where someone had laid down a few squares of

AstroTurf and a collection of mismatched Adirondack chairs. Sandy lowered herself into a chair and invited him to do the same. She rummaged through her big colorful sack, produced sanitary wipes, and offered Terry one with the comment, "The birds poop all over the place; good idea to wipe the armrests."

"That's quite a distinctive bag," Terry said.

She held up a packet of cigarettes and offered him one, which he refused. "Yep, my grammy passed that to me; called it her Mary Poppins bag. It's great for security – no one's going to steal a bag that sticks out like a stetson in San Francisco."

She lit up with a silver Harley Davidson lighter, inhaled deeply, and blew out the smoke, "How do you like my aery?"

The double-decker Bay Bridge with its dinky toy cars stretched across the water toward Treasure Island. Across the bay lay the Berkeley Hills. A container ship, pulled by two tugs, was plowing towards Oakland harbor. From up here, the human toil seemed so ant-like, so insignificant.

"It's beautiful," he said.

She smiled, "Only thing that keeps me sane around here."

He tapped the chair and asked, "Did you set this up?"

She shook her head, "Found it by chance; whenever I went into the street for a smoke, I had to endure the wrinkled noses and judgmental stares from passersby." She took a deep drag and lifted her chin in defiance, "San Franciscans are an obnoxiously sanctimonious and superior swarm of arseholes – try saying that fast, three times in a row." She grinned.

He thought about his ex-mother-in-law, who took pride in being a fourth-generation San Franciscan and said, "No argument from me on that score. Where are you from?"

"Madison, Wisconsin."

Terry found out that Sandy had double-majored in behavioral science and statistics and that she was a self-proclaimed data analytics junkie. She was an expressive talker. In the glow of the afternoon sun, her skin radiated, and her eyes sparkled when she spoke. Her lips were as full as her chest, and he had to repeatedly force himself to stop fantasizing. *Terry Reynolds – you're acting like a pubescent teenager. You can't let Chloe throw you off balance like this. Get a grip!*

Sandy said, "We're living through a most extraordinary historical discontinuity. The whole foundation of scientific inquiry is being turned on its head." She leaned forward, warming to a favorite topic, "For more than two thousand years, going back to antiquity, scientists have always started with a hypothesis – and then designed experiments to collect the data to prove that hypothesis."

She played absentmindedly with her braid, brushing its tail like a paintbrush across her throat. He wondered whether she was aware of the effect she was having on him. Terry couldn't remember ever meeting anyone so sensuous and yet so unpretentious. He said, "Go on."

"Galileo and Copernicus postulated that the planets turned around the sun; Newton hypothesized that an apple and the Earth attract each other. Often scientists died before their hypotheses could be proven. Physicists have only recently developed telescopes that can observe black holes and prove stuff that Einstein predicted fifty years ago. But we," she snapped her fingers, "we have at our disposable a limitless amount of data and the computing power to establish correlations almost instantaneously. And then we can figure out why there is a correlation."

Terry interjected, "If indeed there is a reason, a cause, for the correlation."

"Ah," she said, "You're a good student. You listened. But isn't it exhilarating to establish insights into the world, into human behavior, so rapidly and so efficiently?"

Terry nodded slowly, "But it's also terrifying. Just from the glimpse I got today, it looks to me like we have access to almost anything – health data, gun ownership, affiliations, purchasing behaviors, web surfing history, location data. I see we even bring the DNA analyses into the lake from all those DNA-kit providers. What about data privacy? I would have expected more segregation of data."

She stubbed out her cigarette and looked at him sideways from under her eyelashes, "You're right, but the customers can't do that on their own. Our value proposition is to integrate data from disparate sources. That's where the fascinating and surprising insights come from." The sparkle was back in her voice, "When you work with the data of one company or one industry, it's like going exploring in an urban park. You might be pleased to see a bird or an early spring blossom. But what we do is more like exploring in the jungle. You find tigers and boa constrictors and plants that no one has ever seen before. It's the ultimate rush."

Her cheeks were flushed, and she looked at Terry with such intensity that he let his gaze drift to the sea of red lights on the Bay Bridge. All those people, he thought, and they have no idea that we sit up here analyzing their every move, their purchases, their secrets, and their desires. And then the information is sold to the highest bidder to manipulate them.

He looked at this watch, "What time does everyone knock off?"

Sandy shrugged, "Some of the guys keep sleeping bags under their desks." She shook another cigarette out of her packet and said, "Great job today, Terry. You'll be an asset to the team. Go on home; I'm going to stay and enjoy one more." She leaned back in the chair and lit the cigarette.

Terry said, "I don't have anywhere I need to be. I'll carry on a bit – make sure I understand all the various data sources. It's just mind-boggling how many there are." He gave her a smile, "See yous guys."

She laughed, "Is that sad attempt supposed to be a Wisconsin accent?"

***

Once Sandy was sure that Terry was back in the stairwell, she reached deep into her sack, retrieved a cellphone, and dialed.

After four rings, a man answered, "Clyde Curry."

His deep, unhurried voice always gave her goosebumps.

"Hello, Professor Curry." She knew it embarrassed and irritated him when she called him by his title, but it amused her.

He sighed, "Hi Sandy, what's up?"

"I think I've come across a ray of sunshine in the darkness here." She took a drag on her cigarette, "But just to be sure, I thought one of your team should run his name through the system."

Clyde started to say, "Not over the phone …"

Sandy interrupted, "I know, I know. Jeez, what do you take me for? I'll bring the name around later. Just wanted to make sure we have someone there who can run the search on your cranky old system."

He protested, and she chuckled, "I know you keep up to date, but man, you should see the latest search algorithm they have here at BDA, *un-be-lievable*. The university will have to give you more money to keep up." She continued in a rush, "Anyway, I have no idea why *he's* working here – he seems to have a deep concern for data privacy. He's so genuine and guileless that either he's the real deal or one hell of an actor."

"We'll find out," the prof said. "But if he's got a moral conscience, won't they fire him?"

"I'll coach him to be careful in his utterings – share his concerns only with me."

"And you think you can control him?"

A smile crossed Sandy's lips, and she brushed the tip of her plait across her cleavage, "Oh yes."

***

When Terry got back to his workspace, the office had started to empty out, and there was no one in his immediate vicinity. He logged on and navigated through the master data sources. Whoever had designed this system was a gifted IT professional. The catalog of metadata was a thing of beauty. Every data source was meticulously documented – upload frequency, purpose, data owner, time of latest upload, data quality rating, etc. There were feeds from retailers, banks, insurance companies, search engines, hospitals, doctors, government sources, and airline reservation systems. Even CCTV footage from the highway patrol and thousands of private security cameras was fed into the data banks together with the live streaming of police reports and traffic accidents. The interface was equally impressive – a fifth grader could have sat down and started building reports.

Terry couldn't resist the temptation to look for a few exploratory, wild correlations. He decided to test one counter-intuitive correlation that he'd heard about on NPR: "annual rainfall" vs. "acres burnt in wildfires." Combining data from the weather office and the California Department of Forestry, he had his answer in minutes. The more rain, the worse the fires. The correlation became stronger when offset by a year.

Terry lost track of time and didn't notice that most of the other workers had left. He dragged himself away from the data sources and clicked on the "current and prospective customers" section. The list read like a who's who of major West Coast companies with a heavy emphasis on insurance, health care, and financial services. He scrolled down the list and felt a rush of adrenalin when he saw *The Settlement Bureau.* As he clicked on the link, he got an "access denied" message. A minute later, he was startled to receive an Instant Message from someone called Rajiv.

> **Rajiv:** *I see u r taking an interest in what the company does.*

Terry's heart skipped a few beats, and his mind raced through his actions over the last two hours. What exactly had he done to attract attention? He leaned forward and peered at the small round photograph that accompanied the IM. Then it struck him; this was Rajiv Patel, the charismatic founder and CEO of BDA, the same man he'd seen at Starbucks this morning. Terry's fingers shook as he typed.

> **Terry:** *Just trying to get up to speed.*

> **Rajiv:** *r u free tonight? u could join me for a dinner presentation to prospective clients.*

This is beyond bizarre, Terry thought. How did the guy even know his name? He was busy typing *why me?* but before he could hit send, the next message came through.

Rajiv: *heard great things about u from a contact at Facebook.*

It dawned on Terry that Jake must have lobbied much harder than he'd thought. That would explain why he was employed on the spot without even an interview.

Terry: *no dinner plans.*

Rajiv: *come one floor up to my office – will give u details.*

It was past seven when Rajiv waved Terry into his office and greeted him with a warm smile. Rajiv looked like he'd just had an invigorating workout followed by a shower and was now ready to take on the world. Terry caught a whiff of an expensive-smelling sandalwood cologne. Rajiv's tailor-made navy suit and muted tie, which picked up the amethyst color in his cufflinks, would have made some of Chloe's law-firm partners swoon. He was acutely aware of his own Macy's suit and wished he'd given his shoes a shine before coming up to see Rajiv.

Rajiv said, "I know this must seem strange to you, but here we do everything at Mach speed. I like to get new staff exposed to our customers as quickly as possible – it's the only way to ensure that everything we do is customer-driven."

He had a deep, melodious voice that inspired confidence. Terry thought he could probably tell an audience, "We'll land a man on Jupiter next year," and people would think of it as something achievable by the sheer power of his tone and presence.

Terry nodded, and Rajiv continued, "Some of our clients get a little flustered when they see how young our workforce is." He smiled, "And how diverse in their culture, their world views, their dress code."

Before Terry could stop himself, he blurted, "So I'm going along tonight because I'm a white male over thirty?"

Rajiv appeared to be bemused. One side of his mouth lifted in a smile, "And you wear a suit. Very important, since we're meeting with a group of city bankers." He clapped Terry on the shoulder and said, "Hey, I don't use those demographic markers to decide whom I trust and respect, but these clients do. They would, of course, deny it, but unconscious bias is a reality." He paused and looked Terry directly in the eyes, "I know you've spent time working in the banking industry, and you've seen some of our capabilities. Now tell me, how would you use our tools and data to improve the risk management at Bank of America?"

Terry took a moment to compose himself. It was an intriguing question. He walked to the window from where he could see the Bank of America pyramid and other city landmarks in the fading light. Down below, cars and people were bustling along the street. Lights in various glass towers twinkled in random geometric patterns. Not random, Terry thought, in fact, quite the opposite.

He turned to Rajiv and said, "What if I told you that it is entirely predictable when each light in that apartment complex will be turned on?"

Rajiv made an encouraging gesture with his hand.

"It's really quite simple. All you need is to cross-reference the identities of the occupants with their smartphone geo data, and you would probably be eighty to ninety percent correct. If you then added the data of their Fitbits or Garmins, you could improve the accuracy. By further analyzing their daily pattern of behavior over time, you'd get to within 98% accuracy. Then, just for good measure, one could pull in data from their car or even air travel and get longer-range predictions. Imagine what that could do for security and law enforcement? If anyone

119

doesn't show up where they're supposed to be, instantaneous action can be taken. Now imagine the same principles applied to managing banking risk. By analyzing the individual's personal and professional issues, you can update the risk profile in real-time. A car accident, job loss, an expensive health issue in the family, a child having to repeat a year at college. These are all predictors of financial risk. But to date, it simply hasn't been possible to integrate that data fast enough to be meaningful. Well, now it is – we make it possible."

Rajiv slowly clapped his hands and said, "Do it exactly like that tonight."

Terry gaped, "What? Me?"

"You come across fresh, unrehearsed, authentic – that's exactly what I want."

He opened a credenza, pulled out a leather pouch with *Harry D. Koenig* branded onto it, and gave it to Terry. "You can keep this." He pointed to a door on the far side of his office, "There's a dressing room and bathroom through there; grab a quick shave." He smiled his sardonic smile and added, "Bankers trust white males over thirty who are clean-shaven. I'll call an Uber. Be ready in ten minutes."

Chapter 12, Somewhere over Africa
Saturday, Early Morning, 3rd Week of June

KATIE

Katie was numbed by the steady drone of the plane that had the smell and feel of a well-worn sofa. Thirty hours of travel across ten time zones had made her catatonic. She could not sleep, nor could she bring herself to work or even watch a movie. The monitor showed them crossing the border between Angola and Namibia. Two hours to Windhoek. Eerie moonlight reflected off the plane's wing. She wriggled her numb toes and felt a little envious of her father, who had been upgraded to business class.

A hint of discoloration appeared in the east. Then it morphed to purple, and the horizon appeared in scissor-cut silhouette. Soon, a splash of orange infused the purple, giving the impression of a cosmic bruised eye. When last had she watched the night give way to day? When exactly does the new day start? When exactly does a new life begin in the womb?

The sun's golden orb rose with such triumph that it ought to have been accompanied by trumpets and trombones. Then the landscape took on form – gentle hills with scraggly bushes and sparse trees. The earth had the color of dried lentils. Dusty riverbeds and dirt roads connected tiny settlements. Quietly, she hummed, "A new day, all I want is a new day."

The stewardess, a young African woman in a dark blue uniform and a scarf in the cheerful colors of the Namibian flag came up the aisle and whispered to Katie, "Can I get you anything, madam? Water, juice, coffee?" Katie shook her head.

Isaac was asleep next to her. On his other side, an old lady's head had slid sideways against his shoulders. Her glasses and the book she'd been reading were threatening to slide off her lap. The stewardess knelt to stow away the glasses and book before tucking a blanket around the woman's shoulders. Katie was touched by the care of the gesture and pulled up her own blanket.

The old woman had befriended Isaac as the plane had taken off. Her name was Anneliese Wallenberg, and she was a proud Namibian of German descent. She was returning from Berlin, where she had celebrated her eighty-fifth birthday with her son and his family. Anneliese spoke good English with a German accent and, once she'd declared that Isaac reminded her of her grandson, there was no stopping her. She was a font of knowledge about the land she loved, and Katie learned that Namibia was one of the most sparsely-populated countries in the world. "Twice the size of California with only two-and-a-half million people. Imagine that? But of course, most of the country is desert; beautiful – we have many, many artists – but not very good for agriculture. They call it *The Land God Made in Anger*."

Katie couldn't help but feel a sense of foreboding. This mission seemed like it was destined to arouse God's anger. She must have dozed off because she awoke to the announcement that it was time to prepare the cabin for landing.

"Good morning," Isaac beamed at her, "Didn't want to wake you for breakfast, but I saved a yogurt for you." He pointed out the window, "Isn't it amazing? The sky looks bluer than back home."

Katie yawned, "Do you think they'd still give me a coffee?"

"Nope, only the early bird gets the coffee." He continued, "I suspect you haven't had a chance to go over the itinerary I sent you, so I'll give you a quick rundown. We're going to be picked up by a ranger from the Oshinawa Game Lodge. He's going to take us to a hotel, where we have a few hours to freshen up, hit the gym, or catch up on sleep…"

Katie closed her eyes and mumbled, "That's all I need to know. Tell me the rest when I wake up." She pulled her eye mask down over her eyes.

Isaac chuckled and was not dissuaded, "We'll have lunch in Windhoek and then set off for the lodge. It's a three-hour drive. Tomorrow we have our first round of presentations to the investors and, hopefully, also get a chance to go on a game drive."

Anneliese pitched in, "You will have a lovely time." She dragged out the word lu-ve-ly, pronouncing each syllable separately. "When my husband had his first heart attack, the doctor prescribed for us to spend ten days at a game reserve. Just to relax, be with nature, de-stress."

Katie pushed up her eye mask and glanced sideways, "Did it work? Did your husband get better?"

"For a while…he died of a second heart attack."

Isaac gave Katie a look that made her feel like she'd kicked a puppy.

The pilot's voice interrupted, "Ladies and gentlemen, we have started our descent and will land in twenty minutes. For those of you who are new to Windhoek, a word of warning – it will be bumpy. Please buckle up."

Anneliese tightened her grip on the armrests, her mouth set and her eyes staring fixedly ahead of her. Suddenly, the plane lurched and bucked, and shrieks could be heard throughout the cabin. Katie gasped as the seat belt bit into her stomach. Isaac was wide-eyed next to her. The plane reared again and swayed from side to side. Katie dared a quick glance outside, but there was only clear blue sky. Another violent lurch and a shudder went through the plane. She and Isaac both looked at the luggage compartments, expecting roller bags to rain down on them at any minute.

Then, as suddenly as it had started, the lurching stopped, and the voice of the pilot came over the speakers, "Well folks, that's the worst of it behind us. In case you're interested, the thermal updrafts around Windhoek airport are legendary. This is where they set world records for gliders and bring new planes for stress testing." He added with a laugh, "And we get to have this fun every day."

When they deplaned, Isaac and one of the stewardesses fussed about helping Anneliese off the plane. The stewardess ensured that the old woman was bundled up against the crisp coldness of the winter morning. Isaac carried her roller bag, and she beamed when he offered her his arm down the steps and across the tarmac to the airport building.

Is this it – the airport of a capital city? Katie counted a total of eight planes lined up within walking distance of the corrugated iron building.

As if reading her thoughts, Anneliese said, "Isn't this nice, after the craziness of Frankfurt and all those other big airports? Here, everything is like a family."

***

It would have been hard to miss the Oshinawa ranger, Petrus Mabumba. He was over six foot and dressed in Khaki shorts, a matching shirt, and army-style boots. His head resembled a polished bowling ball, and his ebony skin gleamed in contrast to the perfect white teeth he displayed in a broad smile. When they emerged from the baggage area, Petrus was at the center of a group of rangers, drivers, and others who'd come to pick up tourists. They were talking in a language Katie could not understand. Still, it was clear that this man was a leader – he carried an air of authority to rival even Pastor Jeremiah, and when he laughed, which he did frequently, everyone joined in.

He sauntered over and greeted them each with a handshake. Katie was awed by the size of his hands and grateful that he had the grace not to crush her own. He surveyed their luggage, "Is that it? I'm impressed. Usually, when we pick up Americans, we have to bring an extra trailer."

His voice was deep, and there was something vibrant, impish lurking under the surface. Katie was intrigued by the accent. He pronounced "a" as "u" and emphasized different syllables from what she was used to. Hence *Americans* sounded like *Umericuns,* with the emphasis on *cuns*.

It was silly, but she was pleased to have met with his approval as far as her luggage was concerned.

Petrus said, "I hope you don't mind; the people in Namibia don't mince their words. We say it as it is."

"We've noticed," Isaac said and winked at Katie.

Petrus took control of their bags, led them out into the brilliant sunshine and stowed everything in the back of a dark green Land Rover. It was agreed that Pastor Jeremiah would take the front passenger seat. When the pastor went

125

to open the door, Petrus smiled and said, "Do you want to drive? You're welcome."

Katie did not often see her father flustered. It must have been a function of the long journey that he stood for a full five seconds, looking at the steering wheel in bewilderment.

Then he said, "Of course, they drive on the wrong side here."

Petrus graced the pastor with a disarming smile and said, "Did God decree a wrong and a right side for driving, Pastor Jeremiah? I would simply say we drive on the *other* side of the road."

They set off for Windhoek with Petrus indulging Pastor Jeremiah's questions about the land and its people. Katie couldn't fall asleep on the upright back seat, so she was forced to absorb more Namibia facts. *I can write a darn book when I get back*, she thought. She studied Petrus' broad shoulders and muscular arms; one hand was on the steering wheel, the other trailing out the open window as if to stay in touch with nature. It was hard to gauge how old he was. There wasn't a wrinkle on his face, but his demeanor and confidence made her think that he was at least her own age.

Pastor Jeremiah was delighted to hear that eighty percent of the population were practicing Christians. She wasn't sure if Petrus was being ironic when he said, "The European missionaries did a thorough job." But then he continued, "I got a great education at a missionary school. If I had been left to the government education, I would be nothing."

They followed a narrow, well-paved road winding through the mountains. A sign proclaimed *Windhoek 15km*. Every couple of minutes, there would be a car coming in the opposite direction, flashing its lights.

"Why are they flashing their lights?" Isaac asked.

"They're warning us that the traffic cops have put up a speed trap to catch the morning rush."

"This is the morning rush?" Katie snorted, thinking of the drive she faced between San Francisco and Tracy.

There was a sudden, loud clanging noise from beneath the Land Rover, and it started to lose speed. Petrus pumped the gas pedal and muttered in Oshivambo as he guided the sputtering Land Rover off the road. They all got out, and Petrus popped the hood to inspect the engine.

"Well, it's not the engine," he proclaimed. "Must be the diff. He patted the side of the car. She's getting old." He turned to the group and asked, "Anyone up for a morning stroll into the city?"

Katie, Isaac, and Jeremiah looked at each other, then at the road stretching off into the distance. It only had a very narrow shoulder; they'd have to walk on the actual surface of the road. The sun was gaining strength.

"Are there any wild animals here?" Katie asked.

"No big predators. Only antelopes, rock rabbits...that sort of thing. You do have to keep an eye out for snakes; they like to come and warm themselves on the asphalt."

Katie shuddered and scanned the road.

"Can't you phone the Triple-A?" Isaac asked.

Petrus snorted, "Firstly, there's no cell phone signal here, and secondly, we'd be lucky if they send someone before sunset."

Jeremiah was the first to square his shoulders and say, "Well then, just let me get at my bag for a different pair of shoes. A brisk walk will do us good."

Petrus laughed and clapped the older man on the shoulder, "Good sport, but I wouldn't do that to you. I'll have this fixed in no time." He yanked a toolbox out of the vehicle, spread a tarpaulin, and disappeared under the car. They could hear him clanging and grunting. Ten minutes later, he emerged with a satisfied grin, wiped his hands on a rag, and said, "She'll get us into town, but I'll have to take her to a workshop while you all chill at the hotel."

She? Katie thought. *Do beasts of burden, even mechanical ones, always have to be female?*

***

When Katie stirred in her bed three hours later, she had no idea where she was and had to claw her way to consciousness. She had a long shower and felt guilty when, afterward, she saw multiple signs exhorting visitors to use the precious water sparingly. She found Isaac on a patio overlooking the city center. At the waiter's recommendation, they each ordered a Windhoek Lager and goulash soup with crusty rye bread. Katie hadn't realized how hungry she was till she inhaled the aroma of the soup. The waiter, who looked like he might have been Petrus' younger brother, hovered. He beamed when Isaac proclaimed that it was one of the most delicious soups he'd ever tasted. The waiter took that as an invitation to point out the city's sights.

What is it with everyone around here – are they all official tour guides? Katie thought.

"You see up there, Madam, on the side of the hill, that is *our* houses of parliament. We call it the ink palace – lots of writing." The waiter laughed. "And next to it, the new supreme court. Behind, on the highest hill, that is the Christus Church – built by the Germans."

Isaac said, "Your father has gone for a walk to the church. He wanted to see it up close. The receptionist said it's quite safe to walk around; just take the usual precautions against pickpockets – no flashy jewelry and keep a close eye on your purse."

She nodded and pointed at the bustling street below, "What's down there?"

The waiter said, "That's Independence Avenue, *our* main street, with all the shops. What you see over there is the craft market – beautiful carvings, things made with beads, baskets – it is very nice and very cheap. You should go." He displayed white teeth in a disarming smile.

She peered at his name tag on the crisp, maroon jacket and said, "Thank you, Francis. I think I will. A bit of sunshine and a walk is supposed to help one get over jet lag."

Isaac declined to join her; he wanted to get caught up on emails before heading into the wilderness.

Katie meandered up one side of the street and down the other, frequently stopping to look at shop windows or to inspect the street hawkers' intricate soapstone carvings. Now she regretted that she'd only brought a small suitcase. The street was crowded and, when Kaite suddenly stopped, a woman bumped into her. The woman gave her a toothy grin, apologized, and asked if she could help Katie find something. Katie quickly checked her bag, but no, it hadn't been a scam to steal her wallet.

She began to relax and felt a little intoxicated by the babel of languages and the foreignness of it all. There was a *Baeckerei* with delectable pastries. Next to it was a shoe shop called *Sapados.* The price tags, in Namibian Dollars, bewildered her, and she regretted not paying more attention to Isaac's preparatory materials. There were beer gardens, vendors with bratwurst, Chinese take-outs, and discount stores that sold cell phones like the one she'd had as a teenager. She was fascinated to see tall African women in ankle-length, billowing dresses like characters from a Jane Austen novel. Except Jane Austen heroines never wore

129

African prints in vibrant reds, yellows, and greens. They also did not wear a turban, which provided a convenient cushion to balance huge plastic containers full of socks, T-shirts, and underwear. Katie gaped in awe as three women glided past in stately fashion – their posture something that any finishing school mistress would have been proud of – till they found a convenient spot to squat down on their haunches and set up their shop-in-a-bucket.

She stopped in front of a glitzy fashion boutique called "Rakulia." It had an exquisite, full-length coat in a shiny, textured material in the window. It made Katie think of Chloe and, on an impulse, she went inside. The contrast to the street outside was staggering. The shop, with its mezzanine area, felt like an art gallery. Every piece of clothing was displayed separately and discretely lit by spotlights. Two customers were sipping coffee near a Nespresso machine.

A middle-aged woman in a pencil skirt and white blouse approached. She would have been quite at home in any boutique in Paris or Berlin. The woman smiled and asked in a hushed tone, "*Darf ich Ihnen behilflich sein?*"

"Um…I'm afraid I don't speak–"

"Oh, so sorry," the manageress immediately switched to English. "This time of year we get so many German tourists that I just assumed. My apologies; how may I assist you?"

Katie stroked one of the coats and said, "It's beautiful."

"Yes, would you like to try it on? It suits the color of your hair. All the items here are made by our own master furriers."

Katie stopped mid-stroke and asked, "What exactly is this fabric?"

The woman raised an eyebrow, "It is not a fabric. Karakul refers to a breed of lamb that survives in arid climates like here and in Afghanistan. The coats are made from the hide of prematurely-born Karakul lambs. You can feel how soft…"

Katie drew back her hand as though she'd had an electric shock. She croaked, "The hide of unborn lambs?"

The image that came to mind made her stomach heave. She turned on her heels and staggered out of the store. She could see the hotel diagonally across the street, so quickly looked to her left and stepped into the road. She didn't even register the squeal of tires and the shouts of bystanders before a minibus taxi hit her from the right.

When Katie regained consciousness, she was aware of the blinding sun right above her and a cacophony of people and faces swarming around her. She couldn't understand what they were saying. She tried to sit up, but the searing pain in her right arm made her gasp. One of the African women in the long dresses gently pressed her back down and said, "You have been hit, Madam; you are hurt. Please lie still." A strange calm came over as she thought, *so this is it, I am going die on a street corner in Africa, surrounded by strangers.* She closed her eyes. *Not exactly marrying material.*

Someone was slapping her face, "Wake up, Madam, wake up!" She saw the waiter, Francis, through lidded eyes. Next to him, Isaac leaned into her vision, "Kate, Katie, you must stay awake." He turned to the crowd and yelled, "Call 911. Someone call an ambulance."

Francis said, "No 911; an ambulance takes too long. Look – she is bleeding. We must take her in the taxi." A torrent of Oshivambo ensued, and the last thing Katie remembered was being lifted into a crowded minibus taxi and stretched across the laps of four African women, who cluck-clucked and shook their heads but accepted this detour on their journey with grace.

Safe in the arms of Mary, Katie thought, before she passed out again.

Chapter 13, Renaissance Institute
Saturday, 3rd Week of June

DANNY

Danny pushed himself to keep up with Gerald as the older boy moved effortlessly up the side of the canyon. The mouth to the secret valley lay in the shade, several hundred feet below them, and the terrain was getting steep. Perspiration ran down Danny's back, and he tried to keep his voice even when he asked, "How much further is this 'big surprise'?"

"Nearly there," Gerald said and pointed. "This last bit is tricky; you're going to have to use your hands and feet to scale up to that ledge."

Ten minutes later, he beamed at Danny's look of surprise and wonder. They had scaled the ledge and squeezed through a fissure in the rock wall to find themselves standing at the mouth of a five-foot-high by four-foot-wide cave. The walls glistened damp, and there were signs of animal habitation.

"Wow," Danny exclaimed, peering into the darkness, "how deep do you think this is?"

"That's what we're going to find out." Gerald shucked his backpack and methodically went through the contents. He laid out water bottles, gloves, flashlights, and batteries – borrowed from an emergency cabinet – as well as a long ball of string and a bundle of rags from the workshop.

"Tie the rags around your knees," he commanded as he set about anchoring the string to a boulder. "We'll try and get by with one flashlight – we're short on batteries."

They set off into the darkness and had to crawl through a two-foot gap, then navigate over and around several boulders. The morning light with circling falcons faded away behind them. All Danny could hear was the squeal of their trainers on the slippery floor and his own pounding heart. He was reminded of Lord of the Rings, where Frodo and his friends had to navigate past the monster spider, Shelob. *There won't be any Shelob or skeletons here,* he reasoned. *And hopefully no bats!*

"This is as far as I came last time," Gerald said. "Put some water on your finger and hold it up." Danny was perplexed but was not going to argue with Gerald, whose face appeared ghoulish in the small circle of light.

"There's air coming from inside the cave," Danny said. "Is that what you'd expect?"

"No, most certainly not. We are so far in that the air should be rank and damp by now. This is unusual. It means that this is a connector tunnel to something else." There was excitement in his voice, "Possibly a large cavern or another tunnel leading to the surface."

They continued in silence until Gerald suddenly held up his hand, "Shh, d'you hear that?"

Danny strained his ears. There was a faint thrumming. "It sounds like running water," he said. He had no idea why they were whispering but kept his voice down,

"There might be an underground lake or river? That would be so cool."

"We can't go much further," Gerald said, "Running out of string." He held up what was left of the ball.

"Let's just continue a bit; it would be so amazing to find a cavern with water."

"You've read too much Harry Potter," Gerald said, but he turned and led the way further into the mountain.

A few minutes later, there was a series of zig-zag turns, and then Gerald stopped so suddenly that Danny bumped into him. Danny whispered, "What the hell?"

He was the first to recover his wits. He crouched down behind a boulder and pulled Gerald down, hissing, "Turn off the flash!"

In front of them was a massive, dimly-lit cavern as high as a double-story building. Judging by the symmetry and the concrete finish, it was man-made. The thrumming noise they'd heard before was now very pronounced – a generator or air conditioning, or maybe both?

"What do you think?" Gerald whispered. "A wine cellar?"

"Glory be…" Danny said. He took in the myriad of blinking lights and suddenly remembered the delivery of Cisco servers. "It might have been a wine cellar originally, but this is a data center." There were hundreds of computer racks, eight feet tall, lined up like a regiment of soldiers. A sliver of daylight was visible in the far distance.

"I wish Timothy could see this," Danny said, "He'd wet himself with excitement."

Gerald murmured, "It's a perfect location – cheap to air-condition and physically secure."

"Except for this back entrance. I don't see anyone around this end of the place. Let's go have a look."

They crept out of hiding, scrambled down to the floor of the cavern, and crouched behind the computers. Danny waited for his breathing to steady, then listened. Nothing but the thrum. Was this place completely unmanned? He crept towards the mouth of the cavern, with Gerald close behind him. It was eerie to be caught up in this regiment of soldiers, humming, flashing, and bristling with life – ready to do what? And at whose command?

Danny stumbled over something and cursed. As he picked himself up, he and Gerald both stared at the labeling on a box – security cameras.

Danny whispered, "They haven't finished the security set up yet."

They were halfway to the entrance when they heard voices. Carefully, they crept from one rack to another until they came upon a control room set-up with two consoles and a neat kitchen area. Danny's eyes fell on the espresso machine. *One of these days, I'm going to break out of the damn institute just to get a decent cappuccino.*

One man sat at a console, talking into a radio, "I can see 54-WR3 now; that's live. But the one next to it, 53-WR3, has gone dead. What are you doing – over?"

A clear voice responded, "I swear if I get my hands on the techies who installed this. The wire labeling is totally up to maggots. Check it now – over."

"Okay, now I can see them both. Shall I put them into production – over?"

"No, let's let them run in test mode for a couple of hours." He chuckled, "Leave it for the night shift. If the servers crap out, they can deal with it – over and out."

Gerald and Danny froze as they heard footsteps behind them. Mercifully, the technician came down an adjacent aisle and didn't notice the two boys. The man sat down at the second console and said, "Time for a security sweep, your turn."

The first man grumbled, "This is such a waste of time. I didn't go to college to be a friggin' security guard."

"It's protocol. Quit the whining. Just get off your ass and do the rounds."

"When are they going to install those infrared cameras and save us the trouble?" The man's hands roamed across the touch screen. Suddenly, the cavern was bathed in bright light, and the computer operator pushed back his chair with a sigh.

"Go!" Danny whispered and gave Gerald a push. They crouched low and hurried back. As they rounded the boulder into the tunnel, Danny stopped for a moment to take in the sight. In the brilliant fluorescent light, the sheer magnitude of the data center was awe-inspiring. It pulsated like an alien life-form. He didn't linger to find out why it made him feel so uneasy.

Chapter 14, San Francisco
Saturday, 3rd Week of June

TERRY

Charlie was ecstatic when Terry put on his running shoes for their Saturday routine. He seemed to have saved up enough pee to give every tree in Golden Gate Park an extra helping. Jake had joined them, and Terry kept up a pace that had his friend panting, unable to make conversation.

When they reached their bench at the lake and Jake had caught his breath, he asked, "So, how's your first week been?"

"Bit of roller coaster, or rather a bullet train. You didn't tell me that I was hired before I even stepped into the door," Terry grumbled.

"Told you, my recruiter is a magician," Jake said. "And she owed us a favor."

Terry let it go and gave Jake a rundown, describing the meeting with the prospective clients on the very first evening. He couldn't help but let his pride show when he mentioned how pleased Rajiv had been with his performance.

Jake whistled through his teeth, "I knew you'd go out there and slay the dragons. You just needed a foot in the door. Well done, man." He high-fived Terry. "So, what have you found out so far?"

"Jeez, give me a break. Yesterday I had to wrap things up at NorCal. Fortunately, they were decent about me ducking out so abruptly. I've only had two days at BDA; work starts in earnest on Monday."

Jake appeared not to have heard him, "Any early impressions, any co-workers that look dodgy, could be up to bad things, any dirt?"

Terry stared at him, "Are you serious? There are a few hundred millennial geeks. Depending on your perspective, they either *all* look dodgy, or *all* look perfectly normal." He decided not to tell Jake about Sandy, who had invited him to meet her 'for a surprise' later that afternoon – what was there to tell, anyway? Jake would just make crude insinuations. So instead, he said, "I can tell you that the systems are impressive. The architecture is elegant, and the interface usability is...wow."

Jake raised his eyebrows, "That good, eh? Coming from you, that's high praise."

"Yep, and I hate to disappoint you, but from what I've seen, they have pretty good data governance in place. They're doing a lot of fascinating trend analysis, but it's all done on anonymized data. Did you know that San Francisco traffic will be gridlocked six hours per day within five years? One of the clients is a Realty Firm that uses this and other information to bet on a collapse of the property market. The tech firms won't be able to recruit and top talent will leave the city."

Jake nodded, "Well, let me know if you come across anything interesting."

"One thing you might be interested to know – Rajiv has asked me to play basketball with him at his club tomorrow."

"Seriously? That's amazing. Rajiv is famous for his aloofness. I've never heard of him fraternizing with staff – but he loves his basketball. Just as well our resume writer remembered to mention that you were on the UCLA 2nd team."

"She put that on my resume?"

Jake nodded, "Of course. You were good."

On the way home, Terry picked up a coffee and bagel for Joe Doe. Charlie tried to lick the old man's face, and Joe smiled as he bent down to hug the dog.

"Wonderful creatures, dogs," Joe said. "If they could talk…" He shook his head, "our innermost secrets would be revealed." He looked at Terry and said, "Their sense of smell is incredible. Charlie can tell who passed here in the last twenty-four hours, who lingered, what I've eaten, where in the neighborhood I've been. Did you know that dogs tell time through their sense of smell?"

"Really?" Terry said. "How so?"

"They have a sense of smell decaying over time. When you leave in the morning, Charlie gets your full odor. He measures time by the way that odor slowly dwindles. And he knows when it reaches a certain level, he can expect you to come home." He looked at Terry and added, "If you do the decent thing and maintain a regular routine."

Terry felt a prickle run down his neck. Was the old man keeping tabs on his movements? Was it a warning? Where did Joe come up with these stories? Did he read them in the newspapers that he used for bedding?

***

Terry met Sandy in a coffee shop near Lake Merritt in Oakland, from where she gave him a ride to the top end of the East Bay University campus. They parked outside a gray, three-story building typical of the soviet-style architecture afflicting cash-strapped universities everywhere. Terry couldn't imagine what surprise might await him in this office block. Maybe a rooftop bar?

"Nearly there," Sandy said with a smile. She wore jeans and a bedazzled black T-shirt with her trademark Doc Martens.

They entered a lobby where time and the shuffling shoes of thousands of students had worn the glazing off the terra cotta tiles. The walls were mustard-colored. She led him down a staircase and into a basement, to a door with the sign, *Welcome to 1984*.

They entered a surprisingly-large basement that looked like Terry's new work environment at Big Data Analytica. Dozens of young programmers were glued to their keyboards and monitors. The only difference was that the setup appeared more organic. Mismatched desks and chairs had been lumped together and embellished with personal touches such as potted plants and lamps. The whitewashed concrete walls were plastered with posters advertising current events but also depicting idols such as Nelson Mandela, Che Guevara, Rosa Parks, Barack Obama, Anne Frank, and Martin Luther King.

Sandy zigzagged her way through the maze with Terry in tow. Everyone seemed to know her, and she stopped to chat several times. One young girl with braces on her teeth and a T-shirt that proclaimed *SOS, Save our Squirrels* wanted to show Sandy what she'd been working on.

"Look at this map," the girl said, "We got the latest WWF satellite images of migrating herds in the Serengeti.

141

Trevor's new app can distinguish different species *and* count them with 99.4% accuracy. That's allowed us to speed up our analysis of the factors impacting herd size."

Sandy nodded and asked, "And anything interesting so far?"

"We'd been using the rate of environment encroachment, temperature, and rainfall as predictors. But now we can also factor in the fluctuating size of the predator population. And," she beamed, "there's a near-perfect oscillating sine curve correlation, offset by about a year. So it's still good old predators rather than other influences that impact herd size."

"Good job," Sandy said, "I look forward to reading the analysis."

Next, Sandy was cornered by a shy Chinese boy, "I've completed the analysis of the factors that determine how fast the Ebola virus will spread after an outbreak."

"And?" Sandy asked. "Is it the usual culprits – overcrowding and lack of sanitation?"

The boy grinned and shook his head, "No, it's internet availability."

"Are you sure?"

He nodded emphatically, "I've discussed it with Clyde. He agrees. The best way to contain the spread of Ebola is through communication and warning people to stay away from infected areas. If there's no effective way to communicate, the disease goes rampant."

Sandy nodded, "That makes sense – well done, Hui."

At the far end of the room, Sandy rapped her knuckles against a door and, without waiting, entered. A tall man with poor posture and black-framed spectacles rose from behind his desk to greet them. He was a few years older than Terry, and wore jeans, a T-shirt, and a sleeveless sweater. His careless man-bun had dreadlocks poking out like snakes to proclaim that this man had more important things to do than worry about his appearance. He gave a boyish grin when Sandy kissed him on the cheek and blushed when she declared, "This is Professor Clyde Curry, one of the youngest professors ever appointed at the East Bay University."

Terry shook the professor's hand. He had the strangest feeling that he had met the professor before. There was something familiar about the ascetic face, with its linear nose and high forehead. Where had he seen this man?

Terry shook the thought and asked, "What's your field of study, professor?"

The professor invited them to sit and shot Sandy a glance. "Please call me Clyde; no one but Sandy and my mother refer to me as a professor."

The office was windowless and spartan in its furnishings. An oar had been mounted on the wall behind Clyde. Terry pointed to it, "You rowed for Oxford?"

Clyde nodded, "Yes, I think the rowing was even more character-building than the work I put into my thesis." He smiled.

Sandy chipped in, "Don't get him started on the book *Boys in the Boat*; he thinks it's the best story ever."

Terry said, "*I* enjoyed it – a great story about the underdogs persevering and winning the day."

Clyde cleared his throat, "You asked about my field of study. We've compiled a curriculum entitled *Data and Society*. It's very hands-on and practical. It seems to have found favor with the students."

"That's the understatement of the year," Sandy said. "There's a waiting list a mile long to get into Clyde's classes." She waved in the direction of the programmers they had passed, "As you can see, these students are very committed, willing to put in twice as much effort as any of the indentured laborers at BDA."

Terry raised an eyebrow and said, "I'm confused. I thought you liked working at BDA?"

Sandy said to the professor, "I always get things muddled when I'm excited; that's why I brought him here – you'd better explain."

Clyde folded his hands on the desk in front of him and fixed Terry with a penetrating look, "Do you ever think about where society is headed with all this surveillance? With the capability to capture and analyze petabytes of data in real-time? Not just to watch people, but to analyze their mood, their behavior, their dreams, and their fears?" He didn't wait for an answer, "How much financial value is associated with information? How much power is associated with it? And, most importantly, who gets to wield that power?"

The man in front of Terry was growing in stature and glowing with conviction. Terry couldn't help but be mesmerized as Clyde continued, "We look back and scoff at the feudal system where a handful of nobles," Clyde made air quotes, "ruled with an iron fist over a population of peasants and serfs. That will appear a benign social order compared to what we're facing. In the information age, a few moguls can literally rule the entire world."

He thumped the desk with his fist. "The peasants at least knew they were being shafted – the modern serfdom comes stealthily, hidden behind a phrase like, 'It's worth giving up some freedom for the sake of security.' I feel ill every time someone says, 'I have nothing to hide; I don't care if they monitor what I do.' That's so naïve, because you never know who *they* will be. What if *they* end up being a bunch of Nazis who only need to find out that you're Jewish to haul you away to a gas chamber?"

Clyde was in full stride; his cheeks had taken on a pink hue, and his eyes blazed. Sandy had her lips parted as if to drink in the words. "What if *they* are a bunch of crazies who believe in astrology? Anyone born under the star signs Pisces and Libra is superior, but you are inherently bad if you are born under Scorpio and need to be locked up. I exaggerate, of course, to illustrate the point. But it is, for example, quite feasible to deduce from medical records whether someone has had an abortion. What if the powers that be in Alabama decide to prosecute citizens who've had an out-of-state termination?"

"Overreach by the state," Terry said. "Hence 1984."

"Precisely. We live in a dystopia far worse than anything George Orwell could ever have imagined. The level of invasiveness that we accept is mind-blowing. We're worse than sheep." He paused to catch his breath. "We here are dedicated to studying this phenomenon and to promoting debate around what kind of society we want to be, and how we want to use the power of information."

"And who exactly are 'we'?" Terry asked.

He noticed Clyde's sidewise glance to Sandy, who gave a brief nod.

Clyde continued, "Officially, *Data and Society* is a department within the university. It's well endowed by a consortium of companies and organizations that all espouse – and I stress that word, *espouse* – a desire to use information for the good of mankind and the planet."

Sandy jumped in and said, "We get money and data feeds from the WWF, The Climate Reality Project, The Gates Foundation, The World Health Organization, and many more." She paused. "But you'd be interested to know that we also get support, mainly in the form of access to computational power, from Facebook, Google, and Amazon. It's a truly collaborative effort."

Terry looked from one to the other and said, "This all sounds pretty fantastical. Wow! So do I take it that you're the good people of the Federation and Big Data Analytica out there is the Death Star? What is Rajiv's role – is he Darth Vader?"

Sandy gaped at him, but Clyde took it in his stride. The corners of his mouth twitched with amusement, "A

145

cynic and a Star Wars fan. But of course, I knew that because I did a little research the moment Sandy told me that you'd surfaced at BDA. Shall I tell you which Star Wars character you identify with?"

Terry blinked, but before he could answer, Clyde read from a document on his computer screen,

"May 1993. Essay entitled, 'Who do you admire?'. Written by Terry Gunderson, 4th Grade."

He looked up and said, "This was obviously before your mother changed her and your last name to her maiden name – Reynolds."

Then he continued reading, *"My favorite movie of all times is Star Wars Episode 3, The Return of the Jedi. The film was made in the year I was born. That is why it has special meaning to me. I admire Luke Skywalker, but my favorite hero is Han Solo and his friend the Wookie..."*

"My school essays?" Terry spluttered, "Where the hell...? I haven't seen those in decades."

Clyde shrugged, "That essay tells me more about you than any job interview could. But, like I say, people don't have the faintest idea of how everything about them can be found, exposed, and used against them." Terry looked at him sharply, and Clyde added, "If the information gets into the wrong hands."

Terry placed the palms of his hands over his eyes and pressed down hard. Then he sighed, "What is it you want from me?"

Clyde said, "We have a common goal. You want to find out who's behind *The Settlement Bureau* and why they're blackmailing you. We believe they are coercing *hundreds* of people. We need to get detailed insights and evidence about their operation because we want to expose them and shut them down once and for all."

"I don't know that I can contribute anything."

"Well, it seems as though you wandered onto the playing field and joined the wrong team." The corners of his mouth quirked up in a smile again, "The thing is, Han Solo, one way or other, you've landed in a position of trust on the Death Star. I believe you're playing basketball with Rajiv later today – a rare honor. We need allies on the inside. Sandy is one of the few people we have been able to, how shall I say, infuse into that organization without raising suspicion. But she can't do it alone." He went on, addressing Sandy, "Incidentally, how is it coming along? Have you found out anything about the COLD index?"

Sandy said, "It's there. I found a directory labeled COLD index, but it is in the highly restricted zone. If I dig too aggressively, the cybersecurity monitoring group will be onto me in seconds."

Clyde produced a six-pack of cold beers, and they discussed potential strategies. Terry declined the beer but felt a rush of warmth and adrenalin at the thought of gaining allies and being part of a team. Sandy knocked back two beers in quick succession and then mused that maybe she could dig up dirt on one of the cybersecurity analysts at BDA and coerce him.

Clyde responded with a perfect Yoda imitation, "Stoop to the level of the enemy, we must not."

***

Later that afternoon, Terry and Rajiv were recovering from basketball-for-two on the balcony of the club. Rajiv had won, but Terry was pleased to have given him a good game. The CEO had at least broken a sweat, and his tousled hair made him look younger than when Terry had seen him at the office. Rajiv sipped his mineral water and said, "By the way, I may need you to tackle a special project that's near and dear to the heart of one of our directors."

"Sure," Terry said, "What's it about?"

"Your ex-wife."

Terry's head whipped around to look at Rajiv, "What? Chloe?"

"It shouldn't surprise you that Ms. Chloe McGrath has political ambitions. We've been asked to do voter research to develop a political platform for her. And it occurred to me: who better than you to figure out a compromise between what voters want and what your ex-wife might genuinely believe or be willing to embrace as a political stance?" He quirked an eyebrow and smiled, "Quite brilliant, don't you think?"

Terry said, "There's a reason I'm her ex; it might have something to do with the fact that I'm not very good at figuring out what's going on in her brain." He shook his head, "I know Chloe has political aspirations, or rather her mother has political aspirations for her, but I'm surprised that she is getting so serious about it."

Rajiv shrugged, "Like I said, speed is everything these days. Seems like every democrat with a pulse is plotting to get into the White House." He studied his fingernails, "I'm only doing this because Katie Blanchard wants it. I told her, two weeks. I'm prepared to invest no more than two weeks of your time. Think you can put aside personal feelings and do it?"

Terry didn't know how he felt about this assignment. Why hadn't Chloe mentioned that she was getting ready to start a political campaign in earnest? Was that why she had divorced him? Was he such a millstone that he'd held her back from her aspirations? It hurt to feel he'd been discarded like an old sweater. His jaw muscles tightened, but he shrugged and said, "Sure. How do you know Katie Blanchard?"

"She and I go back a long way. We were at college together, and of course, the Church of Holy Redemption owns BDA."

Terry choked on the sip of water he'd just taken. He spluttered, "That church owns Big Data Analytica?"

"I thought you knew. It was Katie who had the vision to build a tech company and use its profits to fund the Church's operations." He grimaced, "Donations alone couldn't fund Pastor Jeremiah's ambitions in a million years."

Chapter 15, Namibia
Sunday, 3rd Week of June

KATIE

Katie felt a chill and looked at the dark clouds obliterating the daylight. She was barefoot and wore nothing but a thin linen nightshirt. Her body ached, but she knew she had to drag herself up to the top of Golgotha. A flash of lightning illuminated three crosses, and she fell to her knees in front of Jesus and begged, "Let me wash your feet, Lord." A basin with water appeared, and a soldier held out his foot. The man sneered down at her, "Get on with it, woman, we have things to do."

As she dipped her hands in the water, it turned crimson with blood. She raised up her hands in bewilderment. The guard wore a Karakul coat and had a slaughtered lamb slung over his shoulder; its glassy eyes stared at Katie. She recoiled. The guard's face seemed familiar; he had the dimpled chin of a man she had met – somewhere in an inn. He looked at her bloodstained hands and growled, "Do not touch me with those hands; all you are good for is this!" Then, he flung open the coat, thrust his erection in her face, and commanded, "Do it."

Above him, she saw Jesus on the cross, looking down at her with tear-filled eyes. She could see his dry, cracked lips and stammered, "I'm thirsty." Something moist touched her lips, and she shrank back in revulsion from the grinning soldier.

The face of Jesus morphed into her father's face, and she tried to hide her bloodstained hands. Finally, she looked up at him and cried, "Kyrie Eleison – father, have mercy – *please* understand!" But her father averted his face and said, "Some sins cannot be forgiven."

She wrestled to free herself from the soldier's grip and woke up to find a woman in uniform pressing her gently back into the pillows. The nurse said, "Miss, you must please lie still so as not to pull out the IV drip."

Katie stared around the neat hospital room. It appeared to be night because the only light came from a dimmed bedside lamp. On the wall straight ahead of her was a wooden, carved crucifix, and she shuddered as remnants of the dream flitted through her consciousness. The nurse adjusted the drip, and Katie noticed another African woman standing on the other side of the bed. She was tall, with full lips and high cheekbones. Despite being dressed in a tracksuit, there was something regal and calming about her. She held up what looked like a popsicle - a small sponge on the end of a stick – and said, "You kept asking for water, but then you did not want to drink."

Katie asked, "Who are you? Where am I?"

"You are in very good care at the St. Elizabeth hospital. You were brought here yesterday after a taxi bus knocked you down in the street."

Memories came flooding back. Katie tried to sit, but a bolt of pain in her right shoulder, and the nurse's staying hand, prevented her. The nurse said, "You were fortunate,

Miss; nothing is broken, but you have a nasty bruise on your shoulder and a few stitches in your arm. In addition, you were concussed, and you were dehydrated after your long flight – you must drink on the plane, Miss – which is why the doctor insisted on keeping you overnight."

"My father, Isaac…Oh God, they're going to miss the meeting. I must…"

The other woman leaned forward and said, "Don't worry, everything has been organized and arranged. They obviously did not want to leave you here, and the doctor did not want to let you go." She chuckled, "Your father is a very persuasive man, but our doctor is very, very stubborn." She made the clucking sound that Katie was beginning to recognize among the Namibians. She took Katie's hand into hers and continued, "In the end, Petrus, my son, called me. I promised that I would stay right here by your side, all the time, and I have been texting regular updates." She smiled, "Your father is an extraordinary man. We have heard of him, even here in Namibia, and he cares about you very, very much."

Katie tried to process the dilemma her father and Isaac had been in. She was filled with gratitude for the kindness of strangers. She said, "So you're Petrus' mother?"

The woman nodded, "Ida Mabumba. Now, can we get you something to eat or drink?" When Katie did not answer, Ida leaned forward and whispered, "I heard the doctor say that when your appetite has returned, we can call Petrus to come and fetch you and take you to Oshinawa."

Katie thought for a moment, then responded, "You know, I am feeling a little hungry."

Ida winked at her, and the nurse said, "Stay here, sis Ida; I'll go find something in the kitchen."

Ida nodded, got out her cellphone, and said to Katie, "Now, smile for a nice photo for your father."

***

At 5:00 a.m., the management team at Oshinawa lodge was assembled for their daily meeting at a table in the dining hall. Angelica Geingob, the manageress, warmed her hands on a mug of coffee and studied the schedules on her laptop. When she looked up, she saw that every table in the hall was set for breakfast. Starched table cloths and polished glassware contrasted with the rustic thatch ceiling, hammered copper sconces, and carved masks on the walls. Beyond the glass doors, dim lights illuminated the water hole. There was no sign of life, though Angelica knew that what appeared to be five gleaming boulders at the edge of the waterhole were, in fact, sleeping hippos.

Angelica was a no-nonsense leader dressed in sensible brown shoes and a khaki skirt and blouse – the standard uniform at the lodge. She had grown up in the sub-tropical northern region of Ovamboland and did not like these cold mornings. Hence she wore her parka jacket and a woolen hat, knitted by her aunt. Her reading glasses betrayed that she was on the mature side of forty-five.

Opposite her sat Martha Khumalo, the chief cook. Martha was a large woman with an ever-ready smile and, despite the iciness of the morning, her dark skin gleamed with perspiration. She had already been up for two hours to ensure that the crispy breakfast rolls, croissants, and rye bread were baked per the exacting standards she had learned under a German master baker in Windhoek. She split her attention between the management meeting and the staff setting up the breakfast buffet, "Watch the oatmeal, I don't want it burnt; look at that milk jug – it's dirty – wipe it, man. Wake up! *Hakahanna* with those breakfast packs, the guests need them for their game drives. Julius, where's the coffee for the people?"

Angelica turned to her and asked, "Have you got what you need for those VIPs in the conference room?"

Martha rolled her eyes, "What is wrong with those people? They expect to be served food out there all day. Don't they have legs? Why can't they come to the dining hall like normal people? And to sit in a conference room all day – why don't they go out on a game drive, so we can get in there and clean?" She clucked and muttered, "*Attatatat*– it's Sunday. My people have their day off. I don't have a waiter to be there all day just to fill their glasses and pour coffee and bring them pancakes. Pancakes – with syrup! I ask you, why don't they eat scones like normal people?" She wiped her brow with her apron.

Angelica consulted her schedules and looked at the other two members of her leadership team, Petrus Mabumba, the chief game warden, and Johannes Witbooi, the facilities manager. Johannes was a short, wiry man. He looked emaciated, despite Martha's efforts to fatten him up. His fingers and teeth bore testament to a lifetime of smoking. Before Angelica could ask, he wheezed, "With eighty people in the lodge, I have no hands to spare. Number twenty-one has no hot water; thirty-two is complaining that the door does not lock. Those people in the conference room want help in setting up a satellite dish for their computers…"

Angelica held up her hand and turned to Petrus. She scowled and cleared her throat when she saw him glancing at his cellphone. Petrus said, "Sorry, Angelica, just checking up on that guest in the hospital in Windhoek, Miss Blanchard."

"Yes, how is she?"

"My mother says she was awake for half an hour and is now sleeping again. But they think I can come through and fetch her after lunch."

"That's good," Angelica said. "Please be sure to thank sis Ida for helping out. Now, what suggestion might you have for helping out with the VIPs?"

He shrugged, "My team is all scheduled, but I was on the roster to take those people for a game drive. Since they don't seem to be interested, I can be their waiter."

"You!" Martha pointed at him and laughed, "with your big mouth?"

Petrus leaped up, draped a napkin over his wrist, and stood rigidly to attention. He gestured with his free hand that his mouth was zipped. Then he picked up a glass from a nearby table and delicately placed it in front of Martha, "What would be madam's pleasure – I can recommend Moët or maybe a mimosa for breakfast?"

Martha chuckled and nudged him with her elbow. Johannes laughed till he broke into a coughing fit. Even Angelica cracked a smile as Petrus joined in the laughter. Angelica thanked him and said, "You'd better go see if we have a uniform that fits you. Martha, you must stop feeding this man; he's getting too big."

Martha gave a shy titter. Food and love were synonymous to her, and no one was showered with more special treats than Petrus.

***

The conference room was set apart from the guest chalets and communal areas. A vaulted thatch roof gave it an airy feeling. Ten hand-carved chairs surrounded a polished mahogany table. One wall had large windows that provided a view of the waterhole, where five elephants were enjoying their morning bath. Two of the walls were hung with tapestries and African masks. The fourth wall had a projection screen that showed the logo of CAFCA: a thick black circle with two crossed rifles against a blood-red backdrop. The top half of the circle read *CAFCA – Civil Action for Carrying Arms.* The lower had the words, *Defenders of the Second Amendment.*

Pastor Jeremiah was inspired to say a stirring prayer about the bounty and beauty of nature. His 'Amen' still hung in the air when Colonel Wilbur Hink, Chairman of CAFCA, brought the meeting to order and suggested a round of introductions. The Colonel himself needed none. He regularly appeared on cable TV, was a respected veteran of the first Gulf War, and the photogenic face of CAFCA. He was in his late fifties and still attracted plenty of female attention with his cropped gray hair and tanned, chiseled face.

Petrus, who hovered in the shadows near the door to the kitchenette, noticed that the Colonel's khakis were ironed with military precision.

The man to his left introduced himself, speaking with a thick, southern drawl, "Chuck Thibodeaux, secretary of CAFCA. I'm from good ol' Louisiana." He was a large, gregarious man with a ready smile and long strands of hair valiantly straining to cover his baldness. He wore shorts, and Petrus could not help but wonder how those spindly white legs could carry the man's bulk. As if sensing Petrus' eyes on him, Chuck waved in his direction and pointed at his coffee cup. "More...coffee," he said loudly and slowly in the insolent manner of foreigners around the world trying to make themselves understood.

The man next to him did not appear much older than Isaac. He wore jeans and a cotton shirt and sported fashionable dark stubble to match his glasses. "Hi, I'm Robbie Gardner; I have a systems background from MIT. My portfolio is defensive systems. I'm based in Virginia."

The Colonel turned to his right and said, "Last, but not least…"

"Hi," the woman on his right said, "I'm Antoinette Bussey. I look after legal and public relations." She smiled directly at Pastor Jeremiah. "It is such an honor to meet you, Pastor Jeremiah." Her accent slid from East Coast to pure Southern when she continued, "I'm a huge fan, and I believe we have so much in common; I also grew up in Mississippi."

Pastor Jeremiah beamed, "Well, what good providence that brought us together in this here fair land."

Ms. Bussey looked like she was dressed for a meeting with lawmakers in Washington or arms dealers in Chicago. Her only concession to her surrounding was that her tight-fitting business suit and accessories were entirely zebra-colored. The black stiletto heels were as sharp as her perfectly cut raven hair and immaculate makeup.

The Colonel mentioned that they were in "divide and conquer mode" and that two of their party were attending other business. They were Major McCullum, in charge of the offensive weapons portfolio, and Mr. Carl Gunderson, an independent advisor for Africa and the Middle East. But, he assured them, the four members present had the full authority to continue with the meeting and make the necessary decisions.

With the introductions completed, Kim joined via video link from California to conduct a presentation. Petrus had a few tense moments when the signal faded into gray static, but eventually, the technology settled down. He remained in the shadows and was mesmerized to see the gigantic church; it seemed to have more seats than the national soccer stadium in Windhoek.

As Kim launched into the minutiae of the technology deployed, Petrus couldn't help but shake his head. It seemed so incongruous, particularly in a church.

The man called Robbie looked at his iPad and said, "Hang on a moment, just give me a run down again of the technology you've deployed."

Kim answered, "Every seat is fitted with heart rate monitors as well as temperature, perspiration, and blood pressure sensors. In addition, we now have facial-recognition cameras that sweep every seat. The facial recognition is linked to our BDA database, which allows us to tap into a broad array of the individual's information, like medical, financial–"

The large man, Chuck Thibodaux, cut in, "Yes, yes, we're quite familiar with BDA's capabilities. We've been using them for a while. But I still don't see how this can be of benefit to our members."

"If you'll allow me, sir," Kim answered, "I'll show you an example from last Sunday's service." The screen was split in two. On one side was a picture of the congregation, following Pastor Jeremiah's homily with rapt attention. On the other half of the screen, a thick band of curves appeared, pulsing in a uniform rhythm.

"Here, you see a pictorial representation of how the congregation is responding to Pastor Jeremiah's sermon. The changes in temperature, pulse rate, and perspiration are amalgamated to represent their emotional response – it rises and falls in unison with what the Pastor is preaching or if people are stirred by the music. But notice here," he pointed to a few lines that looked like loose strands. "These are outliers; people whose response does not follow the norm." His mouse pointer clicked on one of the strands, and the screen filled with the picture of a young woman and a brief synopsis.

> *Carrie D., aged 35, married, one child. Church member since 2014, lives in Tracy.*
> *Two calls to 911 for domestic disputes over the last nine months. Husband suspected of abusive*

behavior based on medical visits by Ms. D.;
perceived threat level orange.
Ms. D. has limited financial means. No relatives in
the state for support.
Recommended action: Visit by church elder; place
on the heightened alert watch list.

Kim continued, "Our real breakthrough lies in the fact that the algorithms automatically pick out non-standard responses. In this case, Ms. D. is probably preoccupied with her domestic issues, and we can focus on preventative measures. You see what a powerful defensive system this could be in any stadium, church, school hall, or venue where crowds are gathered. Instead of screening everyone, the AI algorithms hone in on those whose behavior is out of the ordinary. Say, heaven forbid, there were a bomber or shooter in the audience – their bodily readings would betray the fact that their emotions were out of sync with a sports crowd or a church congregation. The link to their profile, assembled from hundreds of sources, would very quickly allow security to pinpoint genuine threats."

Robbie Gardner nodded and said, "It is indeed impressive. But, of course, we would have to verify the accuracy of the algorithms."

The other members of CAFCA joined in a lively debate. There were questions like, "What about metal detectors at every seat?" The answer was, "We have them at the doors, that's more cost-effective, and we can automatically lockdown and shut any door within the church."

"Why do you bother to fit every chair with all the other detectors? Can't you just pick up the data from people's fitness devices?" The answer was, "Excellent question, but not everyone has one of those devices, and we are all about welcoming the stranger. Also, from CAFCA's perspective, your average suicide bomber is probably not concerned with wearing his fitness device."

Petrus heard sniggers. He missed the rest of the question and answer session because he went off to fetch scones, muffins, and more coffee. When he returned, the meeting appeared to have moved towards commercial discussions.

The Colonel said, "Now, let me get this straight. Pastor Jeremiah, you're looking for us to invest thirty million dollars. This money would allow you to perfect the system and would grant our members a license to build, sell and deploy similar systems throughout the United States. Is that right?"

Pastor Jeremiah said, "That is exactly the proposal. We think this system has the potential to do tremendous good. Of course, we'd love to simply share it for free, but it requires significant investment."

The Colonel nodded and looked across the table, "Robbie, your thoughts?"

Robbie adjusted his glasses and looked at his notes, "It would appeal to those of our members who are in the defensive space. With ongoing school shootings, there's a growing market for defensive technologies. I would, however, propose a licensing arrangement where the members who actually sell the system pay an ongoing royalty – if we invest a lump sum, we take on an enormous financial risk."

Pastor Jeremiah paled, and Isaac chipped in, "Can one do a combination of up-front investment and then an ongoing royalty scheme?"

Petrus thought there was something a little desperate in his voice.

For the first time, Antoinette spoke, her voice soothing with southern charm. "We have, of course, done considerable homework, and we realize that you are...how shall I say...a little overextended in terms of cash flow. And this is not the sort of project that a bank would easily finance." She tapped a crimson fingernail on the table, "But we do see great potential, and I want to put forward a slightly different proposal. Do you gentlemen still have time?" She smiled. Jeremiah and Isaac nodded in unison.

Antoinette put up a hand and waved with one finger. Without looking at Petrus, she said, "Waiter, can you connect my laptop to the projector?"

A minute later, she projected an organization chart. The top block was entitled "Church of Holy Redemption." Below it were three additional blocks next to each other – "Big Data Analytica (BDA)," "The Settlement Bureau," and "God's Eye."

Antoinette said, "This is a most intriguing set of companies, all privately owned. Pastor Jeremiah, won't you be so kind as to explain the genesis of these three organizations – just briefly."

"I'd be glad to," Pastor Jeremiah said, "A decade ago, as our church grew, we set up a member database. The intent was to get to know our congregation better. We recorded the normal demographic information, income, key events like deaths and births, etcetera. We quickly realized that we could save ourselves and our members a lot of time by pulling data from existing sources. Our members trust us with their data and don't hesitate to give us permission. From there, things just grew. Other organizations asked us to provide similar data aggregation and analytical services, and we realized that we had something on our hands that could help us understand not only our members but trends in the community, the state, and the country."

"And of course, it generates an income stream," Chuck Thibodaux chimed in.

Pastor Jeremiah said, "Indeed it does, though at the moment it's growing so fast that the investment outstrips income."

161

Isaac added, "The demand for our services is phenomenal, and we have to capitalize on that first-mover advantage."

Pastor Jeremiah took over again, "*The Settlement Bureau* likewise had very humble beginnings. Several of our flock own contracting businesses. During the financial crisis of oh-eight, the central valley was hard hit. Contractors felt awkward about having to foreclose on fellow church members. Both parties came to us, and we negotiated debt reduction or extended payment periods. Sometimes we provided bridging finance. But it was all predicated on our database of accurate income and family circumstance data to ensure that the contractors weren't being taken advantage of. If someone's circumstances changed for the better, we expected them to pay back faster. It has grown to become a tool for members to pay their dues and, since we now know our members pretty well, to nudge them if they seem to be shirking their obligation to share their blessings."

Chuck leaned over to the Colonel and said in a stage whisper, "There are quite a few people in Washington that I'd like to nudge to do what is right." He chuckled.

The pastor continued, pride in his voice, "Around that time, my daughter Katie graduated with a double master's in applied statistics and behavioral psychology. At university, she'd met a computer whiz with a very shrewd brain for business, Rajiv Patel. They formed a team to develop the algorithms that tie together data and behavior. And then, of course, we took it to the next logical step: predictive behavioral analytics. That's what God's Eye is all about, identifying people in distress so that we can pray for them, help them, and support them."

He looked around the room and said, "I'd be more than happy to answer any specific questions you might have?"

The CAFCA board members looked at each other, and Antoinette took the lead again. "Pastor Jeremiah, I have to compliment you – any one of these three organizations would attract the attention of venture capitalists if they were for sale, and together they provide so much synergy. Our proposal is quite simple – we want to buy into that synergy. We are prepared to offer you the thirty million you're asking for, but we want a twenty-five percent stake in all three ventures."

Petrus noticed the quick glances that Isaac shot in the pastor's direction. Finally, after a minute of silence, Jeremiah uttered a single word, "Why?"

Ms. Bussey seemed to be well prepared for this question. "Firstly, we have been somewhat frustrated with being mere clients of BDA. There are so many privacy restrictions and red tape." She waved her hand dismissively. "But, if we gain ownership, then we legally become controllers and can better utilize the information assets.

"Secondly, as you've pointed out, the benefit lies in the integration. I will be frank, Pastor Jeremiah, I know how much you value your," she held up her hands to do air quotes, "army of soldiers in the service of God. But you will appreciate that we, too, mobilize an army of committed citizens in the service of freedom. And an army needs to be disciplined." She smiled and reached out toward the Pastor, as though introducing him to an adoring crowd. "You of all people understand that. The wayward sheep must be guided to follow the shepherd. You have devised great tools for guiding people, and we appreciate the potential. The potential to instill discipline and to prod those who want to water down the second amendment – a core value of what it means to be American. So, that is our proposal."

Pastor Jeremiah was silent. He looked out of the window towards a lone giraffe with its front legs splayed in comical supplication to get its head down to the water.

Overhead, birds of prey made lazy circles. Then he said, "We will have to discuss this among ourselves."

The Colonel resumed control of the meeting, "By all means – we totally understand. He waved in the direction of the waterhole. This is such a wonderful place to contemplate. We have other business this afternoon, so take your time, as long as you give us an answer by five o'clock." Then the Colonel smiled. "Gentlemen, it's been a pleasure."

Antoinette slid two binders across the table.

As Pastor Jeremiah and Isaac gathered their papers, the chairman said, "There is one more thing. We certainly don't want to interfere in the running of the church. But we think your three babies," he smiled and gestured at the screen with the organization chart, "are well on their way to becoming unruly teenagers. And if we invest in them, we can help put them on the right path. So, one of our conditions would be that Ms. Bussey here joins your board of directors. It's all in the papers – study them at your leisure.

"Oh, and a word of advice from someone who's been in the military and in corporate life for a long time. You really need to work on your succession strategy, Pastor. It's not good for any organization to be so dependent on a single leader, with no successor in sight."

Petrus was just in time to see Isaac's reaction. He saw a mask slip, and a mixture of bewilderment and anger cross the man's face. Isaac slipped out of the room without a formal goodbye.

Pastor Jeremiah shook hands with the four CAFCA directors and said he would get back to them.

As Petrus started to clear the table, his phone buzzed. He read the update from his mother and followed Isaac and Jeremiah towards the dining hall. He hurried to catch up and overheard their conversation.

The pastor said, "Isaac, are we making a pact with the devil here?"

"We have no choice. Rajiv tells me he doesn't have the cash to make payroll, and he cannot stall the landlord much longer." His voice was urgent, "We need a deal."

"What do I tell Katie? She's not going to like this one little bit."

Isaac replied, "Respectfully, sir, she's just been in a car accident and suffered a concussion. So she should not be subjected to any undue stress. Hence I don't think we need to give her all the details right now."

Petrus cleared his throat, "Good news! I just got the call that Ms. Katie has been cleared to leave the hospital. I'm driving to Windhoek straight away." He looked at his watch and declared with a broad smile, "She will be able to join you for supper."

Chapter 16, San Francisco

Sunday, 3rd Week of June

TERRY

Charlie watched as Terry lifted his bicycle from behind the couch and strapped on his helmet. The dog lay down and rested his head on his outstretched front legs. A frown appeared in the folds above his doleful eyes, and he whimpered.

"Come on, Charlie, don't make me feel bad," Terry said, "I'll take you out when I get back."

The traffic was less hectic on Sunday afternoons than during the week, but Terry still got an adrenalin rush as he dodged buses and double-parked Ubers. He headed north on Divisadero and played his usual game of trying to see how many lights he could cross without stopping. Since his divorce, the record had climbed almost every week and now stood at fourteen.

It was a beautiful, fog-free day, and crowds were spilling out of restaurants onto the sidewalks and ambling across the intersections, regardless of the traffic lights. By the time Terry got to Bush Street, he knew he wouldn't break any records today. He could have detoured down the level path provided by Van Ness or the scenic route through the Presidio, but Terry plowed on straight through the Pacific Heights, where the roads were so steep that cars parked perpendicular to the sidewalk. He stood in his pedals and panted up to the crest, where he was rewarded with an iconic, movie-worthy San Francisco view. From there, the road plummeted down towards the Marina and the Marin Headlands beyond. The mansions of the rich and famous were bathed in the afternoon sun and vied with each other for the best views.

Terry enjoyed the thrill of the descent, where he clocked 34 mph and attracted the honking ire of at least two motorists as he shot through yellow – okay, just gone red – lights. When he reached the Marina, he turned left towards Golden Gate Bridge and weaved through throngs of tourists meandering along on their rent-a-bikes. Terry was on autopilot and only stopped when he reached the first of the mighty bridge towers. Chloe and his psychiatrist would have disapproved if they knew that he was conducting what they termed a 'self-flagellation ritual', but he didn't care. The sun was warm on his back as he looked towards a swarm of sailing boats playing in the bay.

He ignored the chatter of tourists and let his fingers glide below the railing till they found the tiny silver cross he had affixed there. No one paid him any attention, and he felt a familiar resentment at the indifference. Why had no one paid any attention to Lily as she'd stood there, staring into the depths? Could it really have been so fast? Had Lily not hesitated at all? According to the police report, there'd been a single Swedish tourist that day, but her account of events had been so garbled that it didn't shed much light – the only useful information she could provide was the spot where Lily had jumped.

He leaned over the rust-colored railing and stared at the foam crests twenty-two stories below him. The waters in the Golden Gate were always restless, as though hidden creatures below the surface were churning them up and beckoning to the mere mortals high above: *Come, come join us – it's quiet down here, cool and calm; all your worries will be over.* He leaned down further, unable to take his eyes off a spot right below, where there seemed to be a vortex. *Come…*

One thousand and one, one thousand and two, one thousand and three… It was unfathomable to think what would have gone through Lily's head in those endless seconds.

Terry closed his eyes and straightened up. His fingers gripped the railing and Lily's cross. In his mind's eye, he could see her, standing next to him, looking over the bay. She was much shorter than him, and the wind played with her hair. She turned to him with the tiniest smile on her lips and wiped the hair out of her face. No matter how often their mother had told her to tie it up, she liked wearing her hair loose; it was forever swirling about her head.

I'm so sorry, Lily – so, so sorry. I let you down. When Mom got sick, you were the one who put your life on hold to take care of her. I couldn't bear to watch her suffering, struggling to even visit for an hour on Sundays, yet you sat with her through those endless chemo sessions, nursed her through the nights.

He tasted the saltiness of tears running down his face but was powerless to stop them. He clutched at the cross, willing Lily's image to stay with him. There was no judgment in her face. She said nothing, just looked out over the ocean with the wind tugging at her hair.

I miss you, Lily. You were such an excellent listener, and I took that for granted. I never made the effort to listen to you *– to find out what was going on in the inner depths of your mind. And when Mom died…* He blinked his eyes behind the sunglasses and looked at the blurry image of Alcatraz. *When Mom died, I just assumed that you were as relieved as I was. I should have listened and realized how significant the loss was for you – caring for our mother had become your whole life.*

Terry jumped when a hand landed on his shoulder, and a voice said, "You okay, mate?"

He turned to see a man his own age wearing shorts and a T-shirt proclaiming "Property of Alcatraz."

Terry stammered, "Yes, sure. I'm fine." He was grateful for his sunglasses and made a show of wiping perspiration off his forehead and face.

"Magnificent view, isn't it?" The man said. "Reminds me of Sydney Harbor Bridge. D'ya mind taking a photie of me with Alcatraz in the background?"

Terry obliged the tourist, then set off back towards home. At Chrissy Field park, he stopped for a drink of water and surveyed the crowd enjoying the warm weather. A high-school-age girl was helping a six- or seven-year-old boy get a listless kite into the air. She ran barefoot, holding the kite's string in one hand and shielding her eyes with the other. Her dark hair flowed down her back, and her white dress billowed out behind her. She was light on her feet, and Terry thought there was something fairy-like about her. The laughing boy cheered and bounced up and down with excitement. Then, when the kite had found the ocean breeze and steadied above them, the girl handed the string to the boy. There was such concentration and radiant happiness on his face that it made Terry smile.

The wind played with the girl's hair and, when she reached up to wipe it out of her face, Terry's heart lurched. The way she let her fingers glide through her hair, trying to tuck it behind her ear – suddenly he remembered the tea-tree smell of Lily's long curls. Their mother had always said that Lily had hair fit for a movie star.

169

Terry looked at the two and was overcome with memories of Lily and… Danny. He distinctly remembered a beach holiday where Lily had helped the kiddo fly a kite. The little runt had jumped up and down with excitement just like this kid. God, Danny had been full of beans. Always desperate to do stuff with them, just like a puppy.

The boy in front of him shrieked with delight as the kite did a series of loops. The girl clapped her hands and cast a shy smile in Terry's direction. His vision blurred, and he had to swallow hard. He felt a pain in his chest, but it wasn't the pain that came with his anxiety attacks. Instead, it was the fathomless pain of loss. The feeling that his insides had been scooped out like the seeds of a honeydew melon. There was nothing but a void. Lily. *Why? Why didn't you talk to me? Why didn't you speak to* someone? *We would have been able to fix things.*

And then a new thought struck him. Danny! The kid had only ever existed on the periphery of his life as the son of his estranged father. But now, looking at these two, he thought about him. The kiddo had worshipped Lily. It had been a year since Lily's death. How was he dealing with her loss? Was he feeling it as a loss at all? Terry had broken all ties with his father's new family. Hadn't thought about them in a long time and assumed that they'd gotten on with their own lives. But thinking about it now, he had punished Danny as well because he was angry with their father.

Other images flooded his brain – Danny and Lily ice skating. Danny shrieking with delight on Christmas morning as he opened a present: a CSI detective kit consisting of a magnifying glass, notepad, and a few evidence bags. Lily with Danny on her lap, reading him a story. Terry teaching Danny how to shoot hoops. Suddenly, Danny's six-year-old face appeared in front of him – a picture of concentration as he positioned himself to shoot for the ring, and then the glow of pleasure when Terry had high-fived him.

It was as though the universe shouted at Terry, "Of course Danny is missing his sister, you dumb, self-absorbed prick."

The pain in his chest twisted around and took on a whole new form, enlisting the aid of his abdomen. He felt an overwhelming wave of shame. He had been so preoccupied with his grief, with anger at his father, and the fact that he had been the only family member to bury Lily that he had never even thought about how Danny might have been affected. And worse, he had a dim memory of Danny reaching out to him when he was in the hospital. That period was such a blur – whole days were missing in his memory – but he was sure Danny had called him.

Danny, my brother. That was a whole new thought. He had a brother, someone who would share memories of Lily with him.

The demons in his chest and abdomen retreated a little, and Terry shouted to the girl, "Thanks!"

She smiled and asked, "What for?"

"For reminding me that I need to go find my little brother."

The thought of Danny caused the void in his chest to shrink a little. Terry raced home, left his bike in the hallway – which would earn him the ire of Mrs. Nagly downstairs – and Googled "Danny Gunderson." He got 708,422 hits.

An hour later, he had finally narrowed it down to the Facebook profile of someone who looked like he could be the almost-grown-up version of the little runt Terry had known. It was hard to be sure, because there was no mention of this Danny's parents or any siblings. Terry gleaned as much as he could, but something bothered him. It took him ten minutes to figure out what it was – the site hadn't been updated in almost a year. What teenager left his Facebook page without a single update for a year? Maybe Danny had just moved on to a different social media

171

platform? Terry tried some cross-referencing but couldn't find a profile for the same East-Coast-based Danny/Daniel/Dan Gunderson anywhere.

Terry's psychiatrist had warned him that he tended to "catastrophize"; he always assumed the worst. And though he was aware of this tendency and tried to countermand it with positive thoughts, he felt an unease welling up. Had something terrible happened to Danny? A car accident, gun violence, cancer, someone punishing him because of their father? Surely someone would have told Terry? Would they?

He typed a message, *Hi kiddo, this is your big brother, Terry. Would love to get in touch.*

Terry started to think about more things that could have befallen Danny and sensed that awful fist getting ready to clutch and squeeze his heart. That was when Charlie intervened, placing his paws on Terry's lap and licking his face.

"Okay, Charlie boy," Terry stroked the dog. "I guess I did promise you a walk. Let's go."

***

On Monday morning, Terry found that he had been granted "elevated access", and Simon suggested he start with the previously-locked data lakes for CAFCA and *The Settlement Bureau* because BDA did social attitudes research for both organizations. The CAFCA research included attitudes to everything from gun control and immigration to the death penalty. There was extensive research, all sliced and diced and rendered in sophisticated graphics by gender, age, education level, ethnicity, and political affiliation. Terry was like someone who had discovered the internet for the first time. He got pulled from one thread to another, diving down rabbit holes and coming up with all manner of random but fascinating information. With his new access rights, he could see not only the attitudes of demographic groups but also the attitudes of organizations, individual lawmakers, CEOs, journalists, and celebrities.

The Settlement Bureau data was even more granular and tailored to researching individuals. There was data to predict when someone was likely to go into bankruptcy, studies on the effectiveness of training programs, crime prevention initiatives, and the predictors of violence in families. He delved around till he came across a database containing the data of thousands of people associated with the Church of Holy Redemption. He randomly clicked on "Sarah Bates" and a detailed profile page came up. Her photo showed an anxious-looking woman with stiffly-set gray hair. She appeared to be a widow in her sixties, with two grown children. She managed the hospitality after church services. After a mastectomy in 2017, she lived in constant fear that the cancer might return.

As Terry read, he marveled at the level of detail. The profile page was a high-level summary with extensive, categorized links. Under education, there were links to Sarah's Alma Mater – San Luis Obispo – where she had studied librarianship. Under "Medical" he could drill down to her healthcare provider. There was even a link to the DMV site, where Terry learned that Sarah was convicted of a DUI ten years ago. Under "Daily Life", he could get to her Fitbit readouts.

Terry felt like he had stumbled into some kind of *Matrix* horror movie. The most disturbing thing wasn't just the access to information about every aspect of Sarah's life, but the cold summary conclusions and inferences that dehumanized her. He might as well have looked at the records of a dairy cow: *past breeding age, milk flow diminishing, consider disposal.*

He called up a few more profiles and noticed that they seemed to hone in on people's frailties, weaknesses, and mistakes in life. It made him feel like a peeping tom, and he was ashamed for even looking.

Terry was about to log out of the secure database when, on a whim, he typed in "Daniel Gunderson," and, to his surprise, a profile picture came up. Terry's hand trembled over the keyboard as he stared at the young surfer boy – the same person he'd tracked down on the internet the night before. Danny had a defiant expression as he dipped his head and looked at the camera. The eyes! Terry would have recognized their father's Nordic blue eyes anywhere.

A quick scan of the profile told him that Danny's mother was remarried, that Danny never spent more than one year in any school and that he seemed to have had some brushes with the law. Then, scrolling down, he saw, "Currently enrolled at the Renaissance Institute for young men in California."

California! Danny was in California. Terry's eyes raced down the page, but when he clicked on the "Education Detail" button, he got the message, "Access denied".

"What the…" Terry muttered and tried clicking on other buttons, but it was always the same pop-up.

Kiddo, what are *you up to? Are you teasing me? Are you punishing me for ignoring you all these years?*

A quick internet search produced the phone number of the institute. To get some privacy, he took the elevator to the top floor and stepped out onto the roof. This time, he was oblivious to the beauty of the bay and the city below.

"Come on, come on," Terry muttered as he drummed his fingers on a railing and waited for someone to pick up the phone.

"Renaissance Institute," a man's deep voice said, "how may I assist you?"

Terry explained who he was and that he wanted to speak to his brother, Daniel Gunderson.

He could hear computer tapping, and then the man said, "What's your name again, sir? I don't seem to have you on the register of authorized relatives."

"Authorized relatives? I just told you, I lost touch with my brother but I've found out that he's a student at the institute and want to pick up contact with him. I appreciate that he might be in classes now. So can you just give me his email address and tell me when might be a good time to call? Maybe this afternoon?"

There was silence at the other end. Then the man coughed discreetly, "Sir, I don't think you quite understand the nature of the institute. Our...*clients*," Terry got the impression that the man used the term under duress, "are here under a stringent set of rules. They do not have access to cell phones, email, or other forms of communication. They may speak to an authorized family member once every two weeks."

"What?" Terry exploded. "Are you telling me this is a correctional facility?" He had to breathe deeply. *Oh God, Danny – have I let you down, too?*

"If you would like to get in touch with your...brother, Mr. Reynolds," the voice said, oozing skepticism, "I suggest you contact his mother. I assume you know her, since you claim to be his brother."

Terry wished he could punch the innuendo out of the faceless individual behind that voice.

The man continued, "I have to tell you, though, that in my experience here at the institute, mothers are rarely willing to give up their bi-weekly phone slot for any but the *closest* of relatives."

175

Terry hung up, pounded the railing with his fist, and shouted, "Fuck, fuck, fuck!" across the city.

He spun around when a voice behind him said, "I know some people don't like Mondays, but you take it to a whole new level." Sandy exhaled a ring of smoke. "D'you want to talk about it?"

Terry sighed and deliberated. *What the hell.* He did need to talk to someone, and Sandy was offering. So he told her what he'd found out while she stared into the distance and smoked. Finally, he mused, "Maybe I can look in the database and find the name of the principal or someone in authority I can appeal to. What do you think?"

Sandy stubbed out her cigarette and joined him at the railing. She said, "Or go right to the top. Find someone at the Church of Holy Redemption. They own the institute and ought to be open to a compassionate plea." She smirked, "Prodigal son and all that good stuff."

Terry frowned and stared out over the bay. Then he beamed at Sandy. "Of course! Katie Blanchard is a bigwig at the church, and she was Chloe's bridesmaid at our wedding."

Sandy gaped. "You mean you know *the* Katie Blanchard personally? The woman that's regularly on TV? The one who was on the Meredith de Frey show the other evening?"

Terry nodded.

Sandy shook her head. "Man, you are full of surprises." She smiled, "Well, there's your answer. Ring up your pal Katie. I mean, she's virtually all-powerful. There's only the Pastor Jeremiah between her and God."

"You're brilliant," Terry said. On an impulse, he embraced Sandy in a bear hug and planted a kiss on her cheek. When he went to pull away, her hand came up behind his head and held him. She sought out his mouth and kissed him. For a moment, Terry was too surprised to react. Then he felt her breasts against his chest, and his hands seemed to take on a life of their own, stroking Sandy's back and hair. His breath caught as she squeezed his ass. They kissed with more urgency.

When he reached for the straining top button of her blouse, Sandy drew away, her face flushed.

Terry stammered, "I'm…so sorry. I don't know what came over me…that was…unforgivable…"

She cocked her head, and there was a sparkle in her eyes when she said, "Believe me, no one kisses me unless I want them to." Then she smiled, "We may want to continue this conversation some other time at a more appropriate location."

Terry couldn't take his eyes off her as she straightened her dress and motioned for them to sit in the Adirondack chairs. Sandy said, "Okay, now tell me all you've found out since you've been granted the keys to the kingdom. I still can't believe that you've been here a week, and you get elevated access – I've been busting my gut for nearly a year…ugh. Boys networks make me so mad."

Terry grinned, "You look hot when you're mad."

She rolled her eyes, "Focus, Terry. If your blood is in your dick, your brain gets oxygen deprived."

Terry blushed and crossed his legs.

He told her about the vast array of ready-made queries for CAFCA and the detailed individual profiles for The Settlement Bureau. "It's like stepping into a parallel universe, like the *Matrix* or *Westworld,* where suddenly you find that the people aren't real, they're puppets being manipulated by unseen hands. It's ultra-creepy and yet also fascinating – totally de-humanizing when people are boiled down to just a few key conclusions. I can't believe a church would do this to its members."

Sandy scowled, and Terry continued, "There was one I came across that said, 'Gay democratic lawmaker, in a committed relationship, having an affair.' And when you click on it, it's like reading a detective's report. The thing is, though, all the data seems to be automatically assembled from a gazillion data points feeding into an AI algorithm twenty-four seven. So it's not just surveilling; it's surveilling and *automatically* drawing behavioral conclusions on everything from phone records and geo-positioning to credit card spending and CCTV facial recognition." He leaned forward, "Would you believe that for this guy, the algorithm had sucked in data from a wearable device that measures sleep quality. That way the AI could establish when there was sex happening in his bedroom? Mash that with who was in the house at the time, and voila – it's the next best thing to having webcams in the bedroom."

Sandy shuddered, "That is *so* disturbing. How many profiles did you trawl through?"

"Just enough to get a gist of the level of detail. This lawmaker caught my attention because the little box marked 'COLD Index' was red with a score of eight. All the others–"

Sandy's hand flew up to her mouth, and she whispered, "Did you say cold as in C-O-L-D?"

Terry nodded, "I remember you and Professor Curry saying that you were keen to find out what it was about. I noticed that every profile had a little box with a number and a color. If I had to guess, I'd say it's a score from one to ten. Most of the profiles were green, with scores between one and three. Then there were a few orange scores around four and five. As I say, I only came across one red with a score of eight."

Sandy bit her lower lip and stared into space, "But what does it mean?"

Terry shrugged, "Maybe it is an indicator of how far away from God you are." He chuckled, "If you get into the red zone, you're a bad, bad boy, getting closer to hell – and the congregation had better pray for you."

Sandy whipped her head around and looked at him. Looked at him as though she saw him for the first time. "That's it!" she exclaimed. "You're not just a pretty face; you've figured it out. Of course, that's it!"

Terry looked at her without comprehension.

"Think about it," Sandy's face was flushed with excitement. "Think about how, for thousands of years, people avoided going to hell. Hmm? What did good Catholics do to atone for their sins? Come on, you're Irish."

"That doesn't mean I'm a good Catholic," Terry mumbled and strained his memory back to Sunday School days. He shrugged, "They paid the church to forgive their sins. It's called an indulgence."

Sandy said, "Exactly! All this bullshit about collecting data so the church can help its members and pray for them." She snorted in a most unladylike manner. "They're blackmailing their flock. Plain and simple. What I don't understand is why people stay with a church that blackmails them. It must be like some kind of sect."

"Oh my God," Terry said. "I've been so thick. I got so carried away digging into the member profiles that it never occurred to me to look for my own. Remember, *The Settlement Bureau* tried to squeeze money out of me. They're not just blackmailing their members; they're blackmailing *anyone* with *anything* to hide."

"Fucking hell!" Sandy said and the words hung in the air. They didn't even begin to express what Terry felt.

They sat in silence, contemplating the enormity of it. Then Sandy roused herself and said, "You've done an awesome job, Terry. We need you to go in there and try and ascertain how big this is – how far the reach is. Are they sucking in data for the county, for California, the whole United States?" She shook her head and continued, "I need to talk to Clyde; he's either going to have an orgasm or his

179

brain will explode when he finds out the scale of this operation."

Chapter 17, Namibia

Monday, 4th Week of June

KATIE

Over breakfast, Pastor Jeremiah extracted a promise from Katie that she would follow doctor's orders and have a day of complete rest. To underscore his seriousness, he took possession of her PC and cell phone before he and Isaac went for their follow-up meetings with the CAFCA team.

Mid-morning, Katie found herself sitting on the verandah overlooking the waterhole. She had moved her chair to a spot where she could feel the winter sun on her face. There was absolutely nothing to see or do. She closed her eyes and listened to the sound of silence – nothing but the chirping of cicadas. The dining room and verandah were deserted except for an elderly couple reading their books. She flicked through the three-day-old *Windhoek Observer* and several well-thumbed magazines that seemed to obsess over British Royalty. She tossed them back on the coffee table. Then Katie picked fluff off her sweater and examined her fingernails, which were cracking in the dry weather.

She was touched that her father was so concerned about her health, but wondered whether she could ask reception for a spare key to his room to get her laptop. It seemed ridiculous to sit here and do nothing while her work piled up.

A shadow fell over her, and Petrus said, "Good morning; I hope you slept well. How are you feeling?"

Petrus was dressed in his Khaki shorts and shirt. His only concession to the chill air was a steaming mug held in both hands. He followed her gaze and asked, "Would you like some tea and maybe a scone? Cook has just baked fresh scones, and they're *good.*" He stretched out the word "good" and licked his lips.

Katie smiled, "How many have you had?"

Petrus laughed, "I go into a trance and lose count when I eat cook's scones with clotted cream. But there are more."

"Tea and scones would be lovely," Katie said, and Petrus gestured to a waiter, who seemed to understand the wordless request.

Katie asked, "Where are the animals?"

Petrus made a broad gesture encompassing the water hole and the bushveld beyond. He crouched next to her chair and handed her his binoculars. It was like the clearing of vision after cataract surgery. The two muddy logs at the edge of the water turned out to be crocodiles. Beyond them, hidden in the bushes, a family of Springbuck was waiting – torn between thirst and fear of the crocodiles. There were guinea fowl and sandpiper mamas shooing their teenage broods and pecking about for grubs.

"Watch over there, where those two trees make a gateway," Petrus said.

Katie waited then dropped the binoculars, "I don't see anything – what am I looking for?"

"Wait…they're coming."

Katie gasped when an enormous elephant sauntered into view, immediately followed by a herd of, "One…two…three…" she counted. "Oh, look at the baby!" She was mesmerized to watch the herd of seven elephants as they began sucking water up their trunks and squirting it into their mouths. The crocodiles slid away, and the Springbuck took their cue and joined the elephants to drink. Katie marveled at the comings and goings of the animals and only took a break to sample the scones, which were as good as Petrus had predicted. He laughed when she licked the last of the cream off her fingers.

Then they sat side by side and enjoyed the serenity of the graceful parade at the waterhole. There were zebras and wildebeest, impala, wild dogs, and giraffes. Occasionally, Petrus would tell her things, like how a particular elephant bull had broken off a tusk in a fight or how to spot the difference between male and female giraffes by looking at the tufts of hair on their comical little horns.

Katie became so entranced that she barely noticed the verandah and dining room filling up until Petrus said, "Well, it's time for lunch. I have to go look after some of our other guests."

She felt a pang of disappointment at the thought that she was just "another guest" but chided herself for being silly. Petrus was a professional – and it was his job to take care of the guests.

Petrus coughed, and she looked at him. He said, "I'm not scheduled for any sunset game drive this evening. And since you missed out, that is…if you like…I could take you out this afternoon?"

"That would be lovely," she said, and wondered, *when did I start picking up words like "lovely"? It must be all those magazines about British Royalty.*

She joined her father and Isaac for lunch. The buffet included vegetable soup, salads, beef stew, and braised chicken thighs in a delicious sauce. Pastor Jeremiah beamed when Katie went back for seconds, "Glad to see you've developed an appetite. Looks like the fresh air agrees with you."

Isaac commented, "It must be quite a logistical challenge to produce this kind of food for dozens of people when the nearest shop is fifty miles away."

Katie nodded, "And the baking! I had scones this morning; they were fantastic." She sipped her water and asked, "So, how are the negotiations going?"

The two men glanced at each other, then her father said, "It's all pretty much wrapped up. You won't have to worry about our cash flow situation anymore."

"That's a relief," Katie said. "Do you want me to join this afternoon?" She placed a hand on her father's forearm and smiled, "I know how you hate going through contract details. I can do that for you."

"No, no," Pastor Jeremiah said, "Isaac is doing a splendid job shielding me from the detail. You just carry on enjoying the peace and quiet around here."

***

At 3:30 p.m., she and Petrus headed west along dusty tracks in an open Land Rover. Katie loved the wind in her hair and the sun on her face. She marveled at the contrast to San Francisco. The soil was so different from the clay she was used to. It was pale grayish-brown with patches of ochre. The vegetation was hardy – mainly camel thorn bush with slender white spikes. An earthy smell filled the air. Every few minutes, Petrus would tell her to "duck" and she had to lean in towards him to avoid the gauntlet of thorns that spread their branches to resist the intrusion of civilization. *These would make a phenomenal crown of thorns*, she thought.

They drove for twenty minutes without encountering another soul. Then Petrus turned off the road and the vehicle bumped cross-country around eight-foot-high ant heaps that dotted the landscape like a network of sentries. Finally, when they got to a clearing with a muddy pond, Petrus turned off the engine; the silence was overwhelming.

"And now?" Katie asked.

"Now we wait."

"For what?" She asked.

He grinned, "Patience will be rewarded."

They sat in silence, then Katie whispered, "So I gather from your mother that you have a master's in Environmental Management from Oxford."

He rolled his eyes and chuckled, "Mothers and their bragging. It's insufferable. What else did she tell you?"

Now it was Katie's turn to grin, "Wouldn't you like to know – knowledge is power."

"She couldn't have told you that much. You were asleep most of the time."

Katie started counting off on her fingers, "I know that you were a Rhodes scholar; that you've always wanted to be a game ranger; that you're on the board of the Namibian Save-the-Rhino foundation and an internationally-respected authority on eco-tourism and wildlife conservation."

Petrus hid his face in his hands, "I'm going to kill that woman."

"I also know," Katie said, "That you have two younger sisters and that your mother thinks you walk on water except for one small omission…"

"Oh, God no," Petrus groaned, but he was smiling.

"You haven't produced any grandbabies for her yet," Katie said and laughed.

"Shhh," Petrus held a finger to his mouth.

A group of six zebras emerged from the bushes, and Katie was astounded at how quiet they were. They made for the pond, stopping every few feet to watch for predators. *Such a harsh existence when one tiny mistake could mean the end.* They all stopped at the water's edge and waited while the old matriarch sniffed the air. When she moved to drink, the others followed. Every so often, one or other zebra raised its head, craned its neck, and sniffed.

"They look so skittish," Katie whispered.

Petrus held his finger to his lips and whispered, "With good …"

Two lionesses burst from the bushes to their left. The zebras squealed in alarm. The matriarch turned to face the lions, allowing her brood to scatter. She reared on her hind legs and kicked frantically. Katie was amazed by the agility of the cats. One of them snarled directly at the zebra, and when she rose again, the second lioness leaped onto her back. The huntress' nails tore into her prey as she clawed her way up to the neck. The zebra's thrashing veiled the scene in a cloud of dust. Then she uttered an unearthly squeal that ended in a gurgle and a thump. It made Katie's blood run cold.

The kill had taken seconds, but it felt like an eternity. Katie looked at Petrus and realized she had gripped his arm so hard that her fingernails were digging into his bicep. "Sorry," she mumbled and unclamped her hands. She released a long breath and whispered, "That was…amazing…and incredibly sad. She sacrificed herself for the herd."

Petrus nodded, "It's how it should be; nature's way. She's had a good inning, and if she'd run, the lions would have killed one of the youngsters. Also, she was losing her touch – should have smelled the lions much earlier. It's time for a new leader."

Katie watched as the lionesses ripped into the carcass. A few minutes later, a splendid specimen of male lionhood emerged to join the feast. He growled once. The lionesses did not appear happy but yielded to him.

"Let's leave them to their dinner," Petrus said and started the Land Rover back towards the road. They stopped several times to admire a lone kudu bull, a herd of impala, and a family of warthogs. Katie smiled at the comical animals with their big heads, short legs, and curly little tails. The sun was nearing the horizon when Petrus veered off the road again. Katie clung to the grip bar as they bumped up the side of a hill across a field of grapefruit-sized rocks. They stopped near the top of the hill, and Petrus spread out cushions for Katie to sit on the ground. He opened the back of the Land Rover, and within minutes was able to offer a full bar service, complete with snacks: chips, olives, biltong, crackers, and cheese.

With a flourish, he said, "What would be Madam's pleasure? We have scotch, gin and tonic, the finest of South African box wine, Windhoek Lager, Savannah cider – highly recommended. There's also Baileys, Kahlua, and the local favorite, Amarula."

She smiled, "Just water, thanks."

He pulled a face of mock disappointment and poured water into an enamel mug. Katie took a sip and studied a hardy little plant that grew out of a crevice in the rocks. It was barely more than a twig with a few stunted leaves, but it stood erect and even seemed to have produced a few seed pods. *Poor thing; some seeds fall on stony ground. And yet, even they must try.*

She dipped her hands in the mug and splashed water on the plant.

She hadn't realized that Petrus was watching her till he said, "Sometimes, all we can do is help one of the many in need." He gestured at the field of rocks below them and the many plants struggling for survival among them.

The sun touched the horizon and cast an orange glow over the land. Katie pulled up her knees and hugged them to stay warm. Petrus produced a blanket and wrapped it around her shoulders.

"Aren't you cold?" she asked, watching him in his summer uniform. There was something very rooted and proprietary in the way he stood surveying the land below them. The last rays of the sun gave his skin a bronze sheen. His sculpted muscles looked like tempered steel.

"Guardian of the Land," Katie mumbled.

He turned to her with a quizzical look.

"Sorry, did I say that out loud?" Her face flushed. "I was just thinking that, if Marvel ever came up with an eco-hero, you could play the part – Guardian of the Land."

He said nothing and returned his attention to the veld. A minute later, he pointed out the silhouettes of two giraffes, their heads and necks gliding above the canopy of camel thorn trees. It was such a peaceful tableau that it made Katie smile. She kept her eyes on the sun, which was now reduced to a glowing crescent intent on not letting this singular, precious day pass without a final flare of deepest amber.

When was I last so relaxed, so at ease with someone? A small voice in her head said, *you don't have to live the life your father has mapped out; you could go somewhere far away and...* She suppressed the thought and looked up to find Petrus gazing at her.

"What?" she asked and touched her cheek, which felt dry as parchment.

Before he could answer, the radio in the Land Rover cackled, "Oshinawa ranger one, are you there, over?" A pause and the message was repeated. Petrus went to the vehicle to answer and started a conversation in Oshivambo. It sounded like pleasantries were being exchanged. The only word she could understand was "over" as Petrus and an unknown man tossed the conversational ball back and forth. Katie tried to think whether she'd ever heard a radio conversation outside of the movies. It seemed like a quaint throwback to a pre-cell-phone era. Petrus' counterpart was agitated about something. He started to monopolize the conversation, and she thought she heard the terms "Americans" and "CAFCA." The man cackled with laughter, and Petrus repeatedly pressed the button on his radio. When the other man finally gave him a chance to speak, he said in English, "Aish, not on the open channel. I will call you from camp, over and out." He rammed the radio into its holder with more force than necessary.

Katie studied his grim expression and said, "What was that about?"

He did not seem to have heard her and started to pack up. She waited, and finally, he said, "That was a friend who works at the neighboring hunting lodge. Those CAFCA people that your father is meeting with, they were at the lodge before they came here. They did a lot of hunting. I guess that's why they chose Namibia for their conference; just an excuse for a hunting trip." He sounded bitter.

Katie said, "Oh. Is that illegal?"

"No, it's part of Namibia's sustainable eco-tourism program. The hunting lodges are issued permits to allow a certain number of animals to be culled – hunters pay well for that. But my friend says these people were crazy. They kept offering the manager of the lodge money to shoot more than the permits allowed. When the group left on Saturday, two stayed behind and bribed him to hunt rhino. And that," he added with emphasis, "*that* is crossing every conceivable boundary and is highly illegal."

His jaw was set tight.

189

She thought of the lion kill and the zebra's death squeal; she felt sick at the image of an endangered animal, like a rhino, shot simply for its trophy. Her voice was constricted and sounded small when she asked, "What happened? Did they get the rhino?"

A slow smile spread across Petrus' face, and he shook his head. "That's why my friend was laughing so much. I have taught them a scheme whereby they 'accidentally' mix up the signals from the tracking devices. When the hunters tracked down what they thought was a rhino, it turned out to be an ancient wildebeest. They were not happy and swore at the manager, but what could they do? Report him to the police?" He smirked. "Anyway, they left this morning to join the others here at Oshinawa."

Katie studied him, "That's a pretty ingenious scheme of subterfuge you've come up with."

"I can't take credit. It was the idea of my Oxford roommate. He's a systems guru and an ardent conservationist. In fact, all the breeding and migration observations we make here get fed into his global database to improve conservation methods. You may have heard of him, Clyde Curry. He's a professor at EBU – East Bay University in Oakland."

Katie's throat constricted, and she had trouble breathing. She broke out in a cold sweat; her wonderful feeling of calm evaporated. EBU, the analytics department, professor Curry. Would she ever be able to rid herself of the memories? She pulled the blanket tighter around her shoulders.

Fortunately, Petrus didn't seem to notice her distress. He laughed and said, "Sorry, here in Namibia, if you say, 'Do you know Joey Mashonga?' there's a good chance the answer is yes. People know each other. I forget just how big the Bay Area is."

Katie swallowed the last of her water. Every instinct told her to just shut up – say nothing – let it pass. But her mouth opened, and she heard herself confide, "That's such a coincidence. I've never met Clyde, but I know him by reputation. You know what's even stranger? His father was my thesis supervisor when I studied for my master's in behavioral psychology and analytics."

"Aish!" Petrus exclaimed, "that's so amazing – so you actually know the famous Nobel-laureate professor Sean Curry? The world is indeed a village."

It was getting dark now, and the evening star, accompanied by a phalanx of twinkling beacons, appeared in the eastern sky. Katie could no longer make out Petrus' features but was very aware of his presence. His body seemed to radiate heat. Neither of them was keen to get back to camp.

Petrus launched into reminiscences of his time at Oxford with Clyde – the parties, the protests, the way he had missed his mother's cooking.

"What do you miss most about your time in Oxford?" Katie eventually asked.

He answered without hesitation. "Two things. I miss the rowing, the feeling of being part of a team. I love what I do here, but it gets lonely." She felt herself blushing in the dark. Quickly she said, "And the second thing?"

"I miss the rain." She could hear the smile in his voice. "Those English people thought I was crazy. It could rain for ten days in a row, and my smile would just get broader and broader. When you grow up in Namibia, you can never get enough of rain." Then he said, "We'd better get going or else they'll worry back at camp."

As they got into the vehicle, she asked, "What are you going to do about the CAFCA people trying to bribe the lodge manager?"

"I think, after dinner, I'm going to Skype with Clyde and see what he thinks." Then he added, "Do you want to

191

join me for the call? He'll be so amazed that one of his father's students pitched up here with me."

She hesitated then shrugged, "Okay, why not?"

Petrus suddenly looked pensive, "I cannot invite you to my room – it is shared with two other rangers. But I can maybe ask Angel if I can borrow the boardroom. Of course, she has rules about all these things, but I'm sure…"

"Just come to my room," Katie said. "I've been very impressed with the Internet speed. It's much better than expected."

***

The guest chalets were spread out on an earthen dam wall along one side of the waterhole. Hedges of bougainvillea, banana plants and the indigenous bush between the buildings afforded each guest privacy and the ability to enjoy watching the animals from their own patios.

Isaac sat on his patio, wine glass in hand, and stared towards the dimly-lit water, where a pack of hyenas was tussling over the remains of an unfortunate buck. They could be heard grunting and squabbling. He paid them no attention as he indulged in his favorite fantasy – him and Katie as a power couple, in charge of the church and all its holdings. His mood darkened as he thought of Colonel Hink's comment that Jeremiah needed to find himself a successor. How dare he, when Isaac was right there. Sure, his style would be different from Jeremiah's – the old man had a certain charisma – but Jeremiah was a fool when it came to business and politics. The man was totally out of his depth. Isaac was convinced that, with Katie at his side, and the money and power flowing from *The Settlement*

Bureau, he would be unstoppable. He visualized himself with the miter on his head, leading a procession; the eyes of the world would be on him and people would pay him the respect he deserved. More importantly, he would be safe. If there was one thing he'd learned in all those endless History of Religion classes, it was that power made you untouchable.

Katie's chalet was closest to his; he could hear running water and assumed she was taking a shower. He closed his eyes and let his fantasy shift to a naked Katie soaping herself down. He pictured her washing her hair and the suds running down between her breasts. Isaac savored an image of Katie stretched across the bed, ready to fulfill his every wish and desire. And he, her lord and master, had a long wish list. He smiled into the darkness.

A hyena's laugh broke the spell. He knew that Katie viewed him as a brother rather than a potential lover, but she would see the light – it was their destiny. By God, he'd given her enough rope to play out her depraved little fantasies. He thought with disgust of the evenings he'd spent watching as she donned that hateful wig and picked up strangers in bars. He had always intended to woo her but, if that didn't work, there were other means of putting the leash on her. He was tempted to get out his laptop and review the cache of documents he had assembled on Katie and her secrets. It always made him feel better to see the evidence that would seal her fate – she would be his, or her life would not be worth living. But he decided it was better not to access these files across the dodgy internet connection in this godforsaken corner of the earth. God only knew what security, if any, they had in place.

The Colonel's comments had rattled him and what had been a vision of the future with no specific timeline had morphed into an urgent plan. Over dinner, he had noticed how radiant Katie was, how relaxed, prattling about the animals she'd seen. There was no telling when she would next be in such a receptive frame of mind, and she probably considered this a romantic setting. He had to make his move with Katie – now.

Isaac picked up a half-empty wine bottle, as well as two clean glasses, and walked towards her chalet. He was about to pass through a gap in the bougainvillea hedge when he stopped abruptly and listened. He heard Katie's voice, "Hi, come in. Excuse my wet hair – I just got out of the shower."

Petrus' voice, "The wet look suits you – pity that in this weather it'll dry in minutes."

He heard Katie's laugh, and then the door closed.

Isaac stood rooted. All his instincts raged and urged him to march into her room. He pictured the scene. She had probably only had a towel wrapped around her and would have already let it drop to the floor, clawing to rip off the black man's clothes and drag him onto the bed with her. He would walk in and be icy, "You are mine, Katie Blanchard, and as of this minute, you will stop fucking random strangers." Petrus would be horrified at her unfaithfulness and skulk off.

But the rational voices in his head prevailed. He took a deep draught from the wine bottle and hurled it in the direction of the waterhole. *Hopefully it'll hit some stupid lion on the head,* he thought. He was so sick of the way Katie went gaga over the lions. For God's sake, they were just bloody animals, and not even edible – they were of fuck all use to anyone.

Isaac couldn't bear the thought of sitting in his room and imagining the fuck fest going on next door. He made his way to the bar, where he found Antoinette Bussey and Robbie Gardner with two unknown men. Antoinette waved him over with a smile, "Isaac, please come and join us. Now you can meet the final members of our team. This is

Major McCullum; he heads up the portfolio of offensive weapons."

Isaac shook hands with Major McCullum, a short man who held himself very erectly. It was hard to gauge the man's age. He wore a designer shirt and chinos. With his tanned, smooth skin and short, jet-black hair, he looked like he might be in his forties. Close-up, though, Isaac got the impression that the smooth skin resulted from cosmetic surgery, and the hair color must have come out of a bottle. He was probably closer to sixty. He and Antoinette seemed cut from the same cloth – city people who did not even make a pretense of trying to fit into this rustic setting.

The major smiled and said, "Antoinette here has filled me in on the negotiations and," he lowered his voice, "she's told me that you're the brains of the operation; the power behind the throne." He winked, and Isaac blushed. This was excellent news that lifted his spirits. Antoinette raised a finger in the direction of the barman. "Let's get this man something to drink – a flight of your special liqueurs."

Then she introduced the other man, "And this is Carl Gunderson. He's a special advisor to CAFCA for the Middle East and Africa regions."

Isaac couldn't precisely determine Carl's portfolio but thought the man promoted weapons sales for CAFCA members. Carl was quite the opposite of Major McCullum. He spoke with a charming accent and looked very Nordic – tall, with silver hair worn down to the shoulders and stylish European glasses. The burst veins on his nose, and the puffiness around his blue eyes, hinted at a fondness for alcohol. He wore an open-necked white shirt, shorts and sandals, and greeted Isaac with a warm smile and a firm handshake. Isaac thought that Carl Gunderson was the sort of person everyone would want to befriend – someone who looked like they didn't have a care in the world as they sailed off on a yacht to an exotic location.

The flight of liqueurs arrived and, with some coaxing, Isaac was initiated into the delights of "Namibia's finest" – sweet apple liqueur, followed by Pamplemousse and gin. Then there was the ghastly bitter taste of Jaegermeister, which was mercifully washed away with creamy Baileys, Amarula and Sambuca. Isaac downed one after the other to the cheers of the CAFCA gang. He felt a warmth spread throughout his body as his new friends clapped him on the shoulder and encouraged him. Even Antoinette fluttered her eyelashes and said that he was clearly a man of many hidden talents. Isaac grinned.

To his disappointment, Antoinette soon excused herself, but the men wanted to stay and talk with him. The major pulled his barstool closer and lowered his voice, "Isaac, I don't think the good pastor fully appreciates what a gold mine he's sitting on." The world around Isaac was beginning to swim. He barely heard the major, but was overwhelmed by the familiarity of the man's cologne – Paco Rabanne. Isaac stiffened when the major placed a hand on his shoulder. The older man's lips were so close, he could feel his breath against his ear. Isaac suppressed a shudder. The major leaned in and whispered, "Can I let you in on a secret?" His hand moved, massaging Isaac's neck as if to dispel a knot of tension.

A wave of nausea swept over Isaac. He mumbled an apology as he slid off his barstool and stumbled through the glass door onto the deserted terrace. He clutched the banister as he lost the fight against his rebellious insides and vomited the alcohol into the bushes below. His eyes filled with tears, and when the retching finally stopped, he remained bent over the banister. Memories, as sharp and fresh as yesterday, assailed him. He, in his new altar boy robes, nervous and desperate to please. The priest back home in Chicago who had placed a hand on his neck, gently massaging, telling him it would be all right. Then, over time, suggesting ways – adult ways – to fully relax and dispel all anxiety. "It will be our secret."

Isaac's body shook with silent sobs. After a few moments, his nightmare memories were interrupted by the melodious voice of the surfer dude, "Hey man, I'm sorry. Those liqueurs are a bitch. I guess these guys have never outgrown their little hazing jokes. Are you okay?"

Isaac was grateful that the man, Carl, kept his distance. He remained bent over the banister, gripping till his knuckles turned white. He would grin and bear it, the way he had done so many years ago in the little chapel in Chicago. He would grin and bear it one more time because he needed these people to get the power that would forever make him untouchable. *Mine* is the power, and the glory, and the *vengeance*. The thought gave him strength.

He straightened up and nodded, "Just give me a minute."

When Isaac rejoined them, after a detour to the bathroom, the major picked up the conversation, "To date, we've spoken about defensive capabilities. The melding of defensive hardware and analytics is great. But of course, like yin and yang, for full security, one must have a solution that includes both defensive and offensive capabilities."

Isaac nodded, and the major described a system that CAFCA had invested in. It entailed hundreds of tiny drones clustered in innocuous objects that looked like a chandelier or a sculpture. The drones functioned like their literal counterparts – they delivered a sting with anything one wanted to arm them with – from a hallucinogenic drug to deadly venom or anthrax. And they could either disperse at random into a crowd or be set upon specific targets based on facial recognition.

Isaac's speech was slurred when he said, "Amazing...so you could have these...little drones pop out...and go sting a specific person?"

"Exactly," the major said, and his two compatriots, Carl and Robbie, nodded their heads in unison. "The thing is, we want to find an opportunity where we can put all the pieces together and demonstrate them in a real-life setting."

Isaac wasn't sure what they were driving at. Damn those liqueurs. "Go on," he intoned.

Carl Gunderson chipped in, "Imagine a situation where we have the full suite of capabilities installed at your church. And then there is," he made air quotes, "a terrorist attack by some deranged nutter. Of course, you'd identify the terrorist with your analytics and neutralize him with a targeted drone sting."

Carl's voice was smooth and seductive like a mature cabernet. He continued, "If this were to happen during one of the major televised services, can you imagine the publicity? Can you imagine what a hero you'd be when it was revealed that you'd had the foresight to install all these systems to foil the attack? And of course, yourselves and CAFCA would profit greatly when the orders started streaming in for similar systems all over the country – all over the world."

Isaac was mesmerized. He said, "I don't know what Pastor Jeremiah..."

Carl nodded in acknowledgment and gave an appreciative smile. "You *are* quick on the uptake. We've thought about that, and we also got the impression that the pastor is somewhat...old school. That's why we wanted to talk to you. I mean, you're the future of the organization, aren't you?" He paused. "The pastor doesn't need to know. No one needs to know until the big reveal at the end when, of course, you would get the credit for your strategic thinking and action." He smiled. "If that doesn't cement your position as the leader of the church, then God alone knows what would."

Isaac's mind drifted. He saw himself interviewed on CNN, on Fox, the Today show. Every cable network in the country would want to talk to him. And Katie – he saw the look of admiration and wonder in her eyes, "Gosh Isaac, I've underestimated you. How could I have been so blind – you're all I've ever wanted."

He struggled to focus, looking from the major to Carl and back, then said, "There's a televised mega-event planned for the middle of July. It's an interfaith service."

Chapter 18, Renaissance Institute
Saturday, 4th Week of June

DANNY

According to the Renaissance Institute's website and glossy brochures, the labs were "a cornerstone for preparing our students for 21st-century jobs". There were pictures of boys in white coats doing experiments, using spectrometers, designing circuit boards, building a solar-powered buggy, and dissecting everything from a frog to a wind turbine.

Danny, Timothy, and Gerald were the only boys who had decided to spend their Saturday "passion time" in the labs. Danny would never admit this to anyone but, if all the fences at the institute were removed, he'd probably stay anyway – because of the labs. They far exceeded anything he had seen in the many expensive schools he'd attended.

Like a master chef, he'd set out all the ingredients he needed on one of the benches: a microscope with a digital camera, fingerprinting powder with a brush, latex gloves, strips of gelatin, a hot water bath, and more. He put on the gloves and inspected the glass container that had Carlos' fingerprints on it.

Gerald watched and said, "So, you're telling me that you are going to lift Carlos' fingerprints off that container and somehow make a replica fingerprint that will be good enough to fool the fingerprint readers at the main gates?"

"That's right," Danny said as he started to apply fingerprinting dust with a feather-light touch. "The security systems here are pretty basic – this is five-year-old technology. So I just need to get a half-ways decent print, put it under the microscope, take a digital picture, enhance that picture to fill in any missing lines, imprint it on the gel substrate, and then fix it to the latex gloves I borrowed from the clinic."

He continued, "Just as well they don't have iris scanners; I would've had to rip out Carlos' eyeball."

Gerald shuddered and pulled a face, "Gross! Don't say things like that." He reached for a shoebox that Danny had placed at the end of the bench and peered inside at what looked like latex gloves in labeled zip lock bags. "What are all these?"

"Be careful," Danny said. "That's my collection of keys – that is, my collection of fingerprints."

Gerald read the labels, "Coach Jamey; Principal; Matron Holly…" He looked up, "You lifted the matron's fingerprints? What on earth for?"

"Access to the pantry," Danny chuckled, "sometimes a guy feels like a midnight snack."

Gerald picked up the next bag and read, "Dr. Roberts." He gaped, "Seriously, you've even got your therapist's fingerprint?"

Danny used scotch tape to lift a print off the glass and placed it under the microscope.

"He keeps bragging to me about how he can open and start his Tesla with the touch of a finger." Danny looked up and grinned, "Now that I have Carlos' fingerprint to open the main gate, maybe one of these days I can take that Tesla for a spin. D'you want to come? Where would you like to go?"

Gerald shook his head, "Where did you learn all this stuff?"

"I've wanted to be a detective since I was six. I've watched every episode of CSI ever made, and I started to play around in labs from a young age." He peered into the microscope and adjusted the tape. "It's amazing how much fun you can have in a lab if you do a little research on the internet." He looked up at Gerald and said, "Didn't you ever blow anything up in the lab?"

"No," Gerald said with indignation in his voice, "I wasn't very good at science and tried to spend as little time in the labs as possible."

Danny turned his attention back to the microscope. "What a beauty, this will work." After a pause, he asked, "Do you know what my nickname was in Middle School?"

Timothy, who sat bent over a circuit board and soldering iron at a neighboring bench, piped up, "They called you *double-M-seven*."

"Thanks for stealing my punch line," Danny muttered as he positioned the microscope's camera and started to snap images of the enlarged fingerprint.

Gerald looked from one to the other and said, "Am I to figure this out by myself, or is someone going to tell me? I assume the name is a play on Agent 007, but why the double-M?"

Danny said, "The double-M stands for Mayhem Machine; I can't even remember how many things I 'accidentally' blew up, both inside the lab and out. For 4th of July one year, I scored a hat trick – one of the rockets I made smashed the neighbors' picture window; the second landed smack-bang in a 4th of July party and caused utter pandemonium. The third got tangled in a Eucalyptus tree and started a fire for which the fire brigade had to come out."

Timothy interrupted, "I have just had a message from Mykyta. He confirms that the only way to get access to your mysterious computer center is to do a physical implant."

Danny and Gerald walked over to where Timothy was busy connecting the circuit board to the innards of a disassembled cell phone.

"A what?" Gerald asked.

Timothy had the tone of a lecturer forced to teach a group of rather dim freshmen. He said, "Danny asked me to enlist my friend Mykyta's help to find out what is in that data center. Mykyta has figured out that the data center belongs to a company called BDA – Big Data Analytica. Mykyta is highly impressed with their level of security – he has tried every known vulnerability and says their perimeter defenses are hardened to the highest standard."

Danny asked, "Okay, but there has to be a way – there always is, no?"

Timothy ignored him and continued, "It is like a castle with a moat. If you can sneak in through some back gate, you can roam around the castle wherever you want. All we have to do is implant this circuit board with the cellphone transmitter in one of the network servers, and Mykyta thinks we'll be able to gain access to most of the systems."

Danny was about to slap Timothy on the shoulder but remembered his aversion to physical contact. He said, "Good job! We'll go up there tomorrow afternoon. We know that they're so cocksure of all their digital security that it'll be a piece of cake to get in via our backdoor tunnel."

Gerald looked from one to the other, "Aren't I glad that you two spymasters are my friends and not my enemies. If my mother knew that I was hanging out with…"

Danny raised an eyebrow, "*Investigating* is an essential and noble profession – it keeps people honest. It's one of the oldest professions…"

Gerald cut in with a laugh, "You're not going to persuade me. I think it has rather a lot in common with that other oldest profession." He did a double take and pointed at the cell phone, "Where did you get that? I thought they were banned?"

Timothy shrugged and pointed at Danny.

"Ask no questions, hear no lies," Danny said. "Actually, it was easy. You know Juanito, the fat Latino who thinks he's Al Capone? I just picked the lock on his closet. It's full of stuff."

Gerald rolled his eyes, "I'm going to leave before you two incriminate me any further."

Timothy said, "I have done nothing wrong. Tell him, Danny. You said everything I'm doing is a legitimate defense against very bad people." His voice rose, "I would never do anything wrong. Tell him, Danny!" Timothy's hands started to shake, and behind his back, Danny was playing out an urgent pantomime pleading with Gerald to retract the insinuation of wrongdoing.

Gerald said, "You're absolutely right, Timothy. I admire what the two of you are doing; I just don't have the experience to understand it all." He let Danny see the crossed fingers behind his back and said, "I'm one hundred percent with you."

This seemed to appease Timothy, who bent down to continue soldering.

Gerald changed the subject, "Are you guys coming to the church service tomorrow? The reverend Isaac O'Neill is coming up from Tracy – he's going to show a video from his recent trip to Africa. And," he paused, "I've been asked to sing a solo."

Timothy showed no sign of having heard the request. Danny squirmed, "You know I don't do church – and I'd like to go for a run before it gets hot."

Gerald smiled, "No worries, just thought I'd mention it."

***

On Sunday, Danny went for his run. All the way up the mountain, he was plagued by a bad conscience. Gerald had never asked him for anything, and although the older boy had shrugged it off, Danny had seen the look of disappointment in his eyes when Danny had refused his invitation.

He checked up on his plants and contemplated a cooling dip in the pond. But then he looked at his watch and calculated that he could make it back down the hill for the latter half of the 9 a.m. service. His feet seemed to develop a mind of their own. He could hear the bells tolling when he was a mile away and, by the time he reached the church, sweaty and panting, it was 9:15.

He'd never been inside the squat structure and felt embarrassed to barge in late in his running shorts and vest, so he walked around the building, thinking he might peer through a window. Instead, Danny found the outside door of the sacristy unlocked. He slipped into the cool, dimly-lit room and crept along the wall towards the sanctuary door. He jumped when something brushed against his shoulder. It turned out to be a jacket – probably the reverend's – hanging on a hook.

The door to the sanctuary was open a crack, and Danny pushed it open another half-inch to give himself a good view of the altar area where the reverend Isaac stood, hands outstretched in prayer. Danny thought the man's long, silky gown, with a richly embroidered golden stole, looked ridiculous in the simple whitewashed church with its rustic granite altar. The reverend was praying "for all the animals of the wild that are such an important part of the Lord's creation" and "for all the poor people in Africa that they might turn to God's ways and share in his bounty."

Danny had to suppress a gag reflex when he noticed the heavy golden wristwatch on the reverend's arm. He was instantly reminded of why he disliked institutionalized religion and wondered how much of this he could stomach. To his relief, Isaac announced, "And now, I call on Gerald Myers, who will share a special gift with us; the gift of his voice."

Gerald stepped up with his guitar and sat on a high stool in front of the altar. He adjusted the microphone and announced in his Texan drawl, "This one's for a special friend." He started to strum the guitar and began to sing. Danny immediately recognized the Lady Gaga/Bradley Cooper song.

> *"Tell me somethin', girl*
> *Are you happy in this modern world?*
> *Or do you need more?*
> *Is there somethin' else you're searchin' for?*
>
> *I'm falling*
> *In all the good times I find myself*
> *Longin' for change*
> *And in the bad times I fear myself."*

The light from a stained glass window cast a glow around Gerald, and there wasn't a rustle or movement among the boys that formed the congregation. They were as mesmerized as Danny by the power of Gerald's voice. He seemed transformed, oblivious to anything but pouring his soul into the music. Gerald rotated on the stool to avoid the glare of the light. When he opened his eyes, he looked directly at Danny, and a smile of recognition lit his face. He continued,

> *"Tell me something, boy*
> *Aren't you tired tryin' to fill that void?*
> *Or do you need more?*
> *Ain't it hard keeping it so hardcore?*
>
> *I'm falling..."*

Danny swallowed hard as the music swirled around him

"...We're far from the shallow now

In the shallow, shallow
In the shallow, shallow
In the shallow, shallow
We're far..."

Danny pulled the door shut as the last notes faded away and the boys erupted into applause. His eyes were moist, and he felt a lump in his throat as the refrain kept echoing in his mind, *we're far from the shallow now.* Not I, *we*! He felt a swelling in his chest. It was such a strange sensation to feel that someone was in his corner; he was not alone.

A buzzing sound startled him, and it took a few seconds to figure out that it came from the jacket that had given him a fright as he'd entered the sacristy. The annoying sound continued as he patted down the coat until he retrieved an iPhone from an inner pocket. Danny looked at the screen and nearly dropped the phone as he read the caller ID: *Carl Gunderson.*

He raced for the outer door and punched the phone's green button, "Dad," he whispered into the phone. "Dad, is that you? It's me, Danny…how?" He looked at the phone and shook it. The screen read, "missed WhatsApp call." Danny cursed and frantically tried to punch buttons, but the phone's keypad was locked. The call had eluded him like a shooting star in the night sky.

"Fuck, fuck, fuuuuuuck!" Danny beat a fist against the whitewashed wall. He contemplated his next step. Should he wait for the reverend and ask him? He thought of the outstretched arm with the gold watch and the sanctimonious prayer – his deep-seated distrust of the church kicked in and he decided on a different course of action. He sprinted to his room, where Timothy sat in his pajamas, working at his laptop.

Danny didn't waste time with explanations, "Timothy, get dressed and meet me in the lab."

Timothy looked at him, "Where is my bagel and banana? I am hungry, and you are late. Where is …"

Danny cut him off, "Timothy, please. Just this once, please, please just do as I ask. I'll explain when you get to the lab. And bring your laptop."

Danny assembled the fingerprint-copying equipment in record time. He cursed himself for having punched wildly at the phone; *Dear God, let there be a usable index fingerprint; come on, God, you owe me one. Jeez, to have a call from my father so close, so close.*

Timothy appeared and grumbled, "What's the emergency?"

"I need to get into this phone, and I need to do it fast – it'll be missed very soon, so I want to download whatever's on it. Can you do that?"

Timothy scratched his head and mumbled, "I've read about it; it should be straightforward if you can unlock it."

"That's what I'm doing now. You start getting your computer ready."

Timothy sat down and started to work. After a few minutes, he looked up and asked, "Danny, are we still catching bad guys? You know you told me I must not do anything illegal. I don't want to go to one of those prisons."

Danny looked at him and wrestled with his conscience. Could he truthfully say the reverend was a bad guy? He might be a sanctimonious twat, but Danny doubted that he was up to anything *bad*. And his father? Did he want Timothy to think that his father was a bad guy?

He breathed deeply and said, "In this case, I honestly don't know. Remember how I've been trying to find my father? The strangest thing happened; I think he might be trying to find me. There was a missed call from him on this phone – I want to, I *need* to, phone him back."

Timothy nodded once and said, "I understand."

It took Danny only a record eight minutes to add the reverend Isaac O'Neill's fingerprint to his collection and to unlock the phone. He was desperate to make the call, but he handed the phone to Timothy to download its content. Danny paced the room, trying to think of what he would say to his father. *Four years, four fucking long years, and you never called me once. Four birthdays, four Christmases, court appearances, hospital stays – and nothing, nothing ever, from you. Why?*

He breathed deeply and thought, no, don't put him on the defensive, be cool. *Hey Dad, what a surprise; great to hear your voice. What are you up to?* He rolled his eyes; *I'm cool, great school out in California, still as passionate as ever about CSI. They have the most fantastic lab here.* This was going to be harder than he had thought. *Mom's great; can't say I'm wild about her new man, but whatever. She's happy. What about you? Any love interest in your life?*

Timothy said, "Okay, I have most of it. We can go through it later and if you can find another spare iPhone, I can upload whatever you want accessible."

"Thanks a ton," Danny said, "And I'm sorry about your breakfast. If you go by the kitchen, I'm sure matron Holly would give you…"

Timothy picked up his laptop and said, "I will be fine. Are we still going to that cave this afternoon?"

Danny nodded and waited until the lab door had closed behind Timothy.

He slipped on the glove with Reverend Isaac's fingerprint, picked up the phone and gently touched the reader. His heart thumped violently until…the screen unlocked. "Yes!" With trembling fingers, he navigated to recent WhatsApp calls, pressed the video call button, and waited. For an agonizing while there was nothing. He was about to try again when he heard a sound like gears clicking into place when a lock is picked, then a ringtone – one, two, three, four, five… "Hallo, Isaac? Is that you?"

"No, Dad, it is me… Danny." His father's face appeared on the screen. Danny did a double-take. The man was unmistakably his father, but he looked different. Danny blurted, "What's with the long hair and glasses?" He gave a nervous laugh. "Looks kind of cool."

His father's eyes were wide with surprise, and Danny thought he saw a hint of pleasure before his father's expression turned into a frown – a very familiar expression, "Daniel? What the heck…? Where…? How did you get hold of this phone?"

"I think it belongs to the reverend Isaac O'Neill. He left it lying around, and I saw a call from you. Naturally…"

"He left it lying around? The man is an imbecile." The icy disapproval in his father's voice brought back a flood of memories. That tone was mainly reserved for Terry. No wonder Terry stopped visiting, Danny thought as he started to come down from the adrenalin high he'd felt since first hearing the buzz of the phone.

"Now, Daniel, listen to me," his father said, "and don't roll your eyes, I can see you. You *must* return this phone immediately, and Isaac must never ever find out that you borrowed it – never. It's imperative. Do you hear me?"

Danny sat in silence. Did his father think he was still thirteen? The man had no idea of the things Danny had done. Seriously, how much shit could there be from "accidentally" picking up a phone and making a few calls?

His father must have sensed his reluctance because his tone changed and he said, "Danny, I don't have a right to ask you to do anything – I know that. I also know that I owe you a lot of explanation; but this is simply not the time for it. *Please*," there seemed to be genuine concern in his voice, "please believe me when I say that you *must* return that phone. It could land you in horrible trouble."

"With the church, with the institute?" Danny asked, unable to hide his skepticism. "I don't give a crap about them."

Danny could see the strain on his father's face as he fought for self-control. Carl said, "There's a hell of a lot more than meets the eye with this church. Seriously, the less you know, the better."

Danny thought for a moment. "My inclination is to just keep the phone; I can use it." Before his father could interject, he continued, "But I will return it, as you have asked, on one condition. You said you owe me some explanations – I want those explanations. If you promise to contact me for a proper conversation, I'll return the phone."

Danny saw the relief on his father's face, and it made him wonder what the hell his father, Isaac and the

Church of Holy Redemption were involved in that could be so important and so dangerous.

Carl said, "I promise; I swear, I'll contact you." He looked directly at his son and added, "I've put you through a lot, Daniel; I'm truly sorry for that." Then the call was disconnected.

When Danny got back to the church, the last of the congregation were leaving. He rushed down the aisle towards the altar, where three boys were tidying away sound equipment. There was no sign of Reverend Isaac O'Neill. Gerald was packing his guitar into its case and beamed when he saw Danny. He gave Danny a fist bump and said, "Thanks for coming."

"You were awesome!" Danny looked around and whispered, "Where's the reverend?"

Gerald pointed towards the sacristy, "Getting changed, I presume."

"Can you somehow distract him? I need to get in there for a minute."

"What?"

"Pleaaaase." Danny begged, "I'll explain later. I saw something in there earlier."

Gerald sighed, "Okay, grab those two music stands – they need to be taken to the sacristy. Go!"

Danny had barely grabbed the music stands when Gerald uttered a howl of pain and collapsed onto the front pew, clutching his ankle. The three boys in the altar space stared at him, and the door to the sacristy swung open.

Reverend Isaac looked alarmed, "What's the matter, Gerald? What happened?"

Gerald moaned, "My ankle; I twisted it coming down that step – so stupid of me."

As everyone crowded around Gerald, Danny ducked into the sacristy and slipped the phone into the jacket pocket. Then he went to join the others, and Gerald made a show of being sheepish, tested his weight on the ankle, and said he would be able to hobble over to the kitchen and get some ice. Danny offered to go with him.

Reverend Isaac turned to Danny and said, "Where did you come from? I didn't see you in church." He looked Danny up and down, no doubt taking in the running gear. When his eyes came to rest on Danny's face, Danny had the feeling of a scanner ingesting data and feeding it into a facial recognition system – looking for a match. A frown appeared on the reverend's face, and Danny felt a prickling of sweat between his shoulder blades. He thought back to the image of his father, with his long hair, blue eyes and aging surfer looks. It suddenly struck him that the family resemblance had become very strong over the last three years.

The reverend asked, "What's your name?"

Danny produced his most disarming smile and extended his hand, "Daniel Reynolds. Pleased to meet you, reverend; Gerald has told me a lot about you. He is a great admirer of what you and the church are doing." Gerald didn't miss a beat and chipped in, "Sorry Danny, I'll have to do a rain check on the run we were going to do. But do you mind giving me a hand across to matron? I'd like to get some ice on this ankle before it swells up."

Danny could feel the reverend's eyes burning on his back as he made his way up the aisle, with Gerald leaning heavily on his shoulder and limping in a remarkably convincing manner.

Once outside, they picked up the pace but continued the charade in case someone was watching.

Danny chuckled and said, "You're not only a great singer, you're also a good actor."

"I swear, Danny *Reynolds*," Gerald put so much sarcastic emphasis on the surname that Danny winced, "you're turning me into a liar and cheat."

"You worry too much," Danny said, "worst that can happen is that your soul gets downgraded from first class to business on its way up to heaven."

"Don't mock. Seriously, what was all that about?"

"I'll explain it this afternoon." He gave Gerald's shoulder a squeeze and added, "For what it's worth, thank you. You're a great friend, and I think you're still in the running for sainthood."

Gerald sighed in exasperation but couldn't suppress a smile. They parted at the entrance to the kitchen.

***

The three friends set off shortly after lunch. They had bummed muffins and apples from matron Holly, mainly to underpin the story that they were off for a hike and a picnic. She had beamed when she saw that Timothy was going with them, and insisted on adding chocolate chip cookies to Danny's backpack. Meanwhile, Gerald's pack contained flashlights and rope, as well as Timothy's laptop, the carefully packaged circuit board, and an extra iPhone, which Danny had liberated from Juanito's stash.

Along the way, Danny told his friends about the conversation with his father and, despite some wild and imaginative speculations, they could not come up with any plausible theory as to what could possibly link the reverend O'Neill, the Church of Holy Redemption, and Carl Gunderson. Danny suspected that, given his father's history, it was some get-rich-quick scheme involving the church's money. Was the reverend diverting funds for Carl to "invest" somewhere? And how had they even met? Gerald supplemented this information with the fact that the reverend had just returned from a safari to Namibia –

wherever that might be. Danny fervently hoped that they might find some answers in the computer center, *if* the plan to implant a snooping device succeeded.

Danny made sure to distract Timothy with questions about cybersecurity as they quickly ushered him past the marijuana patch. He didn't want to burden Timothy with more legally "gray space" activities. To Gerald and Danny's surprise, Timothy had no problem climbing the rockface. When they reached the crevice that hid the entrance to the tunnel, Timothy was flushed with a sense of achievement and his friends' praise. He even allowed them to fist bump him.

The tunnel was more of a challenge. When they reached the section where they had to crawl through a two-foot gap under a flat rock, Timothy refused point-blank. "Come on, Tim," Danny coaxed, "you've done awesome so far. It's perfectly okay." He crawled back and forth through the gap twice, trying to make it look easy. But it was no use; Timothy dug in like a dog at the vet's door. His jaw clenched, and his breathing became more rapid. The more Danny coaxed, the more panicked he became, constantly looking back at the path they had come, ready to bolt. Finally, he said, "That rock above the gap doesn't look stable – I'm not going underneath it."

Danny decided to change tack, "Okay then, let's think of a different solution. Can you explain to me exactly where the computer board has to go?"

Timothy shook his head.

"Why not?"

Through clenched teeth, Timothy said, "Because I do not know. Mykyta showed me pictures of what to look for, but I will only know the right server and the right slot when I see it." He added miserably, "If I see it."

Danny fought his exasperation. As he was about to open his mouth again, Gerald placed a hand on his arm, shook his head, and said, "We're all just going to sit here and relax a while. We're not in any hurry. And you know what? I'm going to turn off the flashlight to conserve the batteries. Is that okay with you, Timmy?"

Timothy's eyes grew wide, but he nodded. "It makes sense to save the batteries. But don't leave me!"

Gerald smiled, "We'd never leave you, and to stay connected, we're each going to hold onto this rope." He placed the rope in Timothy's hands, careful not to touch him, and gave a tug to which Timothy responded. Danny took hold of the other end of the rope. Then Gerald turned off the flashlight, and darkness enveloped them. Danny could feel the trembling of Timothy's hands transmitted through the rope. Every few seconds, there was a tug as the boys reassured one another that they were there and connected.

Gerald began to hum a tune and started to sing something that Danny had never heard before. It sounded like country and western, not a genre that Danny was familiar with. But in this weird womb, isolated from the world, Gerald's song enveloped them like a mother soothing her unborn child.

> *"I met God's will on a Halloween night*
> *He was dressed as a bag of leaves*
> *It hid the braces on his legs at first..."*

Gerald hummed a few bars, and Danny asked, "Whose song is this? "

"Martina McBride. I grew up on her songs." He tugged the rope and said, "Timothy, now if I keep singing and we both hold on very tight to the rope, do you think you can follow my voice?"

There was a long silence before Timothy croaked, "I will try."

"Okay then, get down onto your stomach and just follow my voice and the rope. Danny will be right behind you." He started singing again, and Danny had no idea how Gerald was accomplishing the feat of crawling through the gap and singing in that sweet, haunting voice, making it sound effortless.

> *"Will don't walk too good*
> *Will don't talk too good*
> *He won't do the things that the other kids do*
> *In our neighborhood...*
>
> *"He was a boy without a father*
> *And his mother's miracle..."*

Danny kept listening, and only when he felt a strong tug, and saw the glimmer of Gerald's flashlight, did he shimmy through the gap where the other two were dusting off their clothes.

They made it all the way to the cavern without incident and were relieved to find that the security arrangements had not progressed since their previous visit. The cameras were still in their boxes.

Gerald and Timothy scrambled down to the cave floor and disappeared among the rows of servers, while Danny worked his way up along an elevated ledge to a lookout point above the control center from which he had a commanding view of the entire cave, as though he were looking down onto a gloomy, dimly-lit maze. He found a rock behind which he could shelter and peek out from time to time. There was music and indistinct conversation between the two controllers. One had his feet on the console and was eating popcorn; the other sat hunched over a laptop at a bistro table. *Probably playing Words with Friends or watching sports*, Danny thought. His assumption was confirmed when he heard the man say, "Come on, Giants! I'm sick of supporting a bunch of losers."

Time passed at a crawl in the gloomy cavern. There was no sound other than the eerie thrum of cooling fans. Then, suddenly, a clanging noise echoed through the darkness. The first controller whipped his feet off the console while the other spun around from his computer and asked, "What was that?"

Oh no! Shoot, crap, bugger, Danny thought as the first controller punched a few buttons, and the cavern was flooded in light. Danny's birds-eye view allowed him to see everyone below, even though they could not see each other. Gerald and Timothy were frozen statues, looking in horror at a metal panel that had dropped onto the floor. They were three rows to the right of the data center controllers, who were looking at each other.

"I'll go have a look," one of them said and grabbed a taser from a hook. He headed up the path towards the main aisle that ran like a highway through the middle of the cavern. *Turn left, turn left,* Danny prayed as the man hesitated. But the man turned right. Gerald and Timothy spotted Danny and looked at him wide-eyed, silently pleading for help and direction. There was no time to think. Danny picked up a pebble and hurled it as far as he could to his left. It hit with a loud clang, and while the sound was still reverberating through the cavern, Danny let loose with a loud "meow", hoping it would sound like an injured wild cat.

The man at the junction hesitated and cocked his ear. Danny followed up with another pebble in the same direction, and the man headed to where the stones had landed. The other man followed. Danny gestured in a wild pantomime for Gerald and Timothy to put back the metal plate and get out. Then, as he started his own retreat, he heard one of the controllers say, "Bloody wild cats, what next? What a dumb idea to stick a data center out here."

The other said, "At least the cat will keep rodents at bay. The last thing we need out here is rats chewing through the cables. Maybe we should put out some food for the cat."

His colleague scoffed, "Maybe I should bring my son's BB gun and put some lead in its ass."

The boys regrouped, and Timothy had no hesitation scooting through the gap. When they emerged at the end of the tunnel, and could look down on the hidden valley, they stopped, panting.

"Did you find it? Did you find the right spot?" Danny asked.

"I think so," Timothy answered. He made himself comfortable on a rock with his laptop and cellphone. The signal was weak, but he managed to create a hotspot and started furiously punching away at his computer. Danny and Gerald desperately tried to contain their impatience and give Timothy space.

It took five tense minutes, and then a stream of letters and symbols appeared on the screen. Timothy smiled. "We have first contact."

Danny whooped and pumped his fist into the air, "We did it!" He gave Gerald a bear hug and Timothy another fist bump – two in one day. Timothy was becoming positively cuddly.

Chapter 19, San Francisco
Wednesday, 1st Week of July

TERRY

Terry clutched an envelope with the research and analysis for Chloe's political campaign. Rajiv had been abundantly clear in his directive: Terry was to bring him, *and no one else*, a printed copy. If this blew up, Terry knew he would be the one hung out to dry like apricots in Turkey.

Despite misgivings, he'd warmed to the subject and was fascinated to see the myriad of opportunities for defining positions on issues from crime to public transport, health care and immigration. He had even added suggestions for crafting messages to appeal to target groups. He sighed, *Man, Chloe, I could have really helped you with your campaign.* Maybe in a different life.

He went up the stairs and was just in time to see Rajiv entering the elevator at the far end of the corridor. Rajiv was probably on his way to a lunch meeting. After a moment of indecision, Terry walked to Rajiv's office and found it unlocked. He decided to leave the sealed package, with a note, on Rajiv's desk. The only snag: the desk was as pristine as a frozen lake. Terry opened the top drawer to look for a post-it pad and pen. The drawer contained an engraved Mont Blanc fountain pen that looked like it had never been used, a square tin filled with small change, and a pile of ticket stubs – all for Warriors games. Terry blew out a breath; *it must be nice to drop two thousand dollars on a ticket.*

He sat at Rajiv's desk and looked around. It was clear that Rajiv had digitized his life, because there wasn't a single photograph, picture, artwork or personal item in the office. The sterility reminded him of the many cubicles he had worked in as a contractor. The second drawer was locked, and the bottom drawer appeared empty. Terry was about to close it when he noticed what looked like a hand-written card. It turned out to be the back of a photo frame, with an inscription, "We dare not forget. Remember your promise." The message was signed by Katie Blanchard.

Terry turned the frame over – a picture of Golden Gate Bridge. He inhaled sharply. *What the...?* The photographer had captured one of those days where the bridge was shrouded in fog; the tops of the towers reached up into brilliant sunshine while the lower half sank away into a gloomy cloud. He placed the photograph on the desk and stared at it. The picture made him think of Lily.

What does this mean?

He shrugged. Maybe Rajiv and Katie had had a romantic date that involved the Golden Gate Bridge. He forced the picture from his mind and shifted his gaze to Rajiv's screen saver. It showed Rajiv posing in front of the Taj Mahal. Terry let his fingers glide over the keyboard. If only he could get into this machine somehow; Sandy and Clyde were convinced that Rajiv had answers to so many questions. There was bound to be proof of the extortion scheme run by the Church of Holy Redemption through *The Settlement Bureau.* Why had they targeted Terry? What algorithms decided who was to be squeezed and who went scot-free? Someone was playing God, and Terry was determined to find out who it was.

He placed the cursor over the password prompt and typed *Rajiv123*. Yeah, right, a top computer expert would have such a lame password. *RajivPatel@BDA*. Nothing. Rajiv didn't look like the type to own a dog. Did he have a girlfriend, siblings? When was he born? Mother's maiden name? Terry knew it was hopeless. He picked up the photo frame and stared at it, mesmerized, as the pain and loss of Lily's suicide washed over him.

He was ripped out of his reverie by the sound of voices outside; one of them was Rajiv's. Shit! Terry leaped up as though the seat had burst into flames, dropped the photo frame in its drawer, and dashed into the anteroom. He cursed himself for being irrational. He could have just told Rajiv he'd stepped into the office to drop off the envelope. But then, Rajiv would wonder why he had lingered there the whole time it took for Rajiv to walk from the elevators to the office.

It was too late now. Terry closed the door behind him just as Rajiv and a group of visitors entered the office. From his previous visit, when Rajiv had let him shave in the bathroom, Terry knew there was no backdoor. He was trapped, so he looked around for a place to hide. The dressing room was just a wide passage where one wall was an open closet with everything from sports gear to dinner jackets arranged as neatly as the cans in Terry's kitchen. A couch faced the closet.

He placed his ear against the door and, for a moment, worried that the wooden door would amplify the pounding beat of his heart. But, once he got his breathing under control, he could discern the voices of a man and a woman, as well as Rajiv's. The woman said, "I'm so sorry that I didn't have time for a proper tour, but from what I saw, it seems like you have a strikingly... *vibrant* setup here. So many young people; it makes me feel my age." She gave a dry laugh.

The man's voice said, "Not a person in that room that can hold a candle to you, Antoinette."

Rajiv spoke, "I have to say, this is all rather unexpected, Miss Bussey…"

"Oh, do call me Antoinette," the woman interrupted. "Since you, me and Robbie here are going to be working closely together, we might as well drop the formalities."

"Thank you…Antoinette," Rajiv said, and it sounded as though he was tasting something unfamiliar and unpleasant. "You say the deal was signed between CAFCA and Pastor Jeremiah last week in Namibia? I know that Pastor Jeremiah was looking for a cash injection to progress development of the God's Eye technology, but there had never been any mention of selling shares in any of the church's ventures."

"It's all there in the papers," the woman said. "And, from what I'm told, you're someone who is familiar with a fast-paced world." There was a pause, and her voice was silky when she continued, "I certainly hope so, Rajiv. CAFCA views this as a strategic investment, and we intend to be very hands-on. We'll be assessing the performance of key staff and, where necessary, will make recommendations for change."

Terry wished he could see the expressions of the three. The woman's voice conjured up an image of Cruella De Ville.

The pregnant silence in the room was broken by the man called Robbie, "Well, I don't think *you* have anything to worry about." He gave a nervous laugh. "I'm dying to just learn and understand what you're doing here. I checked out some of your patents; it's groundbreaking stuff, and there's so much value in the way you manipulate data. Maybe you can give me a run-down of the data acquisition and scrubbing model? Data quality is something I've always..."

The woman broke in, "You two can geek out later. Robbie, please be a darling and call the driver to take me to the airport. Better get moving; I do so hate the San Francisco traffic." She paused, then said, "Rajiv, I don't know why you put this facility here among the homeless and drug addicts. Why not out in Tracy, where the church is? It's so much more convenient – and cheaper."

Terry heard a sharp intake of breath. The woman continued, "Why don't you send me a copy of the lease agreement for this place? I'm sure I can find a way to nullify it."

Rajiv said, "We specifically chose this location to attract the right kind of talent, and..."

Robbie interrupted, "Your driver is waiting downstairs."

Antoinette said, "Rajiv, please find an office for Robbie. I want him to move in here as soon as possible. We'll set up a weekly call to improve coordination between BDA, *The Settlement Bureau*, and God's Eye. We have to find a different name for that project."

Her voice faded as she moved to the door. "I'll see myself out. Robbie, please give Rajiv the starter list of the ten congressmen that we need to be investigated."

Rajiv's voice, "What? We work with anonymized data. We don't just do random investigations..."

Antionette cut him off, "You do now. I expect a dossier on each congressman by Monday."

There was a pause and the clacking of heels down the corridor. Then Robbie said, "Antoinette can come across a little strong at times, but you get used to her."

"Get used to her?" Terry had only known Rajiv for a few weeks, but it was clear that the man was on the verge of losing his cool. "I have no intention of getting used to her. There's been some mistake. I cannot, for one minute, believe that Katie would have been part of an agreement that gives CAFCA these rights. It runs counter to everything she stands for."

Robbie's voice was placating, "She wasn't part of the discussions. She'd been involved in a hit and run accident."

"What? Where? Out in Africa? Is she okay?"

Robbie said, "She's fine. I only met her over dinner one evening. I believe she'd suffered a concussion, and the doctors had recommended she take it easy. So she played tourist while the pastor and Isaac handled the negotiations."

Rajiv groaned audibly, and Robbie continued, "Look, I know you've been caught unawares, but I think we can make this work. I very much admire what you do here, and I can help you deal with Antoinette. You just have to give her what she wants, and she'll leave you alone."

Rajiv's voice rose two notches. "Give her what she wants? And what exactly is that? Dirt on congressmen and others so she can pressurize them to support the gun lobby? That's not what I do."

"Come on, Rajiv. You can't be so naïve." There was a hard edge in Robbie's voice. "Don't tell me you don't know how Isaac and *The Settlement Bureau* are using the data in these systems? Do you really think people are making generous donations to the church just because they're being asked nicely?"

There was a pause, then Robbie continued in a placating voice, "This isn't anything new. All Antoinette wants to do is expand the scope of the operation. And I can tell you, she's orgasmic at the thought of all this power. Power is the only thing she gets off on. So don't even think of getting in her way."

Rajiv said in a monotone, "I would appreciate it if you left now."

"Here's the list," Robbie said. "I'll see you tomorrow."

225

***

There was a long silence, punctuated only by a sigh from Rajiv. Then Terry heard him dial a number and, from his tone, it sounded like he was speaking to an answering machine. "Isaac, I just had a visit from a group of people who claim to be our new business partners. What the fuck have you and the old man negotiated with them? They carry on like they own the place. Call me the minute you get this. I'm going to be at the gym for the next hour, but I'll have my cell with me."

The gym! He's got to come in here and change. Terry broke out in a cold sweat. In an act of desperation, he dove behind the couch, squeezing into the narrow gap between the leather back and the wall. The door opened, and Terry tried to calm his breathing. Rajiv was close enough for Terry to smell his cologne, and his nostrils were further assailed by the dust emanating from the carpet. He felt a sneeze well up inside him. *No, no, no! Not now. Keep it together, Terry.*

To his intense relief, Rajiv merely picked up a gym bag and left. Terry waited until he heard the outer door shut before sneezing into his elbow. Then he waited another two minutes just to be sure. Finally, he scrambled up from behind the couch. As he passed Rajiv's desk, his eyes landed on a folder with a distinctive logo that he'd seen in some of his research. It was the CAFCA logo: two black, crossed rifles against a red background. From a distance, it could be mistaken for a Swastika.

Terry grabbed the folder, amazed that Rajiv would leave something like this lying on the desk. He looked inside – empty. Then Terry yanked open the drawers –

nothing. He tugged at the locked drawer and cursed; clearly, Rajiv was more careful than Terry had given him credit for.

He put the folder back where he had found it, hurried down the stairs, and texted Sandy to meet him on the roof.

***

It was past 9:00 p.m. when Sandy, Terry, and Professor Clyde Curry met at EBU in Oakland. Clyde picked through the remnants of Chinese take-outs and listened as Terry recounted all he had heard. Sandy chimed in, "Remember what I told you about how they coerce not only their members but just about anybody? Can you imagine that kind of power in the hands of CAFCA?" She barely paused for breath, "What are we going to do? Should we go to the Washington Post? Is there an authority we can go to? Maybe the FTC?"

Clyde dropped the last food container in a waste bin, folded his hands behind his head and rocked back in his chair, "We only have hearsay and conjecture, not a shred of evidence…"

Terry said, "What about the attempt to blackmail me? There must be lots of others."

Sandy offered, "We could start an online support group. #victimsofsettlementbureau."

Clyde tipped his seat forward and splayed his hands on the desk, "It is an angle." He stroked his goatee, "But how do we do that without showing our hand and having *The Settlement Bureau* quickly change tack and cover their tracks?" He looked from one to the other, "I'm convinced the evidence we need is at BDA. Look what all Terry has uncovered in a week. We just need to persevere – if we can find some incriminating emails, documents, code, then we can go to the media."

227

Sandy picked up a piece of paper and fanned herself, "Is the air-con on the blink again? Man, it's hot."

Clyde ignored her comment and said, "There's someone I want you to meet." He looked at his watch and frowned, "It's six o'clock in Namibia; this should be a good time to catch him." He placed a call via his computer and swung the monitor so the others could see. The face of an African man with a broad smile appeared. He said, "Howzit Clyde, what's up?"

"Hey, Petrus, sorry to catch you so early – what's the time over there?"

"It's okay," Petrus said, "six o'clock; I've already had breakfast, but I can't talk long. I have a group chomping at the bit to go and find lions." He laughed, "There are one or two that I'd like to leave out there as bait."

Clyde introduced everybody and explained Petrus' involvement with data gathering on the migration and habits of endangered species. Then he said, "Petrus, last week you shared with me observations of a different kind; that is your impressions of the CAFCA leadership. Can you give Sandy and Terry a run down?"

Petrus looked uncomfortable, and Clyde had to assure him that this was in the strictest confidence. First, the game ranger gave them a brief overview of Katie Blanchard's accident, the CAFCA retreat, and the meetings with Pastor Jeremiah and Isaac O'Neill. Then, at Clyde's prompting, he gave his impressions of the CAFCA members, and Terry had to smile when he described Antoinette Bussey, "That one – I'd be scared to give her a blunt kitchen knife!" Terry hadn't seen her, but Petrus' description of Antoinette complemented the impression he'd formed from listening to her voice.

Petrus went on to describe the colonel, "Tight ass, who thinks he's playing a movie part in his starched uniform and cropped hair," and the major, "who may well be a descendant of Hitler's right-hand man, Goebbels."

"Oh, there was one other who didn't seem to fit in with that crowd. A nice man with a Scandinavian accent. All the staff at the lodge liked him – he remembered everyone's names, spoke to them about their jobs and families. Totally different from the CAFCA lot – he looked like a surfer; he was introduced as an advisor…"

Clyde frowned, "You didn't mention him to me last week."

"I forgot; I was more focused on the others. The man's name is Carl Gunderson."

"What?" Terry was half out of his chair, leaning over the desk. "You can't be serious. Are you sure?"

Sandy and Clyde looked at each other, and Sandy tugged at Terry's sleeve to pull him back into his chair. Terry whipped out his cell phone and Googled. He held up the iPhone to the computer and asked, "Is this the man?"

Petrus leaned in to study the photo. His brow creased with concentration as he said, "He's older, with long hair and glasses but…yes…that's Carl Gunderson. How do you know him?"

Terry turned the phone around and stared at the screen, "He's my father."

Terry struggled for breath as an anxiety attack gathered steam. Between wheezes, he said, "This is… utterly bizarre. You know who he is… don't you?" He looked from one blank face to the other, "Big scandal in 2017 where thousands of people lost their investments? Carl Gunderson, conman extraordinaire, charmer of rich widows and pension fund managers…he escaped from the US and has been hiding out God knows where ever since."

Realization dawned on his audience, and Clyde said, "*The* Carl Gunderson is your father? Wow! But your last name is Reynolds."

Terry answered, "My mother reverted to her maiden name and changed my and my sister's names when she divorced him."

Everyone was silent, then Terry said, "How on earth is he connected? This can't be good."

Petrus said, "From some of the conversation, I got the impression that Carl Gunderson is based in the Middle East to facilitate arms sales for CAFCA members." He paused, "I still have a tough time reconciling the charming man I met with…"

Terry, unable to suppress his bitterness, interrupted, "Oh, he can be as charming as a thousand-dollar-a-night hooker – and as vicious. He'll do anything for money."

Petrus continued, "I guess we have to assume that he probably is well connected with all manner of governments, militia, and possibly even terrorists in the Middle East."

"Sanction busting?" Sandy commented. "But what does it all have to do with the church?"

Petrus said, "From the presentation I saw, the church has stumbled on some pretty amazing tech capabilities to analyze, predict, and manipulate human behavior. But they've run out of cash to keep developing it. CAFCA also wants to analyze, predict, and manipulate human behavior, and they agreed to provide money, but only if they could become partners – old pastor Jeremiah doesn't know it yet, but I suspect he's soon going to find himself in the position of junior partner or completely ousted."

"That's consistent with what you heard in the conversation with Rajiv," Clyde said. "They sure aren't wasting any time."

Petrus said his goodbyes, and the other three brainstormed ways to dig into the morass they had uncovered. They agreed that Sandy and Terry would continue searching at BDA, and Clyde's team was going to see if they could penetrate the CAFCA systems. Clyde said, "There have to be emails, or contracts, or something that can give us an idea of what exactly their plans are. We've found in the past that CAFCA are arrogant enough to think no one will try and get into their systems; keep your fingers crossed that they haven't closed the loopholes."

Terry's phone pinged, and he looked at his messages.

> **Rajiv:** *Good job with the report. Katie wants u to deliver a copy and walk her through it. Meet at Holy Redemption after Sunday service.*

Terry said, "Guess I know where I'm going this Sunday."

Chapter 20, Tracy, California
Sunday, 1ˢᵗ Week of July

TERRY

Terry had done some online research but was not prepared for the magnitude of the church. His mother had taken him and Lily on a tour of Europe when he was sixteen. His secret hopes of finding weed in Amsterdam, or at least a glimpse of the red-light district, were non-starters. In later years the trip was always referred to as the "all-saints tour" – St. Mark's in Venice, followed by St. Peter's in Rome, St. Paul's in London and St. Patrick's in Dublin; plus Westminster cathedral for good measure. Terry had rolled his eyes about being dragged from one "petrified-papal-wet-dream" to another, but the glory of the cathedrals had impressed him. For a while, he'd thought of becoming an architect.

He sat near the back and couldn't decide how he felt about this building. The old churches in Europe were limited by construction constraints, which meant that thick pillars obscured the view from many seats. The massive open space of this church had the advantage of excellent visibility from everywhere – there was no place to hide from God's beady eye. But with its plush red carpets, it was more akin to a Vegas show venue than a church. Above him, he could see a maze of catwalks supporting a constellation of spotlights and cameras. There was no feeling of "sanctuary".

Two TV monitors, which could have served a football stadium, gave Terry an excellent view of the proceedings. The cameras panned across the congregation during the opening hymn and allowed Terry a glimpse of Chloe next to Katie Blanchard in the front row. Chloe wore an elegant emerald dress and tailored jacket. Her hair shone under the lights. With her mouth open in song, she reminded Terry of the Lladro porcelain angel that had been his grandmother's prized possession. He felt a tell-tale cramp in the region of his heart as emotions of regret, admiration and desire for Chloe rose up.

He wondered where things had gone so wrong. Chloe's mother was a factor, but most everyone had impossible mothers-in-law; Lily's suicide had been pivotal, but again, other couples overcame a death in the family. Maybe if they'd had a child? But he immediately dismissed that idea – it was never a good plan to have a baby in an attempt to chain people together.

He fingered the envelope with the research report. Chloe had the potential to be a great politician; she could go far. He closed his eyes and could no longer ignore the little voice that had been nagging in the back of his mind for months. Had he been scared that he would lose her, that she would leave him behind as she climbed up the ranks in the law firm and in politics? And, instead of confronting this fear, had he precipitated the split rather than keeping living in the shadow of the ax?

He was jolted out of his reverie by the sounds of rustling clothes and shuffling feet. The congregation were on their feet and holding hands for prayer. Dear God, he thought, give me a good Catholic service any day, where at least no one expects to touch me.

A plump woman approached from his left, took hold of his hand, and pulled him to his feet with a wide smile. She nudged him to move along the pew towards a man who looked at least as uneasy as Terry felt. He was younger than Terry, with brown hair in need of a decent wash and cut.

Next, there was the awkward tussle to agree who had their palms up and who had them down. Both men avoided eye contact and, looking down, Terry was amused by the contrast of the three pairs of shoes he saw. The woman on his left had swollen feet and thick ankles bulging from formal beige shoes that were deformed by her bunions. In the middle were his tan loafers, and on his right was a pair of highly polished, brown, military-style boots. His neighbor wore jeans and a khaki shirt.

Then Terry did a double-take; he noticed a red-and-black tattoo, no bigger than a quarter, on the inside of the stranger's wrist. Terry flinched and nearly yanked his hand away. The stranger shook his arm a second later, and the shirt sleeve slid over the tattoo.

Pastor Jeremiah's voice had the quality of chocolate mousse as he intoned, "For whom and for what do we pray today?"

A group of select congregants at the front of the church took turns to pray for the poor, for immigrants, the sick, the elderly, all that were lonely, children everywhere, that world leaders might see the perils of climate change, that cancer might be conquered, and that AIDS might be banished. The prayers were punctuated with "Amens" on his left, and Terry thought, *jeez, you don't want much, do you?*

By the time they got to praying for the Giants to win the Western Conference and for the local swim team to make it to regionals, he was getting thoroughly annoyed and was pretty sure that God, in case he was listening, was getting pissed off with these petty requests. Terry's right hand was going numb from the stranger's firm grip, and he was deeply grateful when the congregation chanted a final, "God, in your mercy, hear our prayer."

Pastor Jeremiah had barely said, "We greet each other in peace," when the woman on his left embraced him in a hug that took his breath away. Once she turned her attention to the people on her left, he extended his hand to the stranger. The man had pale skin and the remnants of baby fat. Terry caught a strong garlic smell. He wanted to gag and had to fight to keep a straight face as they shook hands.

Just as Terry thought it was an appropriate time to bring the service to a close, Pastor Jeremiah announced that it was time for the "unveiling". The camera crews sprang into action, and the pastor drew everyone's attention to a black curtain covering a piece of art high up behind the altar. Apparently, the congregation had spent months fundraising for this project and were eagerly awaiting the big reveal. Terry looked at his watch and sighed.

The organ started up and the music built to something akin to drum roll; two young altar kids approached the curtain with solemn steps and grabbed hold of the dangling golden cords on either side. The organ held a single, deafening chord, and pastor Jeremiah nodded. The kids pulled their ropes and the curtain seemed to take on a life of its own as it furled and floated up into the rafters. The music stopped and there was utter silence. Then a gasp went through the crowd, followed by chattering, pointing, and applause that grew to a crescendo. The cameras rolled over the picture, showing it in minute detail on the big screens.

It took Terry a while to grasp what it was – a modern rendition of Leonardo da Vinci's Last Supper with figures at least five times the size of real-life people. The subjects in the painting were familiar: Christ sitting in the middle of the table with the apostles in groups of three. On Jesus' right were John, Peter and Judas. All the familiar detail was there: the loaves of bread, fish and a salt cellar tipped over by Judas' elbow. The positioning of the figures was unmistakable, but they were dressed in jeans and T-shirts; one wore a hoody, and another a bandana. Their hairstyles were thoroughly modern. Jesus' hair was not quite down to his shoulders and tousled; one of the disciples had a shorn head, another had the kind of mohawk that one might see anywhere in San Francisco or New York. The beards were in line with twenty-first-century fashions.

Terry gaped. He had seen the Giampietrino copy of the painting in a London gallery. It was a monumental, awe-inspiring artwork, but this was something else in terms of its sheer size and realism. The symmetrical layout was precisely as Terry remembered from the original, but the feel of the room could have been a diner anywhere in middle America. The most surprising aspect was that the figures weren't stationary; they moved! Terry finally figured that this was not a painting but rather a digital burst photograph, displayed on a state-of-the-art, high-definition monitor like one might find in an Apple store. The picture represented the moment in which Jesus revealed that one of his disciples would betray him. The movement and the changes in the expressions portrayed the shock and horror of the moment in a whole new dimension.

Pastor Jeremiah beamed and gestured to the back of the church. Thirteen young men walked in and the applause became thunderous when the congregation realized that they were the models in the photograph. The woman on Terry's left put two fingers in her mouth and produced a loud whistle. She leaned to Terry and said, "They're all members of the congregation. The man on the right, in the purple T-shirt, that's my nephew." She whistled again.

Pastor Jeremiah held up his hands. When the applause subsided, he said, "I'm so glad that the congregation approves. This work of art symbolizes our conviction that the spirit of the Lord dwells among us *today*. Every meal could be our last, every good deed we do, our last. Hence, go forth in the spirit of the Lord, and be sure to welcome the stranger to your table. For all you know, they might be Christ dressed in jeans, a torn T-shirt, or a hoody."

After the service, Terry sipped a surprisingly good coffee and watched as people milled about in the gathering hall. Pastor Jeremiah stood like a boulder in the middle of a swirling river of people, who all wanted a chance to shake his hand and exchange a few words as they flowed towards the refreshments. Terry was fascinated by the pastor's ability to entirely focus on one individual at a time. His parishioners might only be in his presence for seconds, but for that time, he made them feel like they were the only thing in the world that mattered. Invariably, those who left his presence had a beatific smile and looked truly uplifted.

Katie and Chloe were at the center of another knot of people. He watched Chloe as she smiled and shook hands but sensed that her heart was not entirely in it. When a young mother held up a baby for her to admire, Chloe took a step backward and looked positively panicked. Terry was relieved that there were no TV crews nearby. Chloe would have to step up her baby-cooing game.

Katie spotted him across the room and waved him over. There was a moment of awkwardness as he stood in front of the two women like a schoolboy called into the office by Mother Superior and her acolyte. Then Katie leaned forward and gave him an air kiss; Chloe followed suit, and it annoyed him. Christ, this was the woman he'd slept with for ten years. A handshake would have been preferable to the fake familiarity of the kiss. It must have been how Jesus felt when Judas kissed him, Terry thought, and had to suppress a smile when he realized how melodramatic he was. *Chloe is not going to crucify me – at least not literally.* Thank God for small mercies.

"How do you like the art installation?" Katie asked.

"It's pretty awesome. Wow. Very different; extremely lifelike. I admire the model that had himself immortalized as the face of Judas up there – that takes guts."

Chloe chipped in, "Would you have wanted to volunteer for that?"

Terry shot her a look and retorted, "To really bring it into the twenty-first century, they probably should have portrayed Judas as a female."

Katie gave a brittle smile, "Now, play nice, you two, or I'll put you in time-out." She looked at her watch. "Let's go over to the conference room. Father will join us once he's finished here so we can go over the details for the interfaith service."

The conference room was lavish by any standards – ten leather chairs surrounded a gleaming maple wood table, and Katie handed out Perrier bottles from a concealed wet bar. One side of the room had floor-to-ceiling stained-glass windows, and Terry thought it was an effective way to deal with the view of the parking lot and the drab industrial landscape beyond. Other than the window, the boardroom distinguished itself from corporate boardrooms through the art that had been chosen to adorn the walls. It showcased a collection of Pietas through the ages, including Van Gogh, El Greco, Picasso and Salvador Dali. *So many ways to see the same thing, so many versions of the truth.*

He handed out copies of his report and outlined some of the findings. It didn't surprise Katie or Chloe to hear how polarized the voters were on almost any issue. Terry focused on one group that the analysis had shown as "target-rich": recently naturalized immigrants.

"This is a sizeable group," he said, "and one which many politicians misunderstand. People assume that recent immigrants would be sympathetic to the plight of undocumented people in the US, but the opposite is true. Many immigrants, who have fought their way through the system to get legal status, resent anyone who comes in via a shortcut."

He pointed to a section of the report that substantiated these findings, then went on. "If the GOP were not so blatantly Caucasian, they'd do very well in this group, who tend to be pro-life, tough on crime, and socially conservative. And, especially in California, many have a strong religious background." He paused and addressed Chloe, "Much as I hate to say it, your mother is right. One effective way to differentiate yourself from the average Democrat, and make some inroads towards the center, is to associate yourself with the Church of Holy Redemption. It allows you to tread the fine line of appealing to religious voters without veering too far from the Democratic mainstream."

The two women exchanged glances and Katie sighed, "I suspected this would be the case. We'll have to think long and hard about the implications of endorsing a political candidate…"

"Nothing to think about," Pastor Jeremiah interjected as he shut the door behind him. "Chloe and her parents are members of this flock. We're not endorsing any particular politician, just one of our members setting out to put her God-given talents to good use."

One of our own indeed, Terry thought. *So how come in ten years of marriage, Chloe not once expressed a desire to be with the flock – not even for a single Sunday?*

It was on the tip of his tongue to call bullshit when he caught Katie's eye. She gave him a wry smile and an eye-roll to indicate that she wasn't buying any of it – she also made a small gesture with her hand, asking him to let it rest.

Pastor Jeremiah took a seat at the head of the table, and Chloe congratulated him on the inspirational art installation. The pastor was aglow with the last hour's adrenalin, success, and adoration. Terry thought he looked like someone who had just had particularly satisfying sex. That made him look at Chloe, and the ache welled up inside him. Damn, she looked good. How did she manage to simultaneously look so tough and yet so vulnerable?

Katie took charge and projected her iPad onto the big monitor. She shared a draft outline for the Interfaith service on July 12th. Terry assumed they had what they needed from him and started to excuse himself, but Katie stopped him, "If you can spare us another half hour, Terry, I'd really like your perspective on a couple of things."

"Sure," he said, somewhat surprised but also flattered. He could see that Chloe was equally surprised, but she kept quiet.

Katie looked straight at her father and said, "If we're going to introduce Chloe, it has to be done the right way. It should be a component of the service, not the centerpiece – we can't deviate from the key message of bridge-building. If our interfaith brethren think we're just using them to sponsor a politician – no offense, Chloe – things could backfire horribly; for Chloe and for us."

Pastor Jeremiah nodded slowly, "Katie, why don't you take my place during the service? You did such a great job during that interview, and I think it would add a whole new dimension if the service were led by two up-and-coming women."

"Nice try, father," Katie scoffed. "We've been over this before. I'm not ordained; I have no qualifications to stand up there and preach. It could also be taken the wrong way by some of our guests. The catholic archbishop of San Francisco has accepted; so has the Iman, and Rabbi

Feltenstein. All people who have a...*complicated* relationship with the idea of women in leadership positions. We need to be respectful of that."

She pointed at the agenda and said, "My biggest concern is time management. For example, the Korean community wants to bring their choir. They're outstanding, but they extended their four-minute slot to fifteen last year. And as for that Buddhist lady..."

Pastor Jeremiah made a dismissive gesture and said, "Leave that to Isaac. After last year's experience, he's implemented some new protocols – he's going to give them time warning signals and simply fade out the microphones one minute after their allotted time." He leaned forward and squinted at the screen, "Can you make that a little bigger?"

Katie muttered, "Can you overcome your vanity and wear your glasses?" She enlarged the typeface, and Pastor Jeremiah said, "I see we have Chloe near the start, reading the lessons, and then a 'musical gift' from Gerald Myers...who's that?"

"He's one of our students at Renaissance. Isaac says he has an amazing voice and 'radiates a deep Christian conviction' – Isaac's words, not mine. We thought it'd be a good way to touch on the work we do in our ministries. Here, let me show you – we've got a video of the young man."

Within a minute, Gerald's voice had captivated everyone in the room. When he sang, "We're far from the shallows now," Terry thought he heard Chloe suppress a sob.

Pastor Jeremiah was the first to speak, "I like it, but I want him to come up here beforehand so I can hear him and he can get used to the setting."

Katie said, "Oh ye of little faith."

Pastor Jeremiah smiled, "Attention to detail is everything."

241

Chloe asked, "Why is he at the institute? Did he commit a crime?"

Katie answered, "I believe he's there for the sexual affirmation program."

Chloe's eyes narrowed, and she asked, "Are you running one of those pray-the-gay-away programs? I don't think that's something that would go down well at all with democratic voters."

Pastor Jeremiah interjected, "It's not like that. We just recognize that sexuality falls on a spectrum and young people, young men in particular, are often confused as to where they fall on that spectrum. So we provide them a safe space to pray, discuss and examine their sexual orientation before committing to a choice that can have irrevocable consequences for their lives."

"Sounds like a pray-the-gay-away program to me," Terry said and earned himself a look of pity and disdain from Pastor Jeremiah, as though he were a simpleton that couldn't understand the nuances of what had just been explained to him.

Katie muttered under her breath, "This is why we shouldn't mix politics with our calling."

Pastor Jeremiah turned to Chloe, "Would you like to see our new command center downstairs?" Then, as an afterthought, he turned to Terry and added, "You're also welcome. I believe you're into computers – you might learn a thing or two."

Smug old goat, Terry thought as he politely accepted the invitation.

Pastor Jeremiah offered his arm to Chloe and led the way. Katie and Terry followed, and he seized the opportunity to ask her for help in contacting his brother, Daniel, at the Renaissance Institute. It took Katie a few moments to make the connection between Terry Reynolds on the one hand and Daniel Gunderson on the other. But then she remembered her conversation with Eleanor

McGrath, Chloe's mother. The latter had referred to "all the baggage" of Terry's impossible family, including the father – a con man on the run from the authorities.

Terry said, "I have to admit to my shame that I haven't paid much attention to my little half-brother. After Lily…after Lily's death, I was just so consumed with myself." He paused, "I only recently found out that he was at the institute. I don't even know how or why he's enrolled there. Last thing I knew, he was with his mother on the East Coast."

Katie said, "I don't get involved with every person who is enrolled in our various programs, but I do remember Daniel's case. He's had a tough time of it with all the publicity surrounding your father. He went through quite a rebellious phase, changed school a few times, and had several brushes with the law."

She put a hand on his arm, "Nothing serious – brawls, petty vandalism, public disorder. That sort of thing. I believe he had a lucky break that an enlightened judge decided that he was more of a victim than a perpetrator and needed to be shielded from the tabloids, TMZ, and constant scrutiny via social media. That's why they sent him to Renaissance – it's a kind of protective custody for him. I remember because the probation officer came personally to make sure that the boys at the institute had no cell phones; that TV, Internet and contact with the outside world were appropriately restricted, and that access was tightly controlled."

Terry said, "I understand, but I'm his brother. Who gets to decide whether I can visit him or not?"

"I'll see what I can do. The normal protocol is to work through the legal guardian. Ideally, you'd contact your stepmother and have her give consent…"

Terry interrupted with tight lips, "She and I don't speak."

"Well, I'm sure we can figure something out; I'll let you know tomorrow afternoon."

They came to a halt in a wide, windowless corridor underneath the church. The walls were painted gray, and concealed lighting lent a clinical atmosphere. Pastor Jeremiah placed a finger on a biometric reader; a door slid sideways, giving access to a foyer the size of a large elevator. In front of them was another door – stainless steel with a porthole that allowed a glimpse of the control room ahead. When the door had whooshed shut behind them, the pastor placed his finger on a second reader. A suction fan started to vacuum dust off them.

Airlock double doors, Terry thought. They take physical protection very seriously.

The inner door slid open. Pastor Jeremiah had his hand on a green button and motioned for them to pass him. He said, "You have to be very careful with these doors – they're equipped with active intruder prevention."

"What does that mean?" Chloe asked.

"It means that when you press the red button to tell this door to close, it *will* close, regardless of any arms or legs that get in the way."

"Isn't that a little harsh?" Chloe asked. "You could hurt someone."

"It is, unfortunately, a necessary safety precaution. A physical intruder could do untold damage – it's a changing world we live in."

Chloe and Terry both eyed the large red button with suspicion and gave it a wide berth.

Terry had seen many data centers and control rooms. Through his work at Big Data Analytica, he also had a sense of how The Church of Holy Redemption operated. But he gaped at the sophistication and scale of the setup. A bank of monitors cycled through every conceivable angle of the church and its facilities in high definition. One camera was panning across the newly-installed Last Supper, and

Terry could make out strands of gray in the hair of St. Thomas and a small scar across the brow of the apostle, Peter. Other monitors showed trend graphs and color-coded geolocation maps of California, the USA, and the world. Pastor Jeremiah proudly explained that the maps indicated the intensity of social media engagement – a visual representation of where the church had its most significant influence. "Trending topics" from Facebook and Instagram scrolled down yet another screen.

A politician's dream, Terry thought. A ready-made, ultra-sophisticated campaign headquarters. A sidewise glance at Chloe, and the rapt wonder on her face, told him that the opportunity was not lost on her.

There were only a handful of people at the controls and two men, deep in conversation, at the far end of the room. They both turned to look at the newcomers. Pastor Jeremiah was in full throttle and didn't pay them any attention, but Terry noticed the look of annoyance on the face of the boyish man with curly brown hair. He had seen the same man at Starbucks, talking to Rajiv. He now knew him to be Isaac O'Neill, Pastor Jeremiah's right-hand man. The other man, to his surprise, was the young man with the military boots who had sat next to Terry in church. What was he doing here?

Isaac whispered to the man, who turned and stepped into an office, closing the door behind him. Only then did Isaac walk over to them. By the time Pastor Jeremiah introduced him to Chloe and Terry, he was oozing boyish charm: *What an honor to meet Chloe; such an admirer of her father's work in the senate; delighted to be able to help her start her political career.*

Terry wanted to gag.

Isaac said, "We're bringing on some extra security for the event; I was just talking to one of the new guards." He made a vague gesture in the direction of the office. He looked from one to the other and smiled, "Well, you've seen our control room. Pastor Jeremiah has done a great job explaining the setup, and I believe you've worked through the order of the interfaith service. It makes me feel downright superfluous."

There was something petulant and aggressive in the way he said that he was superfluous. Terry wondered what the underlying dynamic was between the pastor and Isaac. But the older man appeared completely oblivious. Pastor Jeremiah said, "Let's just have a look at the server room." He chuckled, "I confess that I find all those blinking lights quite mesmerizing."

Isaac led the way to a door on their left and said, "There's nothing much to see." He addressed Chloe, "We used to have all our servers down here, but we've outgrown this space. It's all been relocated to a remote location."

"Where?" Chloe asked.

Isaac wagged his finger, "If I told you, I'd have to shoot you." Then he added in a stage whisper, "I'll give you a hint; we've hidden them where the dwarfs dwell."

Chloe laughed and touched Isaac's arm as they stepped into a cavernous room, where only two dozen server racks stood blinking.

Terry was getting hot under the collar watching the interaction between his ex and Isaac. To get away from them, he followed Katie to the far end of the room, where she examined a pile of boxes on pallets. Then, without preamble, he asked, "What's the C.O.L.D. index?"

Katie's head snapped around and her nostrils flared, "The *what*?"

"The C.O.L.D. index. I've heard the term mentioned at Big Data Analytica and elsewhere."

For a fleeting second, Katie's eyes went wide and wild, like a trapped animal. Terry was intrigued. What deep secrets did Katie have to hide? Then it was as though a shutter came down, and she looked at him impassively, "Why ask me? I don't …"

"Funny thing is," Terry interjected, "that every time I ask someone, they give me an oblique answer. Though a few people have said that you're an authority on the subject and that I should ask you."

She let out a breath and shook her head, "Whoever pointed you in my direction is mistaken. I have no idea what this…this cold index is about. Presumably, a temperature indicator? Sorry, can't help you on that one." She turned her back on him and called, "Isaac, Father, what's in these boxes? Don't tell me you've been buying more equipment. We really can't afford to spend any more money on all this stuff."

Isaac walked over and said, "I don't second guess what you do, Katie. I wish you would occasionally trust me to do my job."

Katie looked taken aback, "Of course I trust you, it's just …"

Isaac interrupted, "Well, it doesn't feel that way. We didn't spend a dime on this. It was provided to us by CAFCA as part of our new partnership agreement. Just some technology they want us to test for them."

As Isaac nudged everyone toward the door, Terry lingered to take a last look at the inscription on the boxes. It said something about drones. How utterly weird. Were they going to have drones fly around the sanctuary? Maybe they were meant to enhance security around the parking lot.

"Come on, Terry," Isaac called. "You wouldn't want us to 'accidentally' leave you in here." Despite his light tone, there was something malicious in his voice when he said, "The room's soundproofed – no one would hear your cries for help."

Just to annoy Isaac, Terry stalled, pointed at a fixed installation ladder on the side of the room, and asked where it led.

Isaac said, "That provides access to the lighting gantries in the sanctuary. The technicians sometimes use it to go up and adjust the lights or lay cables. Why?"

Terry shrugged, "Just curious." He chuckled, "Looking for an escape route in case you do lock me in here." He shot Isaac a broad grin and followed Pastor Jeremiah toward the airlock. As he was leaving, he overheard Katie say to Isaac, "I'm not happy at all with this CAFCA deal; Rajiv called me yesterday – he was fuming about the way they've marched in and are throwing their weight around. I want to know the details of the deal you struck with them."

Isaac's voice was dripping sarcasm as he mimicked Katie's voice, "Really, you're not happy. What a shame." His voice turned cold, "It's about time you – and your father – gave me the recognition and trust I deserve…"

Then the door closed. Terry would have loved to have heard the rest of the conversation. It sounded like Isaac was a cauldron of pent-up anger about to blow.

A few minutes later, he and Chloe stood outside the massive front portal of the church. She was fidgeting with her car keys. Terry noticed that she still had the keyring he had bought her on their honeymoon in Spain – a sliver flip-flop sandal to remind them to find time for vacations. It was ridiculously comforting to know that she had kept the souvenir.

Chloe said, "Quite a setup they have here."

He nodded, "Somewhat beyond what you'd expect for a church."

She shrugged, "People are always skeptical of innovators and trailblazers."

"Don't you find it creepy – the way they monitor everything? They don't just surveil the premises, you know.

They collect the most detailed and intimate data about their members and anyone else in their sphere. And now they're getting into bed with CAFCA." He paused, then added, "Do you really want to be associated with this lot?"

Chloe put on her sunglasses, and though he couldn't see her eyes, there was no mistaking the ice in her voice, "You just can't bear the thought of me moving on, Terry. Give it a rest and get used to it."

She swung around and headed off toward her car.

Terry watched her and thought, *you are so wrong*. His analysis had strengthened his belief that Chloe had a brilliant political career ahead of her, and she was enough of her father's daughter to remain a decent human being and do her best, even in the fray of politics. But he was concerned that the association with the church and CAFCA would backfire horribly. He stood and watched until her Volvo had disappeared into the shimmering heat of the day.

Chapter 21, Renaissance Institute
Sunday, 1st Week of July

DANNY

The weather forecast had predicted windy conditions, and Danny did his best to secure the dried marijuana leaves in his secret garden. He stuffed a few extra packets of the precious foliage into his running shorts, then jogged back to the dormitory via the kitchen to pick up a bagel and banana for Timothy.

The door to their room was ajar, and Danny had a sense of foreboding. "Timothy?" he called.

There was no answer. It only took seconds to ascertain that his friend was not asleep under the covers nor in the bathroom. The only thing he could think of was that Juanito and his gang had come to exact revenge for the humiliation they had suffered. Danny dumped the food and weed, ran up the stairs to the seniors' dormitory, and charged into Juanito's room. The big guy was sprawled in a chair, smoking. He made a feeble attempt to lurch up and toss the cigarette out the window, but gravity dragged his bulk back into the chair. He quickly regained his composure when he saw that it wasn't a teacher or security guard.

"What the fuck do you think you're doing barging into my room? Didn't your mother teach you any manners?"

"Where's Timothy?"

Juanito snarled, "How should I know where your crazy little fuck-buddy's gone? Maybe to the cuckoo farm where he belongs." He blew out a cloud of smoke.

Danny clenched his fists and forced himself to speak calmly, "If you or your goons have touched him, so help me, I'll…"

Juanito smirked and said in a high-pitched voice, "Ooh. Now you're giving me ideas. What will you do, eh? What? Throw your toys out the pram? Run to Mommy?" He grunted, "Why don't you just fuck off before I get angry?" He took a deep drag and blew out more smoke.

Through the haze, Danny noticed that Juanito's eyes had shifted to a spot behind him. He spun around and came face to face with one of Juanito's guys, who asked, "Is there a problem, Juanito? I heard voices."

"Yeah," Danny said, "I'm sure you hear voices all the time. They're in your head, asshole." He elbowed past the boy. At the door, he turned and said, "You want to know what I'll do if you touch Timothy? I'll blow up your whole little smuggling operation, including the security guards that you keep bribing. They'll know that you dropped the ball, so they'll probably come and cut off yours."

Juanito scooped up a shoe and threw it, but Danny was already halfway down the corridor. *Where the hell was Timothy?*

He stopped by Gerald's room, and together they roamed the corridors, the common room and the kitchen. Ten minutes later, they found him – in the science lab.

Danny exclaimed, "Timothy! *What* are you doing here? You gave me a scare."

Timothy looked up from his computer and pointed to a whiteboard, "I needed to draw."

The whiteboard was covered in what looked like organizational diagrams – boxes, lines, question marks, annotations.

"What's all this?" Danny asked.

"The corporate structure of the Church of Holy Redemption and all its holdings."

Danny and Gerald stared at him before Danny said, "And you're drawing this up because…?"

Timothy blinked, "The data center. You asked me to find out what it's all about."

Danny said, "What? That whole ginormous data center is used to run a church? You're kidding me."

Timothy shook his head.

Of course, Danny thought, *he's not kidding. He never kids.*

Timothy walked to the board, "Mykyta and I have been delving into the systems, but I had to create a picture of the various entities to be able to organize and understand what we are looking at." He went on to explain that there was the church itself with its direct subsidiaries, including the Renaissance Institute, the various shelters, youth groups, and ministries. He pointed at the box in the middle with a cross on it and said, "Once inside the system, their security is remarkably lax. You can see all the financial data, personnel records, information about members and people they serve…"

Gerald interjected, "You mean you can access Danny's or my records?"

"Oh yes," Timothy said, "I told Mykyta you two were my friends. He looked at your academic and health records and psychiatrist's notes. He says you're both boring."

Gerald and Danny gaped at each other.

Timothy continued, "Now, the other entities are more interesting." He pointed at the next block on the board, "BDA – short for Big Data Analytica – is based in San Francisco. It is a massive data vacuuming operation." He explained how BDA tapped into hundreds of sources to gather information and perform trend analyses for several clients.

"We have hit a challenge," Timothy explained. "BDA has a classified data zone that is extremely tightly protected. No idea what they are trying to hide, but they have information crown jewels that they don't want anyone to see." He demonstrated on the keyboard how specific directories popped up with a bold, red *Access denied* message. "The encryption is based on modern multifactor authentication."

Gerald shrugged helplessly and said, "I don't think I understand."

"You need fingerprint ID to get to this data. Mykyta is working it with some of his friends to help us get into that zone."

Danny decided not to point out to Timothy that his friend Mykyta clearly was still in the business of hacking. So what the hell was the church doing with all this data?

The answer came when Timothy explained that the BDA data lake was being accessed by *The Settlement Bureau,* which specialized in collating data about individuals and then "exerting pressure" on them. He pulled up examples of letters being sent to people and showed how this practice bolstered the organization's cash flow.

"That's… that's unbelievable," Danny said. "This is a wholesale blackmail and racketeering syndicate."

"That's not how they see it," Gerald said. "From the research I did before I came here, they speak quite openly about 'nudging' their flock to do the right thing."

Danny was outraged, "There are many ways to 'nudge' people. The crusaders nudged them with their swords, the popes nudge them with fear of eternal damnation, and Hitler nudged them at gunpoint into the gas chambers."

Timothy said, "There is nothing about the crusades, the pope, or Hitler in this system. You are being irrational."

Danny was about to retort when his eye caught a live-streaming picture in the corner of Timothy's screen. "What's that?" he asked.

"We've managed to tap into the church's video surveillance system; they have dozens of cameras. There is a service going on right now." He enlarged the picture and flicked through various camera angles from the parking lot to the lobby, to a sinister-looking maze of corridors and finally, to the sanctuary itself, where a camera was focused on Pastor Jeremiah.

Gerald said, "Hold it on that camera." He leaned forward, and there was awe in his voice when he said, "I do hope I get to meet the pastor; he's amazing. At home, we watch his sermons every week."

Timothy turned up the volume, and they were just in time to witness the dedication of the Last Supper. Gerald's eyes shone; he was enthralled, "The man is such a visionary. Imagine taking the Last Supper and making it totally relevant for us today."

Danny countered, "Fleecing people through blackmail – all in the name of God – is hardly visionary. That's been done for millennia."

"Don't be such a cynic," Gerald said, "he's giving hope and direction to thousands. Look at them!" The congregation were on their feet, holding hands in prayer, enveloped in organ music. Gerald sighed as they watched the camera pan across the earnest faces of the parishioners. Most had their eyes closed, their faces turned upwards; many were mouthing prayers. There were young people with rapturous smiles, men with the disappointments of a lifetime etched on their faces, and women with tears escaping from under their eyelids.

Pastor Jeremiah's voice melded with the organ as he intoned, "You are talking to your God. I'm not feeling it; put your heart and soul into your prayer, and God *will* listen!"

The camera showed faces scrunched up in redoubled effort. Danny would have laughed, but he didn't want to offend Gerald, who had his eyes closed and his hands outstretched, his lips moving silently.

Suddenly, Danny shouted, "Stop! Can you rewind?"

Timothy nodded and tapped the keyboard.

"There! Stop, hold it."

All three leaned in to study the freeze-frame of an earnest man, whose dark eyes seemed to bore into them via the camera.

"Who is it?" Gerald asked.

Danny looked like he might climb into the screen, "That's my brother, Terry," he whispered. "What on earth is he doing at an evangelical church?"

The three friends got so engrossed they barely made it to lunch before the cafeteria closed.

Danny's dam of memories and longing had burst. He shared story after story about his big brother and was only interested in ideas for tracking Terry down. "If he's a member, he must be in the database," Danny said. "Timothy, after lunch, we have to find his email address and phone number." Doubt started to gnaw at him as he swallowed a mouthful of lukewarm Brussels sprouts. "Maybe he was just there for that picture dedication. Then, of course, he might not be in the system."

Gerald said, "Wasn't it amazing? When they brought out the real live subjects of that painting, I thought…I thought my heart would stop. It was like being there with Jesus."

Timothy interjected, "It was a photo, Jesus was *not* there," before continuing his explanation of the encryption challenges he and Mykyta were facing.

The lunch conversation continued like something out of a modern play, where each character obsessively followed his own train of thought – a three-way monologue.

Chapter 22, San Francisco

Monday, 2nd Week of July

TERRY

Sandy and Terry met at their usual rooftop spot. She smoked while he devoured the first half of a chicken wrap for lunch.

"Are you asking me on a date?" Sandy said with a smile that Terry found hard to interpret.

He swallowed an unchewed piece of chicken and experienced a momentary short circuit between his brain and his tongue, "Well…I'd like us to go for a drink after work, maybe grab a bite to eat…"

She gave him a sideways glance as she blew out smoke. "Where? If it's somewhere with linen tablecloths and candles, then it's definitely a date."

Terry thought of his depleted finances. "Eh…I hadn't really thought of a candle-lit dinner; more like grab a drink and a bite somewhere at the Embarcadero."

She pursed her lips in a sulk, "Is that all I'm worth?"

Oh, God. I'm so out of practice with this dating game. Terry looked down at the remains of his wrap. He wasn't hungry anymore. *I really suck at this. Maybe it's time to let Jake and Britney fix me up with a blind date – I'm clearly not going to get anywhere by myself.*

Suddenly, Sandy broke out in a laugh and punched him on the shoulder. She laughed till she started coughing. He looked up with a scowl, "What's so funny?"

"You," she spluttered between coughs. "I'm just messing with you. Of course I'd like to go for a drink with you. I don't care where we go; we can go to McDonald's." She paused, "No, wait, we have to go somewhere that at least serves alcohol." Then she took the wrap out of his hand and said, "Did I manage to spoil your appetite?" She winked, "Your face is an open book – I'd love to play poker against you."

He grunted, "For that very reason, I don't play poker."

Sandy put the wrap to her mouth and enveloped it with her lips in a way that made Terry blush. He took a quick peek over his shoulder to make sure that no one else was on the rooftop terrace. She took a bite and handed it back. When she'd swallowed, she looked at her watch and got up, "See you after work. I hope you've got your appetite back by this evening."

***

They ended up at the Slanted Door – a Vietnamese restaurant with good food and a great view of the Bay Bridge. It was a compromise between a fast-food joint and a seriously expensive, linen-candles-and-stuck-up-waiters type place. Over dinner, they talked about anything except work, and Terry became more relaxed than he had been for weeks. Sandy regaled him with stories of her childhood on a farm in Wisconsin. She adored her older brother. "He was my fiercest critic and my most enthusiastic cheerleader," she said. "He encouraged me to climb trees, go down a raging river in an inner tube, jump my horse over impossible hurdles – I could do these things because I always felt that he was there to catch me."

For a moment, Terry dwelled on his own big brother performance. Had he been there for Lily? For Daniel? He felt ashamed, but Sandy distracted him with stories of going hunting before anyone had realized that she was quite nearsighted. After she'd mistaken a chicken for a wild cat and shredded it with a shotgun, her brother decided that hunting was not for her.

After dinner, they got into an Uber. Terry felt mellow and a little buzzed as he savored the scent and feel of Sandy snuggled up against him. He kissed the top of her head, and she stroked his chest. Terry stifled a groan of pleasure as she nibbled at his earlobe. He caught the driver smirking at them in the rearview mirror. "Eyes on the road," he wanted to say, but only another groan escaped his lips as Sandy's other hand moved up his thigh.

The Uber dropped them near Terry's apartment, and they walked arm-in-arm. It was a clear night with glimpses of starlight above the city. Terry breathed deeply and looked at his companion. She smiled at him and touched the tip of his nose with her finger. At the door to his building, Terry said, "Do you mind waiting here a minute? I'm going to bring Charlie down so he can meet you on neutral territory – he gets a little possessive, and he needs to be let out for a pee anyway."

Sandy smiled, "I grew up with dogs; I look forward to meeting Charlie."

Terry bounded up the stairs and straight into the jumping-jack excitement of his furry roommate. "Best behavior, Charlie. I don't want any attitude from you."

The apartment was pristine, but still, Terry raced through to straighten cushions, give the basin a quick wipe, and shove toiletries into the bathroom cabinet.

He need not have worried about attitude from Charlie toward Sandy. The dog's tail swished like a car's windshield wipers in a downpour when Sandy knelt down to let him lick her neck.

Suddenly, Charlie growled and turned to stare across the street. They both followed his gaze. There was a commotion in the shadows of a tree. Then Terry heard a frail, plaintive voice, "No, no, leave me. That's mine. Let go!" Terry knew that voice; it was Joe. What sort of low-life attacks an old homeless man? There was a thud and a howl of pain. Charlie was the first to react; he raced across the street with Terry behind him. Under the streetlamp, he could make out the old man's face, bleeding and distorted with fear, as he shouted, "You imbecile, you don't know..." The attacker was dressed in black, and was at least six inches taller than Joe. Joe clung to the man to prevent him from escaping. The assailant pushed Joe hard, then his fist smashed into the old man's face. Joe slumped against the tree, and the thug pulled back his fist for another punch.

Terry shouted, "Hey, leave him!"

The man briefly turned and hesitated. Then, before he could plant the fist again, Charlie lunged and sank his teeth into the man's wrist. The attacker cursed, and a knife appeared in his other hand. The blade glinted in the streetlight, and Charlie's bark turned into a surprised yelp, then a whimper. The attacker ran.

For a split second, Terry's rage commanded him to follow the attacker, but the sight of Joe and Charlie, both crumpled and bleeding on the ground, stopped him in his tracks. He knelt by the old man, whose face was smeared with blood, one eye beginning to swell. His breath was coming in desperate rasps.

"It's okay, Joe," Terry soothed, "We're here; we'll get you to a hospital." He whipped off his jacket and propped it under the old man's head. Behind him, Sandy was on the phone to 911. She crouched next to him and used her sweater to stem the bleeding from a cut above the old man's eye. Joe seemed to drift in and out of consciousness, and Terry tried to keep his voice calm, "Ambulance should be here any minute now, Joe. We'll take good care of you. You just try and relax; you're safe now."

"You know him?" Sandy asked.

Terry nodded. "Sort of. We chat – he's great friends with Charlie."

At the mention of his name, Charlie whimpered. Terry and Sandy looked at each other, and, by unspoken agreement, Sandy shifted to attend to the dog while Terry continued to try and soothe the old man. *Where is that damn ambulance?* Terry wrapped Joe's coat more tightly around the old man, then peered towards Sandy and Charlie.

"Brave dog," Sandy said and as her hands ghosted over the dog's body, searching for injuries. She glanced at Terry, "I think he was lucky; it looks like a cut on his shoulder, but it isn't bleeding much. Pass me my bag; I'll go over it with a sanitizing wipe."

Joe's eyes suddenly flew open, and his hands shot up to grip Terry's shirt. He croaked, "Where is it?"

"Shh, Joe, you've had a bad shock. You've been attacked. Just lie still."

"Where is it?" The old man implored. His feeble hands shook, "You must get it back. You must…"

"The police will find him," Terry said, "Try not to worry." Gently, he prized the old man's hands from his shirt.

Joe sank back. A look of infinite sadness and resignation crossed his face. His hands shook as he patted his coat. Terry tried to hold Joe's hands still, but the old vagrant insisted on fumbling with the coat's buttons. Joe was so agitated that Terry undid the top two buttons, all the while soothing, "Try and take it easy, Joe. I know that's trite, but please, just lie still." He pricked his ears. "Hear that? The ambulance is on its way."

Joe ignored him and reached into the depth of his coat from where he pulled a small item. He pressed it into Terry's hands and said, "Please, you must tell my son…" He coughed and winced with pain. Terry was aware of Sandy right next to him. Concern was etched on her face as they both leaned forward to better hear Joe, "…tell my son that *they* got it."

Terry and Sandy exchanged looks. Joe was in a bad way. His breath was irregular, and his right eye was beginning to swell up. But what was more concerning was the grayish-green color of his face. Terry wondered what manner of internal injuries the old man had sustained. He'd been so frail and gaunt to start off with – he had no reserves. Terry reached for Joe's wrist to feel his racing pulse. *Come on, old man,* he willed. The ambulance is nearly here.

Joe opened his eye again and fixed a glassy stare on Terry. Anguish stole across his face as he gripped Terry's arm, "Clyde, my son, I'm *so* sorry. I kept a copy of the COLD index research. And now they've got it." Tears welled in the old man's eyes as he clutched Terry's arm and repeated, "I'm so sorry, Clyde. Please don't leave me." He sighed, and his head rolled to one side as the ambulance, followed by a police vehicle, screeched to a halt amid the deafening sound of sirens.

In the minutes it took for the EMTs to stabilize the old man, Terry looked at the item Joe had pressed into his hand. It was a well-worn business card. Someone had written in shaky letters across the top of the card, "next of kin". The card bore the printed logo of the East Bay University and below it: *Clyde Curry, Professor of Data Analytics*, plus a phone number.

He showed the card to Sandy, and they both stared numbly back and forth between the card and the old man on the gurney. Sandy was the first to find her voice. She whispered, "So, old homeless Joe is, in fact, the Nobel laureate Professor Sean Curry. And he's just been beaten to within an inch of his life…"

Terry finished her sentence, "…for a copy of the COLD index research." He shook his head, "Why? Why now?"

A policeman approached notepad in hand and said, "Good evening, ma'am, I assume you're the one who called 911. Care to tell me what happened here?"

"I've got to go with him," Terry blurted and pointed towards the ambulance. The policeman was about to object, but Terry cut him off, "Joe is scared, and he begged me not to leave him." He held out his keys to Sandy, "Can you please put Charlie back in the apartment? I'll call Clyde from the hospital."

Sandy took the keys, "Go!"

Terry stepped into the ambulance just as the EMT was about to shut it. He sat next to the still figure and took his hand, "Hang in there, Joe. Please, please, hang in – for Clyde's sake."

Mercifully, the ER was quiet. Terry did his best to deal with the paperwork and answer the myriad of questions posed by administrators and nurses. What was Joe's age, address, medical history, previous surgeries, allergies, medications, blood type? Did he have a living will, a do-not-resuscitate? Was he an organ donor? Terry felt equal parts frustration and guilt as he kept saying, "I don't know." His conscience was on an auto-repeat loop, *Terry Reynolds, you could have spent a little time getting to know the old man.* Only when the doctor asked questions about the nature of the attack did Terry feel he could add some value. The doctor quickly confirmed that Joe had at least two broken ribs, a concussion, and most likely damage to his internal organs. He was rushed to the operating theater, and Terry sought out a corner in the waiting room.

He was about to dial Clyde Curry's number when his phone rang: *unknown caller.*

A deep voice, with an accent he couldn't place, asked, "Is this Mr. Terrence Reynolds?"

When Terry answered in the affirmative, the caller said, "I am Sergeant DeVries with the Johannesburg branch of the South African Police – serious crimes division." The caller paused to let this information sink in. If he could have seen Terry, he would have known that the pause was pointless.

"What? Who?" Terry's brain was like cotton wool. He would have hung up but for the fact that the caller seemed to know him by name. "Say that again?"

The caller repeated his credentials and went on, "I am calling on behalf of your father, Mr. Carl Gunderson. We have him under police guard at the Johannesburg General Hospital. He is allowed one call, and since he is about to go into surgery, he insisted on making the call now. You are his next of kin."

Terry's mind reeled. His father, in custody, in a hospital? That seemed impossible; the man hadn't been sick a single day in his life. Terry looked around as though suspecting a candid camera joke. But the words that had struck him most were, "you are his next of kin". He had shut his father out of his life years ago and had just assumed that his father had somehow rebuilt his own without him. Yet there it was: "you are his next of kin".

There was a shuffling at the other end of the phone, and a jolt went through Terry when he heard the familiar, thick, Nordic accent, "Terrence, I don't have much time." With one sentence, a decade had been erased. I don't have time. *Wasn't that the truth?* Terry thought bitterly. Some things clearly never changed.

"Terrence, are you there? Can you hear me…say something?" his father said, and Terry detected something else in the voice – a note of pleading. That certainly was new.

"I'm here," he said and wiped a hand over his eyes. "What happened? The man said you're in custody – and in a hospital?"

"Fate happened," Carl Gunderson said with a dry laugh. "I was in transit at Johannesburg airport, on my way from Namibia to the Middle East. Had a heart attack. They rushed me through immigration and to the hospital. Half an hour later, the police showed up. My passport was flagged. South Africa, unlike Namibia, has an extradition treaty with the US."

"Oh…" Terry said, "But your heart; are you okay?"

"I'm being wheeled to the OR as we speak. Apparently, the doctors here are pretty good. Heck, they did the first heart transplant. They're going to do a triple bypass."

Terry said, "Oh, wow. I don't know what to say."

Carl ignored him, and there was urgency in his voice when he said, "Terry, that's not why I called." Terry realized with a jolt that his father had called him "Terry" instead of "Terrence" for the first time in his life.

Carl continued, "I'm so tired of running, I don't give a shit what happens to me. But I'm worried about Daniel. He's stumbled across some secrets relating to that Church of Holy Redemption in California, and he knows more than is good for him. He's in danger."

"What?!" Terry exclaimed. "What kind of danger? I thought he was up in that institute precisely to keep him safe."

"Listen to me," Carl pleaded. "Those people are playing dangerous games, and CAFCA is involved." There was a shuffling, and the voice grew muffled. Terry heard the sergeant's voice trying to get his father to end the call. Then Carl said, "Terry, please take care of your brother." His father's voice choked up as he added, "We can't lose him, too."

"Dad?" Terry shouted, and a few people in the waiting room looked at him.

The last thing he heard was Carl's strangled voice, "I love you, son."

The phone went dead, and Terry collapsed into a chair.

Chapter 23, San Francisco

Monday, 2nd Week of July

KATIE

Katie was exhausted as she drove home. The day had been a whirl of unforeseen crises, starting with an allegation of harassment at the women's shelter. Then, a spat among the catering volunteers was blown out of proportion right after the building maintenance manager lobbied her for support to get more funds. On top of it, she ran into a brick wall when she tried to facilitate contact between Terry and his brother, Daniel. On the plus side, she had to concede that the privacy protocols to protect the young men at the center were working, but it was still infuriating. She'd even called Daniel's mother, who'd been singularly unhelpful. Initially, Natasha Gunderson-Pombo had followed the line of, "My baby is troubled; it would upset him to meet with Terrence." Then, when Katie tried to explain that family visits were an important part of helping the boys reintegrate, she'd become arch and defensive, "I thought we paid you to keep him isolated."

A quick review of the records showed Katie that, in nine months, Daniel had not received a single visit, and his "half-hour" calls with his mother rarely lasted more than six minutes. So much for the family's commitment to support. She had decided that, the following day, she would drive to the institute and meet with Danny's counselor. Her hope was that the counselor might have the power to insist that brotherly contact would be helpful for Daniel.

By the time she pulled into the parking garage at her apartment block, she was too exhausted to think about Terry and Daniel. Underlying everything else was the mounting anxiety about the deal her father and Isaac had struck with CAFCA. What were they thinking? Katie couldn't shake the feeling that her absence at the meeting had been exploited to rush through something ominous. She didn't admit to herself that she felt betrayed by her father, but she certainly felt hurt and upset – and what was with Isaac? He was acting strangely.

She let herself into her apartment, put down her laptop bag, and dropped her keys into a ceramic bowl near the front door. The foyer led to the lounge, and straight ahead through the windows, she could see the silhouette of treetops that reached the third floor. A glimmer of dusk reflected off the bay; the sky was losing the last of its orange glow, sliding into the color of a ripe eggplant. Her home, her sanctuary – it never failed to calm and restore her.

Her study was to the right, the kitchen to the left. She flicked a light switch as she stepped into her study, and a warm glow illuminated her inner sanctum. The room had cream walls and drapes that were prone to waft like a gossamer mist in the faintest breeze. Katie had confided to her interior designer that her secret fantasy was to have a room reminiscent of the elves' castle in *Lord of the Rings*. Hence there were lamps with whimsical parchment shades and art pieces inspired by ancient Celtic ruins and forest scenes. Katie's favorite was a painting she had commissioned, based on a photograph of her mother in Muir Woods. It captured the essence of Amelia Blanchard. The painting had a dreamy, flower-child quality and exuded the serenity of a person at peace with herself and with the world around her.

The only item in the room that was at odds with the décor was a curvaceous Ikea chair with black leather upholstery. Despite the designer's exasperated pleas for her to get rid of the chair, it retained pride of place in the corner by the window. Amelia had assembled that chair with "help" from an eight-year-old Katie. There was a hole in the upholstery where Katie's hand had slipped while trying to use a screwdriver for the myriad of screws. Katie smiled as she looked at the tear. She'd been mortified when it happened, but her mother had simply said, "It's okay to make mistakes, Katie, as long as you learn from them." And she had insisted that Katie tackle the next three screws.

"How's your day been, Mr. Spot?" she said to the stuffed toy sitting on the chair. She picked up the toy, flopped into the chair, and let her hands run through the silky hair of the animal, which looked at her with its permanently-woebegone expression. "Boring day for you, I imagine."

God, listen to me, talking to a stuffed animal. Pathetic. She kicked off her shoes and thought back to the day she got Mr. Spot – her seventh birthday. She'd been desperate to get a puppy and had begged her parents for one. Jeremiah was dead against it for reasons Katie never fully understood. She'd held out hope right up to her birthday and had fought back tears when her parents presented her with a new bicycle – but no dog. That afternoon, at her birthday party, Mitch McGrath had appeared, tugging spot along behind him on a leash. He had whispered to Katie, "Don't tell your father, but this is a real dog. He just pretends to be a toy."

At night, in bed, cuddling Mr. Spot, it had been easy to imagine that he was real.

Katie's stomach told her that, unlike Mr. Spot, she needed food. She hadn't eaten since she'd picked up a bagel and coffee mid-morning. She gave the dog a final hug and crossed the hall. The kitchen – all stainless steel, dark granite, and LED spotlights – typified the designer look of kitchens that never get used for anything but cocktails and take-out food. She opened the fridge with no enthusiasm, knowing that there would be little other than yogurt and sliced cheese. Oh well, cheese and crackers wasn't the worst meal, and at least it went with wine.

Suddenly, a voice behind her said, "I hope you don't mind that I've opened the bottle without you."

Katie got such a fright she dropped the cheese. Her heart pounded as she spun around and peered into the darkness of the lounge.

"What on earth? Isaac, is that you? How…what are you doing here?"

A switch was flicked, and the light of Katie's reading lamp illuminated Isaac. He sat in an armchair, his legs stretched out in front of him, a glass of wine in his hand.

Katie regained her composure and repeated, "What are you doing in my apartment?"

He looked about the room, letting his eyes linger on a large photograph of the Golden Gate Bridge, the elegant gray sofas, an outsized coffee table on wheels, and the gleaming hardwood floors.

"Nice place," he said, "I always wondered what it looked like inside." He crossed his legs and continued, "A bit clinical though, don't you think? I presume it was all put here by a decorator – there's not a single personal item in sight."

"Isaac…" she said in a voice that did not sound as commanding as she wanted it to.

He held the wine glass to the light and carried on as though she hadn't spoken, "This wine is mediocre. You should let me choose for you."

Irritation helped Katie find her voice. She retorted, "Well, yes, we all know that you're a wine snob. I find it perfectly to my taste. Now answer my question."

For the first time, he looked her straight in the eye, and Katie felt her neck hairs prickle. There was something dark and unpredictable in those eyes, and bitterness in his voice, when he said, "Eight years, Kate. Eight years we've worked together, supposedly been friends. And not once have you invited me here. Not once!" He jerked his thumb towards the bedroom behind him, "How many men have you fucked in there?"

Katie was stunned. Hot rage bubbled up in her, "How dare you? It's none of …"

Again, he ignored her and carried on, "And me. Not even so much as a coffee or a drink – let alone a meal." He leaped out of the chair and crossed the room in a few strides, "How do you think that makes me feel, Kate? Isn't that what they taught you in all your behavioral science classes, to be mindful of people's feelings?"

Katie's mind was reeling. She could not think of anything to say as she tried to process what was going on. She wondered how much he'd drunk. His normally boyish face had taken on a blotchy color. He leaned forward and enunciated every word, "Well? Let's talk about feelings. *My* feelings."

Katie shrank back. She steadied herself on the kitchen counter and tried to focus her breathing; tried to remember everything she'd ever learned about anger management and diffusing potentially violent situations. It

271

all seemed so logical in the training sessions, but now her mind was blank.

"Isaac," she managed, "I can see that you're upset, but this is no way to resolve–"

"Upset!" He barked and slammed his fist on the counter, inches from her hand. She jumped. "Upset doesn't even begin to describe it." He waved his arm in an expansive gesture and then pointed his finger right under her nose, "*You* second guess my decisions and actions. Your father treats me like his boot licker when in fact, I do *everything*. I plan the services, oversee the systems, the whole operation. I find money and contractors for his grand schemes. Hell, I feed him just about every word that comes out of his mouth. Without me, he'd be an empty vessel." He closed his eyes momentarily, then fixed her with a stare, "I am not upset; I'm pissed off beyond belief. I'm sick and tired of being taken for granted and treated like a nobody."

Katie tried to soothe him, "You know my father is very appreciative; he's always viewed you as the son he never had."

Isaac snorted, "Rubbish! The only things he cares about are the church and you. During the trip to Africa, when CAFCA prodded him about succession, he didn't say a word in my defense." He breathed deeply, and Katie was relieved to see that he appeared to have regained some measure of control over his emotions. He continued, "I've invested years of my life in the Church and its businesses; I'm not going be tossed aside. From now on, I'm taking control."

Katie chose her words carefully, "I think this business with CAFCA has thrown us all a bit off balance. As I said on Sunday, I'd really like to better understand what ..."

He was back in her face, growling, his features distorted with anger, "Sunday morning was the last time that you use that imperial tone with me. Who do you think I am? Your servant? Your slave?" His face was flushed and he spat out the words, "I demand that you give me the respect I deserve!"

Katie involuntarily stepped back, but Isaac gripped her wrist and held it.

"Isaac," she gasped. "You're hurting me. I don't know what's gotten into you. Please..."

He gave a short, hollow laugh, "You put on the image of St. Katherine for all the world, but you don't fool me, Kate Blanchard; you are a common harlot, a whore…"

Katie slapped him with her free hand, "How dare you?!" She pulled her arm with all her strength, but his hand gripped it like a vice.

Isaac continued, "I have hours of video footage of you in that shameful red wig, picking up strangers – married men – and bringing them back here for your carnal pleasure. What would the world say, what would Pastor Jeremiah say, if those videos were released?"

Katie tried to hide her shock. Her eyes flitted about the room. Were there hidden cameras inside the apartment, inside her bedroom? The thought horrified and angered her. She tried to keep her voice level, "My private life is my business."

"Ah, but that's where you're wrong. You're wrong on two counts. Firstly, you're in the public eye, so the public deems it their right to know the real Kate Blanchard. And secondly," he paused, "you're destined to be mine."

"What?" she gasped, but he didn't seem to notice. There was a frightening fervor in his voice when he continued, "You and I are going to be married. Can't you see – it's our destiny, it always has been. We're the power couple who will take the Church of Holy Redemption from its humble beginnings to being a global force." His eyes shone as he looked right through her at his vision of the future.

Katie's mind was a maelstrom of astonishment, fear and anger. She tried to process the revelation that Isaac, whom she had only ever thought of as a colleague, a friend or a substitute brother, harbored these intense feelings for her. But they were not feelings of affection or love; he merely thought of her as the queen in an elaborate chess game that had been festering behind his genial façade. She could only imagine his vision; the hunger for power, money, influence.

She kept her eyes down. Her survival instinct told her to avoid confrontation, buy time, and learn more.

He said, "Luckily for you, I'm prepared to forgive your whoring and sinning. But that will end right now. You will learn to obey me, and we will do great things together."

Part of Katie wanted to burst out laughing, and part of her was afraid that Isaac was on drugs and might hurt her. She said, "Isaac, I'm very flattered; I never knew that you had such strong feelings for me. But the future you see with me is an illusion – this isn't going to happen. Please, let's just forget that this conversation ever …"

He yanked her from behind the counter and roughly pulled her into the lounge, where he commanded, "Sit!" He pushed her down into a chair and said, "You and I are going to watch a bit of *very interesting* TV, and then we'll see who's living in the real world and who's living a delusional lie."

"Isaac…"

"Shut up," he interrupted. He flicked on the TV with the remote, and pressed a button on his laptop. Katie noticed that his computer was set up on her coffee table and already wirelessly connected to her TV. How on earth? It gave her chills to think how meticulously Isaac had planned this invasion.

The screen was filled with gray static, and then a picture of a study emerged. The washed-out colors and a faint hum pronounced this to be a home video. A date stamp appeared in the bottom right of the picture: 31 October 1997. There was something familiar about the room, but before Katie could fully place it, her mother stepped into the scene, sat behind the desk, and held up the crossed fingers of both hands. It was such a familiar gesture that it hit Katie like a blow to the stomach.

On-screen, Amelia Blanchard smiled with the upheld fingers and said, "Well, I hope this works, given my challenges with technology."

She folded her hands on the desk in front of her and spoke straight into the camera, "Darling Katie; if ever you get to see this video, then one thing is for certain – I will have died." She shrugged and smiled, "You know death holds no fear for me. I would just be very sorry to miss seeing you grow up and seeing you shape your life. Whatever it is you choose to do – career, family, both – nothing would have given me greater pleasure than to be your cheerleader-in-chief and maybe a source of advice." She chuckled, "Or at least to comfort you when you hit the bumps in the road that are an inevitable part of life."

Katie had almost forgotten about Isaac. Tears blurred her vision. This was so unexpected, surreal. Amelia looked vibrant and full of life. Katie felt like she could reach out and touch her mother. She glanced again at the date stamp. In 1997 her mother would have been thirty-nine, not that much older than Katie was now. God, how she missed her mother.

Amelia said, "I probably should have made some notes, got my story straight. You know how your father always says I ramble – especially when I'm a little nervous." She gave a small laugh, bit her lip, and stared sideways out towards a window. The view from that window was etched into Katie's memory; it was as though she was looking through her mother's eyes at the small, neat garden, the pine trees and a golden-brown hill stretching off to the horizon, maybe with a pair of Kestrels circling above, searching for prey. Katie had often sat across the desk from her mother to do her homework, draw pictures, or simply just be with her. They had both been people who could enjoy quiet companionship.

Amelia started to hum a tune, and Katie felt a jolt to the heart. Her mother had had a beautiful alto voice, and she began to sing softly,

> *"Look into my eyes*
> *You will see*
> *What you mean to me..."*

Tears prickled at Katie's eyelids. She remembered the Bryan Adams song so well. It had been one of her mother's favorites. Amelia had sung it in church and had brought the whole congregation to its feet with applause.

> *"...Don't tell me it's not worth tryin' for*
> *You can't tell me it's not worth dyin' for*
> *You know it's true;* everything I do, I do it for you.*"

Her mother stressed the song's last words and folded her hands in front of her. Katie turned to Isaac, "Where did you...?"

"Listen!" he commanded.

Amelia continued, "Katie, I guess there's just no easy way to do this. I want you to hear it from me." She paused as if to gather strength, then blurted out, "Jeremiah isn't your father." She looked up into the camera and rushed ahead, the sentences tumbling out, "I know, I know – this must be a shock. I'm sure you have a million questions; I'll try to answer them. I so wish I could be there, hold you, explain to you." She sighed.

"Your father and I wanted to have a baby, and it just wasn't happening for us. You know what a proud man he is. And of course, his faith is strong." She looked up, and there was exasperation in her voice, "He kept reminding me of Abraham and Sarah but," a short, humorless laugh, "my faith wasn't strong enough to wait till I was 90 to get pregnant. Jeremiah wouldn't hear of going to a fertility clinic." She sighed. "I'll spare you the detail, but I did get a sample of his sperm tested, and the sperm count was so low that we had virtually zero chance of conceiving."

Katie was numb. At one level, she could totally understand and empathize with her mother. Jeremiah was a proud man – the thought that he might be infertile would undoubtedly have tested his faith to the limit. Where was this headed? She tried to brace herself.

Amelia looked down, her voice so soft that Katie had to strain to hear, "I went to my old college buddy, one of my best friends in the whole world, Mitch McGrath." She looked up. "The answer was so obvious to both of us – no clinic with medical records that could leak, no unknown donor. Mitch and Jeremiah have a lot in common physically…" She trailed off and sighed. "I timed it carefully, slept with him – once – and a month later, I was pregnant."

Katie was aware of Isaac's eyes boring into her, looking for a reaction. She was in turmoil but kept her expression neutral, determined not to give him any satisfaction. Her poor mother, what a secret to carry around with her.

Amelia continued, "I'm not proud of what I did, Katie, of deceiving Jeremiah. But even now, twelve years later, if I were faced with the same situation, I'd do it again in a heartbeat. And you know why?" She smiled and, despite the quality of the recording, it was as though a hand reached across the years and touched Katie. Her breath caught as she felt her mother's aura.

"Because *you* were the end product. You, who are the sun and the moon and stars – not just to me – but also to Jeremiah. What choice did I have?"

Her mother concluded, "Darling Katie, I hope you can understand and forgive me. Of course, the only other person in the world who knows this secret is Mitch. I'll give this recording to him for safekeeping with the instruction to only share it with you if there is a life-threatening medical reason for you to be informed. I don't know what that might be, but there are possibilities – he might discover a hereditary medical condition, or you might have a baby that falls in love with Chloe's child." Amelia's voice faltered, and she dabbed her eyes with a tissue. "Silly me, thinking of matchmaking your baby. Anyway, it's my choice, so please don't blame Mitch for keeping this to himself. He is fulfilling my wishes."

Amelia blew a kiss at the camera, got up from the chair, and the screen went blank.

Katie closed her eyes to stem the tears and emotion that threatened to overwhelm her. She suppressed everything except anger – anger at Isaac for betraying her mother. She rounded on him, "Where did you get this?"

He flopped into a chair opposite her and said, "What does it matter? The more important question is, what should we do with this recording?"

He sat forward, steepled his hands under his chin, and said, "If it were made available to the public, there could be very interesting consequences. For example, what would it do for the stature of the sainted Pastor Jeremiah if it became known that he is just a cuckolded old fool – God would not even grant him a child?" He pursed his lips, "That might make him contemplate an early retirement, which would open up an opportunity for…me."

"You wouldn't dare," Katie said through clenched teeth. "Have you no shame? Any damage to my father or the church would just be cutting off your own nose to spite your face."

He bobbed his head from side to side and said, "Maybe, maybe not. But of course, it is not just Jeremiah who would be impacted, but also your father – your real father – and his family. I wonder how that bitch, Eleanor McGrath, would spin this one away." He gave a dry laugh, "To see her squirm and be publicly humiliated is almost reason enough to go public."

Katie paled. Her first thoughts had been for Jeremiah and how this revelation would crush him. She hadn't even thought about Senator McGrath, Eleanor, and Chloe.

As if reading her mind, Isaac continued, "And dear Chloe, on the cusp of starting her political career in the footsteps of her fine, upstanding father. Suddenly the whole family comes under suspicion and scrutiny. Stoke that a little with the concerns about her ex-husband and his family, and I think Chloe's political career would be stillborn."

Katie closed her eyes and let her head fall into her hands. She sighed, "What do you want?"

"Marry me," he said.

"No, Isaac. I mean, what do you really want? You don't actually love me; heck, I don't know whether you even like me? Whether we're even friends anymore. This," she gestured at the computer, "isn't something you do to a person you want to spend the rest of your life with. I don't think you would even do it to a person you dislike – you actually have to hate a person…"

She opened her eyes and looked directly at him. "Is that it? You hate me? You hate me enough to inflict whatever hurt you can?"

He returned her gaze and said, "In this world, you have to fight for what you want. I want you, and believe me, Katie," an innocent-looking smile curled at the corners of his mouth, "I will stop at nothing to get you."

His words were in such contrast to the boyish smile that her blood ran cold. In the space of half an hour, she'd had to reverse all her perceptions of this man. Isaac's helpfulness, his sweet smile, they were all a façade. Every time she had thought he was being nice, he had, in fact, been inwardly seething, feeding his hatred. How could she have missed it? She sighed and got up, "I think we're done here. Do your damndest – give the tape to the press – whatever. I'm not going to be held hostage by this information for the rest of my life. I think you underestimate the Christian spirit of our following. This will change nothing in the long run. I'll call Jeremiah and Mitch in the morning and give them a heads-up." She gestured to the door, "I think you know your way out."

Katie did not feel half as confident as she had tried to act, and, to her horror, Isaac's smile broadened as he lounged back, showing not the slightest inclination to leave. *What the heck do I do, scream? Run for the door and call the police?*

Isaac clapped his hands in mock applause, "Bravo, what a performance. Just as well you didn't take up acting as a career. You suck at it. You know those TV infomercials where they say, 'But wait, that's not everything. There's more?'" He pointed at her seat and continued, "Do sit. You'll love this next piece."

He paused dramatically, and it flashed across Katie's mind that, if she'd had a gun in her hand, she would have shot him right there and then. She was shocked by the vehemence of her anger and revulsion. What was the man up to? What else could he have dug up? As she sat, Isaac worked the computer. The unassuming front cover of an academic dissertation appeared on the screen. The paper seemed dog-eared and grimy, and had been folded. Who folds up a dissertation?

Katie paled as she read, "Shaping human behavior through data analytics and predictive modeling." The subheading was, "Research conducted by Katherine Blanchard and Rajiv Patel in fulfilling the requirements for a master's degree in behavioral psychology at the East Bay University of Oakland, California. July 2013. Thesis supervisor – Professor Sean Curry."

Katie shot a glance heavenward, *Dear God, not the investigation. Please, please, don't tell me he found a copy of the investigation.*

Out of the corner of her eye, she saw the look of triumph on Isaac's face, and she knew her prayers were in vain. He advanced the screen, and a similar page appeared, though this one had the word "confidential" stamped across it in large, blood-red letters.

The title on the page read,

"Investigation of the collateral damage attributable to a research experiment conducted at East Bay University, Oakland, California.

Aug 2013. Author – Professor Sean Curry."

"Original study title…" Katie didn't need to read it. She closed her eyes and was transported back to 2013, when she had been a conscientious, bright-eyed student, determined to make the world a better place, or more specifically, to help her father and his church make the world a better place. She and Rajiv had complemented each other from day one, and Professor Curry had encouraged the collaboration of his two star students. Rajiv had an incredible brain for computers, data and analytics. Katie had a deep understanding of human behavior and, through growing up in the shadow of Pastor Jeremiah, a profound belief and passion for shaping that behavior. How naïve she'd been, believing that everyone had a vast store of goodness – that one just needed to nudge them to unlock it, let their better nature shine through. And thus, they had started to hypothesize about the minimum "nudge" people needed to do the right thing. She knew now, with hindsight, that what they had embarked on was blackmail, plain and simple. Dig up dirt about people and see how long they could resist the escalating threat of exposure before they caved in and modified their behavior.

It had not felt like it at the time. They had seen themselves engaged in a grand social experiment to quantify the relative strength of levers. Were people more concerned about having their tax evasion exposed or the fact that they'd cheated on their spouses? How much were they willing to pay to hide the fact that they lied on resumes, or that they had a misdemeanor against their name, or that they had a communicable disease? Social media was like the Wild West, and someone like Rajiv could trawl through it and come up with a net bursting full of squirming fish any day of the week. It was easy to find information to "leverage".

They set out to develop an index by which one could mathematically compute how much pressure an individual needed, on a scale from 1 to 10, to change their behavior. It was positioned as something a religious institution like the Church of Redemption might use to guide errant members of the flock back onto the straight and narrow. A service to society, a way to reduce everything from petty theft and embezzlement to wife-beating. The proposal seemed innocent enough and was endorsed by the EBU ethics board.

Katie remembered the long and admittedly-exhilarating hours she and Rajiv spent working on the project. Rajiv's algorithms dug through the details of thousands of students in the Cal system until they could identify a list of one hundred study subjects. Then they started their campaign of reaching out to apply pressure. The term "collection bureau" was invented – an innocuous-sounding organization that could help make problems go away for a small fee and a promise to mend one's behavior.

They worked all summer, monitoring responses. Who pushed back and argued, who just paid up, who ignored a first request, a second request, or even a third request? And most importantly, who went to the authorities to complain? That was one of the key research objectives: "How far can you push someone to modify their behavior before they rebel and withdraw from your influence?" The individuals who rebelled were deemed collateral damage, and hence the *COLD index* was born.

Katie rubbed her arms. She had goosebumps and was feeling nauseous, but she couldn't suppress the memory of what came next. She could still see the headline in the San Francisco Chronicle: *Summer Suicide Epidemic among Cal Students.* According to the newspaper, there had been an inexplicable spate of suicides – three, to be exact. No one could understand why. The Cal system was accused of everything from excessive academic stress to financial pressure and lack of support. But the students came from various walks of life with different financial means and varying academic abilities. It was a mystery.

It was a mystery to everyone except the three shell-shocked individuals poring over the article in Professor Curry's study. A whole new category of collateral damage stared them in the face. How could they have been so stupid, so irresponsible? They hadn't thought through the possibility that some people, before reaching out to authorities, would simply fall into despair and commit suicide. Three out of a hundred. Katie still felt physically ill whenever she thought about it. She'd murdered these people as sure as if she'd put poison into the cafeteria's food or shot into a crowd with an assault rifle.

She had wanted to run to her father, to the police, the chancellor. Anywhere she could confess her crime and unburden herself. But the professor had stopped her, and had insisted that they owed it to the suicide victims to conduct an investigation and fully understand what happened before considering a course of action.

Four weeks, four weeks in which they had barely slept. Rajiv had churned through mountains of data on the suicide victims to look for unrelated causes – desperate to find some common thread. But it always came back to their research.

Initially, Katie had pleaded with Professor Curry to destroy the research – delete it, burn it, throw their computers off the Golden Gate Bridge. But the professor countered that human knowledge could not be undone, just channeled. "You cannot undo the discovery of the atom or of DNA, but you can promote a thorough understanding of the dangers." He was obsessive in his desire that, at the very least, the tragedy be used to fine-tune the mathematical models and to build in more safeguards. They had dug through the data, supplemented it with more, picked up on social media and other clues that they'd missed, and had then come up with models that would have predicted the suicides. The new models were simply referred to as the COLD index. Professor Curry personally wrote the investigation report.

Katie looked up at that screen. The last time she had seen this document was on the day that Professor Curry took it to the University's Chancellor on a sunny afternoon at 4:00 p.m. She'd been so wrung out and exhausted by then that she did not care what happened to her – expulsion, jail, being stoned to death in front of the students' union. It all seemed appropriate and reasonable to her. She had just wanted it to be over and done with.

She and Rajiv had waited. By 6 p.m., they had started to get worried; at 7 p.m., they dared send the professor a text. No answer. Katie felt bile rising in her throat at the memory of the anxiety. She had convinced herself that the professor had been summarily thrown into jail, or that he had committed suicide in solidarity with the victims or, at the very least, been hit by a car.

When professor Curry did walk in at 7:35 p.m., it was clear that he'd had a few drinks. He had sunk into a chair like a man ten years his senior and had stared into space until Katie had squeaked in a small voice, "What did the chancellor say? What's going to happen to us?"

The faraway look had found her face and focused. Then, in the precise tones of someone trying to hide his drunkenness, the professor had said, "Nothing, nyet, nada."

Rajiv and Katie had exchanged glances, and the professor had continued in a voice mimicking the chancellor's, "Despite the investigation, we are of the opinion that there is no definitive causal relationship between this research and the unfortunate spate of suicides. From time to time, there will be unexpected outcomes to research, but such is the nature of science and progress. I need not remind you that the physicist J.R. Oppenheimer, father of the atomic bomb, did much of his research a stone's throw away from here at Berkeley. So, a case like this is not without precedent."

He'd looked from Katie to Rajiv and back before continuing in his own voice, "The modified algorithm will be designated as 'anonymous student research output'. All the supporting documentation is to be destroyed. You will both get your degrees based on coursework presented, and I," he paused, "I will take a sabbatical."

"You mean…" Katie had asked, "That's it? That's all...surely…"

"Believe me, Katie," the professor had said. "We will suffer consequences. One consequence is not being given credit for our research. The second, well, it depends on how strong your conscience is."

That was the last time she had seen Professor Curry. He'd gone off on his sabbatical and had simply disappeared. She had often thought of his words, though – especially when she woke up sweat-drenched from the nightmares that had been her constant companions for the last decade.

Isaac broke into her thoughts, "So, my darling Katie, we were talking about living in the real world." He pointed at the photograph of the Golden Gate Bridge and said, "I guess this is a daily reminder, a kind of penitence?"

She said nothing and wondered whether Rajiv ever looked at the small framed photograph of the Golden Gate Bridge she had given him when they had both sworn tearfully to Professor Curry that they would use the algorithms for good.

Isaac said, "Don't you think it might be cathartic for you if you could share the burdens of your past with someone; someone with whom you are bound together, in a bond of absolute trust – with your husband?"

Katie looked at him and, for the first time that evening, there was a glimmer of the old Isaac – a good friend through thick and thin. And when he put it like that, the thought of sharing the burden of her guilt was enticing. She sighed.

Isaac got up, and there was compassion in his voice when he said, "I know this is a lot to process. I'll give you a few days."

She was too numb to say anything and just nodded.

At the door, he turned and said, "Katie, in your mother's words, everything I do, I do for you."

He flashed her a boyish smile and was about to leave when she said, "Isaac?"

He paused and looked at her.

Katie cleared her throat. She was almost too scared to ask the question, but she had to know, "Tell me honestly, since those first three…victims, have there been more?"

He avoided her eyes and, even before he answered her, realization swept over her, *oh, God, no. Please no*. She had persuaded herself that the algorithms had been tuned down to a level where collateral damage was restricted to the odd letter of inquiry or protest.

Isaac shrugged and said, "A few. We keep tuning the algorithm. There haven't been any suicides in the last six months."

He turned and closed the door as Katie's world imploded. She heard her mother's voice, not kind and supportive, but full of sarcasm, "It is okay to make a mistake once and learn from it. But to make the same mistake again and again…"

Katie took one of the plush seat cushions and hugged it. She rocked back and forth while the images and emotions of the evening ricocheted through her mind like bullets in the saloon of a western movie. Her brain felt like it was going to explode. All these years Jeremiah had been under the illusion that it was his charisma and God's will that had kept the money coming in, "with a little bit of help from the behavior modification program." He had trusted her implicitly and it had suited her not to dispel his belief. Meanwhile, she had trusted Isaac.

Oh God, what a fool, I've been. If only I had come clean to Dad years ago. If only I had paid more close attention. If it all comes out now, the lawsuits and negative publicity will destroy the church and that will crush father. It will make all our lives pointless.

Katie slid onto her side and curled up in a fetal position. She had just progressed to the ranks of a mass murderer. A part of her was numb with shock. A part was relieved that the terrible secret was out. It had been a festering boil waiting to burst for years. Isaac had taken a lance to it. But he'd also taken a lance to the heart of Katie Blanchard. There was no Katie Blanchard. Who was she anyway if she wasn't her father's daughter? How was she going to tell him – and Mitch?

She pressed her face into the cushion and tried to stifle her sobs. But, once she had started, there was no stopping. Katie wept.

Chapter 24, Renaissance Institute

Wednesday, 2nd Week of July

KATIE

Since her encounter with Isaac two days earlier, Katie had barely eaten or slept. She was exhausted and labored under the weight of the ticking clock Isaac had set off. After the weekend, he would want a decision. The last thirty-six hours had been agonizing, and the dark cloud that enveloped her got heavier with every minute.

She had raged at his impertinence and the betrayal of her trust. But by the second morning, a numb acceptance had started to set in. Isaac held all the cards. How could she refuse when she factored in the consequences for Jeremiah, the church, for Mitch and Chloe – and for Eleanor? Oh God, how would Eleanor react to the revelation that her husband had fathered a child with another woman? What would it do to the memory of her mother? And Katie had to consider BDA and its hundreds of employees; and Rajiv – a loyal friend. Her head spun as she imagined the ever-increasing circle of implications that would sprout from

Isaac's revelation. Like blight hitting the land, turning everything good and green to dust.

Katie left Dr. Roberts's office at the Renaissance Institute and sighed. Why was this so difficult? Dr. Roberts had been sympathetic but had cited any number of federal and state laws pertaining to minors. It was frustrating and ridiculous. No wonder there were so many troubled youngsters and strained family relationships. The system was broken.

She walked out into the heat and paused when she reached her car. She didn't want to go back to work in Tracy; she couldn't bear the thought of bumping into Isaac – or her father, *who isn't my father*. Nor did she want to go back to her apartment. Katie was overcome by the extent of her loneliness. She felt like she stood on a tiny outcrop in a sea of lava. There was nowhere to go and no one she could confide in. The heat was creeping through the soles of her shoes. *For God's sake, make a decision, woman*, she scolded herself. *You cannot just stand here and fry.*

Suddenly, music came from the little square church and Katie remembered that the stone building was wonderfully cool in summer. She walked inside and slid onto a pew at the back. Five young men were rehearsing gospel songs. One of them looked familiar. Only when she heard his voice did she recognize him as Gerald Myers, the man who was supposed to sing at the big service on Sunday.

Katie closed her eyes and listened to the familiar melodies. When they struck up *Nobody Knows the Trouble I've Seen* in perfect three-part harmony, tears leaked from her eyes and she thought of her mother. The video reeled off in her mind, over and over again. *If only you'd told me, Mom. What am I supposed to do with this information now? Tell Dad? Go to Chloe, throw my arms around her and say, "Hi, guess what, I'm your sister – for real!" Who am I now anyway? My life is a lie. Why did you make that stupid tape? What good did you think could possibly come out of it?*

The music shifted to *Bridge Over Troubled Waters.* The irony of it. A part of her kept marveling at the quality of the singing. These young men were good. Then her mind raced back to the confrontation with Isaac. She wanted to retreat from the memory, but it held the morbid fascination of a car crash or a burning building.

The singers finished their rehearsal and, as they left the church, she felt a wave of panic and wanted to call after them, "Don't leave me here alone." But instead, she sank back into her seat and stared at the stained glass window. Anything to distract her mind from the grinning Isaac, who now didn't only infest her dreams but even intruded on her waking hours. Was she losing her grip on reality? Images of her father, Chloe, Amelia, Mitch and Eleanor rushed at her in a babel of voices. She shut her eyes tightly and put her hands to her ears, but the noise only intensified. Finally, another group of pictures rose in her mind – seven, to be exact – and Katie shrank back further, tears streaming from her eyes, "I'm sorry, I am so sorry."

That morning she had delved into the highly-secured inner sanctum of *The Settlement Bureau*'s computer systems to confirm what Isaac had already told her. There had been more suicides. There had also been a string of out-of-court settlements, gag orders, and non-disclosure agreements to contain collateral damage. But the most shocking thing had been the list of four more deaths. In her purse, she carried a list of seven names. That piece of paper weighed a ton and would inflict a fresh paper cut to her soul every day for the rest of her life. And the worst of it was that Lily Reynolds was one of the latest victims. Lily, her best friend's sister-in-law. It was unfathomable. How could she ever again look Chloe or Terry in the eye, knowing that she could and should have prevented Lily's death?

I can't even ask their forgiveness, she thought. *All I can do is join them in solidarity.*

Katie was startled when she heard a few guitar chords. Gerald had not left with the others. He sat on a stool, and a shaft of light illuminated him from behind, giving him an ethereal quality. His voice drifted through the sanctuary to touch Katie.

> *"What if God was one of us?*
> *Just a slob like one of us*
> *Just a stranger on the bus*
> *Tryin' to make his way home?"*

Gerald seemed to be in his own world, and Katie was ridiculously thankful for the presence of another human being. When she regained her composure and opened her eyes, Gerald sat beside her. His face betrayed no emotion, as though it was the most natural thing in the world to have a woman in the throes of a breakdown right next to him. No judgment, not even concern, just acceptance. His eyes radiated the type of compassion that she had only ever seen in the wisest and oldest of people.

"Do you want to talk about it?" he asked.

Of course not, she wanted to shout. *Don't be ridiculous; you're half my age. I'm fine.*

"You don't have to tell me; you can tell God," he said, and his voice reminded her of a time she had burned her hand in the kitchen. Her mother had sprayed on a cooling salve that couldn't immediately heal the wound, but oh, it had felt good. When she remained quiet, he smiled and got up to leave. Katie didn't know what possessed her. She appeared to have lost control of her own body because her hand reached out and touched his arm while her mouth said, "Please stay. I'd rather talk to you. God seems… a little distant these days."

And once she started to talk, she couldn't stop. Never in her life had she bared her soul so completely to another human being. It was an out-of-body experience, to look down on herself and see herself sharing her deepest secrets. No one was more surprised than Katie herself. She told the young man about her complicity in causing, and then covering up, the deaths of three innocent people. And when he didn't recoil in horror or run screaming for the doors, it gave her the slightest glimmer of hope that maybe she wasn't a total monster. And that hope was like a drug; it lifted the dark clouds just a little. She wanted more of it, so she kept unburdening herself like a balloonist shedding ballast to try and avoid a crash landing.

The sun had moved around to one of the west facing windows when she turned to him and said, "It's ironic, really. All I ever wanted was to be like my mother – strong, free-spirited, supportive of my father's mission. He once said to me that she was the rock on which his life, his mission, 'God's work', was built. And now...? I'm nothing like my mother. Everything my father has built in the name of God is going to go to pieces."

Gerald had not interrupted her once in all the time she had spoken. He hadn't asked a single question – he had just let her talk. Now, he said, "God can take care of his own mission. Neither you nor your father needs to put it on yourselves to fight his battles for him."

Tears flowed from her eyes and she said, "I never really cared that much about 'the mission' – I just wanted my father to need me, to be proud of me, to lean on me the way he leaned on my mother." She blew her nose into a crumpled tissue and asked in a small voice, "What should I do?"

He was silent for so long that she thought he was going to ignore the question. But then he said, "The more important question is: who are you, Katie?"

Gerald took both her hands in his and looked at her intently, "Irrespective of your parents, your upbringing, your past successes and mistakes, who is the person that only you can see? The person that you want to be for the rest of your life. What would that Katie do?"

There was something about his hands. Despite the apocalypse in her mind, Katie was conscious of their strength. Not the grip; it was a different kind of strength. She took a deep breath and said, "If I recorded a video message and wanted it released to the world at a specific time, how would I do that?"

"I'm sure your IT people can help distribute..."

"No," she interrupted. "No one must know in advance. They'd quell and sabotage it." There was a hint of the old, decisive Katie in her voice when she said, "I want to record the message here and now, and I want it released this Sunday during the church service. Will you help me?"

He thought for a moment, then nodded, "We'll need help from my friend, Timothy; he's an internet whizz. Is that okay?"

By the time the two young men returned with an iPhone, Katie had settled herself on Gerald's stool in front of the altar. She had splashed water on her face and brushed her hair. Her hands, which held a single sheet of paper, were steady.

When Timothy gave the thumbs up, she began, "Many of you know me as Katie Blanchard, Public Relations Officer of the Church of Holy Redemption. I have a confession to make." Her voice faltered and her throat constricted, but one look at Gerald strengthened her resolve and she continued, "In fact, I have several confessions to make."

Katie spoke for ten minutes before she got to the list of names. She did not need the piece of paper – the names were seared into her soul. She spoke them one by one before ending with, "There is no excuse for what I have done. Words cannot express how sorry I am."

Then she sat motionless until Timothy turned off the iPhone. None of them spoke, but the silence was more companionable than it was awkward. Finally, Katie turned to Timothy and said, "I seem to recall your case. You got into trouble for computer hacking. You're quite the genius in that space, aren't you?"

Timothy shot a look in Gerald's direction before nodding.

Katie said, "I've never concerned myself much with the physical protection of information; there were always other people who took care of that. But do you think it is feasible to unleash a virus or something that would corrupt and destroy all of our computer systems? I want this abomination rooted out once and for all."

Timothy beamed, "It would be easier than you might think, especially since Mykyta and I already have full access."

Katie looked from one to the other, and Gerald quickly filled her in on how they'd stumbled on a back entrance to the cave and how Danny had come into possession of Isaac's phone, which had given them all the passwords needed to access the system.

She felt the strangest sensation, as though her body and soul were being inflated. Another, almost forgotten feeling rose up in her – laughter! For the first time in days, she laughed. She shook her head and said, "There is a God in heaven after all."

Timothy stared at her and said, "That makes no sense at all. That is not a logical deduction."

Katie got off her stool, gave Gerald a hug, and Timothy a kiss on the cheek, "Now listen, Sunday at 10:30 a.m., I want you to release that video to the world, and then unleash the meanest virus you can find to destroy the entire computer system. Can you do that?"

Timothy nodded.

"Good," Katie said, "and not a word to anyone. I trust you completely."

She walked out into the afternoon sun and took a deep breath of the fresh mountain air.

Chapter 25, San Francisco

Thursday, 2nd Week of July

TERRY

Terry rubbed his eyes and tried to focus on the computer monitor in front of him. Every muscle in his upper body hurt. He got up to stretch and cast a longing look in the direction of the windows, where the late-afternoon sun reflected off a neighboring building. He thought of Charlie, who was still at the animal hospital, though he was out of immediate danger. He really needed to make time to visit.

An IM message pinged on his screen.

Rajiv: *Those CAFCA people are on my neck. When will you have the analysis?*

Terry: *15 minutes.*

Rajiv: *Thx, I owe you.*

Twelve minutes later, Rajiv was at Terry's desk. He looked like he needed a shave, and the wrinkles in his shirt gave the impression that he'd slept in the clothes he was wearing. He motioned for Terry to follow him into a huddle room. As soon as the door was shut, he crumpled into a chair and started to massage his temples. "I don't know how much more of this crap I can take. That Ronnie character from CAFCA is there *all* the time – literally peering over my shoulder. And I can't get hold of Katie. I can't believe that she's okay with this." He banged his hand on the table. "They're going to ruin everything we've built. How could Isaac and the old man have been so stupid? So greedy?"

Terry waited.

Rajiv continued, "I'm sorry that I've dumped all this extra work on you. You're one of the few people I can trust." He waved in the direction of the cubicles outside and said, "Most of them are good kids, but they have no sense of perspective or what's at stake. They'd blab on social media or run to MSNBC if they had any sense of where CAFCA is trying to push us."

"What are we going to do?" Terry asked.

Rajiv looked out the window, "We have to stall and contain the damage as best we can. You're an outstanding analyst." He smiled sardonically, "Too good; my eyes popped when I saw the detail of your last report on those two senators. Makes one lose faith in humanity. I want you to dial it back, and then I want you to start digging up whatever you can find about these fucking CAFCA guys themselves. Nothing via email, though. Give it to me on a flash drive."

Terry said, "I'll do my damnedest." He looked at his watch, "I just have time for a quick edit of the senators' analyses, and then I have to get over to the hospital to see old Joe...I mean Prof Curry."

Rajiv said, "I'm such an ass; I haven't even asked – how is the prof? I still can't believe that he's been here under our noses all this time. Katie and I were convinced that he'd gone off to Greece. He was always on about the Greek philosophers, Greek governance, Greek warfare – everything worth knowing the Greeks had figured out."

"He's regained consciousness, but he's totally out of it. Doesn't know where he is or what happened. He gets me and his son confused, which is why Clyde's asked me to come by. I'm going to take the night shift – give Clyde a break and a chance to go home for a sleep and a shave. Talking of which…"

"Yeah, yeah," Rajiv said. "I probably smell like ripe cheese." He got up, "Thanks, man; I don't know what I'd do without you."

Terry wrapped up the edits and called an Uber. He picked up three poke bowls en route to the hospital. This made him an instant hero when he met up with Clyde and Sandy in the waiting room. They ate their dinner, Sandy went off for a smoke, and Clyde filled Terry in on the professor's condition. There were hopeful signs that the swelling on the professor's brain was receding; he had appeared to be remarkably lucid for a twenty-minute spell.

Clyde rubbed his chin. "I just don't know what to believe anymore, but my father seems to think it was a targeted attack to steal research papers, which he'd been carrying around with him for nearly a decade. Can you imagine, all this time he was hoarding a single paper copy of the COLD index research that was supposed to be destroyed."

"Did you know that he was on the streets all this time?"

Clyde nodded, "For the first two years, I had regular contact with him and tried desperately to get him to come home to me. But then…I got to understand that, for him, it was a kind of penance for something that had gone horribly wrong. He never told me the full detail, but it consumed him. After a while, bit by bit, I saw that he was coping out on the streets." He gave a hollow laugh, "He even seemed to have friends, a community – that was novel. You must understand that, when I grew up, he was a distant presence in his cocoon of intellectual superiority – not to be disturbed by a pesky kid or any mundane everyday concerns." He sighed, "So it was kind of strange, in a good way, to see him being human."

Sandy rejoined them, and they speculated at length about who might have attacked the professor, but couldn't come to any conclusions. Of course, they suspected BDA, but Terry was unconvinced. Why now? Rajiv seemed to have genuine liking and respect for the professor and had been as surprised as anyone to find that the Nobel laureate had been living on the streets. If it was BDA, it was a rogue element not sanctioned by Rajiv.

The hospital's pulse had slowed into a dimly-lit near-sleep when Sandy dragged Clyde to his feet and said, "I'm going to take you home and put you to bed. Terry can let us know if anything changes – won't you?"

Terry nodded.

At the door, Clyde turned and said, "Thank you; I really appreciate the way you've stepped in to help. Hopefully, tomorrow we can get my dad to fill in a few of the blanks. It's like I can just about touch the full picture, but every time I reach out, it wriggles out of my hands."

***

Something disturbed Terry's sleep. He had to grope through a thicket of the mind before he could piece together why he sat in a lounger in a dark hospital room. He felt the vibration in his pocket and retrieved his cell phone, 4:02 a.m. Who the hell would call him at four in the morning?

"Hello," he whispered, his voice as dry as a Californian creek in October. He cleared his throat and kept an eye on the professor. Something was wrong; the old man was groaning.

"Is this Mr. Reynolds?" The caller spoke in the South African accent that Terry had come to recognize over the past few days. "I just wanted to give you an update..."

Terry was alarmed, not by the voice on the phone, but by the sight of Professor Curry. The old man had ripped away his bedsheets and was thrashing about, froth at his mouth. Then Terry noticed that the monitor, which had been turned to silent mode, was furiously flashing red alarms.

"Nurse!" he called and rushed into the corridor, "Nurse!"

The voice on the phone was indignant, "No, no, I am not a nurse, I am doctor–"

"Sorry," Terry said, "I have a crisis here. Just tell me, is my father okay?"

"Yes, he is still sedated but expected to make a full recovery. We just ..."

Terry saw the nurse hurrying down the corridor and waved. He said, "Doctor, I don't mean to be rude, but this is a terrible time; I'll call in the morning."

He hung up and turned to the bed, instinctively trying to help the nurse restrain the professor's convulsing body. She was forcing some object into Joe's mouth.

"What's happening?" Terry asked.

"He's having a seizure. Dr. Wong said this might happen. He's going to need surgery to relieve the pressure on his brain. I need to stay with him. Can you please ask my colleague to page the on-call neuro surgeon and alert the OR?"

Terry did as he was told.

Twenty minutes later, he sat alone in the darkened room, staring at the void where the professor's bed had been before the orderlies had wheeled him out. Absurdly, the combination of dim light, empty space, and his own sweating palms made him think of his first school dance in the gym when he'd tried to pluck up the courage to ask Mandy de Vos for a dance. He shook his head and deliberated whether he should call Clyde. It was 4:30 a.m. Clyde could do nothing, and the man hadn't had any significant sleep in days. Still, if it was his father; wouldn't he want to know? Instantly Terry was overcome by guilt. He hadn't been particularly interested to find out how his father was doing. In fact, he had been far more concerned about a man he'd only known in passing as a vagrant. God, he was a bad son. And then he remembered that he still hadn't done anything about Danny, and his guilt mushroomed into a physical presence, threatening to choke him.

Terry lurched out of the chair and switched on the lights to dispel the demons. He scrolled through his messages, hoping to find something from Katie to tell him he could talk to his brother. Nothing. He sighed. *This Sunday – no matter what – this Sunday I am going to rent a car and, right after Chloe's coming out event at the church, I am going to drive to the Renaissance Institute.* It was ridiculous to deny him access to his brother. He would do whatever it took. Bring in a lawyer, call the media, camp at their gates. He would not leave till they let him speak to Danny.

With that decision made, Terry could breathe a little easier. He texted Clyde and Sandy.

Chapter 26, Renaissance Institute
Saturday, 2nd Week of July

DANNY

Danny tried to resist the force propelling him from a delicious dream into consciousness. He kept his eyes shut, desperate to prolong the warm feeling of his sibling's admiration. In his dream, the three of them were roommates – equals. They'd been out all day on a lake, fishing, swimming, and sunbathing. He had beat Terry at basketball while Lily had cheered them on and laughed; laughed as only Lily could. The birds had stopped singing to listen to her laughter.

And that evening, in the cozy kitchen of their cabin by the lake, Danny had cooked for them – herb and nut-crusted fish with roasted vegetables and mashed potatoes. Terry had said it was the best meal he'd ever had. After dinner, they'd sat on the porch and let the serenity of the lake and the mountains beyond wash over them. They passed around a joint, which he had provided. The smell of marijuana filled the air.

Danny's eyes flew open, "What the…Timothy? What the fuck are you doing? Give me that. You can't smoke in here."

He leaped out of bed, snatched the joint from Timothy, and threw open the windows.

Timothy looked at him, actually looked at him, and said, "Your hair." He chuckled and pointed at Danny, "You look like a rooster."

Oh God, Danny thought. *I've had to deal with morbid Timothy, stubborn Timothy, fraternizing-with-Russian-hackers Timothy, and now stoned Timothy.* He guided his roommate to the bathroom and instructed him to shower. Guttural noises, that might have been construed as song, mixed with the sound of running water. Danny sprayed Axe deodorant around the room and attempted to remove ash and other evidence as he tried to suppress his anxiety. If Timothy ended up in the "cooler"… Fuck! He couldn't let that happen. Thank God it was Dr. Roberts on duty for the weekend. Danny had spotted the doctor's Tesla the previous evening and persuaded himself that the doctor wouldn't allow Timothy to be locked up. But still, he decided to forego his run, stay in the room, and keep an eye on Timothy.

An hour later, Timothy was sufficiently recovered that Danny could leave him for ten minutes to nip down to the dining hall for bagels and bananas. They ate in silence until Timothy suddenly said, "It is not right." He looked at a spot somewhere on the wall behind Danny and repeated, "It is not right. You have often told me it is not right to lie."

Danny nodded, wondering where this was going and aware that he'd better keep his options open. Timothy saw the world in black and white, right and wrong, and Danny was painfully aware that he had tried to guide him through some gray zones. As though Timothy could read his mind, he asked, "When you know something that someone else should know, and you don't tell them, is it lying?"

Danny thought for a moment. "I guess it depends, but yes, in general, I would say it is lying if you withhold information that could help someone else."

"Then she has no right to ask me not to tell you. You need to know. She is making me lie." There was a fleeting moment where Timothy's gaze made contact with Danny's, and it was gut-wrenching to see the anguish and indecision in his eyes. Timothy continued, "And Mykyta also lied to me. He said the virus would destroy all the systems, but I went through the code; the virus will do no such thing. It is designed to siphon all key data to Mykyta's servers. Mykyta lied; it is not right to lie."

Danny swallowed the last of his bagel together with rising exasperation. The marijuana had really done a number on Timothy.

"Slow down, Tim; you've lost me completely. Who is *she*? And what does Mykyta have to do with this?"

Timothy bowed his head and concentrated on picking bits of dough from his bagel to rub them between his thumb and forefinger into equal-sized balls.

"Timothy?"

"If I tell you, I will have lied to her. Because I said I wouldn't tell."

Danny wished Gerald were there, but Gerald had been driven to Tracy the previous afternoon so that he could rehearse for some big deal church service on Sunday. He was going to spend the weekend as a guest of the Church of Holy Redemption. Danny had never seen him so excited; the prospect of meeting Pastor Jeremiah in person had made Gerald vibrate with anticipation. Danny took a deep breath, "Let's look at it logically, Timothy. If she, whoever she is, asked you to withhold important information from someone who should have it, then she is asking you to lie. Right?"

Timothy nodded.

"And if she is asking you to do something that is wrong, then that's an invalid request. Hence, any promise you made to her is invalidated. You're not bound by it. You can talk freely, and it wouldn't be considered a lie."

Timothy rolled two more dough balls, the size of peas, and lined them up with the others.

"*She* is Ms. Katie Blanchard," Timothy said.

Danny nodded, "Yeah, I saw her yesterday on my way to Doc Roberts. She looked...unhappy. How did you meet her?"

"Gerald called me." Then the whole story poured out as Timothy unburdened himself. He explained how he had recorded Katie and set up the video for worldwide distribution. Danny was flabbergasted to learn about Katie's request to annihilate the computer systems of the church and all its affiliates. Timothy had spent the last two days with Mykyta identifying a virus to do just that, but now Mykyta was trying to double-cross him and appropriate the very algorithms that had wreaked so much havoc.

"Mykyta doesn't respect me," Timothy mumbled. "He must think I'm stupid."

"Buddy, you know and I know that that's not true. You are the smartest person I've ever met. What are you going to do about it?"

Timothy stopped rolling dough balls and looked out the window. Then he said, "I'm going to modify the virus and teach him a lesson."

Danny grinned, "Good. But now, can you please show me that video? You said that it contained something I should know."

Timothy picked up his laptop and set it up for Danny. "Just press play," he said and walked to the door.

"Where are you going?"

Timothy said, "You will want to be alone when you see this. I will go to the lab."

The empathetic gesture was so unusual that Danny was overcome by a wave of dread. It came out of nowhere and washed over him like a misjudged breaker on a bad surfing day. His finger hovered over the *play* button. What could it possibly be? His father was a fugitive on the run, his sister had died by suicide, his mother was a distant non-caring presence, and he was locked up in a facility. What else could fate possibly throw at him? Terry! Something terrible must have happened to Terry. He closed his eyes. If there was a God in heaven, then this would be a good time to reveal himself with a grain of compassion. *Please, God, not Terry*. He pressed play.

***

Timothy was itching to work on the virus modification, but since he'd left his computer with Danny, he had to contend himself with letting the code take shape in his head. He had decided to call the virus *Nyx*, after the Greek goddess of the night. His virus would nix the systems.

An hour and twenty minutes later, Danny walked into the lab. He was dressed in running gear and drenched in sweat from his limp hair to his dirty sneakers. Timothy wondered whether he'd been for a swim but decided that that made no sense. He stole a glance at Danny's impassive face. His eyes were red-rimmed and blazing. It was like looking from a great height down into the smoldering red vent of a volcano ready to blow. Timothy got scared and looked away.

Danny put a backpack on the lab bench and took out Timothy's laptop. His voice was calm when he said, "Right, here's the plan. We're going to pay the Church of Holy Redemption a visit."

"But how, when? How are we going to get out of here?"

Danny said, "Let that be my worry. In the meantime, you're going to use Isaac's passwords to find out what the hell they're up to. Those fuckers drove my sister to suicide, and there is something nasty going down. I feel it in my gut, and I'll be damned if I let Gerald get hurt. Search for everything you can find out about tomorrow's service – who'll be there, the order of service, the security arrangements. I also want you to download the detailed floorplan of the whole church compound onto our cellphone. I want to know where their security cameras are, the roster of guards – everything."

Timothy queried, "You're going to break in?"

"We," Danny pointed back and forth between them, "I want to be there to see Katie go through with her confession. I want to see the faces of those holier-than-thou shits when their world collapses and the cops cart them away. I want to be there when we unleash your virus and turn that place into mush. And maybe I want to start a few well-placed fires to burn the whole place down – once everyone has left the building, of course."

Despite all the exercises Timothy had been through with Dr. Roberts, he couldn't tell whether Danny was serious or joking. But, on balance, he leaned towards thinking that his friend was serious.

Timothy reached for his laptop while Danny went to his locker and started to search out the items he would need. Apparently, he didn't find everything he wanted because he moved to other lockers and cracked them open without a hint of his usual humor and wit. It was scary to see his friend being so methodical and cold. An impressive pile of items accumulated on the bench.

Gloves with fingerprints of Dr. Roberts, Carlos the Security Guard, Isaac, and Katie (the latter lifted from her car the day before)
Two cellphones
Marijuana cookies, joints, and dog treats
Firelighters and a ball of string
A roll of duct tape
A set of Allen keys, a screwdriver, and a Swiss army knife
A tiny microphone bug
Two webcams
A nylon rope.

Danny said, "Do you still have those Ambien sleeping tablets the doctor prescribed?"

Timothy nodded, and Danny said, "I'll want a few to press into these cookies. I don't trust the weed to do the job; the guard must be out cold when we leave. It's a two-hour trip to Tracy, and we don't want Isaac to have any forewarning."

Timothy asked, "What's your plan with Isaac?"

Danny shrugged, "I'll think of something. Put Ambien in his coffee, hit him over the head, or lure him into one of the many rooms they have down in the basement and lock him up till the police get there."

"But he can get out of anywhere; it's all fingerprint operated."

"Then we'll just have to cut off his finger. Remind me to pick up a big knife from the kitchen."

Timothy's eyes rounded in shock, and Danny said, "What? That monster drove my sister to suicide; do you think I'm going to think twice about cutting off his finger?"

Timothy stared at his screen, trying to dispel the image of a severed finger, blood spouting from the stump like a red fountain. It made him think of the colorful fountains he'd seen in Las Vegas – and the noise! The noise of the crowds everywhere in Las Vegas had been torture.

He said, "If you cut off his finger, he'll make a lot of noise."

Danny said, "Just kidding. I won't cut off anything. We'll bind him with duct tape – I'll figure out something."

"I don't like your jokes – they scare me. And I don't like it when you have no plan."

Danny grinned malevolently and picked up a pad of paper and a pen. "Who says I don't have a plan?" He started to write.

Timothy turned his attention to the computer and fed in one search term after another, combining and extrapolating to narrow down the hundreds of results that came up. He continued to be in awe of the system. It was constructed on a state-of-the-art platform; everything was integrated and fast. His searches cut across time and space, across Word documents, spreadsheets, emails, and even IM messages. He absorbed the content and the design. The system's power was also its greatest vulnerability – *Nyx* was going to tear through it like a Californian wildfire.

They sat side by side and started to uncover useful tidbits – biometric reader locations, shift changes of guards, the agenda for the Sunday service. It gave Timothy comfort to see Danny filling page after page with neatly-written notes.

"Hey, what's that?" Danny said, "Go back."

They both looked at an email from Isaac to the control center team leader. It was copied to the head of security. In a very enthusiastic tone, Isaac informed the team that this Sunday, they were going to test their ability to control operations from the remote center in the Sierra. The team leader had voiced some concerns, but Isaac had assured him that this was Pastor Jeremiah's wish and that he, Isaac, would be in the Tracy control center in case anything went wrong.

"Okay," Danny said, "so he's sending everyone away to have the control center to himself. Interesting."

Timothy continued his search. One email string, which referenced the interfaith service, popped up for the third time – an encrypted email exchange between Isaac and someone called Major McCullum from CAFCA. Timothy had to try a variety of Isaac's passwords before he could read it. He angled the computer for Danny to get a better look at the email string.

Major: *Did you get the semi that was shipped with the modified attack drones?*

Isaac: *Yes, I have it secured.*

Major: *Ammo there as well? I had them pack rubber bullets.*

Isaac: *All waiting for your boy.*

Major: *I'll meet you at 9.00 and J will join us at 9.30. That will give us time to get him situated before the service starts. I don't want him there too early in case he gets nervous. What about your control room personnel?*

Isaac: *All taken care of. I'll be the only one onsite.*

"Holy crap!" Danny exclaimed, his eyes wide. "I knew it, I knew it! Something is going down. The 'semi' is obviously a semi-automatic gun." He closed his eyes and scrunched up his face. "But why? Why on earth would

Isaac want to situate someone with a semi-automatic gun in his own church? It makes no sense."

Timothy could just about hear the cogs working in Danny's brain as he watched his friend, sitting in deep concentration at the bench. Then Danny said, "Show me that agenda again." Timothy pulled it up from the multitude of open files on his screen.

"Look at this!" Danny exclaimed, "Guests of honor – Senator McGrath, his wife Eleanor, and their daughter, Chloe McGrath. She's my brother's ex-wife! I didn't spot it earlier because she's gone back to her maiden name." Then the color drained from Danny's face, "It's an assassination plot; they're going to shoot the Senator – CAFCA and the whole gun lobby hate him. Can you imagine the pandemonium when someone opens fire with a semi-automatic in a packed church? And if Chloe's right next to the senator…"

Timothy frowned, "But why would they use rubber bullets?"

"I have no idea. But at close range you can do a lot of damage with a hail of rubber bullets."

Timothy flicked back to the email chain and said, "There must be something else; something we're missing. What's with these modified attack drones?"

Danny shrugged, "God knows, keep digging. The more we can find out, the better prepared we'll be."

"Shouldn't we tell someone; warn them?"

Danny snorted, "Yeah, right. Two teenagers, locked up in a detention facility, happen to have hacked into the systems of a highly-respected church organization where they've uncovered a blackmail scheme that has led to the death of half a dozen people. And," he paused dramatically, "they've uncovered an assassination plot." He shook his head, "No, Timothy; no one would believe us. I wouldn't believe us. We're going to have to stop this by ourselves."

Timothy looked at his watch. He needed to start coding the virus, so he said, "If you want to know what goes on at that church and how it all works, why don't you just look here."

With a few keystrokes, Timothy brought up the feed from several cameras. He flitted from one camera to another, allowing a virtual tour of the outside and the inside of the building. Danny couldn't keep up with the lighting speed at which Timothy went through camera feeds and floor plans that held an endless array of icons in different colors – doors, lights, sensors, speakers, microphones.

Timothy said, "Don't you remember? I can get into their control system."

"Of course! God, I'm so thick. You mean it's not just a case of looking in via the cameras? You can actually effect changes? Show me."

Timothy pulled up a camera angle that showed the twelve-foot-high door to the sanctuary. He found the corresponding icon on the floor plan and pressed a key – the door swung open.

"Wow!" Danny said.

Then they heard a voice come through the laptop speaker, "Hey, Sierra control. What are you doing? We've told you guys a million times to give us a heads-up when you test the controls."

A petulant voice said, "We're not doing anything. You've got full control."

The first voice from Tracy said, "How can the damn door just decide to open by itself?"

"Probably another bug in the system. I guess that's why Isaac wants to run a full test tomorrow. Uncover all the bugs."

A grunt emanated from the speakers, "It's going to be a cluster fuck of epic proportions. I'm just glad it's my day off."

313

Danny whispered, "Are you sure they can't hear us?"

Timothy nodded and pressed a few keys, "Oh yes, I made very sure to have us in stealth mode. I've given back control, but we can still see through the cameras." He looked at his watch, "Danny, I have to start working on that virus, but I'll channel the camera feed to one of the iPhones, then you can keep studying the layout."

Danny gave him two thumbs up.

***

When the alarm rang at 2:30 a.m., Danny was instantly awake. He wasn't sure whether he had slept at all; his mind had churned through every conceivable eventuality to develop countermeasures. He and Timothy dressed in dark jeans and hoodies, picked up their backpacks, and slid out of the building. He wished Gerald were with them, but of course the older boy was already in Tracy at the church's guest house. They hadn't been able to contact him, since Gerald had no cell phone.

Danny was pretty sure that Carlos would be fast asleep. The guard had been delighted to receive a batch of cookies earlier in the evening. Danny had spent half an hour practicing his Spanish with Carlos.

How do I say, *nothing ever happens around here*?

How many children do you have? Don't they miss you? Until what time is your shift?

Do you like Dr. Roberts' car? A Tesla. It's very nice.

The doctor told me he must leave very early in the morning to get a flight from SFO.

314

They hugged the shadows till they reached Dr. Roberts' Tesla. Danny sent a silent prayer heavenward as he pressed his latex-gloved hand on the biometric reader. The door clicked open, and minutes later, they rolled silently towards the main gate. The hoody covered Danny's blond hair and Timothy crouched low in the back seat. Danny stopped twenty feet away from the gate, just outside the cone of fluorescent light. If Carlos were awake, he would hopefully recognize the familiar vehicle and let them out without double-checking who the driver was.

They waited in silence for a full minute. One of the dogs started to bark and Danny cursed. He leaped from the car, making soothing noises till the dog whimpered and quieted. Danny gave it a treat, then crept into the control room. Carlos had dimmed the lights and rolled out a yoga mat in a corner next to the desk. It took Danny only seconds to find the right controls. He sprinted back to the car as the gates started to swing open. Then they were on their way.

Danny whooped and put his foot down. Timothy clambered into the passenger seat and sat rigid as the vehicle's halogen lights touched and discarded bushes, trees, and mile markers at a break-neck pace. After a few miles, Danny curbed his exhilaration and slowed to sixty-five; it would be unforgivable to be pulled over by some lone policeman and have the whole quest blown up. That would be like leaving the reality show *Survivor* with two immunity idols in your pocket.

Timothy's jaw unclenched and he asked, "Where did you learn to drive?"

"When my mother and I returned from California to the East Coast, we took turns driving." Danny was transported back to nights like this, on quiet roads, with the top down – nothing between him and the stars.

"But you were only, what, fourteen?"

315

Danny chuckled, "My mother drove during the day while I slept in the backseat; at night, we'd switch. No one could see that it was a kid behind the steering wheel." He had felt so grown-up then, taking care of her, helping her get out of the bad situation in Los Angeles. They had listened to music; talked like equals about friendship and right and wrong, about their hopes and dreams. Danny smiled to himself and resolved to make more of an effort the next time he called her.

They followed highway 132 till they reached Interstate 580 where, even in the dead of night, trucks roared by in a take-no-prisoner hurry. It was here, where three highways – 205, 580, 5 – formed a triangle, that God had directed Pastor Jeremiah to build his church. Its LED cross towered above a landscape of distribution warehouses, outlet malls, and paved parking lots.

Even though the boys had never been anywhere near the church, they were very familiar with the layout. There was parking in front and to the left of the building. To the right was a walled garden that connected the church to its own compound, or "village". This was a secured facility to provide refuge for abuse victims and other vulnerable individuals. The village was plastered wall-to-wall with cameras and even had guards on foot patrol; it was to be avoided at all costs.

Danny turned off the vehicle's lights and allowed it to glide like a stealth fighter around the left-hand side of the church to a spot behind a shed that housed trash cans. They had figured out that no cameras were covering this area. Timothy used his cellphone to create a Wi-Fi hot spot for his laptop and, within a minute, had gained entry to the church's system. Scrolling through the various cameras, they ascertained that the building was deserted. Timothy called up the floorplan with all its control icons and one by one switched off the cameras along their intended path to the control room under the church. They held their breaths, waiting to see whether this action would trigger any response – nothing. Then Danny put on the latex glove with Isaac's fingerprint, and they scurried to a service entrance. The door opened without a sound, and the two boys, guided by a flashlight, descended a flight of stairs to the broad corridor underneath the church. Finally, they reached the control room door, and Danny placed his finger on the reader. A red light bleeped with the message "access denied." He tried a second time, with the same result.

"What's the matter?" Timothy asked.

"The fingerprint on the latex is really fragile; it wears off. Fuck!"

"What do we do now?" Timothy asked, looking up and down the corridor.

"Can you try and open this remotely?"

Timothy crouched down next to the wall with his laptop and called up the floorplan. He pressed several keys – no response.

"They're not taking any chances with this door," Timothy said. "It needs the fingerprint, and…" anticipating Danny's next move, he urged, "Don't try again! Three false attempts will trigger an alarm with the guards at the compound next door."

Danny sank down on his haunches next to Timothy, looked at his watch, and groaned, "Shit! We have to get in there and turn on the cameras again before shift change in fifteen minutes." He rummaged through his backpack, looking for inspiration. The lock was too sophisticated for his pocketknife or Allen key. Could something be done with masking tape?

"There's a guard coming around the back," Timothy whispered. "He's seen the Tesla."

Oh no, Danny groaned inwardly. They crouched down over Timothy's computer and watched.

"What's he doing?" Danny asked.

Timothy zoomed in on the dark, grainy picture. The guard was taking photos of the vehicle and number plate with an iPad.

Damn, they'll probably run a check and find out it belongs to Doc Roberts. Danny noticed that Timothy had started to tremble and was jerking his head left and right to scan the corridor. His friend was about to freak out. He mustered all the bravado he didn't feel and said, "Thank God we took Doc Roberts' car. If they find it in their system, they'll realize it belongs to a staff member and will just assume he's here to help someone at the shelter."

"Are you…are you sure? I guess we can just wait till the guard leaves and then make a dash back."

Timothy got up and started to move towards the stairs.

Danny closed his eyes. If only Gerald were there. He knew how to calm Timmy. Then he pulled himself together. *We've come this far; we're not going to give up. Concentrate, man. There must be a way.*

Danny smacked his forehead, "Of course, Isaac isn't the only one with access. Come back here, Tim." He rifled through his backpack and retrieved the Katie glove. It worked on the first try, and the door slid open. Danny grinned and punched Timothy's shoulder. They stepped inside and the door shut behind them. They found themselves trapped in a small chamber, with only a porthole giving a view into the dimly-lit control room. What the…?

Timothy just about jumped out of his skin when a rush of ghostly air whooshed out of the darkness beneath their feet and enveloped them. This was scarier than any Disney ride. Timothy yelped, and his cellphone clattered to the grate below. They both scrambled to pick it up and bumped their heads together. Timothy started to flail.

"It's just…" Danny said before being interrupted by a disembodied mechanical voice, "Decontamination complete, please proceed." The door in front of them slid open. Danny scooped up the cellphone and they stepped into the control room. The lights, triggered by a motion detector, bloomed into life. Both boys stood rooted to the spot as they took in the banks of desks and computers, as well as the wall filled with monitors. It made Danny think of a post-apocalyptic sci-fi scene where men, dressed in furs and sandals, stumbled upon the mission control center of *The Ancients* that could transport men to the moon.

"Airlock open," the tinman voice said and, thirty seconds later, repeated the message in the irritating manner that only recorded voices can achieve. There were two lit buttons, red and green, next to the door. Danny pressed the red button and took back a step when the heavy door shot down like a guillotine.

"Right, let's get on with it," Danny said and pointed at the consoles, "You see if you can test drive this baby while I go and plant the bugs and cameras."

Danny didn't know exactly where Isaac, the major, and "the boy" would meet, but it was a fair bet that it would be either in the control room or in Isaac's office – which was unlocked. *Thank you, God. Good to know you're on our side.*

It was easy enough to plant a microphone and webcam among the plethora of equipment in the control room. But Isaac's office was more of a challenge. The reverend was clearly a neat freak; there were no pictures, no potted plants, and no clutter of any kind in his office. After probing the walls and filing cabinets, Danny clambered onto Isaac's desk, removed the plastic cover of a lamp, and made a hole into it with his Swiss army knife. It took eight minutes, but then Timothy gave him the thumbs up that he had a good view of the office via the Webcam.

The first hint of dawn was showing up on the monitors of the building's east-facing cameras when Timothy powered down the control center, and the boys

319

slipped into a storeroom the size of a double garage. The plans had indicated that this room had no cameras installed. Once safely inside, Timothy ensured that he could scroll through all the building's cameras, as well as the newly-installed webcams, on his laptop. He was all set to record whatever conversation transpired so they would have it as evidence.

Danny guessed that the storeroom had previously been used as a staging area for computer servers. There was industrial shelving along one wall and a workbench along another. Cisco boxes and an assortment of discarded office equipment were piled up halfway to the ceiling along the third wall. They dragged out a couple of chairs and made themselves comfortable. From his bag, Danny produced a flask of coffee, as well as some bagels and bananas.

After breakfast, Timothy began to explore every square inch of the room while Danny arranged a few more chairs to make a couch for a cat nap. Unfortunately, lying across four typist chairs was even worse than trying to lie across a row of economy-class airline seats. Every time he moved, one of the chairs would wriggle out of line.

"Hey, look at this," Timothy called, "What do you think these are?"

Danny sighed and went to look at six large boxes, half-hidden behind two desks. Each of the boxes was the size of a two-drawer filing cabinet and, unlike the dusty Cisco ones, the cardboard appeared to be crisp and new. A picture on the outside of the boxes reminded Danny of a giant bunch of grapes.

"I don't know," he said, "looks like an ornate set of chandeliers – just the sort of thing to fit in with the church décor."

Timothy said, "Could be part of a fancy sound system." He peered inside a box and found a lonely sheet of paper. They studied it together, then looked at each other.

Timothy was the first to speak, "Attack drones? These bulbs each conceal a swarm of miniature attack drones?"

Danny turned the box upside and shook it. A metal object, the size of a hummingbird, clanked onto the floor. He picked it up and held it to the light. "Un-be-fucking-lievable," he said. "This is amazing. Look at that pointy…"

"Don't touch!" Timothy interjected, "You don't know what that thing will do if you touch the stinger."

They both stared in awe at the tiny drone.

Chapter 27, Church of Holy Redemption
Sunday, 2nd Week of July

By Saturday evening, Terry had reached such a stage of exhaustion that Sandy had ordered him home to bed. He spent a fitful night in dreams where he was reconciled with Chloe. He could feel her kiss on his arm and woke to find Charlie licking him. He dragged himself out on a walk for Charlie's sake. The dog was well on the road to recovery but not yet up to their usual run.

Afterward, Terry prepared for the church service. He managed to nick himself with a fresh shaving blade and ironed three shirts because he kept changing his mind. Then he hunted through his closet to find the blue tie that had been Chloe's favorite. He hoped that he'd have a chance to see Chloe before the church service – to tell her that he genuinely wished her well, that he was proud of her and rooting for her.

He picked up a Zipcar and found that the drive to Tracy on a Sunday was much quicker than expected. It was only 9 a.m. when he entered the church, where a dozen people were busy setting up long tables for the after-service fellowship time. A friendly woman with tinted hair and sensible shoes welcomed him and introduced herself as

Sarah Bates. When he explained that he'd misjudged the traffic, she laughed and said it often happened to people who came from further away to hear Pastor Jeremiah.

"Come with me," she said and led him into the kitchen, where the smell of coffee and fresh baking sent his appetite into a spasm of desire. Sarah must have heard his stomach. She smiled, "Coffee and snacks usually happen after the service, but you look like you could do with some fattening up." She poured him a mug of coffee and gestured for Terry to help himself to croissant from one of the trays that had just come out of the oven. Terry bit into the warm croissant and thought he might swoon. No wonder people came from far and near to the Church of Holy Redemption.

They moved back into the gathering hall where Sarah could keep an eye on her buzzing team and maintain a stream of conversation about the church, the pastor, and the community. Terry drank his coffee and ate a second croissant. He explained his wish to catch Ms. Chloe McGrath – it still hurt him to refer to her like that – before the service and asked where she might prepare since she was lector for the day.

"I think you'd better speak to the Reverend Isaac O'Neill," Sarah said. "I saw him come in just before you. He'll be down in the control room. I can get one of the helpers here to show you…"

She suddenly brushed past Terry and addressed a man who had entered the gathering hall and made straight for the stairs that led down to the warren beneath. The newcomer was a short man who held himself very erect. He had black hair, which was neatly parted.

"Excuse me, sir," Sarah said with her unfailing smile, "welcome to the Church of Holy Redemption. Can we help you find something? Down there are mainly administrative offices."

323

For a moment, it looked as though the man was going to brush her aside, but then he opted for charm. "Oh, thank you," he said and held out a manicured hand, "I am *Major* McCullum." He waved his hands in the direction of the tables and said, "I can see you run a tight ship and," he winked, "you're mindful of security. Very admirable. Admirable indeed."

Sarah Bates blushed as she shook the major's hand.

"I'll be sure to stop by after the service," he continued, "but right now, I have an appointment with Reverend O'Neill. He said to meet him in the control room." Then, he leaned forward and whispered, "Security matters."

"Oh, well, in that case," Sarah simpered, "would you be so kind as to show Mr. Reynolds here the way? He's also on his way to the reverend."

The major's smile did not reach his eyes, but he nodded curtly and gestured for Terry to follow him. At the control room, Isaac buzzed them in. The major's hair contained so much gel that it didn't move at all during the decontamination blast. The man showed no surprise when the fan whooshed air into the stainless-steel chamber; he'd obviously visited the control room before. The inner door opened, and the reverend emerged with an outstretched hand from his office. It was comical how Isaac's smile froze, together with the outstretched hand, when he noticed Terry.

His eyes darted between the major and Terry. "Mr… Reynolds, was it? I didn't know that you and the major were acquainted."

"We're not," the major said in a clipped tone. "Just a coincidence. The lady in charge of refreshments asked me to show Mr. Reynolds the way. Apparently, he also has an appointment with you?"

Terry picked up a distinctly petulant note of distrust in his voice; that of a man who was used to being the singular point of attention.

Terry jumped in with his most gregarious smile, "No, no. You misunderstand. I don't have an appointment. I merely wanted to know where I might find my wife," he felt himself blushing and babbling, "that is, my ex-wife, Chloe McGrath. She's lector today, and the kind lady upstairs said you would be able to tell me where she'd be before the service."

"Oh, sure, no problem," Isaac said and touched Terry's arm, guiding him toward the door. As Terry brushed past the major, he saw it – the tattoo on the inside of the major's wrist. It was the size of a quarter and looked like a black cross in the middle of a red circle. Suddenly, a synaptic lightning storm erupted in his brain. The young man next to him in church last Sunday had had that same tattoo. And he'd smelled of garlic, to the point of making Terry feel sick. Then that same man had been down here talking to Isaac when Terry toured the control center with Pastor Jeremiah. The whiff of garlic had been in the room, even though Isaac had shooed the young man out of sight. And then, the evening old Joe got attacked – garlic. He remembered now; it had alluded him all along, but now, seeing that tattoo, he remembered.

It was a long shot, and he had no time to consider. The words just came out, "You know, now that I'm here, I might as well ask, what can you tell me about the C.O.L.D. index?"

Isaac's grip tightened and his smile was brittle, "The what? I'm not sure I follow. Is it too cold for you down here in the basement? Maybe we'd better get you on your way."

Terry dug in his heels. He felt the kind of reckless rush that overcame him when he chased traffic lights on his bicycle along Divisadero Road. He took a wild gamble and said, "Oh, come on, Isaac. Surely you know that Professor Curry's been talking. It's only a matter of time before they identify his attacker from the identikit the prof has put together. But I'd bet good money that the young man who was talking to you here last week was involved. He sat next to me during the service; I got a good look at him."

***

Danny and Timothy watched the webcam feed and hung onto every word of the conversation via a set of shared earphones. Danny barely dared to breathe. *What are you playing at, big brother?* he thought. *You're supposed to be the smart one; don't you know Isaac plays for keeps?*

In horror, Danny saw the major, behind Terry, clench his hands together as if to pray and lift them over his head. He gasped as the major's clenched fists smacked down on the side of Terry's neck. Terry crumpled like a discarded T-shirt. The thud of his head on the floor made Danny feel nauseous. Every nerve in his body was on fire, urging him to burst out of hiding and attack the two men standing in the doorway to Isaac's office. He didn't register the worried glances that Timothy shot in his direction until his friend reached out and placed a hand on his arm. Danny breathed deeply.

"Is he dead?" Isaac asked with no inflection in his voice.

The major knelt down, felt Terry's pulse, and spat, "Of course not; that would cause untold complications and derail the mission. But we have to get him out of sight *now*." He looked at his watch, "The last thing we need is for

Joshua to see him and get spooked. He's already jittery as all hell. We'll have to deal with Mr. Reynolds later."

"Will Joshua go through with it?" Isaac asked.

"Certainly," the major snapped. "I'm just saying that something unexpected like this," he pointed at Terry, "could rattle him unnecessarily."

Isaac said, "Just as well we've planned the attack near the beginning of the service." He produced a duct tape roll and they secured Terry's hands behind his back, then bound his feet. As the major started to wrap the tape around Terry's mouth and head, Isaac stepped away to his computer and said, "You know, this guy has just given us a great gift."

"How so?"

"Look at this," Isaac said triumphantly and turned around his computer. Danny could just catch a glimpse of the screen via the webcam. It showed a still photo from the previous Sunday's service. Danny remembered how shocked he'd been to see his brother staring straight into the camera during prayers. Isaac had selected a shot in which the camera had zoomed out to show Terry and an unknown man standing side-by-side, holding hands.

Isaac continued with glee in his voice, "We feed this to the media and we have an instant motive – a lovers' triangle! Mr. Terry Reynolds here harbored such hatred for his ex-wife that he persuaded his gay lover to kill her. I mean… to give her the fright of her life with a salvo of rubber bullets. The media will lap it up, and no one will believe a word he says after that."

A cold shiver ran down Danny's spine. This guy was pure evil.

"Brilliant," the major snorted. "Now, where can we lock him up?"

A beat later, Danny hissed, "Oh, shit! They're bringing him in here." He slammed Timothy's laptop shut,

327

motioned for his friend to hide behind the modesty panel of a desk and lunged across the room to switch off the lights. There was no time to get back to Timothy, so Danny flattened himself against the wall. Seconds later, the door swung open, nearly smashing into his nose. He steadied his breathing in the pathetically-inadequate hiding place behind the door. Had Timothy managed to get out of sight? Oh God, what if the laptop picked up noise from the webcam and transmitted it?

When the lights were switched on, Danny had his eyes shut tight. *You're dumber than an ostrich,* he chided himself, opening his eyes. He could hear the two men grunting as they dragged Terry into the room.

He heard Isaac's voice, "This is strange."

"What?" the major said, panting.

"These chairs."

Danny froze.

"No one's supposed to come in here. Look at these chairs. It looks like someone made themselves a very comfortable little resting place here."

There was silence, and Danny prayed to any and every God that might be out there listening: *don't let him investigate!*

Then Isaac said, "It must be the control room guys goofing off in here. Well, I'll have to surprise them with a hidden camera installation."

The major said, "Maybe add one of those drone nests and prick them into action when they shirk their duty." Both men laughed, then the major said, "My technician tells me the installation of the first drone nest is complete. I can't wait to see the response to our demo today."

"Yes," Isaac said, "your techie and I armed two of the mini-drones. They've been programmed to pick out Joshua's face and will launch right after he starts firing."

The major said, "Well, there's no way we can let him walk out of this alive. I would have felt happier if the whole nest swarmed on him, but I'm told there'd be too much collateral damage. After all, we want to demonstrate the pinpoint precision of the system." There was a pause, then the major continued, "We'd better go; Joshua will be here any minute now."

The light was switched off and the door shut. Danny exhaled carefully, not yet daring to move. Then he heard a key being put into the door and the lock turning. He stifled a groan. Damn! He waited a full minute and would have waited longer if Timothy hadn't called out in a shaky whisper, "Danny, are you there? I don't like the dark."

Danny switched on the light and tried his best to get Timothy out of his hiding spot with the minimum possible noise. Timothy looked at him with big eyes and struggled to breathe. "Did…did you hear? They plan…to…to…kill Joshua? I didn't believe it until…"

Danny feared that Timothy was about to implode, "It's okay, Timmy, breathe. We're going to stop this whole thing. Remember, that's the mission."

Timothy tried to take a deep breath but faltered when he saw the bound and trussed figure that had been dumped near the door, "Is he…is he okay?"

"Timmy, look at me! This is important. You *must* get that webcam going again, and make sure to record everything. Okay? Can you do that for me?"

While Timothy retrieved his laptop, Danny took a knife from his backpack. It was strange to see his big, strong brother like this – vulnerable. Danny noticed the crow's feet around Terry's eyes and even a hint of gray among the dark curls. Then he caught a whiff of Terry's aftershave, the same sandalwood he'd always worn, and a flood of memories threatened to overwhelm him. He had to fight the urge to lie down next to Terry and just hold him. Terry uttered a moan, and Danny decided that the only way to deal with the tape was to rip it off. He managed to peel off enough of an edge to get a grip and yanked. Terry's eyes flew open, and Danny clasped a hand over Terry's mouth. "Shh, be quiet," he whispered.

Terry's entire body writhed as he strained against the tape around his arms and feet. Danny was actually glad that his brother's wrists were bound. Judging by the wild look of panic and anger in Terry's eyes, he might have strangled Danny.

"Shh, stop wriggling – and if you bite my hand, I swear, I'll…" What would he do? Fortunately, Terry appeared to regain his senses. Danny spoke directly into his ear, "You're lucky you shaved this morning, otherwise that would have been a lot more painful." He waited for a few more beats, then whispered, "I'm going to remove my hand, but you have to be very, very quiet."

Terry nodded, and when Danny removed his hand, his brother whispered just one word, "Danny?" The look of incredulity, relief and pure joy that washed over Terry's face would stay with Danny forever, stored in the inner sanctum of his most precious memories.

"How…? I can't believe it! It *is* you." Terry enfolded him in a tight embrace and murmured, "I was so worried I'd lose you, too. What on earth are you doing here?"

Timothy interrupted, "Joshua's here; you'll want to hear this."

When Terry wanted to ask questions, Danny cut him short, "Later, I'll tell you everything later. This here is my friend Timothy who hacked into the church's systems and uncovered mind-blowing things. This place is a cesspool. You'd never believe…"

Terry interrupted, "Trust me, I know they're capable of almost anything."

"Good, then you won't be surprised to hear that they're putting a shooter in the congregation to assassinate Senator McGrath – and possibly hurt Chloe too."

"What?!"

"Shh!" Danny and Timothy mouthed in unison.

Danny cut Terry's bonds with two slashes, and they all crowded around the monitor to see the trio in Isaac's office. Joshua, the man who had sat next to Terry at the previous church service, was dressed in chinos, a white button-down shirt, and a navy jacket. His hair was neatly combed, and only the pallor of his face betrayed nervousness. The major placed a hand on the young man's shoulder and said, "This is a big day, Josh, for all of us; we're going to strike a decisive blow against the liberal forces that want to take away our freedoms."

Joshua's nod was barely perceptible, and Isaac chimed in, "Everything's in place, just like we practiced. The semi is ready and strapped under the seat. I put it there myself." He gave an encouraging smile and continued, "Can you remind me of exactly when you...start?"

Joshua looked from one man to the other. His demeanor reminded Danny of a schoolboy wanting to please his teachers. Finally, he said, "The pastor will welcome the politician lady, who is supposed to read the Old Testament lesson. He then steps in front of the altar, and she goes to the lectern and starts to read. That's when I shoot."

Danny and Terry sucked in their breaths in unison, and Danny gripped his brother's wrist. He knew that it took every iota of Terry's willpower not to storm into the control room. So they were targeting Chloe and Pastor Jeremiah, not the senator; but why?

He watched as Isaac and the major nodded in unison, and the major said, "There will, of course, be panic and confusion. That gives you the cover to walk out to the side exit just like we practiced. I'll be waiting to take you to the airstrip." He held up an envelope and leaned in close, "By noon, you'll be out of state and ready to read your manifesto – a warning to any church that dares to pervert

Christianity in the service of the communist, anti-gun, pro-abortion forces like this Chloe McGrath. We have Fox News and several other channels lined up. You're going to be famous – a heroic defender of the second amendment."

Joshua nodded, his expression serious, "And you guarantee that I'll not go to prison, because no one will get seriously hurt? It's just rubber bullets to scare them, right?"

"My boy," the major grinned, "heroes don't go to prison. And if they try anything, you've met Ms. Bussey, our chief lawyer. If there is even a hint of a legal problem, she'll make it go away. Let's just say there's hardly a judge in the country that can resist her."

Joshua took a printed flyer from his jacket pocket and turned to Isaac, "What about that guy I saw practicing the guitar yesterday? I looked at the order of service. He'll be on stage because he sings right after the readings."

Danny gasped, and all he could hear was a rushing in his ears and the pounding of his heart. Gerald was going to be in the line of fire. Danny's hands were clammy, and his body cycled through hot and cold; he struggled for air and felt he would explode from the effort of suppressing the fight instinct. He registered the concern and confusion in Terry's eyes before Timothy's whispered words reached him, "We're going to stop them, Danny. You said so yourself. We're going to stop them. Gerald will be okay."

Danny let out a breath and turned his attention back to the screen. He was just in time to see Isaac wave dismissively, "Oh, him. Might as well teach him not to associate with the wrong people." His voice turned serious. "Anyone on stage is your target; is that clear?"

The young man nodded, and Isaac continued, "It's a war, Joshua. And in war, there's always collateral damage."

Danny clenched his jaw. He was seething. How dare this man set himself up as arbiter over life, death, and injury – driving people to despair and suicide. Collateral damage indeed. A hail of rubber bullets could blind a person or cause any amount of other damage. Danny looked from Terry to Timothy and back again before hissing, "I swear, this guy is going to rot in hell. Let's just wait till the other two go, then we grab him."

"He's a total psychopath," Terry said and shook his head. "Unbelievable."

Danny said, "And responsible for Lily's death."

"What?" Terry stared at him. Then his eyes started to sweep the room till they landed on something dangling from Danny's backpack. He snatched a nylon rope from the bag, tested it for strength between his hands, and strode towards the door. Danny lunged after him and tackled him to the ground. Before Terry could recover, Danny threw his body over him and pinned him to the ground. He clasped his hand over Terry's mouth and hissed, "For fuck's sake; lie still. The door's locked from the outside, anyway."

Shit, shit, shit. Surely Isaac and the major would have heard the commotion. He could feel the beat of Terry's heart, but his brother didn't stir. They lay like that for what felt like an eternity. Danny peered back towards Timothy, who stared at him with wide eyes. Then Timothy glanced at the screen and gave him a thumbs up.

Danny shut his eyes, heaved a sigh of relief, and released his brother. He whispered, "I'll explain everything later, but keep your fucking Irish temper under control. We have to wait till they split up – then we get them one by one."

Terry's eyes were blazing, and he clutched his chest like he was about to have a heart attack, but he nodded.

They re-joined Timothy just in time to see the major and Joshua leave. Isaac settled down at the main console, and one by one, the screens came to life. The various camera angles showed that the church was, again, filled to near capacity.

It's only rubber bullets, it's only rubber bullets, Danny kept repeating to himself. But, looking at the thousands of people, his throat constricted at the thought of the havoc caused by a stampeding crowd. As if he were able to read Danny's mind, Terry whispered, "I wonder where Joshua will be seated. Rubber bullets at close range can do a lot of damage."

Terry once again clutched at his heart, and Danny said, "Are you okay? You're not about to have a heart attack, are you?"

Terry shook his head. "Keep looking – see if we can spot where he sits. Once we've dealt with Isaac, we'll have to find the security guards and get to Joshua before he suspects anything." Suddenly he pointed at the screen, "Look, there's Chloe, in the front row with her parents."

Danny had only ever seen photos of his sister-in-law. She was stunning in a dark green dress with long sleeves. The camera zoomed in, and he could see her expressive eyes and perfect teeth as she shook hands with various people. She appeared vulnerable next to the bulk of the senator. Danny touched Terry's arm and said, "Let's go."

Timothy said, "The door's locked, remember?"

Danny smirked, "Watch me." He grabbed the Allen keys and a credit card from the bag and had the door unlocked in less than thirty seconds. Then Danny flicked the lights off and opened the door a crack. The three of them crouched there and watched. They could see the back of Isaac's head twenty feet away.

The surround sound in the control room was phenomenal. Isaac's radio conversations, first with the control center in the Sierras and then the on-site security team, were crystal clear. Isaac directed most of the security guards to fan out in the parking lot. The response over the radio was, "But sir, in the past we've always ensured a presence at all doors of the sanctuary, especially for interfaith services when we have the Muslims and the Jews and everyone else here."

"Yes, and in the past, nothing happened other than car break-ins."

When the guard tried to protest again, Isaac cut him off, "Just do it, over and out."

Danny craned his neck to see where the communication buttons were on the console. It was imperative that they prevent Isaac from calling for help.

Isaac muttered under his breath, "Imbeciles."

Danny was just about to give the nod for the attack when a voice boomed over the speaker system, "Isaac, can you hear me?"

"Yes, sir, Pastor Jeremiah. I hear you loud and clear."

His hands fluttered over the keyboard, and the camera view on the center monitor switched to where the procession was ready to enter the church.

The pastor's voice continued, "We have a slight change in plans. Katie's decided to do the welcome and to introduce Chloe. I am…" The voice trailed off, and they watched as Pastor Jeremiah handed an earpiece and battery pack to Katie.

Katie said, "I won't be needing this." She appeared to switch off the battery pack and could be seen handing it to one of the assistants.

Isaac leaped to his feet and howled at the screen, "Katie, no! Dammit, listen! Katie!" He pounded his fist on the console and screamed in frustration. Then he spun around and headed for the door. He had his hand on the green button when Danny and Terry burst from their hiding place like lava from a blown vent.

Isaac's eyes went wide and he gasped, "You…how?" He was halfway inside the airlock chamber when the brothers tackled him against the stainless-steel wall. Terry got his neck in a chokehold and Danny grasped him around the waist. He was surprised at how ferociously the reverend struggled. Unintelligible grunts and squawks emanated from Isaac and his fists rained down in a staccato on Danny's back.

Danny managed to grab hold of one of Isaac's arms and pin it against his side as they started to wrestle the man back into the control room. Then, out of the corner of his eye, Danny saw Isaac reach for the red door button. He shoved hard, but it was too late – Isaac's fist connected with the button. There was no time to think; Danny gave a mighty push and the three of them tumbled in a heap onto the control room floor. As the guillotine door came down, Danny shouted, "Watch your feet!" Then all sound was drowned out by a thud and an ear-piercing howl of pain from Isaac. He went limp, and his cries turned to whimpers, "My leg, my leg; oh God, it hurts."

Danny and Terry scrambled to their feet, panting, and stepped back. The door had come down on Isaac's left shin. Blood was oozing through the trouser leg. Danny wasn't sure, but it seemed to him like he could see a bone splinter. His stomach heaved and he looked away.

Terry was the first to recover his senses. He stepped around Isaac and pressed the green button. They could hear a mechanical noise, but nothing happened. He tried again, with the same result. Terry muttered, "Damn, it's stuck!" He pressed the button for a third time; there was a loud clank and then silence, "Now what?"

Danny felt something touch his leg and yelped. He looked down to see Isaac grasping. There was no fight left in him; he was just trying to get Danny's attention. Isaac's eyes were frantic and his voice raspy when he said, "You've got to get to Katie, get her out."

"Yes, I know; we want to get everyone out before your friend starts spraying around his rubber bullets."

Isaac's hand tightened around Danny's ankle. He coughed, "*Listen* to me!" Isaac's voice rose to strangled crescendo, "They're not rubber bullets!" He gasped for breath and his face contorted with pain, "The semi is loaded with live ammunition."

Danny and Terry exclaimed in unison, "What?! Why?!"

Isaac's face was pale, and he shook his head back and forth, "It doesn't matter. I wanted Pastor Jeremiah dead; everything else is just collateral damage." Tears filled his eyes, "Katie, my Katie, please, you have to save her. He's going to shoot her." Then Isaac lost consciousness.

Danny took command. He dashed to the communications console, picked up two earpieces and lapel mics, and flicked on their corresponding switches. He put on one set and tossed the other to his brother. "Testing, testing," Danny said, and his voice came through the invisible speakers. "Okay, like this we can stay in contact with Timothy and each other. Tim, you operate the console. Call the security team and call 911; tell them it's an active shooter scene. But they mustn't spook him!"

He scanned the monitors showing the congregation, "We have to find out exactly where Joshua's seated. Terry and I will go in; you see if you can spot him from here. Then at least we can direct the security guards or the police. And Tim, try to figure out how to disarm those attack drones; we're going to need Joshua as a witness." He looked at his watch and then up at the screen, "The procession's moving; we've only got minutes." He turned to Terry, "Come on!"

"But...the door's jammed. How...?"

"Follow me," Danny said and held up his phone, the screen displaying the church floor plans.

***

Terry followed Danny into the vacated data center and to the firemen's ladder that took them straight up to a grated metal walkway. They ducked through a low door and the organ music hit them full force. The sound seemed to collect like smoke right under the ceiling – thick and intense. They took in the web of walkways and gantries that clung to the rafters, supporting a constellation of spotlights. Where to begin?

"Let's split up," Terry said, "I'll head over to the other side, and you can move down this side towards the front." He raced towards the center of the church, stopping from time to time to peer at the crowd below. It was impossible to think of picking out a single face in the congregation, but he had to try.

He heard Danny's voice in his earpiece, "Ouch, shit!"

Terry froze. "Danny? Are you okay?"

"Yeah, I just tripped. Watch out. Some fucking arsehole has left light fittings lying around in the walkways. I nearly kicked one down onto people's heads."

"Don't swear in a church," Terry said.

There was a smile in Danny's voice when he retorted, "What are you now – my big brother?"

Terry grinned, "Be careful little bro."

The procession reached the altar and broke up as everyone took their places. A jolt tore through Terry's heart as he watched Chloe shift over to make space for Katie and Pastor Jeremiah.

He heard Danny's voice in his ear, "Timothy, have you found Joshua yet?"

Timothy grunted that he couldn't do miracles.

The organ music seized, and Terry whispered, "We've got to think about this logically. The shooter has to be somewhere with a clear line of sight, and he'd want to be near an exit."

Danny answered, "They're not planning to let him leave, remember. They're going to get him with those mini-drones." There was a pause, then Danny continued with excitement in his voice, "Timothy, look for the drone nest. If we can find that…"

Terry crisscrossed forward along the walkways as fast he could while scanning the church below and keeping an eye open for the bits of equipment that cluttered the path. He saw a young man with a guitar seat himself on a stool near the altar and strum a few chords. When the rich, clear voice filled the church, Terry couldn't help but stop to look down. What a talent!

> *"Tell me something, boy*
> *Aren't you tired tryin' to fill that void?*
>
> *Or do you need more?*
> *Ain't it hard keeping it so hardcore?*

Timothy's voice came through the earpiece, "The song is three minutes and thirty-six seconds."

Danny asked, "Where are the guards?"

"They wouldn't believe me at first, but now they're on their way."

"And the police?"

"Twelve minutes away."

> *"In all the good times, I find myself*
> *Longing for change*
> *And in the bad times, I fear myself…"*

There was a pause during which the haunting words echoed through the church. Then Danny's voice, "I'm

339

going down; this walkway leads to an access point into the sacristy."

Terry felt his insides contract and he lurched forward, scanning across the expanse to see where Danny was. He waved frantically and said, "No, Danny. It's too dangerous. Let me go."

> *"...In the shallow, shallow*
> *We're far from the shallows now... "*

He saw Danny wave in the far distance, near the front of the church. Then Danny said, "I have to do this; you can't get there in time – keep looking for Joshua." And Danny was gone.

Terry barely registered the song's end, but he saw Katie go up to the altar and turn to face the congregation. How could three minutes have gone by so fast? He was frantic. *Think, Terry, think*. Where would a shooter position himself? In soccer, tennis, baseball – most sports – the player always did better going cross-court. The same was true for shooting. If the shooter was right-handed, he'd pull the trigger with his right hand – steadier aim. So, he'd want to be on the right-hand side of the church. Was he right-handed? *Yes*, he'd held his hymnal in his right hand. Terry charged forward as Katie started to welcome the guests.

Timothy's voice reached him, "I've located Joshua. Eastside, fourth row from the front. He's got the aisle seat; it's close to the side exit."

Terry ran, not caring how much noise he made. Timothy's voice broke in again, and he was panicked, "I can't disarm the drones; there's a password on them. I can direct them to someone else's face, but they have to have a target."

Danny's panting voice, "What about Isaac? He must know the password."

"Still passed out. Shall I just leave it locked on Joshua?"

Terry's mind was spinning. Joshua was a fool, a misguided fool. But he sure didn't deserve to have his face blown up. But then, who else? Who could step in to be the sacrifice? It was an impossible choice. He glanced down to where Chloe was stepping up to join Katie.

Then he shouted into the microphone, "Jesus Christ."

"What?"

"Timothy, that big moving picture of the Last Supper; grab the image of Jesus and make it the target."

"But…but that's not a real person. I don't know if the drones…"

Danny's voice cut in, "Just do it, Tim! Please!"

Terry asked, "Where are you, Danny?"

"In the sacristy."

"I see him," Terry shouted and sprinted forward. He saw a man with a blue jacket and dark hair getting up ahead of him. Then Terry saw the weapon and heard the first hesitant shot go off. Oh God, no! Chloe! They were too late. Terry lunged, tripped, righted himself. What had he tripped over? He reached down, barely breaking his stride, and scooped up a light fitting the size of a grapefruit.

The scene that unfolded over the next seconds, and the despair that threatened to paralyze him, would haunt Terry in the days and months to come. The scene would also be played over and over in slow motion on every cable station in the country till Terry would no longer be able to distinguish between what he saw on TV and what was his own memory.

Gerald was positioned closest to the shooter, Chloe at the lectern twenty feet away from him, and Katie another ten feet further to the left, near the altar. When the first shots rang out, all three whipped their heads to the side in almost comic unison, looking straight at the attacker. The

341

bullets hit a vase on the altar that exploded and sent a shower of shards and flowers reaching into thin air.

Chloe was the first to recognize danger, and she drew her head down between her shoulders. The flimsy lectern offered no protection. Katie's face was serene, resigned; she simply stood, waiting, with arms hanging down by her sides. Then Gerald reacted. He gripped the guitar by its neck and stretched out his arms like a rock star at the end of a concert. He made himself as big a shield as he could and stepped forward to place himself between the shooter and the two women. The calmness and resolve in his features at that moment would end up being the subject of nationwide debate and admiration for days to come.

Terry watched in horror as the gunman swung the semi to the right and set off the next rat-tat-tat salvo. The guitar splintered and shattered, and the first screams from the audience could be heard. Gerald took a few steps back to stand right in front of Chloe. Then Katie clasped her upper arm; blood appeared between her fingers.

The door to the sacristy flew open and Danny burst in – a streaking blur in full flight. He ran with his head dipped low. At the same time, Pastor Jeremiah propelled himself out of his seat to embrace and protect his daughter. The gunman appeared momentarily confused. He had taken his finger off the trigger and was waving the semi from left to right, trying to decide where to aim. Terry felt the weight of the light in his hands. He measured the distance to the gunman with his eyes. This was unlike any shot anyone had ever taken on a basketball court, and yet... The rat-tat-tat started again, and Terry launched his projectile with both hands, aiming for the gunman's head.

As the gunfire resumed, Danny hurled himself forward with his arms outstretched. He knocked both Gerald and Chloe off their feet. The three of them sprawled onto the thick carpet as bullets flew over their heads and imprinted a line of dots in the wall behind the altar. The gunman had found his aim, and it looked like someone was creating a long, straight perforation that moved forward relentlessly until it hit...Pastor Jeremiah's back. Three red dots, neatly aligned, erupted on the pastor's ivory satin cassock. The blood spread, and the crowd's hysterical screams rose to a crescendo.

Then the light fitting hit the gunman on the shoulder and the semi slipped from his hands. After a stunned second or two, Joshua tried to reach for the weapon, but a phalanx of congregants wrestled him to the ground and he disappeared under a heap of bodies.

Terry had a sickening vision of the drones finding their way into that knot of humanity and exploding. So he shouted, "Get away from him, just take the weapon!" But it was pointless; no one could hear anything above the crowd's panicked cries. Timothy's voice came through the earpiece, "The drones..."

Terry looked up just in time to see the two specs zoom across the upper void of the sanctuary and smash into the Last Supper – right into the face of Jesus with a barely audible pop, pop sound. Time stood still. Then, the entire sanctuary reverberated with an unearthly creaking as the gigantic glass surface cracked, splintered and crashed down behind the altar like a Niagara Falls of glass. The noise was deafening. There was something majestic in the way the millions of glass pieces shimmered and sparkled as they cascaded down before bouncing and scattering across the area behind the altar.

***

Katie heard the first shots and felt transported into one of those scenes from war movies like *Private Ryan,* where one could see people scream, see the mayhem, but hear only a deafening silence. The visual stimuli bombarded her senses to the point where here brain blurred out sound, smell and touch. Something scratched her arm. Then her father loomed up in front of her, his face etched with determination and concern. He enfolded her in his arms, and she felt safe – safe like when she'd been a little girl and begged, "Make me fly, Daddy." He used to hold her wrists in his strong hands and spin her around in wide circles. Oh, the exhilaration of her feet lifting off the ground and her hair flying loose as she laughed, enjoying the freedom that came from entrusting herself into her father's hands.

Jeremiah's heart pounded against her chest. When had he last held her close enough for her to feel his heartbeat? She realized now that a distance had grown between them since her mother had died; they hardly ever hugged anymore. Katie resolved that she would hug her father every day from now on. She would tell him all she had done, and he would know how to fix it. He always knew how to make things right. Why hadn't she just gone to him long ago? A great calm descended over her.

Then the pop, pop, pop of three jolts transmitted themselves from his chest to hers like three Maverick-wave-size heartbeats.

Over her father's shoulder, she saw the face of the shooter. He was young and pale with cold eyes. Suddenly, his mouth opened, and his eyes darted about in shock and surprise. Poor misguided soul. *Make me an instrument in your hand – but in whose hand? God's hand? Our God works in mysterious ways. Who am I to question?*

An object fell on the shooter. The gun slipped out of his hand, and her father became strangely heavy in her arms. She was tired, oh so tired; she didn't have the strength to support him any longer. *Come on, Dad, I can't do this alone.* She sank down onto the altar step just in time to break his fall. His head came to rest in her lap. She stared at the three red dots on his back without comprehension. It took a while to register that it was blood spreading like circles on a pond. She reached out with both hands to stem the flow.

Her ears woke up to the sound of crashing glass, loud and violent beyond anything she'd ever heard before. Instinctively she bent forward to protect her father from a hail storm of glass, and suddenly the world was turning again at its normal speed. She saw the frantic congregation, the gunman wrestled to the ground, Chloe and Gerald on the floor with another young man. Eleanor's face was anguished as her hands reached outKatie's to her daughter. Mitch was halfway out of his seat, lunging towards Chloe.

Jeremiah opened his eyes. His voice was a whisper, "My Katie – you're the best daughter a father could ever want. I love you."

Then he closed his eyes and exhaled his final breath with a shudder. Katie sat, stunned, unable to comprehend the blank stare in her father's eyes. She touched his face, and her hand left a stain – blood. Quickly she withdrew.

It felt like an eternity before Mitch came over to her. He knelt down, closed the pastor's eyes, and said, "Katie, I'm here for you. Whatever you need."

Katie looked down at Pastor Jeremiah, the only man whose daughter she would ever truly be, and then met Mitch's gaze. "Thank you, Mitch. But Jeremiah will always be my father."

Mitch's eyes widened, and Katie knew that they understood each other.

***

Danny helped Chloe and Gerald to their feet and waited as
Chloe steadied herself against him. She was shaking
uncontrollably. Her eyes darted from Katie to her father, her
mother, the gunman, the crowd, and finally to Danny,
"What happened? I mean…I know what happened…a
gunman. But why? Did anyone get hurt?" Her eyes flitted
back to Katie, "Oh my God, Jeremiah!"

Danny held her back, "The EMTs are on their way;
best to give them space."

Seconds later, Terry was there and crushed them both
against his chest, "It's okay, baby; everything's fine,"
Terry's voice was thick with emotion. "Thank God neither
of you is hurt. I was…" He choked back tears.

Danny and Terry's eyes met over Chloe's head, and
Terry mouthed, "Thank you". Danny had a massive lump in
his throat and didn't trust himself to speak. Instead, he
squeezed his brother's shoulder. Chloe started to cry, and
Danny left her in Terry's arms. He heaved a sigh of relief
when he saw policemen swarming into the sanctuary and
starting to calm the crowd. A team of paramedics came
down the aisle to where a circle of people had formed
around Katie and Jeremiah. There was nothing he could do
to help there.

His eyes fell on Gerald, who stood apart from
everyone else amid the glassy rubble behind the altar.
Danny walked over and got a fright when he saw Gerald's
anguished face. His friend looked as though he might be
sick at any moment. Danny touched his arm, "Hey, it's
over, it's okay." Gerald shook as if in the grip of a fever,
and Danny embraced him, "It's just the shock, buddy;
you'll be fine. It's over. Look, the police are leading the
shooter away; they got him."

When Gerald didn't respond, Danny said, "Come on,
we'd better get you over to the medics. Have someone

check you out." He tried a chuckle, "It's not every day a guy steps out in front of a gunman the way you did. That's bound to knock you." Gerald didn't budge. Instead, he placed his hands on Danny's shoulders and looked him in the eyes. Danny was relieved that a normal color was returning to his friend's face and that there was the usual intense brilliance in his eyes.

"You saved my life," Gerald said.

Danny squirmed and didn't know how to respond. He tried to crack a joke, "I thought you'd be giving God the credit – we're all just pawns in his big scheme and all that." He chuckled sheepishly, but Gerald's expression didn't change.

Gerald took a breath and said, "You know how they say you see your whole life flash by just before you die?" He paused. "When I stepped out in front of that gunman, I experienced that. I saw my life – not every minute of it, but the essence of it – and I was convinced I was going to die."

Danny interrupted, "Gerald, you don't have to do this now. There will be plenty of time…"

"No, you have to hear this. I was sure that this was the end, and you know what? I was okay with that. If this was God's plan for me, so be it, except…" He lowered his gaze. "Except, suddenly I thought of one major regret, and that led me to think of more regrets, and the life I could and should have flashed before me, and suddenly it no longer felt okay to die, not at all."

Gerald's face had become flushed, and his hands were shaking.

Danny grasped his friend's wrists and tried to soothe him, "Hey, that's okay; that's totally fine. Not even a saint marches off to their death without regrets. Don't beat yourself up, for heaven's sake. You did more than anyone could have expected; you were awesome!" He paused and pointed at Chloe and Terry, who were still embracing, "You

347

saved Chloe's life – look at them. After all that Terry's been through. If something had happened to her, I don't know…" He broke off, overcome with emotion.

Danny pulled himself together and put on a smile, "What was your major regret, or is that a big secret?"

Gerald's gaze was so intense that Danny thought the older boy was trying to drink him in with his eyes. Then Gerald moved his hands up Danny's neck, slowly, tentatively, till his hands cupped Danny's face. Finally, he leaned forward and kissed Danny on the mouth. At first, it was a gentle brush of the lips, but then urgency overcame him, and he pressed down hard, his tongue pushing out to explore and to share his newfound passion for life.

Danny wrapped his arms around Gerald, closed his eyes, and allowed himself to sink into this moment. *Let the world turn without me for a while,* he thought.

The spell was broken when a voice filled the church, "Many of you know me as Katie Blanchard, Public Relations Officer of the Church of Holy Redemption in Tracy California, and I have a confession to make. In fact, I have several confessions to make…"

Danny spun around to the larger-than-life picture of Katie that filled the screens behind him. The remaining crowd stilled and watched as Katie' recording filled the sanctuary. Danny turned to look at Katie herself, who appeared to be in a trance, while the paramedics pried her father's body from her hands. Despite his vehement wish to avenge Lily, he felt a pang of pity for her as she held onto the lifeless body of her father.

Timothy's voice came through his earpiece, "Everything is going according to plan. The virus is burning through the systems."

"Thank you, Tim; you've done great."

Tim answered, "You'll be pleased to know that the police and medics have just taken Isaac away." He paused, "You can go back to what you were doing before."

Danny blushed and Gerald gave him a quizzical stare. Danny pointed to the lapel microphone and said, "Timothy's been listening to every word we said." They both broke out into laughter, earning themselves reproachful stares from nearby congregants.

Chapter 28, Aftermath

Sunday afternoon, 2nd Week of July

Sarah Bates watched the kettle, waiting for it to boil. Her eyes were red and puffy, and her hair hung limp about her face. Anyone who might have seen the spritely bundle of efficiency that morning would not have recognized her as the chairperson of the refreshment committee. She dared not move her eyes from the kettle for fear that the alien surroundings would send her into another spasm of tears. Her church – the sanctuary, the gathering hall, the offices – was crawling with FBI agents, policemen, and all manner of other serious-looking people. They went about their business as if this were normal. The only thing normal was the kettle; it still took forever to boil.

The last time she had looked outside, she had been shocked to see that a mobile city, populated by TV crews, law enforcement and their support staff, had sprung up in the parking lot. Satellite dishes, cameras, reporters, and curious onlookers generated a buzzing cacophony. Sarah was a mild-mannered woman, but she had visions of Pastor Jeremiah stepping forth and sending them all on their way, like Jesus when he chased the money changers from the temple.

The thought of Jeremiah brought on another stream of tears and her friend, Jessica, embraced her. They cried together till Sarah spluttered, "I cannot bear to think of him, alone in that cold morgue. And…" she sobbed, pointing to the yellow police tape across the sanctuary door, "his blood on the altar steps. They won't let me go in to clean." She wailed, "His holy blood left for people to trample on."

Jessica tried to comfort her, "I'm sure they're being very respectful. They have to do a thorough investigation. We all want to know how such a terrible thing could happen – here, of all places. That someone could be so filled with hatred; it…" She broke off and buried her face against Sarah's neck.

The kettle started to boil, and Sarah dried her eyes with a dishcloth, "Well, we have to think of the living. Will you take tea to the senator in the board room? I'm going to offer the policemen more coffee."

She placed a coffee jug and mugs on a tray and carried them to the far end of the room, where a group of law enforcement agents were gathered around a TV. She nearly dropped the tray when she saw the breaking news banner, *Terror in Tracy*. How dare they? An older agent stepped forward and took the tray from her, "Thank you very much, ma'am." He looked at her with concern and said, "Maybe you don't want to see this right now?"

Sarah didn't want to see it, but she couldn't tear herself away. The entire incident, in detail, played itself out on the screen. She flinched every time she heard the shots ring out. The splintering guitar above Gerald's serene face was shown in slow motion. And when the camera zoomed in on the blood spurting from the pastor's back, Sarah brought up her hands to cover her eyes. The church's many high-definition cameras showed the events from several angles. Over and over, the scenes repeated with the reporter speculating on the shooter's motivations in breathless tones.

351

It was surreal – like a movie production rather than the shaky cellphone videos one tended to see on the news. For a moment, Sarah had the fervent hope that it was all a nightmare.

"Where did the cable channels get all this camera footage?" Sarah asked.

A young agent, who didn't take his eyes off the screen, said, "Apparently, the guys in the remote-control center were offering to sell the footage before the pastor's body was even cold. Bet they got a good price. This is the sort of thing the cable stations love; real-time footage in high def. Can't ask for more."

Sara gasped and thought of the guards at Golgotha, who had gambled to see who would get Christ's clothes.

The older agent admonished his colleague, "Show some respect."

Then the picture moved to a meeting room inside the church, where the CNN anchor was interviewing three young men. They were the young man with the voice of an angel, who had stepped in front of the gunman, the handsome surfer boy who had burst into the church and saved the lives of several people, and a third boy that Sarah had not seen before.

***

Terry watched as Chloe poured tea for the six people seated around the boardroom table: herself, Katie, Senator McGrath, the deputy attorney general for the state of California, the FBI's lead investigator, and himself. He let his left hand glide over his right arm. Up and down, up and down. Just to feel something real. Something normal to convince him that he wasn't in some *Matrix*-like alternative universe.

They had just finished watching Katie's video confession again. No one seemed to know what to say or where to start. FBI agent Braun and the deputy AG were writing notes, Senator McGrath stared out of the window, and Chloe seemed intent on pouring six perfect cups of tea.

Terry had known parts of the story, suspected some of it, and then got further confirmation from Danny that morning. But ironically, it was near impossible to absorb the facts when they were spelled out so clinically, precisely. An experiment gone wrong was one thing – a terrible thing, but still, understandable. Yet to think that Lily had died because people had continued practices that they knew were lethal was unconscionable. They might as well have gone around putting poison into the city's water supply to see how many people survived what dose.

Terry looked across the table at the puddle of misery that was Katie. She appeared to have shrunk as she sat staring at her hands in her lap. She hadn't had a chance to change, and there were smears of blood on her dress.

Terry was at war with himself. A part of him felt vicious satisfaction that Katie had lost her father; let her feel the pain, see what it's like to have a loved one die an untimely death. And wasn't Pastor Jeremiah ultimately responsible? The buck must stop somewhere. Why didn't he practice better oversight? The man had been a narcissistic fool. He got his just desserts. Another part of him was horrified at these thoughts. Katie carried much of the blame, but Isaac had been the mastermind behind the ongoing deliberate blackmail. Still, she'd played with fire and let the genie out of the bottle. Then again, whom do you blame, the sorcerer or the apprentice? Why hadn't Professor Curry done more? Where was the East Bay University's oversight? *You're thinking like a lowlife lawyer, gravitating towards the deep pockets. Stop that!* But there was individual accountability – Katie was an intelligent woman; how could she have let things get so out of hand?

Terry thought he might explode with the hurt, rage, frustration and sorrow that roiled through him. And then there was the guilt that had been his constant companion since Lily's death. If he'd been there, if he'd paid more attention, then Lily would have confided in him and he could have prevented her death. Could he really unleash all his anger and emotion on Katie when he also carried blame?

Katie lifted her gaze and looked at him, "Terry, I am so, so sorry." Her eyes shifted to Chloe, then back to Terry, "I will take whatever punishment comes my way, and I would totally understand if neither of you ever speaks to me again. I will not insult the memory of your sister by even asking for your forgiveness." She sobbed and wiped her nose with the back of her hand.

Terry took a deep breath. He knew that his next words would be defining for the rest of their lives. For Katie, for Chloe and, most of all, for himself. Beside him, Chloe sat completely still, and he appreciated that. It was an untenable situation for her, too – torn between loyalty to her best friend and the man she had spent ten years of her life with.

He closed his eyes to still the raging demons vying for his soul. What would Lily do? What would Lily want him to do? Finally, he said, "I don't know what the courts will decide, but you're right not to ask for my forgiveness. I cannot forgive you. Ultimately, this is going to be between you and your God."

She looked so miserable that he reached across the table, briefly took her hand in his, and squeezed it. Katie nodded and mouthed thank you.

The deputy attorney general cleared her throat and said, "This is a very delicate situation. I will be totally frank, Miss Blanchard – part of me wants to put you behind bars and throw away the key."

The senator interjected, "Surely not, Allison, the girl has just lost her father…"

"Mitch, I have every sympathy, but you know as well as I do that a person's personal circumstance and tragedy have no bearing whatsoever on crimes that may or may not have been committed. At best, they become a factor during the sentencing phase." She held up her hand when the senator made to interject again, "I will concede that there never appears to have been any malicious intent but, at best, Miss Blanchard is guilty of gross negligence. She was in a position of authority where she could have – and should have – ensured that these...these algorithms...were used with proper care. She, more than anyone, knew how dangerous they were." She turned to her FBI colleague and asked, "Any early insights from the investigation?"

Agent Braun consulted his notes and said, "This is going to take months to unravel, but so far we've learned the following." He started to count off on his fingers, "The computer systems have been annihilated; we're getting cooperation from Mr. Patel and BDA to salvage what evidence we can. CAFCA and the Reverend O'Neill conspired to stage a mock domestic terrorism attack to showcase a new defensive drone technology to generate business. Joshua Snyder, the shooter, seems to have been a pawn in this scenario. He would have been blown up if it had not been for the intervention of–" he looked up and pointed, "Mr. Reynolds here and his brother.

"Reverend Isaac O'Neill had his own secret agenda. He substituted live ammunition for the rubber bullets and wanted to have Pastor Jeremiah assassinated. It speaks to the ruthlessness of the man that he had scant regard for the incidental danger to," he looked up again, "Mrs. Reynolds – I mean Ms. McGrath – and the young man who was on stage to sing. At this stage, Joshua and Major McCullum are clamoring to be state witnesses and to testify against each other and against the Reverend O'Neill."

He looked at his cell phone, "And I've had three messages from Ms. Bussey, CAFCA's chief legal officer; she wants to speak to me."

The deputy AG said, "Yes, she's been trying to contact me as well. Interesting." She played with her pen, then said, "Nothing so far indicates that Miss Blanchard was implicated in *today's* events."

For the first time, Katie showed a sign of life. She leaned forward, her voice hoarse, "Are you suggesting that I would have been part of some plot to…to…" Her voice rose, "to assassinate my own father and one of my very best friends?"

The FBI agent said, "Miss Blanchard, right now we don't know what to believe; we're simply gathering evidence. However, we do have to consider the fact that you were placed under duress by Mr. O'Neill, and you gave the orders to destroy the church's computer systems. That is tampering with evidence."

Katie sank back into her chair and bowed her head. Chloe said, "Surely not. My client here…" Everyone, including Katie, looked at Chloe in surprise. She continued, "What? What did you expect? Everyone's entitled to legal defense. She's my client, at least until a suitably-qualified defense attorney can be found."

Katie was at breaking point. Tears streamed down her face, and her hands were shaking in her lap. Senator McGrath stepped in and said, "Allison, Agent Braun, can we possibly continue this tomorrow? Katie needs a chance to get cleaned up. She also needs to briefly meet with the church elders to delegate leadership. They're a flock of thousands that have just lost their shepherd."

Katie looked at him and said, "My father's funeral; I have to start planning. Will they let me do that from prison?"

The senator placed a hand on hers and said, "Leave that to me. I'll help you as much as you want me to." He looked at the deputy AG and said, "So, where do we go from here?"

She sighed. "We need to see where the investigation takes us; and also open up the case of the original set of suicides and EBU's handling of the matter." She turned to Terry, "How's Professor Curry doing?"

"He's going to pull through. Apparently, he was quite lucid this morning."

"Good. He'll be a crucial witness. Senator, if Ms. Blanchard surrenders her passport as well as her laptop and cellphone, I'm prepared to release her into your custody until a bail hearing can be arranged." She got up, looked from the senator to Chloe, and said, "Both your reputations are on the line."

When she and agent Braun had left, Katie broke down in Mitch's arms. He let her cry, then commandeered a group of security guards who ushered him and Katie out of a side entrance and into the church's center for battered and abused women.

It was the first time Terry and Chloe had been alone since the shooting. She took his hand and brought it to her lips, "Thank you."

"For what?"

Chloe cocked her head, "Where do I start? For being there when I needed you; for saving my life; for believing in me; for…"

He leaned forward and kissed her. When he finally pulled away, he grinned and said, "You'd better stop, or I might get a swollen head."

"Seriously," she said, "you continue to surprise me in the best possible way." She choked back tears and Terry was content to just embrace her. A minute later, she rubbed a hand across his chest and sniffled, "I made your shirt all wet with my bawling."

He stroked her hair, and his voice was raw, "When I thought I was going to lose you…I don't think I would have survived it."

She looked up into his eyes, "Terry, do you think we can try again? I mean, try to really get to know each other. See if there is maybe a future together for us.

Terry thought his chest would explode. He hugged her tight and pulled her hair into the crook of his neck, letting his fingers massage her scalp. "I'd like that very much," he whispered in a thick voice.

The door burst open, and a wholly unapologetic voice said, "Are we interrupting something?"

Danny, Gerald, and Timothy trooped in, followed by the Renaissance Institute's head of security, Captain Flynn. Danny introduced his friends, and Terry thought it was bizarre; he felt like he had known these boys all his life, they'd been through so much together – they had saved Chloe's life, but of course, they hadn't really met. His own brother hadn't met his wife before. Gerald and Danny hugged Chloe and Timothy waved hello to everybody from the edge of their circle.

The boys were still on an adrenalin high, and Danny gave them a run-down of the CCN interview, "You know how she started the interview? She sat there and said, 'Let's start with that kiss; the pictures have gone viral around the world'. I mean, seriously, with all that's gone down?"

Gerald laughed and said, "And you know what Danny answered? He said, no, let's not. Let's start with all the serious shit that has been going on here for years."

Terry couldn't help himself. He said, "You swore, in a church, on national TV?"

"International TV," Timothy corrected, and Terry groaned.

"Anyway," Danny said, "We've just come to say goodbye. Captain Flynn here is taking us back to the institute."

"What?!" Chloe exclaimed. "No way are you going back there. You're coming with us."

"All of us?" Danny asked with a wry smile. "I'm not going anywhere without Timothy and Gerald. Tim's parents are flying in from the East Coast and will be here tomorrow. We haven't heard yet from Gerald's parents."

"We'll make a plan," Chloe said. "I've got space in my apartment."

"Some of us might have to share a bed," Terry smirked and smiled at Chloe, who blushed.

The captain cleared his throat, "Ma'am, I'm afraid I can't allow that. This young man stole a vehicle from one of our staff members, and this one," he pointed at Timothy, "was an accessory to the fact. Dr. Roberts is pressing charges of grand theft auto and insists we bring the young men to the institute."

If Terry had thought the situation was bizarre before, he now thought he had stepped through the looking glass. His maelstrom of emotions found a convenient target and he rounded on the captain, "Tell Dr. Roberts to piss off and get a life."

Chloe put a hand on his arm, "What my husband meant to say is, we strongly urge Dr. Roberts to consider what this action might look like in a court of law. I don't think there is a potential juror in all of California who would not have seen these young men's brave actions on TV. And there is legal precedent for commandeering a vehicle to prevent a serious crime. If the doctor wishes to pursue a legal path, we'd be more than happy to see him in court."

359

The captain huffed, "They cannot just leave the institute at will."

Terry got right up into his face, "We'll sort out whatever paperwork is needed from the courts but they. Are. Not. Going. Back. I guarantee you that by tomorrow evening every judge in the country will fall over themselves to disassociate from the," he spat the words, "Renaissance Institute."

The captain muttered something about this not being the last of it and left.

Danny pointed from Terry to Chloe with a wide grin and said, "You two getting back together again? That's so cool."

Chloe smiled coyly, "Well, we'll see." She looked up at Terry, "At least we are going to give it a try."

"Awesome!"

Raised voices reached them from outside the boardroom – it sounded like a serious altercation. A forceful woman's voice said, "Out of my way, young man. I will not tolerate your interference. My boy is in there." When the guard tried to reason, she continued, "I will count to three, and so help me, God. One…"

Gerald groaned, "Oh no," and went to open the door.

"Gerald, my baby!"

Mrs. Myers steamrolled into the room. She was a commanding presence with bottle-blond hair swept back into a mane and flashing eyes accentuated by dark eyeliner. She wore a billowing gray-and-black pantsuit, offset by crimson shoes and a matching purse that she held like a battering ram in front of her. She engulfed Gerald in a hug. "My baby," she kept repeating. "What an awful, awful business. I came immediately. This," she held up her purse, "is all I brought. I didn't pack a thing. Lina drove me to the airport while Elsie did her online magic to book me a flight."

Terry surveyed the immaculate hair, dress and shoes, and pictured the way Mrs. Myers would usually travel – with a porter wheeling at least three suitcases behind her and a plethora of those hat-and-make-up boxes that were fashionable in the fifties.

"It's…it's good to see you, Mom," Gerald managed to say.

"Poor, poor baby; Mommy's come to take you home. We leave tomorrow at noon." She let her eyes sweep the room to see if there was any dissent to this announcement. Terry wished that Captain Flynn were still there. He would have liked to see him try and go up against this force of nature.

Mrs. Myers noticed Danny for the first time. Her eyes flitted between Gerald and Danny. She held out her hand and said, "I'm Gerald's mother."

Danny shook hands and bowed, "Very pleased to meet you, ma'am. Gerald has told me lots about you."

She smiled, then pulled Gerald to one side. She might have thought she was being discreet, but her voice carried when she whispered, "Your father was…very upset about that image. You know, you and that boy."

Gerald took a step back, and there was an edge in his voice. "Really, is that what father saw? He didn't see me singing in front of five thousand people in the church of his hero, Pastor Jeremiah? He didn't see me in the face of danger? He didn't see the Pastor Jeremiah gunned down in cold blood?"

"Gerald, please. Keep your voice down."

Gerald moved across the room and draped an arm around Danny's neck. He faced his mother and said, "It's a funny thing, Mother. Other people might have seen *that* kiss, but they saw a lot more besides it. What am I supposed to do, so that my father will finally accept me for who I am?"

Mrs. Myers dabbed her eyes with a handkerchief and said, "Gerald, you will not speak to your mother in that tone."

"If you don't like it, you are free to leave."

Mrs. Myers gulped for air and struggled to regain her composure. She tugged at her sleeves, "I know you're upset. I won't hold anything you've said against you, but please, Gerald, you must understand that it's a shock for your father. Just give him some time; he'll come around."

Gerald sighed and gave Danny a squeeze. His voice was calm when he said, "I'll give him time. I'll give him till eight o'clock tomorrow morning. If he texts me by eight a.m. to say that he accepts who I am, then I'll meet you at the airport and fly home with you."

"And if he doesn't?" she asked with a quiver in her voice.

Gerald gave her a lopsided grin. "Then I won't come home. I will no longer go where I'm not accepted."

Before his mother could say anything, he took her by the elbow and guided her toward the door. "Come, let's see if one of these nice security people can help find you an Uber to your hotel. We'll talk in the morning."

When he re-entered the room, he plonked himself into a chair, rested his face in his hands, and groaned. Terry looked at Chloe and Danny, and both raised their shoulders, not knowing what to say or do.

There was a suppressed guffaw from the corner of the room, then another. Everyone stared at Timothy, who tried to stifle his giggles. Finally, he spluttered, "Your mother is very funny."

Everybody, including Gerald, joined in the laughter, and Terry whispered to Chloe, "Makes Eleanor seem like a dream mother-in-law."

The FBI shielded the group as they were whisked through a side exit to a waiting black SUV with tinted windows. Danny lost all sense of direction as the driver sped through side streets and residential neighborhoods to shake off any media or other thrill-seekers. He must have dozed off, because it was dark when he woke up. Gerald and Timothy were asleep on either side of him. He turned to Terry and Chloe in the back row and asked, "Where are we?"

"Change of plans," Terry said. "We got word that Chloe's flat was staked out by the media, so we're headed for the McGrath's cabin at Lake Tahoe."

"It's very rustic," Chloe said, "So don't expect too much. My mother called the neighbor to lay in some supplies for us."

Danny grinned. A barn or tent would have been fine with him; any accommodation without a fence was better than what he was used to.

Twenty minutes later, the vehicle snaked up a winding path and came to a halt in front of the cabin. They got out and Danny turned in a slow circle to take it all in. Below them, the moonlight shimmered off the lake, and beyond that the mountains were a black silhouette against the sky. A coyote howled and an owl answered. A warm, inviting glow spread from the windows across the covered porch where an array of rocking chairs, a lounger, and even a hammock beckoned their welcome.

The others went inside but Danny remained on the porch. He couldn't believe it. This was it! This was the cabin he'd seen in his dreams. A place where he would live with his brother and sister-in-law, like a proper family.

Terry came out, beer in hand. They stood in silence, side by side, and listened to the sounds of the night. Chloe came to stand on Danny's other side. She inhaled deeply and sighed, "Do you like it?"

Danny said, "This is so amazing, being here, with you guys. Yesterday this was a dream...and now." He placed an arm around each of them and held them tight – his family.

"Can I cook for you tomorrow?" Danny blurted.

"You cook?" they both said in unison.

From behind them, Gerald said, "Does he ever. Danny here is an aspiring master chef."

Terry and Chloe high-fived each other, and Terry said, "Man, have we lucked out."

Epilogue
Tahoe, nine months later, last Saturday in May

The morning sun streamed into the room as Danny pulled on his running gear, causing Charlie to whimper and bounce up and down with anticipation.

"Quiet, Charlie," Danny whispered, "Let Terry and Chloe sleep in."

Danny slipped out into the fresh air and stopped to look across the lake. The view from the porch never got old. Danny, Terry and Chloe spent at least one weekend per month at the Tahoe cabin; it had become their sanctuary – a place to regroup and recharge.

Danny, with Charlie beside him, set off south along the lakeshore and reflected on the last nine months. Despite Katie's televised confession, Pastor Jeremiah's memorial service had rivaled the pomp and circumstance of a state funeral. Celebrities from far and wide came to eulogize him. Their voices faded into the mist when, a week later, the AG brought a string of charges, including culpable homicide and racketeering, against the Church of Holy Redemption and its subsidiaries. The facts of the C.O.L.D. index, and the practices of *The Settlement Bureau*, fueled a media frenzy. Every day brought new revelations. CAFCA

365

fought a determined rearguard action to disassociate itself, branding Major McCullum and Joshua Snyder as "rogue elements, operating in a sinister anti-gun conspiracy under the guidance of liberal forces." Their supporters believed them, but nobody else did.

Within weeks, the courts had frozen all of the church's assets in anticipation of payments for the suicide and other blackmail victims. Pastor Jeremiah's memorial service was the last service ever to be held in the church he had built. It was sold to a retail chain and scheduled to be converted into a distribution center.

Gerald and Timothy were out of state and shielded from the tumult, but the McGrath mansion, where Katie stayed under stringent bail conditions, was a fortress under siege. Chloe's apartment, which was now Danny's home, was not much better. Ironically, Danny handled the pressure better than most for two reasons. The first: most of the attention levied at him was positive, bordering on the adulatory. He was a hero. The second: he'd experienced it all before, and this time he was not alone; he had his brother and sister-in-law by his side.

It was harder for Chloe who, as an aspiring politician, was under extreme scrutiny. Terry wasn't given an inch either, once the media connected him to Carl Gunderson. It got so bad that Chloe and the senator employed a public relations firm to deal with social media and the torrent of emails, requests for interviews, book deals, and speaking engagements. The most disturbing aspect of all the attention was that it divided itself into mindless adulation on the one hand and vitriolic hatred on the other. There was no middle ground. Danny, Chloe and Terry spent many a winter evening in front of the fireplace philosophizing about the way social media had amplified the best and worst of human nature.

The sun climbed higher and Danny savored its warmth on his face. In the distance, he could see a beach and the Chapel of the Bells where Terry and Chloe had been remarried the previous September. Danny had never seen a more radiantly-happy couple. Only five guests had been in attendance – Danny as best man, Clyde Curry, Sandy, and the bride's parents. Over drinks, after the ceremony, Chloe had announced that she was resigning from the law firm and quitting any idea of politics. Instead, she and Terry had decided to open a Data Privacy consultancy. Their firsthand experience of what the abuse of information could do to people's lives had fueled a passion for personal data protection.

Danny's wedding gift had been a five-course home-cooked meal at the cabin, and even Eleanor McGrath was moved to compliment him on his ceviche starter and stroganoff main course. Danny smiled at the recollection.

He reached a grassy embankment where he stripped to his speedos and waded into the frigid water. Charlie splashed about happily in the shallows. The water was so clear that Danny could see every pebble on the lake floor. *We're all pebbles in a stream*, he thought, *waiting to reach that wonderful clear lake where all will be calm and peaceful*. He chuckled at his own flawed analogy. *Peace equals death; give me the raging stream any day*.

And a raging stream it had been when the court cases started in October. Danny had divided his time between school, college applications, and the courtroom. It had been harrowing to hear the testimony of the families of suicide victims and others who had been driven to drink, drugs, or despair. Isaac was given life without parole, while Major McCullum and Joshua Snyder would spend at least five years in prison.

Katie received a twelve-year sentence and Rajiv ten years. The judge was severe in her pronouncements and wanted to send a message that those who developed new technologies had a duty to safeguard them. Katie and

Rajiv's failure to allow their tools to be used without adequate protections was considered "unconscionable." The death of Lily Reynolds and three other people was directly attributable to "their reckless disregard." Katie in particular came in for harsh criticism, because she had been in a position of power and, though well-intentioned, had ordered the destruction of vital evidence.

As Danny swam, he remembered his shock and surprise when Carl Gunderson, as Lily's next of kin, was awarded twenty million dollars in compensation. This money was immediately appropriated by a court in New York to compensate victims of the Carl Gunderson fraud. Terry and Danny had been relieved. The last thing they would have wanted was to profit from their sister's death. The New York judge also determined that the trust funds, set up by Carl in Danny and Lily's names, were to be dissolved to repay people defrauded by Carl.

In January, in a separate trial, Professor Curry, Katie, and Rajiv were tried together for the culpable homicide of the original three suicide victims, dating back to the EBU experiments. Katie and the Professor tried to outdo each other in accepting blame. The jury deliberated for five harrowing days and found the defendants guilty of a lesser charge of gross negligence. They were given suspended sentences, hence "Old Joe" a.k.a. Professor Sean Curry, avoided being sent to jail. In her ruling, the judge opened the door wide for civil litigation against the University. She didn't spare anyone, from the chancellor to the research ethics committee, in her tongue lashings regarding governance and oversight practices that were unfit for the 21st century.

Senator McGrath brokered a deal whereby the Renaissance Institute and the women's shelter were placed under the state's care. All other assets went into the victim compensation fund. CAFCA had approached the courts to recoup its investment in the church. A close examination of the contract revealed that CAFCA had usurped controlling powers of the enterprise and, in an ironic twist, the judge promptly ordered them to pay an additional thirty million towards restitution. This judgment was going through an appeals process.

Danny had had one phone conversation with his father. Then, true to form, Carl Gunderson had escaped from the Johannesburg hospital and was presumably hiding somewhere in South Africa. The S.A. police had more pressing matters to deal with than actively searching for a U.S. conman.

Carl had sent an elaborate bouquet for Terry and Chloe's wedding. Terry would have put it straight into the trash if Chloe hadn't prevented him. "What he's done is very wrong. But he is your father, and you can't get away from that."

Danny turned onto his back and spread out his arms to float in the thin layer of warm water near the surface. He wondered whether anyone had taken ownership of his secret garden. He'd never admitted it to anyone, but he missed the Renaissance Institute, especially the daily contact with his friends, Matron Holly, and the endless cat-and-mouse games with the figures in authority. It seemed childlike now, but it had filled him with purpose at the time.

From afar, he heard a car horn honking, and someone calling his name. He lifted his head and saw a figure waving from the shore. Gerald?!

Danny cut a swathe through the water and sprinted towards the grinning Gerald, who gave him a hug.

Gerald pulled away, "Ugh. You've made me all wet."

Danny laughed, "What are you doing here?"

Gerald spread his arms, "Happy birthday! I flew in from Houston last night and drove up this morning. Let's just say there's been a little conspiracy going on to make your eighteenth a special one. Come on, I'll give you a ride up to the cabin."

"Sweet ride!" Danny exclaimed when he saw Gerald's red Jeep Wrangler. "Did the rental car company give you an upgrade or have you won the lottery?" He let his hand glide over the shiny metal, "Can I drive?"

"You most certainly cannot."

Danny pouted, "You're no fun and you drive like a grandma."

Gerald laughed, "Put on your clothes and don't get the seat wet. I don't want to be stung with a penalty charge."

Charlie was allowed to jump into the back and, as Gerald pulled onto the road, Danny asked, "How're things between you and your father?"

Gerald grimaced, "Oh, you know – there's no zealot like a recent convert. I think he's vying to be Sugar Land's foremost advocate of LGBTQ issues. Trying to get our church to set up a support center." He shrugged, "We get on a lot better, but I'll be pleased to head off to college. Home feels claustrophobic."

They inched up the steep road to the cabin and Gerald asked, "And your mother – how's she?"

Danny shrugged, "A couple of magazines interviewed her and she was thrilled with the attention. The drivel she spouted was utterly embarrassing. We speak on the phone every few weeks. I might go out and visit at the end of summer."

Terry and Chloe were drinking coffee on the porch when they got back and greeted them with hugs. Terry gave Danny an extra hug, and said, "Happy birthday, little bro. Now the party can begin."

"Party?" Danny looked from one to the other. "A party at eleven o'clock in the morning?"

Terry pushed the front door open and led the way, "It's always party time somewhere in the world."

The room had been transformed with a large monitor on the dining room table and a birthday cake with eighteen candles. A collective "Surprise!" boomed from the monitor and Danny stopped dead in his tracks. The Zoom screen showed Timothy, sitting on the patio of his parents' home in Boston with a cake in front of him. The frame next to him showed Sandy and Clyde Curry holding up their champagne flutes. On the third frame was Matron Holly with an enormous birthday cake. She, Terry, and Timothy started lighting candles on their respective cakes and a golden glow enveloped everyone. Matron Holly said, "We miss you, Danny, and we're going to have a celebration here in honor of the three of you – the institute's most famous alumni."

Danny blew her a kiss and said, "I miss you too."

Zoom pinged, and another face appeared on the screen.

"Dad?!" Danny exclaimed.

Carl said, "Happy Birthday, Daniel."

"How…where are you?"

Carl smiled, "I can't tell you that, but I hope to be able to make more contact." He looked from Danny to Terry and added, "I'm so very proud of you boys."

Danny looked around the room, feeling tears prick at his eyes. "You guys! This is the best birthday ever. Thank you for organizing this."

Terry grinned and put an arm around Chloe. "You can thank your sister-in-law. She's the brains behind this operation and insisted we invite Dad as well." He looked at Carl and added somewhat reproachfully, "It took all of Clyde's team to find him."

Danny launched himself at Chloe and embraced her in a fierce hug; he buried his face in her hair to hide his tears.

Terry said, "Hey, careful – the baby."

There was an audible gasp around the virtual party, then a collective, "The baby? You're pregnant?"

Terry gave a sheepish grin and Chloe smacked him on the hand, "We were going to wait till after Danny's birthday to announce it. This is supposed to be his big day."

"I'm going to be an uncle!" Danny whooped and hugged his brother.

Gerald remarked, "That's a scary thought."

Sandy raised her champagne glass and said, "Congratulations! How does your mother feel about being a grandmother?"

Chloe rolled her eyes and laughed, "Eleanor is researching pre-schools, schools and colleges; already determined that, since I bowed out of politics, the next generation will have to make a run for the presidency."

Carl and Matron Holly dropped out of the call and the others chatted amiably, getting caught up. Terry enquired after the people at BDA and Sandy filled him in, "Simon and a few of the others have joined 1984. Clyde's father – Joe, as you insist on calling him – is living with us and spending his days volunteering among the homeless."

They ate their cake and the conversation turned to the future. Several ivy league schools were falling over each other to offer Timothy scholarships. He had yet to decide where he wanted to go. Gerald was going to study theology at UC Santa Barbara.

Clyde Curry asked, "So, Danny, have you decided what college you're going to?"

"I've been accepted at UCLA to study chemistry," Danny said. "Don't know yet what I'll do with that. I might become a CSI, or a teacher."

Terry gave a mock sigh. "Gerald in Santa Barbara and you in LA. So near, yet so far. Pity neither of you has a set of wheels."

Danny knew money was tight. Even though Terry and Chloe were off to a good start with their consultancy, they had to plow a lot back into the business. And now, with the baby on the way, there was no way they could afford to buy him a car. He was determined not to be a financial burden to them, so he had already lined up scholarships and loans to manage tuition and living costs.

He smiled and shrugged, "We'll make a plan. I'm sure I can pick up some jobs and hustle to get enough money together for a clunker that gets me to Santa Barbara for the weekend."

Terry arched an eyebrow, "Hustling? What kind of hustling did you have in mind?"

Danny grinned, "Maybe I can act as procurement agent for Juanito; supply him with cellphones and other stuff he needs."

He got a sharp smack to the back of his head from Gerald, who said, "That's not funny."

Chloe laughed and interjected, "Stop torturing him. Give it to him."

When Danny turned around, Gerald dangled the keys of the jeep in front of his nose. The keys to that beautiful, shiny, red, brand-new Jeep Wrangler.

"How…how? You can't be serious. This is too much." He was speechless, staring from one person to the other.

Terry choked up and said in a strangled voice, "My mother bought this car a couple of weeks before she died. To her, it was a symbol of freedom and defiance. I think she'd be very pleased to see you have it."

Danny threw his arms around his brother, too overcome with emotion to speak. Finally, he breathed, "Thank you, brother."

He clutched the keys to freedom and turned to Gerald, "Are you coming for the ride?"

THE END

Book Club Questions

1. What is the significance of the title? Did you find it meaningful, why or why not? What might have been an alternative title?

2. What were some of the main themes of the book? How were those themes brought to life?

3. What did you like most about the book? What did you like the least?

4. How did you experience the book? Were you immediately drawn into the story – or did it take you a while? What emotions did the book evoke?

5. Is Katie Blanchard a bad person? If she had confided in you, what advice would you have given her?

6. Pick a few of the main characters – Terry, Katie, Danny, Isaac, Jeremiah – discuss what motivates them?

7. Was there a particular scene that resonated with you or stayed with you after you finished the novel? Why?

8. What surprised you most about the book? Were there any plot twists that you loved? Hated?

9. Did the author do a good job of organizing the plot and moving it along?

10. Are there any books that you would compare this book to?

11. If you could talk to the author, what question(s) would you want to ask?

I love to hear from my readers. If you have questions or comments, email me at brerlankauthor@gmail.com or contact me via www.brerlank.wordpress.com.

Acknowledgements

This book would never have seen the light of day without the support and encouragement of several people. I owe a debt of gratitude to the many friends, members of Peace Lutheran, my hiking group, work colleagues and others who "kept my feet to the fire", encouraging me to write because they were keen to see my second novel.

I wish to thank Claire Burdett, Libby Flynn and Tony Rund who read raw early drafts and gave me valuable feedback. Pastor Steve Harms was a constant source of inspiration as I grappled to clarify the difference between Christian practices and zealous organized Christian religions.

I had a first-rate quality control team: Mary Hargreaves was my editor, Reese Dante designed the cover and Megan Aldridge is my trusted beta reader. Thanks also go to the authors and staff at Jericho Writers, who so generously share their expertise.

Finally, I want to thank my family for their support. My wife Philippa is my most honest critic. She read numerous versions of *Under the Cloud* and never tired of being a sounding board as I worked through plot and character issues. Everyone else in the family chipped in to bring this book to fruition. Even my 92-year-old mother offered to act as my "typist".

About the Author

Boris Erlank currently lives with his family and two dogs in the foothills of Mount Diablo, east of San Francisco.

He grew up in Southern Africa and has lived in places as diverse as Luanda, Cape Town, Namibia, Singapore and California. Boris has an extensive background in IT and data privacy. He recently gave up his job as Global Privacy Manager with a multi-national company to focus on writing full-time.

"My books are intended first and foremost to entertain and engage the reader with a gripping story. But I also hope that they might promote constructive, reasoned debate about the issues of our time.

"If you enjoyed *Under the Cloud*, please consider leaving a review. You might also want to look up my earlier novel, *Catch You Later*. It is a murder mystery, with a cast of lovable characters, that takes you on a wild ride through Cape Town, South Africa."

Made in the USA
Las Vegas, NV
14 September 2023

77520217R00225